WHEN EVIL WALKS THE LANDS

women trained in the arts of spell or sword must guard the many realms of fantasy. Now let the bards tell of victory and defeat in such tales of magic and mayhem as:

"Stopthrust"—Life is hard and all too often extremely short for those who must fight in the gladiators' arena. When magic suddenly enters the games, will skill or spell prove the winner?

"A Woman's Weapon"—Can Kethry and Tarma solve a riddle of treachery and betrayal before a dealer in death claims another innocent's life?

"Tiger's Eye"—Captured by a magic she scarcely understands can she find the secret means to make her enemy's weapon her own?

SWORD AND SORCERESS IX

SWORD AND SORCERESS IX

AN ANTHOLOGY OF HEROIC FANTASY

Edited by
Marion Zimmer Bradley

DAW BOOKS, INC.
DONALD A. WOLLHEIM, FOUNDER
375 Hudson Street, New York, NY 10014

ELIZABETH R. WOLLHEIM
SHEILA E. GILBERT
PUBLISHERS

DAW Book Collectors No. 878.

First Printing, April 1992

1 2 3 4 5 6 7 8 9

TABLE OF CONTENTS

INTRODUCTION

One of my greatest pleasures is to discover a new vice that is neither immoral, illegal, nor fattening. I really think that reading—anyway, reading fantasy—fills the bill. I've been doing it—addictively—since I was about seven years old; and of course nine-tenths of what I read goes out of my head; anything that I still remember after fifty years, I think, must be quite extraordinary.

For instance, I will never forget the pleasure of reading my first "grown-up" book, with no pictures and with ordinary sized print; my (dull) school readers had a picture on every page. Well, that first book was Dorothy Canfield Fisher's *Understood Betsy*. I am generally not very responsive to illustration; it makes me think of Dick and Jane, or of comic books—which I have never liked. For some reason this makes me very unpopular when I wonder aloud why anyone over ten or twelve would read a comic book. People keep asking me if I've read this or that; and so far each new one I read turns out to be the same old thing—bad art, badly written—which of course reminds me of the old story about Gustav Mahler. An opinionated man, he once stated that he did not like the songs of Hugo Wolf. (I don't either.) His contentious friend said that Hugo Wolf had written over five hundred songs; Mahler couldn't possibly have heard them all and he ought not to make sweeping statements like that, based on incomplete information. Whereupon the composer Mahler stated, "Hugo Wolf wrote five hundred songs; of these I have heard maybe three hundred. Those three hundred *I do not like*."

I feel that way about comics; the ones I have read, without exception, *I do not like*; which even includes some of the new "adult" comics such as the adult Batman, called *The Black Knight*; to read it, I had to have every panel explained to me by my son—who does like comics; but I still call them bad art and idiot writing. Every time I break down and watch anything on television I find myself, more often than not, wondering why I wasted the time when I could have been reading a good book instead. I'm hopelessly print-addicted.

So what sort of books do I remember? Well, I remember the first science fiction I ever read, in *Boy's Life*. By Otis Adelbert Kline or Ray Cummings or somebody like that; it was called "The Crimson Ray," and what I can remember of the plot was a thing to make a cat laugh. (I have never yet seen a cat laugh. Cats have no sense of humor. Neither have I—much.) I also read "Through Space to Mars," about a couple of kids in a space ship called the *Annihilator* or something like that. And I remember *Graustark*, and *The Prisoner of Zenda*, and Rider Haggard's *She* and Chambers' *The King in Yellow*. And there was Haggard's *Allan Quartermain* and *Cleopatra*, Maeterlinck's *Pelleas and Melisande*, and my first real fantasy novel, Kuttner's (Really C.L. Moore's) *The Dark World*, which started me off on a career of reading pulp science fiction magazines. And I've been doing it ever since.

And here I am editing a fantasy anthology, and reading manuscripts for a living. I think I'm very lucky to be able to do what I like best for a living.

I've never lost my sense of wonder about the slush pile, and when I stop and reflect that 90% of what I read is crud, I remember that when somebody commented that 90% of magazine s-f was crud, the late Theodore Sturgeon made the comment, raised later to what's called *Sturgeon's Law*, "ninety per cent of *everything*," he remarked sagely, "is crud."

It's all too true, I fear, but despite the 90%, I still love reading it, because when it's good there's no thrill like it.

Will I ever forget, for instance, when for the first of these volumes, I discovered Emma Bull's "The Rending Dark"? Seldom have I read a first story done with such a sure hand. This year I somehow got a number of first stories like that. And Rachel Pollack's story in S&S II; or Diana Paxson's first salable story, in *Greyhaven*, "Kindred of the Wind." These things are truly Peak Experiences worth remembering. Nor will I soon forget Jennifer Roberson's first story about Tiger and Del, "The Lady and the Tiger" in *S&S II*. Now there are four novels, one of which (*Sword Breaker*) I am reading as I edit this. Well, that's why I keep on doing this—and will keep on doing it as long as Betsy Wollheim keeps on buying them—and my eyesight holds out—and people keep on reading them. It's all I can do to honor the memory of our dear Don Wollheim, who has now left us; but was himself a great discoverer of talent. The list of his discoveries would take up another page and exhaust your patience. I'm sure you're in a hurry to get to my new ones. And that's how I'd like to be remembered; even if my own books are all forgotten, I think I'll be remembered as an editor who loved to discover talent. And who, like John W. Campbell, or Don, discovered lots of it.

SLAVE TO THE SWORD
by Tanya Beaty

As I said in the introduction, I love—almost more than anything else—to discover a first story by a young writer done with a sure hand. Tanya Beaty, like me, has been writing ever since she can remember. She says that the most remarkable thing about her is that in her sixteen years she has moved over twenty times. She loves animals and is the proud owner of a huge German shepherd. Hooray, another dog person. One of many points of resemblance to your editor. May she go on writing as long as I have.

Teral watched the woman walk blindly into the tavern. He had been watching her ever since she had ridden into the town because he had thought, at first, that she was injured or sick. She walked like one afflicted with the mind-blank disease, wobbling slightly and seeing with empty eyes. Her horse had come into the town more by instinct than by guidance. Although, Teral admitted to himself, she had seemed to improve slightly as she walked to the tavern, after realizing that her horse had stopped in front of the dusty town's tying-rail.

The woman stood at the doorway for some time, as if trying to make sense of what her eyes were seeing. By now, everyone in the tavern had noticed the stranger. They couldn't help it. This one had the look of a warrior, with dark, dusty breeches and tunic, and a sword-belt slung at her side. Strangely enough, however, she carried no sword. Her brown hair had once been braided back neatly, but now escaped in long locks to curl about her face and neck. Under all the travel dust she was pale, and her seeming fragility marked her as coming from the south. She was not beautiful, only exotic, but this alone drew all the men's attention to her. Teral beckoned to her quickly, before any other man came to his senses. To his delight, she walked to his table and sat down.

Kira was beyond anything physical. She could no longer think, only feel. Now, sitting here at the very town, the memory of the weeks of traveling, mind-searching yet mind-trapped, were washed away like mist. She probably couldn't remember them anyway; she had been in too much shock. Only one thing filled her mind now: the hunger. The pull of her soul filled her, and she yearned to be whole again.

She barely noticed the man at whose table she sat as she scanned the room. It was near, she knew it! It had to be! The hunger filled her mind, blotting out all thought. She needed—no, she thought, pulling away from that, better to concentrate on the man. Time was quickly running out.

"Will you help me?" Kira was pleased that her voice sounded normal. The man leaned forward slightly, the look in his eyes like that of a predator who had just trapped his next meal. She had herself used that look many a time. She hardened her features instantly—she would not be distracted! The man nodded slightly, recognizing her warning. For now. She leaned back and studied him. He was young and muscular. He seemed shallow, but she didn't care. His sword was old, but well-cared for. And most importantly, he seemed to be comfortable with the people and the town. She needed him. Her mind cleared, for the first time in weeks. She spoke slowly. "I need your help, and I'm willing to pay very well for it." The man's eyes narrowed suspiciously, and his light brown hair fell into his eyes. He brushed an errant lock back with a practiced hand. She met his green eyes with her dark ones. "I just need to find something that was stolen from me."

"What makes you think it's here, lady?" Teral was fascinated by this woman. Under his very eyes, she had shed the crazed look and was now just a normal, albeit determined, woman. She also didn't flinch from his sneering tone.

Instead she replied, in a very flat tone, "I know it's here." She glanced around, and Teral could have sworn that she was looking for it. And then once again she challenged him with that direct stare. "I'll pay you three hundred marks for whatever information or help you give me for two days' time. No conditions."

Three hundred marks! Teral was very impressed. One didn't throw away money without restraint unless one was very crazy, very stupid, or very desperate. There had to be a catch somewhere, he thought. "What happens if you don't find your 'possession' in two days? Not that it would take me that long, of course. If I took the job," he inquired.

Did he imagine the brief flash of—grief?—in her eyes? Then she turned away slightly. "If I don't find it by then," she replied, "it won't much matter."

Teral nodded slightly. Slowly, as if having to force out the words, he said, "I will help."

Kira led the man into her room. He whistled appreciatively at the rich furnishings—she had enough money to pay for the best room at the inn. He wondered if she had a keeper, and if so, who he was. She glanced at him through the corners of her eyes, as if able to read his thoughts. She then collapsed on a chair and motioned for him to sit down. He chose his chair, and then glanced at her expectantly. Kira massaged her aching temples, wishing the pull would go away, even if for one moment. She was so close! She was so close to succeeding! Didn't it know that?

"So, lady, what is it you're looking for?" Teral leaned back into his chair. "I hope, for your sake, that it's worth three hundred." She raised her head at that, and replied wanly that it was. When she volunteered no other information, he became angry. She had an aura of "alien" that unnerved him. "Look, lady, I'm waiting! You can't expect me to find what I don't recognize!" He stopped when she raised her head.

Her eyes fixed his with a feral stare. "I'm looking," she said slowly, "for a sword."

At that information, Teral let out a laugh. "My gods! All this for a *sword?* I thought you would be looking for something important, like a warhorse, or a lord's child!" Kira stiffened. "Why don't you just buy a sword from one of the large city merchants?" He swept his hands across the room. "You obviously have the money. Why risk your life for a mere *sword?*"

He turned back to the woman, only to find her on her feet, and very angry. Her voice rang out in the suddenly silent room. "You could not possibly conceive the value of this sword to me! Do you not recognize my uniform, here in the backwater lands of the Kingdom? I am one of the Enchanted, the Sword-Bound!" At his puzzled look, she began to pace, and to try to explain to this ignorant man what she was. "We are the King's Guard. To ensure our loyalty to the Crown, there is a spell placed on us. Most of the time, however, it seems like a curse." She stopped and sighed. "We are bound to our swords when we take our oath. Our *souls* are bound to the swords." Kira tried to explain the hunger, the madness it brought when she was separated from it. . . . "I cannot be apart from the sword from a long period of time. Therefore, we of the Guard keep our swords near at all times. However, during a scouting trip, my party was set upon by bandits. There were many to our few, but we succeeded in turning them—but not before they had succeeded in gathering up several of our swords. Mine was one of three taken, when I dropped it. . . ." She sighed, and Teral felt, dimly, what she must be feeling. She faced him squarely. "I have to find my sword. Time is running out. Tonight." She paused. "All I can say for sure is that the man who carries it now is in this town. I can feel it calling . . . I must not become lost. . . ." Her voice drifted off, and with a start, Teral realized that she was searching for that lost part of herself, the part stolen from the very fabric of her identity, her sense of self.

Teral shook himself. It had seemed that for one instant, he could feel the despair of her situation. He tried to hide from her the feeling that he was out of his mind to help her. "Well, if you will tell me what it looks like, I might be able to locate him while sitting in this very room. Fellwood Town does not get very many visitors, and many of those here barter with less than legal traders." His grin suggested that he was willing, for a price, to do so himself.

But Kira was almost beyond feeling hope, and so one of the King's Enchanted had hired a sword-carrying thief. "There is no other sword like it. The blade is of unusual metal, has many runes carved on it, and seems to shine of itself. The crossbars are carved into writhing snakes that seem to curl about the bearer's hand." She shrugged. "Having once seen it, none can ever forget it."

Teral could practically smell the gold that would soon be his. No two swords, especially no two of such unusual beauty, could be found in the same town! And Jessen, the horsetrader, had just arrived from one of his long trips. Teral had shown no surprise at the marvels that the fat man had brought, knowing that the man did not confine his tradings to horses. Virgins often brought more money. And on this trip, Jessen had arrived with a sword of unusual quality. Yes, Teral could understand why people would kill for this sword. He remembered the man boasting of the fine deal he had gotten in the city of Riermouth. He had then claimed that he was the best bargainer in the land. And laughed.

Teral had known how he had *really* gotten the sword, but had kept his mouth shut. People died of unusual causes when they told tales of the trader. But even with this warning flashing in his mind, he could not help turning to the woman jubilantly. Fifty marks could easily get him a better horse than his own. "I know who it is!" He was startled by the speed with which she turned to him. "And we can get to it tonight! His house is not more than half a league from here." He swung out of his chair and started toward the door. As he opened the door and let the cool night air in, he started to turn to her and ask her if she had arms, but suddenly decided not to. If she was one of the King's Guard, then she could take care of herself. And he didn't want to remind her that there was more than one way out of a bargain than by paying. To cover up his momentary pause, he smiled and nodded at her. "Well, let's get to his house and prepare him a . . . suitably warm welcome." Teral headed out the door, only vaguely hearing the woman mutter something about "being fed."

Teral crouched in the shadow of the doorway, waiting for his money, in the form of the horsetrader, to walk through the door. Kira had gotten them into the house with the quick twist of a longknife, and now stood a few paces away from him, facing the doorway with an eerie concentration. Teral supposed she was feeling her sword, and trying to "find" it in the night. He decided to calm her. "Don't worry. He always goes to the barn first, to check on his horses. They'll warn us." She didn't show any sign of hearing him, so he turned back to the doorway, just in time to hear a whicker from the barn. Kira stiffened slightly, her brow furrowing as she tried to judge the man's position. Footsteps thundered heavily across the porch of the house, saving her the trouble. Realizing that he was drunk, she did not notice Teral edge closer to the door. All her concentration was on her sword, now thudding up the stairs in the heavy grasp of the lumbering bear. Some distant, unreal part of her mind grew angry at his clumsy handling of the fine weapon.

Teral waited only until Jessen was within reach to lunge at the man. He was easy to bring down, and he was a portly specimen who relied on bodyguards to keep his hide safe on the trade roads. The two men rolled together on the polished wood floor, Teral finally ending on top. He had whipped the sword out of Jessen's sheath and now threw it across the floor, skidding and bouncing, to Kira. That one had made no sound, standing frozen as an ice statue. Teral, his hands full with subduing the trader, turned back to the man, drawing his own knife as he did so. Jessen gasped for breath, the outrage in his expression fading as he caught sight of Teral and the knife near his throat. "Wha–what do you want from me?" he stammered. Sweat trickled down his face and moistened his tunic. Teral decided to simply let the man off with a warning. Jessen didn't know him very well, and he would have no trouble leaving town tonight with a lot of money. Besides, it wouldn't hurt his reputation a bit.

Putting his face as close to the source of a distinct, rank whiskey smell as he could stand, he snarled, "Don't steal from those who are stronger than you, old fool! It will someday get you a knife in your back!" Throwing the man down and whirling up and about, he caught up the arm of the standing woman and the sword at her feet, and propelled them both down the stairs and out of the house. Only when they were safely under the denser trees did he dare stop to catch his breath, and turn to the woman beside him.

Kira had been too caught up in the thrall of having her sword back that she hadn't noticed that the man, Teral, had allowed the creature, Jessen, to escape. The feeling of being whole again had almost sapped her strength. She had caressed the blade, feeling free from the hunger which had clouded her mind for so long . . . until she realized that a vestige of emotion remained. The sword had not been fed . . . NO! She would NOT do this! But it so needed it. . . .

She turned on the man then, remembering that he had let her rightful prey go. She had no choice. She/the sword needed it! He would suffer from his mistake!

Teral backed away from the woman, fear rising to slice through his body at the feral, half-mad gleam in the woman's eyes. "WHAT!" he screamed, his voice cracking with fear. The sound of that seemed to push the woman further in her insanity. "I have found your soul, your sword! I have given it to you! What more could you want? Why?"

Her throaty hiss sent electric shivers up his spine, and she advanced, her face twisted in a gruesome mask of hatred, of fear, and of blood-lust. "I *needed* that man! My sword has not been fed! My sword has not been blooded in a moon! My sword needs—*I* need—the blood of a man! And now *you* will be that man!"

She lifted the sword higher, and it caught a stray moonbeam, which seemed to reflect into Teral's eyes and blind him. His mind shrieked at him, but he tried not to think about the sharpness of the weapon held ready in the woman's hands. Soon, he knew, soon the blade would sink into his body and feed itself on his still-warm blood. "And do you always do what the sword commands?"

She stopped for an instant, and her face fell. A look of sorrow crossed her face, and for one moment, Teral would almost have died just to wipe the sadness from her face—no, he would die—the sadness that would be with her forever, the inner sorrow that had begun the moment she had bound herself to the sword, and realized the price it demanded, and she had become its slave. "I must," she answered, in a voice that wound around the trees and crept through the grass at their feet, a voice that pervaded his very soul with sadness and horror . . . and then he saw the blade slice through the air toward him.

Kira knelt by the man, leaving her sword in the torn chest. She closed her eyes so that she wouldn't see the blood on the blade evaporating, as if the sword was absorbing it . . . which it was. Minutes later, when she opened her eyes again, she discovered a white, bloodless body. A tear crept down her face. It was not the first time she had seen this, nor would it be the last. It would continue for as long as she . . . as long as the sword . . . lived. And in return, she was granted the power of bespelling men, so that they would pause for that one crucial moment it took to take their strength and make it her own. She needed the power granted willingly, and the sword made it possible . . . for a price. And she paid it. She *knew* the price.

With a sigh, the woman stood up and left the body under its tree, pausing only long enough to close the dead man's eyes, forever concealing the terror within at the knowledge of the price.

SHADOWS DO NOT BLEED
by Bruce Arthurs

I remember back before I started doing these anthologies, Anne McCaffrey and I were on some panel or other at some convention or other, and some feminist or other was asking if there was any major difference between men's writing and women's.

Well, we kicked this around for a while and came to the conclusion—wrong, like all generalizations including this one—that men usually wrote more about hardware and scientific theories and women about emotions. Then somebody brought up Ted Sturgeon, who, we all agreed, handled emotions as well as any writer any of us could think of; and Anne drawled, "Yes, Ted writes almost as well as a woman," thus neatly—in those pre-feminist days—turning the tables on those who damned any competent female writer with the faint praise of saying she "wrote like a man."

The reason of telling this basically unedifying little story is to say of Bruce Arthurs that he is living proof that the art of writing emotionally is not limited to females. He appeared in S&S IV with the excellent and almost unbearably intense "Death and the Ugly Woman"; and if I had ever cherished any illusions that emotional writing was limited to women or to Ted Sturgeon, this story would have disabused me of that notion right away. Actually, I find the art of writing well is almost independent of gender; at first I tried to print mostly women's stories in SWORD AND SORCERESS because of a widespread misconception that women could not, or did not write adventure fiction. But if any of us ever believed that—(and after Leigh Brackett it would be hard, if not impossible)—this story would be living proof that we were all wrong. Bruce's first story for us, "Unicorn's Blood" in S&S II, was good enough to dispel my prejudices against unicorns as a cliche; and I chose his "Skycastle" for the cover story of the first issue of *Marion Zimmer Bradley's Fantasy Magazine*.

Bruce is married to writer Margaret Hildebrand, who appeared in S&S V. They have one son, Chris, and four cats.

Bruce has recently devoted much of his time to STAR TREK: THE NEXT GENERATION, for which he provided an episode in early 1991, and probably will have sold other scripts to other TV shows before this appears in print. We hope he'll continue writing for us print junkies in future; a talent like his is—personal opinion coming up—wasted on television, where the general level of talent is pretty low.

Pain. The disciplines of the Order Invisible included mental training to control and lessen the pain of wounds, to allow one to fight on, to complete one's mission. But there were limits to such training.

Being gutstabbed, Jinnell noted, surpassed those limits. She kept one hand pressed against her belly, but she felt the blood pulse out between her fingers. Its odor, sharp and metallic, mixed with the more offensive odor of her own bowels. The pain came in waves of fire, washing over but not obliterating the cold sense of failure.

Her other hand supported her against the cold, dank wall. Her nightsword lay in the dirt behind her, where it had fallen when Obah One-Eye's smashing blow had struck it from her hand.

The tyrant had been so close. Jinnell was hidden in the darkness of the keep's storerooms, had been *part* of the darkness. Moments before, most of Obah's men had been sent to where Prince Ivannan's forces had been making an apparent attempt to breach the castle walls; the ruse had distracted the soldiers within the besieged fortress while the true attack had gone unnoticed. Jinnell, with clawed gloves and bootlets, had scaled a wall thought unscalable and slipped unnoticed within.

Moving from shadow to shadow, she had moved closer to her prey, silently gaining entrance to the castle's inner stronghold. The lower storerooms of the keep had been dark and silent. She had noted that the castle's supplies, although depleted by the long siege, were sufficient to carry Obah and his men through another season.

Ivannan and his rag-tag army of disaffected soldiers and desperate peasants could not afford to wait. They had loosed the tyrant's grip on the country and cornered him in his fortress, but the siege could not be maintained forever.

The meeting in Ivannan's tent two nights before had made that clear. As the various factions had spoken, Jinnell had stood to one side, near Ivannan, unnoticed by most present but constantly alert for the safety of her lord and lover.

The farmers and peasants helping maintain the siege were worried that, with fields untended, their families would face starvation come winter. The native soldiers, those who had finally turned against Obah's excesses and cruelties, were discouraged by the lack of a resolution. And the mercenaries were quarrelsome, bored by the lack of action and booty; fights between the mercenaries and the other forces were becoming more and more common.

Also, the weather had worsened and the rains seemed to drizzle without end; sickness had begun to increase in the besiegers'muddy encampments.

In spite of all Ivannan's efforts, there had seemed no way to continue the siege for more than another month. To consolidate their gains into a final victory, Obah One-Eye had to be either enticed from his refuge, or that refuge must somehow be penetrated.

"I am a weapon, my lord," Jinnell had told Ivannan later that night, as they lay between the blankets in his tent."Use me as such."

"You are more than a weapon, Jinnell," he had answered softly. "You are my protector, my companion, my lover."

"Ivannan . . . my lord . . . I ask this not for your sake alone, or for our long-suffering country. I owe blood-debt. I am the last of the Order Invisible; Obah betrayed them, burned them alive in their own sanctuary. I alone survived."

"Because you were a half-trained acolyte, Jinnell, sent on an errand. I love you. I fear for you. I wish you at my side."

Jinnell had not answered. Seconds had stretched by. "Jinnell?" Ivannan had whispered, then reached out for her . . .

. . . to find empty sheets beneath his fingers, then the cold touch of blackened steel against the side of his neck.

"Half-trained?" Jinnell had asked from behind him.

The argument had concluded as it had to. Two nights later, Jinnell had donned the night-colored shadow-clothing of her order, strapped on her blackened sword, pulled the clawed gloves onto her long-fingered hands, and made the attempt.

Only to fail, she noted bitterly.

She had heard the sound of footsteps approaching the storerooms, and had secreted herself within the shadows there. She had felt a leap of joy, and had thought *The Goddess of Fortune is with me tonight* as she had seen the one to whom the footsteps belonged.

Obah One-Eye himself had entered, accompanied by a servant bearing a lamp. The light from the candle flame made the shadows shift and jump, but Jinnell had silently shifted with them.

Obah had entered, had looked around with his one good eye. He had been close enough for Jinnell to see the long scar that ran down across his face, beneath the black eyepatch that covered his left eye, and out onto his cheek.

He had walked around the storeroom slowly, circling the well that dominated the room's center. Obah was a large man, with coarse features that evinced a lifetime of cruelty and selfishness. But he was also a master swords-man, and the jewel-hilted sword slung from his waist, despite its courtly appearance, had been blooded often and deeply.

Obah had paused by the well, had leaned back on his elbows against the rim.

The servant had shivered in the cold. "My . . . my lord," he began.

A snap of the head, a glare that changed the servant's shivering to trembling. Then a curt dismissing gesture. "Leave the lamp," Obah's deep voice had growled. "I have no need for you."

The servant had scuttled out with an expression of relief, leaving the lamp burning atop a wooden barrel. Obah had looked around the room again, twisting his head this way and that.

Why had he come to the storeroom? Jinnell wondered. Was he aware of her presence? Obah had been the target of assassins before this. But a network of informers and turncoats, and an almost supernatural luck, had kept him alive far too long.

There had been a faint rustle from across the room. Obah's head had snapped in that direction, staring intently. Silence had filled the room for long seconds; Jinnell had scarcely dared breathe. Then there had come the sound of tiny feet moving across the floor, in the deep shadows near where the floor met the far wall.

Obah had untensed, then softly chuckled. "Mice," he had growled, then turned and began to leave the room.

His blind side had been toward Jinnell. She would never have a better chance. She sprang, a shadow sprouting a great black thorn.

It had all happened so fast then. Obah's hand had flashed to his own sword as she had begun to spring. No, *before*, just before she had moved. His swordstroke had not been at her, had not intended to be at her, but had moved across the arc of her own weapon's path, deflecting it upward. Her surprise had given Obah the extra second he needed, the second in which he turned and rushed at her, the second in which the dagger that had dropped from his sleeve into his free hand had slid into her belly.

She had gasped. He had laughed, given the dagger an

extra twist, then pushed her away. Jinnell had fallen to the floor, clutching helplessly at herself.

"Well, well," Obah had muttered, looking down at her from what seemed a great height. "A woman. Are you—?" He had reached down and pulled off her black hood, then laughed, loudly and with vigor.

"Ivannan's killer whore! How rich! He must be desperate, to risk losing such a fine-looking bedmate. Ah, he'll be lonely tonight, I expect."

Grimacing, Jinnell had managed to glare up at him. "Y–you . . . will . . . die, Obah." Her voice had been frighteningly thin.

He had chuckled. "In bed, with white hair, wrinkles, and a woman or two, I assure you." His eyes had roamed over her. "A shame that I acted so quickly. Now that I get a better look, it might have been more enjoyable if I'd used my round-tipped sword on you instead." His hand had suddenly darted out to grab her between her legs; her gut-wound had responded with an explosion of pain so intense that she could only scream in a ragged whisper. Blackness had danced before her eyes.

"Dear me," Obah had continued, drawing back a blood-smeared hand. "It's that time of the moon cycle for you, isn't it? Well, perhaps we'll continue this after your bleeding has stopped. Within an hour, if I'm not mistaken. Won't *that* be more romantic?"

"M–m–monster," she had whispered as he started to rise. "D–demon."

He had looked down at her, smiled, then walked over to the lamp and brought it back close to where Jinnell lay. He squatted down beside her.

"Not a demon or monster at all," he had said. "Just a man with extra . . . resources." He had reached up and lifted the eyepatch away from his face.

Jinnell had expected an empty socket, or an eye rendered unusable and white with scarring. But where Obah's eye had once been, there was an orb of clear crystal, shot through with specks of ruddy gold. As Jinnell watched, she realized that the specks were *moving*, somehow, within the orb.

"Yes," Obah had said. "One of the magic eyes made six hundred years ago by Allurus, the Blind Wizard himself. With this, I can detect all living beings within half a league, shining like sparks lifting into the night sky. As I detected you. As I have detected the number and array of the forces against me. Even when one is a shadow-trained assassin, one of the Invisible. Invisible—oh, I hesitate to disappoint you so—is simply not good enough."

Goddess, Jinnell had thought. *No wonder no one has defeated him.* It was miracle enough that Ivannan had been able to press a siege upon the tyrant.

"Of course, I show you this only because you will not live to tell anyone of it. We shall keep it our little secret, won't we?" Obah had replaced the eyepatch, stood, started to turn away, then looked back at her. "I'll try to get back before you've grown cold, my lovely." His laughter had echoed as he left the room.

Now, moments later, using the cold wall for support, she had slowly, painfully, pulled herself to her feet. She was bare moments from death, but there was one last stroke she could make against Obah. She strained to calm her mind, to gather her last vestiges of strength for what she had to do.

I must be as light as shadow, she thought. *I must leave no mark, no footprint, no sign of what I am about to do. I must not leave a bloody trail. Shadows do not bleed.*

She remembered words that had been drilled into her and the other acolytes of the Invisible. *Where one sword does not succeed, use ten daggers. Where ten daggers do not succeed, use a hundred pins. Where a hundred pins do not succeed. . . .*

Her vision blurred. She had to act now.

Shadows do not bleed. Shadows do not bleed. Shadows do not bleed. The phrase became a mantra in Jinnell's mind. Slowly, the shit-tainted blood oozing between her fingers ceased to flow.

Shadows do not bleed. She took the first step of her last journey.

The captain looked at Ivannan with concern. The rebel leader had achieved his goal; the castle was theirs, had been since that morning when the gates had opened and an officer of Obah's men had stumbled out, weakly waving a white flag. But the captain's commander looked at the fortress around him with sad, half-dead eyes.

Little wonder, though, the captain thought. *His lady vanishing two weeks ago on that ill-fated mission. And then, to finally achieve his goal, but in such a manner. . . .*

Ivannan spoke, his voice muffled by the vinegar-soaked cloth tied across his face. "Have men gather firewood. The dead here will have to be burned. Now, Captain, you say Obah has been found?"

"Aye, sir."

"Take me there."

In a sumptuous room high in one of the towers, Obah had died in bed. He had died alone, trembling and shaking in his own wastes as the killing fever had struck him down.

"Where . . . where is she?" had been the last words he had spoken, but no one had been there to hear them.

If there had been, they might have told Obah that he had already answered that question. He had raged for half a day when he had returned to find the woman vanished. And raged for a day again when the woman's body had been, finally, found. And grown quiet, very quiet, when the first signs of fever and loose bowels began to appear in those around him, and then in himself.

The blood and feces that had leaked from the woman's slashed belly were no longer evident when they had pulled the body up. It had been washed clean by the water of the keep's well.

BEASTLY!
by Lynne Armstrong-Jones

As I think I've said before, Lynne is a perfect example of what I always say about making a sale: if at first you don't succeed, try again—and again—until the editor gets sick and tired of rejecting your work. There was a time when I had just begun editing *Marion Zimmer Bradley's Fantasy Magazine* that I received a new story about every week from Lynne—and sooner or later, as she knew I would, I simply got tired of rejecting them. Persistence usually pays off sooner or later—and if you don't send me your first story, I can hardly buy your fourth or fifth. I think Lynne sent me seven or eight stories before I printed one. Now I consider her a valued old friend and really look forward to reading her new stories because I know if I have room for one it'll be worth reading. And if I don't, she won't take it personally; she'll just send me something else.

Right now Lynne is a part-time instructor in adult English; she lives in Ontario, Canada, and has a five-year-old son—and two thirteen-year-old cats. At least teenage cats don't demand as much emotional support as their human counterparts.

The beast was weary. He'd been wandering for days. But hunger and fatigue had not been his only companions; despair and loneliness seemed to cling to him, pestering him like a determined fly. Yet he continued, desperation urging him onward. There *had* to be a way! He *must* find help!

He lowered his angular head irritably as still another low-hanging branch threatened to scratch at his yellow eyes. He shouldn't *be* in such a state! Why had the fates decreed that he should be the victim of a sorceress' silly whims?

He did *not* deserve this! He spat his fury, his forked tongue flickering. Surely he could find help somewhere . . . somehow! Another sigh escaped him as he quickened his awkward pace. Damn it all anyway. How was he to have known that the female figure hidden beneath the thick robe was that of a sorceress? Who could blame *him*—a strong, muscular, tall, and rather attractive man in every sense of the word—for seeking the comforts of a woman's soft body?

Bah! Yes, he could understand her calling him a "beast" . . . but to curse him to one's form? Rather extreme.

Women. Ladies. Girls. Females . . .

Vixens. Bitches . . .

He'd never understand them! And certainly never *respect* them. Especially not *now*.

His mind simmering with anger and frustration, he stepped into the roadway without thought—and quickly drew himself back into the shelter of the undergrowth, scolding himself for his carelessness. He crouched on short, reptilian legs as the hooves of a large horse trotted by—in the same spot he'd been just a second or two ago.

The black horse was ridden by a woman. She was fair-haired like the women of the north and clad in breeches and tunic, a sword at her side. She scanned the area ahead as though alert for danger. Yet she did not appear frightened. The beast watched as she rode past, then, as the rider and horse continued on their way, he stepped once more into the roadway.

But no sooner had he done so than another horse appeared, moving swiftly toward him! He panicked; felt rooted to the spot and beyond capability of movement.

The white horse was not as large as the black. When it spotted him, it stopped and reared. Yet the tiny woman astride its back seemed to have no difficulty in controlling it. She spoke to the horse and patted its neck, but she was looking at the beast which cowered in the horse's path.

The object of her scrutiny felt his heart pounding. Suddenly he regained his senses, bolting across the roadway and into the underbrush on the other side. He ran as quickly as his legs could carry him and didn't stop until his way was blocked by a broad tree trunk.

He was trembling, heart beating wildly, his memory bursting with the sight of those hooves thrashing the air above him. The beast lay down, folding his legs beneath him. He knew he *must* rest now.

As he regained his composure, he thought of the small woman who'd calmed her horse so quickly and easily. It was true that the horse had not been a large one. But it still seemed that this woman had erased all traces of panic from her mount extremely effectively.

She'd spoken to it, the beast recalled. She had spoken words which were of no language *he* understood. And the last time *that* had happened, he'd found himself like *this!* He shuddered. Sorcery! He was probably fortunate she hadn't struck him dead on a whim!

Damn all those who dabble in magic, he thought.

But still . . . but still there'd been something about this woman. Something strange and unclear. And it made him wish to see her again. . . .

Sorcery! More sorcery! Would he never escape its touch?

He closed his eyes, determined to rest. But when he did, he kept seeing the memory of that woman's eyes. Bright brown eyes, with a deep sense of calmness; a tranquillity, a wisdom about them that was unlike anything he'd ever seen before. Even now they seemed to draw him, pull him. . . .

A prisoner of sorcery, he thought. *That's all I am—*

So hard to believe when only a short time ago he'd been a strapping warrior the likes of whom women dreamed about.

Then a thought hit him.

If she's a sorceress, she might be able to *help!* If he could somehow charm her, make her like him, maybe she'd sense that he wasn't a *real* beast and help him!

Surely even inside this horrid body there was still a trace of that charm which had always brought the wenches his way.

Well, it was certainly worth trying, he reasoned. It was surely more sensible than running around in the forest wishing that he could run right out of this horrible little body!

He rose and moved back to the roadway. He looked in the direction the two women had taken, although he could feel that the hoofbeats no longer shook the ground. They must have passed over the hill already.

He trotted quickly, ensuring that his haste did not bring him too far from the edge of the road. It would certainly not help him to be seen by some lady of the nobility and set her screaming at his appearance.

He began to despair when he saw that the hoofprints had left the main roadway. How would he be able to track them along this grassy route? But he'd forgotten that he was now a beast: when he inhaled he was greeted by the now-recognizable recent scents of horses. Relieved, he headed in the direction which these indicated.

The creature was breathing heavily when he finally arrived at the women's camp. He hesitated, sensing the tingle of enchantment in the air—but desperation sent him crawling toward it anyway.

The sun had completed its journey down to the horizon and the women had supped without incident. The swordswoman was deeply asleep while the sorceress sipped a cup of water, leaning against the tree trunk.

The sorceress, Lucia, closed her eyes and allowed her spirit to drift along the limit of the encircling protective spell. She felt no threat or danger in the surroundings. But suddenly her eyes opened. Through her protective spell she felt a presence, although not a menacing one. Lucia rose. She stood very still, tendrils of her power moving outward, seeking contact.

She did not have far to scan.

There on the ground not far from her stood the strange creature which had frightened the mare. Lucia gazed down at it. How quickly the thing must have hurried for it to have caught up with the horses!

And an unusual beast it was. Its head was like that of a lizard, but its body had the shape of a turtle.

A hoarse whisper came suddenly from beside her. The tall warrior held her sword aloft as she prepared to slash at the creature.

"No," Lucia commanded in a soft voice.

Cal stopped, sword still held high. Her eyes were on Lucia. She didn't see the beast as it scurried back to the shelter of the underbrush.

A sigh escaped the sorceress. She knew her companion was awaiting her explanation. "There's something magical about the creature. I feel some sort of enchantment."

Cal's sword was wavering, as though its owner was not convinced that her blade would not be needed. The swordswoman was intensely uncomfortable about enchantments, even with Lucia close.

But the sorceress' hand was suddenly touching Cal's swordarm. "Go and rest, my friend."

Cal nodded, returning to her place upon the ground. There was no point in expending energy upon useless thoughts: Lucia would let her know if she was needed.

The light of dawn pierced the darkness as thoughts and considerations likewise poked holes in the sorceress' attempts at rest. She had mixed feelings about the creature. Although she'd sensed enchantment, there was no aspect of danger about the beast. She felt an urge to try to locate the creature . . . but they'd been asked to venture to the next town to discuss serving as escorts to a baron's daughter. And they certainly had need of employment.

A noise disturbed her. She turned to see the swordswoman stirring at what remained of the fire. For now, speculations would be set aside.

The creature watched as the women breakfasted and then prepared to ride. He crouched low, concealed by the bushes. He'd been careful to remain outside of the magical protective circle as long as he dared, returning only when he saw the sun begin to rise.

He sighed as he watched the warrior cluck to her mount. He didn't relish the propect of having to hurry after the two once more. But he was certain now that the sorceress might just be the one he needed. He had no choice. His short legs began moving, the awkward body wiggling as it sought the quickest way through the brush. He *had* to get help from that sorceress. No matter what, no matter how. He *must*. Contact with her might be the key to getting his true, handsome body—and his old life—back. . . .

The warrior wiped an arm across her forehead, her other one reaching toward the neck of the black horse as her fingers sought contact.

"Soon, old friend. I promise."

And, as though the fates wished to ensure continued confidence between horse and rider, she could see it not far away now. The glint of sunlight reflected from a shiny surface: a stream.

Smiling broadly, the swordswoman did not need to suggest that they head in that direction. She simply let the stallion go where he wished, then slipped from his back as he pushed his muzzle into the cool wetness. She had just filled her water skin when Lucia's white horse joined them. She looked up, then, to gaze in Lucia's direction near the trees—and gasped, her sword seeming to leap into her grasp.

Lucia stood still as she watched the wolf approach. It was obviously mad, foam dripping from its open jaws. She raised her hand in front of her face, her lips parting as she prepared to utter a spell.

But, out of nowhere it seemed, that strange and ugly little beast appeared. He scurried in front of Lucia, between the sorceress and the rabid wolf. Lucia watched, fascinated, as the beast approached the wolf and then turned in an obvious effort to distract the mad thing.

The wolf eyed the creature slowly, its eyes a horror of fear and suffering. But the lizardlike beast held its eyes with his own. *He had to protect that sorceress! She was the one person he'd found who could help him!*

The wolf had no opportunity to see its killer. Cal advanced quickly from behind it; within seconds it was dead.

The warrior wiped her blade clean, one lip curled in

distaste as she thought of how this was the blood of a mad thing.

But Lucia's gentle voice distracted her.

"What. . . ?" But Cal spoke no further, recognizing the words of a spell.

Her eyes were drawn toward the strange beast which had distracted the wolf. Cal hadn't noticed the little creature harmed in any way. Yet it lay there as though dead. What in the name of the fates was Lucia *doing?*

Suddenly the little beast began to writhe as though in agony. Cal raised her sword once more. Certainly the thing deserved a quick death—

But Lucia stopped her with a look, then both returned their attention to the sight of the little beast. It lay quietly at first, but soon resumed twisting and moaning.

Cal watched in fascination. Lucia moved toward the creature, whose skin seemed to be stretching to its limits as though there could be another beast inside, trying to break through. Slowly the sorceress knelt beside him and placed a hand upon the writhing body.

Pain. Confusion. Flashes of lightning within his own head. Bits of memory bursting into his mind, only to be quickly replaced by others.

Memories of scurrying along a roadway, grasses tickling his nose. Searches for low-hanging branches or holes in tree trunks which might offer shelter to an ugly little beast.

Memories of gazing for the first time into a still pool: memories of the horror which was now him.

And yet other recollections, too. The feel of a sword in a large, strong hand. The feel of a wench's skin beneath his fingers and lips. And a special touch. A wonderful touch. A sensation of gentle warmth as the power left *her*, the woman of enchantments, to enter him.

As human eyes locked with magic ones, he felt his jaw drop in astonishment—

It was a man's jaw. Suddenly, surprise and joy had him trembling like a child.

She smiled that gentle smile, reaching a hand down to him. Still gaping, he took it, and let her help him to his rather unsteady feet.

He heard the other woman ask something, but he was as yet too dazed to understand the words. His mind cleared, though, as the sorceress began her explanation:

"Some incantations have peculiarities about them which relate to the circumstances under which the spell was cast. For instance, sir," she continued, pausing to nod at the man, "it would seem that you were bespelled because your actions were considered base and cruel by the one who bewitched you. Because of this, a true act of selflessness was required to begin the spell's destruction. I helped only a bit." She gazed at him, smiling—but the grin was somewhat awry.

The man could only stammer, his feelings of respect and gratitude for once dominant. "But—but it wasn't selflessness at all! I—I wanted you to *help* me! I don't deserve praises. Why, you should turn me back to beastflesh!"

He stopped, his voice strangled in a gasp as he marveled at his unaccustomed honesty. Wide-eyed, he stared at the sorceress.

Lucia's smile was no longer twisted. "At times something much deeper than words is required for *true* magic. Believe me, your manflesh is now deserved."

Still he gazed upon this small woman in wonder. Then he smiled, touching his lips to her hand as though gallantry and courtesy had been with him forever.

Manflesh or no, whether beast or not might yet be open to conjecture. For like an eager hound he followed at Lucia's heels, knowing he'd be her most loyal friend and companion all the days of his life.

PIPER
by Susan Hanniford Crowley

As I've said often in my rejection slips; we are not a primary market for series. That has to do with one of my eccentricities; I can't stand the cover letter that says, "This story is the first of a series. . . ." It reminds me of that absurdity which speaks of something as the "first annual" something-or-other, or says—for instance, at a college—"From now on it will be a tradition that—"

As I see it, you should first write your first story; if I like that, I'll willingly print the second and after. Think of Mercedes Lackey's Tarma and Kethry stories, or of Diana Paxson's Shanna stories, which have graced these anthologies from Volume I. But I won't commit myself sight unseen.

Susan Crowley's first story "Ladyknight" appeared in my anthology SPELLS OF WONDER (SWORD & SORCERESS 5-½). She has published a book of poetry, while raising two daughters, and a "literary feline," and while she completes a science fiction novel. She dedicates this story to her husband Larry who underwent a successful heart transplant on September 20, 1990." At least she knows he *has* a heart. Having been married—unsuccessfully—twice, I am forced to wonder about the men in my past.

Piper's small fingers clutched the roots of a tree as she suppressed her gasp. Her green eyes were wide with curiosity more than fright. It was true. Zebulona had returned. The treacherous old hag had been banished fourteen years ago for causing the death of a baby, long before Piper's birth. But Piper knew the story. Every child did. It was often told in the evening to scare them and to warn them. Piper knew she should run back and alert the village, but something held her glued to her spot.

Peering through the hole in the cave roof, Piper saw flames dance and lick the spewing cauldron. Zebulona's hands were gnarled like snakes writhing in the half-light, half-dark. Her face was ancient with endless dried canals. None of the adults would believe she still lived after so many years in the wilderness.

"It is almost complete," she laughed, dropping a root into the boiling pot. "Then I shall have my revenge on my village and every village that turned me away. One ingredient more—the black heart of one nobody loves and my revenge will be sweet."

Piper's ebony curls trembled. There in the shadows and dirt of the cave floor was a body. She recognized the long beard of the town butcher. He was a cruel man who tortured the animals before he killed them. Though Piper knew no one would miss him, she felt sorry for him. Tears fell from her innocent young face into the mixture below.

Using a crooked, bloodstained dagger, Zebulona cut open his chest and threw the heart into the cauldron. Though terrified, Piper stayed.

Smoke billowed, black and acrid. The stench was terrible, the smoke blinding. Piper took the scarf off her hair and covered her nose and mouth. Out of the scalding liquid, a creature emerged. It was black and stood tall like a man. The wings on its back beat stronger and faster as they grew and dried. It was some sort of demon that Zebulona intended unleashing on the village.

With all the speed her little legs could muster, Piper ran from the forest and across the barren field. There were children picking up stones to clear the field for planting. She ran up to the oldest—who was almost ten and tugged at his shirt.

"Quinn, it's true. Zebulona's come back. She's made a demon to kill us all."

"Last night my Pa went out to the cave to see. He said no one was there and beat me, so don't bother me." The dirty-faced boy pushed her, and she fell, sprawling in the dust.

Brushing herself off, Piper jumped to her feet and ran over the hill toward the village. The sky blackened behind her. By the time she reached her father, it was too late. Screaming came from the field. Every man armed with a pitchfork or spear rushed to find Quinn and three other children dead, their bodies ripped apart. Those remaining were huddled together crying.

That night fire rings roared high in hopes of keeping the demon at bay. The village elders listened attentively to Piper's story. The parents of the dead children raged, their anger finally disintegrating into weeping. The men organized watches, while the elders determined the best course of action.

Warriors of great renown came to battle the beast, but all were defeated. Their bloody, half-eaten carcasses were dropped through the air, splattering the council hall doorway. The creature mocked the elders, screeching their names and the names of village children.

The meager wealth of the village was offered to any sorceress or sorcerer who could save them. Many tried, but no spell deterred the monster. Every night he claimed a life, even with all doors and shutters locked tight.

That night Piper couldn't sleep. In every dream, the demon searched for her, calling her name. She woke with a start. Looking around, she saw her family sleeping peacefully on the mats placed on the floor of the hut. She rushed to the small cradle of her baby brother. He was gone.

Silently slipping out the door, she saw the creature standing in the moonlight about to take wing. In his arms was her brother.

"Stop," she cried.

The demon looked at her, as she bravely approached him.

"Please, don't take my brother," she said. "Take me." Her little hands reached out to him. There were tears on her face that glistened in the moonlight likes stars. He shivered and placed the baby on the ground.

He hugged himself, quivering, staring at her and backing away. Then Piper realized that her tears were part of him. They had fallen into the bubbling mire of his creation.

"I saw her make you," whispered the small, night-haired girl. "I'm sorry I couldn't save you. You were already dead when she cut out your heart. I'm sorry I couldn't help you."

A sound like the wind surrounded her. A sound like terror unable to find release howled through her. Then she realized the beast was crying.

Piper became aware of the village waking. Every man, woman, and child soon stood in the circle watching. Her mother rushed out and grabbed the baby. Her father reached for Piper, but she moved closer and closer to the monster.

Suddenly, his talons tightened around her, and he flew off. The villagers followed, shouting and throwing stones, but were soon left far behind in the forest. The creature landed near a different cave isolated by mountain walls. He released her gently, and she walked into the rock opening.

"You stupid demon, you were supposed to bring me an infant. Well, I suppose this child will have to do," Zebulona said emerging from the blackness. In her hand was the same crooked dagger now poised to take Piper's life.

The demon fluttered his wings, and the sorceress fell over.

"Do that outside, you witless beast."

She came at Piper with dagger raised. The child cowered against the demon. She looked up at him with fearful, innocent eyes. He closed his wings protectively around her.

The sorceress laughed. "I see. We need a little prodding, do we, to let loose our prey? You can have whatever's left.''

His huge wings remained closed around Piper like a tent keeping out the storm.

Zebulona picked up a torch and burned the creature. He screamed in pain. Piper scrambled through his legs. She was almost at the cave's mouth, when her eyes shimmered on something. In the clutter of weaponry taken from many vanquished heroes, a sword, broadblade with a single emerald in its hilt, glowed warm and inviting. Piper picked it up and found it incredibly light. Turning with sword in hand, she rushed at the hag.

The sword pierced through the hag's middle. Zebulona shuddered and screeched. Black blood gushed. The sorceress fell to the floor, gray and silent as stone.

Piper's tear-stained face turned to the badly burned demon who lay moaning on the damp ground. She sat next to him in the dirt. Her little hands rubbed his beaked face, as she whispered of his courage in protecting her. Her words were soothing and loving and were the last he ever heard. The creature died with the dawn.

After watching morning's rays creep across the cave floor, Piper rose and searched for food and water. She found the scabbard that went with the sword and tied it around her small waist. A round shield with a comet emblazoned across it became her own. Piper tied her supplies into a strong skin bag and began the long journey home.

The forest was dappled with green and gold, but never having been this far she did not know the way back. She walked until her legs failed, and each night she'd huddle beneath a pine. When she thought she would never see her village again and her food and water were almost gone, she heard the wind calling her name.

It wasn't the wind but voices. Several voices came closer and she ran to meet them. Though days of searching had proved fruitless, Piper's father wouldn't give up. She ran to him and was carried home in glory.

When Piper slept that night on her mat inside their hut, her mother covered her with a cloak of blue she'd made for her daughter. It was a large warm mantle meant to cover a warrior against all the cold winds of life. Piper didn't move. She hugged her sword to her and smiled.

The fireplace crackled, casting a warmth over the large room within the living tree. Sorrel de Martaine watched her teacher throw another log on the fire. The winter wind whistled outside. The torn hem of Torn Gown's dress fluttered in the slight breeze. Black hair once short and curly now cascaded down her back, nearly touching the ground. Her very being was grace. Sorrel studied the woman who taught her more than swordplay. She was awed by the quiet beauty of the warrior's tale.

"So when you were a child, they called you Piper?"

Torn Gown laughed. "Yes, just as you will be known in your life under many names. Some will know Sorrel, while others will only know the Ladyknight. Some will witness the warrior, while others will remember the beggar from which you sprang."

"There is one thing I don't understand. Why did your parents call you Piper?"

The teacher only smiled. Her movements across the floor were elegantly silent. In its place of honor on the wall hung the sword with the single emerald blessing its gold hilt with the brilliance of that moment in eternity. Below it on a nail hung a long bag. Torn Gown took it down and drew forth from its depths a beautifully carved wooden flute. She held it to her lips, and a wondrous sound filled the room with unspeakable splendor. It fluttered through her heart. It soared with her soul. Sorrel relaxed in her chair and drifted with each note into dreaming.

In a mountain cave a child was sitting. Only a few feet away was the slain sorceress who had wreaked revenge on the little girl's village, but the child no longer cared about that. Her emerald eyes looking lovingly on the demon who lay his head in her lap. Her small hands touched his face, and the beast sighed. He was safe now. In the arms of compassion, he died.

In her sleep, Sorrel wept for the subtle beauty of the warrior that awed her, and for the kind of warrior she dreamed she might someday be.

STOPTHRUST

by Diana L. Paxson

Diana Paxson married my brother Don, and having married into the family, proceeded to enter, in proper form, the family business. Both my brothers, Don and Paul, write novels; even my ex-husband Walter Breen writes nonfiction coin articles and encyclopedias for a living. So, as one can easily see, in our family, it's nothing unusual to be a writer; it'd be more unusual *not* to be one. And Diana duly became an ornament to the family. By now, in addition to a generous handful of fantasy novels, she has written a couple of major historicals: the splendid THE WHITE RAVEN, a fine retelling of the Tristram and Yseult legend; and her latest, THE SERPENT'S TOOTH, a retelling of the King Lear story, a grim subject, handled better than most people would think possible. But with all this she has still had time to write us another story of her swordswoman heroine Shanna. And I should add that as first founder of the Society for Creative Anachronism, she *does* know a good bit about swordplay. Hence the extreme verisimilitude of the fighting scenes in her work

The enemy blade was a blur in the bright air. Shanna shoved her shield up to meet it, honed instincts swinging the battered wood where the sword would fall. Peripheral vision sighted an expanding shadow beside her. Swearing, Shanna caught an arm-numbing blow from the second sword and the air rumbled with laughter.

Belisama's breastplate! How had Culain gotten so fast? Shanna glared at him over the rim of her practice shield.

"Need a new one soon, Shanna, if you fight with me!" Culain grinned as her swift glance noted the widening crack in the battered boards.

His fair skin was lightly sweated; in the harsh light his luxuriant mustaches glistened like gold wire. Culain should have been wrapped in the brightly chequered mantle of a warrior on the Misty Isles instead of a dun tunic and scuffed fighting leathers. *And I*, her thought continued grimly, *should by rights be swathed in a silken veil*.

But the time for that was fourteen years past. Instead of the golden torque of a royal house, she wore the iron neckring of a slave of Belisama. She had survived three years in the ring, and Culain two; but for most, the Gate of Death was the way out of here, not the Gate of Victory. All around them similarly clad pairs were battering each other back and forth across the beaten earth of the Arena's practice ground. To either side curved barracks with the mess hall and armory opposite the great statue of Belisama that guarded the gate through which her slaves entered the Arena.

Culain's blue eyes glinted as he lifted his leather wound practice swords. He had been generous to offer her this workout. Clearly, she needed practice against two swords. The cut of the longsword was more dangerous, but the short could serve as shield or weapon, changing direction with blurring rapidity. The past meant nothing: in the Arena, there was only the next fight, the next blow. Settling into a balanced crouch, Shanna lifted her shield and waited for it to come.

Blue eyes met dark across the rim of the shield.

You are my enemy. . . . You are my soul. . . .

He blurred toward her, and suddenly it was true. They clashed and parted in perfect rhythm, the clap and clatter of their baired blades like summer thunder. Faster they fought, and all other movement stilled around them. Laughing, Shanna struck Culain's longer blade aside and thrust, knowing how he would turn to evade her, shifting her balance already for the feint to follow—

—and found both breath and laughter driven from her body as she ran full upon the padded tip of his short second sword. The air darkened as she fought to breathe.

Blood pounded in Shanna's ears as her sight began to clear. She was flat on her back in the dust and Culain was bending over her. Nearby, somebody was cheering. Dimly she wondered how this upset would figure in the betting the next time she went through Belisama's door.

"Shanna, Shanna, my dark queen, ye've not been hurt now?" Swiftly Culain knelt, gathering her into his arms.

Culain, no! her heart cried, seeing something deeper than comradely concern blaze suddenly in those blue eyes. But being held by Culain was like being cradled by a large golden bear. She wanted that comfort, even as her mind cried out in silent despair. She had thought she could afford friendship. But that last bout had been too good, like making love.

The slaves of Belisama existed in uneasy alliance, depending on each other to hone their skills, knowing that whatever you taught might one day turn against you if you were set against the one you had befriended by the luck of the draw. In such a community, even comradeship could be a fatal disadvantage. And there was no place for love.

" 'm all right . . . oaf!" Weakly, she punched at him. "Just . . . got guts wrapped round my backbone! How did you *do* that?"

"Stopthrust!" He colored with relief to hear her answering. "But as to *how*, well now, that's my secret!"

Weakly, Shanna returned his grin, too relieved to hear he had not lost all sense of self-preservation to regret being denied.

"Never mind," she whispered. "Next time we bout I'll wring the trick of it from your stubborn northern hide." She pushed at his chest, and reluctantly he set her down.

For a moment, though, his eyes still held hers, and a pain stirred in her belly that had nothing to do with the blow. It had been fourteen years since Shanna had given up her maidenhead at the Baalteyn fire, and when the priestess of the Dark Mother cursed her she had been relieved to be delivered from the dangers of love. But then she had met Tara, who had shown her Ytarra's mirror, and whose gentle touch had reawakened her body and her soul.

She was barren. She could lie with Culain in all safety—until the day when the lots fell against them, and they faced each other with naked steel. In the Arena, only Belisama's embrace was sure.

The fountains in Lord Darios Starenyi's palace ran with blood red wine. The gilded rivets of Shanna's red leather brigandine glittered in the light of countless hanging lanterns as she listened to the tinkle of polite conversation around her and tried to forget the screams of dying men. Today's battles had been particularly bloody. Several favorites had been killed, men who were odds on to make their five hundred victories, and the mood of the city was ugly. Shanna ached still from the buffeting she had received in that last desperate struggle in the sand.

The wine could not give her oblivion. After three years, Shanna knew to a swallow just how much she could drink without impairing her skill. Nor was the company any distraction. The carnage of the afternoon was mirrored in every avid glance. To nobles whose nightmare was the silken cord of the Emperor's executioner, the slaves of Belisama were living talismans of survival. They sought their company as a child walks the top of a wall, enjoying the danger even as he fears to fall.

They live at the pleasure of the Emperor and I at that of the Goddess, thought Shanna. *Are they more free than I?* She took another sip of wine as two of the younger courtiers strolled by, eyeing her with a curious mixture of lust and aversion.

"Does she fight for the Golds or the Greens?" asked one, as if she could not hear.

"For neither," said his companion. "Really, Lars, where have you been? Red Shanna has allowed neither faction to take omens from her victories."

Shanna smiled sourly. That, of course, was the other reason the swordslaves were invited here. As they aligned themselves with one party or another their survival showed the favor of the gods. Passions that might have led to insurrection were exorcised at the Arena as folk cheered their favorites. Some of the fighters collected gold and jewels, gathering a stake for their dream of freedom. Shanna attended these parties to seek news of the brother who had disappeared here so many years ago. The price of her allegiance was information, but so far no one had offered her the right coin.

The nobleman's commentary continued as he moved on, but Shanna had lost interest. Across the room she glimpsed a familiar swirl of violet and her gut tightened as she saw Lord Irenos Aberaisi standing aside to let a smaller figure, rigid as ironwood beneath a cloud of draperies, enter the room.

Lady Amniset! She might not have come if she had known that the woman who had enslaved, addicted, and nearly killed her was going to be here. But all past debts were wiped out when a warrior took oath to Belisama. What could Lord Irenos' Great Wife do to her now?

As if she had felt the force of Shanna's gaze, the Lady turned. On her right hand the great ruby of the Dark Mother blazed balefully. Her maimed left hand, where Shanna had cut off the finger that had once worn that ring, was hidden beneath the folds of her robe. But the woman's eyes still raged.

"You fought well today, Swordlady—"

The voice held an oily assumption of intimacy that set Shanna to bristling even before she turned. But she recognized one of the eunuchs who served the Emperor, and controlled her reaction. No one from the Palace had approached her before.

"Three years—remarkable," he continued. "Perhaps you will be the first of your sex to make your quota of kills. . . ."

Shanna blinked. She had not realized that no woman warrior had ever won her freedom. The eunuch's smile broadened, and she gritted her teeth. He served the Emperor. He might have seen her brother when Janos came to Bindir.

"And aligned with no party—remarkable! Have you no desires?"

"To live through the next two years?" she returned his smile.

"We pray it will be so," he responded smoothly. "But no one can stand alone forever. You should consider making an alliance. Swordlady, you should indeed."

She eyed him, wondering to which faction he belonged. He was wearing the Imperial black and silver, with not even a snip of ribbon to show who had sent him here.

"Lorisos of Norsith wore gold, and his windpipe was crushed by a swinging spear," she said flatly, "and Nambu the Silent's green colors were dyed red by his opponent's sword. The goodwill of their factions could not save them. I will trust in Belisama's favor, and save my allegiance for the Emperor!"

The eunuch made an automatic gesture of reverence, but whether the goddess or the sovereign had evoked it, she could not tell.

"Green and gold are not the only colors . . ." his voice was lower now, and Shanna felt her hackles rise. "What if there were a power whose goodwill could guarantee victory to its devotees?"

Shanna suppressed her first response, which was that such a thing would be the ultimate impiety when the outcome of the fighting was supposed to foretell the will of the gods. Knowledge could be more valuable than gold.

"To what must I swear?" she asked carefully. Or *to whom?*

"If you come to the place that I shall tell you, you will be given the power to gain victory."

"Magic . . ." It was forbidden, of course, its use earning a slow death from the priests instead of a swift one in the ring.

He shrugged. "Swordlady, can you afford to be pious?"

"Can I afford to obligate myself to a power whose purposes I do not know?" Shanna answered him.

"I cannot say. But it is only good—" he assured her earnestly, jowls quivering. "The greater good of Bindir!"

"Do not all the parties say the same? Tell me more. I cannot answer you."

He shrugged, shook his head, and began to back away from her. Even as they talked, Shanna had been watch-

ing the movement of Lady Amniset's violet veiling. The
flicker of black and silver was heading straight toward
it—now the eunuch halted, gesturing, and the swordswoman moved so that she could see. Lady Amniset's
face stilled, but she could not control the single sharp
gesture of denial. The eunuch's face paled.

Interesting, thought Shanna. *He was not supposed to
make that offer to me. . . .*

A third faction in the capital was most likely to involve
the followers of the Dark Mother or that of the war god,
Toyur. Shanna had made enemies of both of them, but
Lady Amniset was a leader of the Children of Saibel.
The Greens stood for conservatism in fashion and in war;
they counseled the Emperor to be content with present
boundaries. The Golds were equally ready to make war
or swear alliance with the Empire's traditional enemies,
eager to create opportunities for new ways, and new
men. Would the followers of Saibel throw their weight
behind one of them, or try to gain power on their own?
And where, in this equation, stood the Emperor?

Frowning, she made her way around the periphery of
the crowd and accepted another goblet of wine. Culain
was standing by one of the pillars, the center of an admiring group who appeared to be going over this afternoon's
victory blow by blow. He blazed in the torchlight like
the barbarian prince he had been born, his powerful
thighs cased in tightly fitting chequered braes, a rich
cloak of lynx furs slung across one bare shoulder. He
was always so elated by victory; it angered her sometimes, but how could she deny him even a momentary
happiness?

As if he had felt her gaze, Culain turned and grinned.
Shanna found herself starting toward him; suddenly she
wanted to forget the plots and dangers, and even her
long search for her brother, and warm herself in his glowing laughter.

Horns blared from the doorway. For a moment all the
bright flutter of movement stilled. On a wave of glittering
steel and scent from a thousand fluttering white rose-
petals, Elisos Teyn Janufen, High Prince of Kateyn, Protector of the Misty Isles, and Emperor of all Bindir, had
arrived. This evening the Emperor was in his bright

mode. Melody shimmered from silver bells as his white clad attendants danced forward, followed by the perfectly drilled ranks of the Valkyr guards.

The Emperor's chair was being borne toward his host by fair-skinned slaves from the far north, but Shanna's gaze followed the warrior women of the guard. They walked with a balanced grace that the past three years had made her even more able to appreciate, and their bared swords glimmered with the beaten wave-patterns of Dorian steel.

The Emperor alighted, and a coverlet of silver-brocade was hastily draped across a dining couch so that he could lie beside his host. He was thin, pale-skinned, speaking with febrile animation to his host, then turning again to survey the crowd. And now the swordslaves were being summoned for inspection. Even Culain's gold was dimmed by all that white splendor. Shanna had thought him a sun, but as they approached the dais she saw that he was only a flickering candle flame in the light of the Emperor's day.

"You were good today," said Shanna, setting down her mug of thin beer. "I have never seen you fight so well."

Culain shrugged and upended his own mug. She could see the strong muscles of his throat working as the beer went down. She pushed the remains of her meat about on her plate. There were not many here for the night-meal. Today's Games had honored the return of the Fourth Legion from the Dorian Wars, and most of the victorious Arena-slaves were celebrating at one of the many banquets being held in Bindir. Even from the mess-hall of the Arena one could hear the sound of revelry. The withdrawal of the Legion favored the Greens' policy of containment, and betting had been heavy to see if the gods agreed. Those who fought for the Golds had been the heaviest losers, and folk were beginning to speak of a resurgence among the followers of Saibel.

"So why aren't you out being lionized? I know you have invitations. You can't have stayed in for the sake of this beer!" Shanna managed to laugh, but Culain was frowning. She had been right, then—something was troubling him.

"I am alive, and you are alive . . ." he rumbled, staring into the empty mug. "No praise means more than that now. But men died who should have won today. How many of the beds in these barracks will still be empty come the dawn?"

"They will be filled . . ." Shanna answered bitterly. "When the generals sort out the captives from this last campaign. Why does it trouble you now?"

"My last fight. . . ." he shook his head unhappily.

"I saw it. What happened? You were like the bear-priests when they go into a rage!"

"Akonu was my friend," muttered Culain. "And he was strong . . ." he shoved the mug away suddenly. "Come outside with me, Shanna. I can't talk to you here!"

"Are you going to teach me your secret thrust?" She tried to laugh.

"Perhaps," he muttered as they came out into the warm darkness. A full moon was edging above the wall of the Arena, and the elongated shadow of Belisama stretched black across the sand of the practice yard. "Perhaps I will do that. Perhaps that secret does not matter any more. . . ."

Shanna stopped, gripping his arm. "What is it, Culain, what happened to you?"

"Work out with me, Shanna—" his teeth flashed in a bitter twist of the mouth that was not quite a grin. "You know I cannot think without a sword in my hand."

Muscles stiffening from the afternoon fight throbbed in protest, but that other pain that was not of the body was twisting beneath her breastbone. Wordless, she followed him to the armory.

Black silhouettes against the white sands of the training ground, they moved through the training dances that awakened the muscles and brought mind and body into singing harmony. Shanna had chosen to work out with a leather-bound practice sword in each hand; if he did intend to reveal the secret of the stopthrust, she might as well be prepared to practice it.

"You look like the Raven of Battle swooping across

the field—" said Culain, watching as both Shanna's swords arced outward, decapitating invisible foes. "We call her Marigan, in the Misty Isles."

"I know . . ." Her weapons swung back around and up to guard, longsword poised over one shoulder, shortsword upright. But she was seeing blood and fire on the walls of Otey while men cried that name.

"I thought the first time it was *her* battle-madness, and was glad," said Culain. "But I should not have felt that way when I killed a friend. The spell has done this. And I am not the only one. It is a blasphemy."

He flowed into motion suddenly and lunged, his second sword snapping around to take advantage of the gap a blade lifting to deflect the first blow would leave. Remembering how the goddess had once possessed her, Shanna was not so sure the madness of the Marigan distinguished between friend and foe. They came to a halt in the lee of the training pelz, its tough wood hacked and haggled by countless sword-cuts.

"What spell?"

"Fight with me, Shanna, I cannot say it standing—" His weapons came up in salute, black bars crossing like a warding sign against the moon-paled sky. "And guard yourself well!"

"The Emperor's eunuch . . . came to me," Culain stalked her. "Kallios, Zennor, and me—invited to a banquet— taken there blindfolded. The drink was drugged . . ." He struck suddenly; her own blades crossed to catch the first sword, parted to dash the second blow aside.

"—got strange after that," Culain said, panting. His swords lifted slowly back to readiness and she faced him once more. "But there was . . . a ritual, and a *word*—" His eyes were white-rimmed like those of a driven horse. "Is it only a way to win money, knowing which fighters will go mad and win? Or do they have some other plan?" He blurred toward her, too fast, too fast—

Crack! And Crack! Shanna's swords were wrenched from her hands; her breath left as he crashed down on top of her, steely fingers vising her shoulders.

For a few moments they lay gasping, until at last the tremors that ran through Culain's big frame began to ease. His breath was warm on her cheek.

"What was the spell, Culain?" she whispered. "What did they do to you?" She was abruptly aware of her unarmored neck, so close to his hands.

"To say the word . . . makes the madness. Instead of opponent, you see a demon . . . even to think it calls the fury . . . even now."

Shanna tensed as he touched her neck, rough fingertips leaving a tingle of sensation where they passed. Then they came to the iron neckring and paused.

"So soft . . . so easy to kill," Culain sighed. His hand moved up to caress her cheek and he kissed her, slowly, thirstily, like a wanderer who finds a spring.

I should stop this, thought Shanna. If she struggled, even his strength could not hold her. But she was thirsty, too.

"I want to love you, Shanna, not kill you," he whispered when they drew breath at last. "I am so tired of the killing . . . so very tired. . . ."

Culain's head dropped down once more upon her shoulder, and she was aware of the living length of him with every fiber of her own body, and knew that what she was feeling was desire.

"Lie with me, Shanna—" She could hardly hear the words. "I want to make life with you. Take off your armor and lie in my arms."

Shanna turned her head away, staring upward at the sterile silver round of Belisama's shield.

"Have you forgotten what our neckrings mean? You know that if we live, one day they will set you against me, and kill us both, slowly, if we refuse to fight."

For a moment he was silent. "I think it is already too late to shield myself against you. . . . I will teach you the secret of the stopthrust, Shanna!" he burst out then. "But let us make one bright flame against the dark!"

"No . . ." she said, and felt the pain in her belly like a sword.

Culain heaved himself away from her. Her hair had come undone in the fighting and lay spread in waves of darkness against the pale sand, but her face must be white in the moonlight, her despair only too easy to see. His own face was in shadow, the light behind him silvering his fair hair. *The Emperor's colors*, she thought grimly, *but which is the face of mercy now?*

"Marigan . . ." his breath came harshly. "I saw you . . . in Otey. Dark Queen, Blood Dancer, it does not matter what you say to me . . . in life or death, you are my destiny!"

"No—" she began once more, but Culain was already up, lurching across the sand. She heard the door of the men's barracks slam and then a babble of greeting as he went inside.

For a time Shanna lay where he had left her. Then, painfully, she got to her feet. The pelz was a lonely pillar of darkness in the white expanse of the yard. She stripped the guarding leathers from her practice sword and began to hack at the post, and the moonlight spun silver from her blade.

Shanna's nostrils flared as the scent of the Arena flowed through the opening door, wondering as always how she could have forgotten that compound of sweat and incense and the faint sweet stench of old blood that no amount of clean sand could ever quite take away. From the stands came a roar like a distant sea. On Arena days the crowd could be heard halfway across Bindir, but Shanna knew that once she stepped out onto the sands, she would hear nothing but the breathing of her foe.

Here, in the shadow of the passageway, she was still painfully aware of Culain. For the past week she had avoided him, but he seemed to have garnered all the peace she had lost.

"A stopthrust—" he spoke without looking at her, "is when you let your enemy's energy bring him to your blade."

Trumpets blared cruelly from above, and the line began to move. Shanna blinked as they emerged beneath the statue of Belisama and the gates clanged shut behind them. With measured tread, those who would fight this day marched the length of the Arena, their armor blazing in the sun. To their left, the iron Gate of Death was set into the wall beneath the stands; to their right, the gilded Gate of Victory.

"Culain—" Shanna whispered. "Forgive me—"

"You strike with the longsword, enemy parries and comes in," he went on as if she had not spoken. "Drop to one knee and thrust out the shortsword. Before he knows he's in range, you've spitted him."

Below the Emperor's box, the flicker of Belisama's fire great steadily larger as they neared. Today, the Lord of Bindir was swathed in a garment like midnight sewn all over with little crystals that glittered in the sun. Great lilies black as bruises garlanded his box, and dark-skinned slaves with black plumes propelled the great fans. The princes of the city were ranked around him. Shanna stiffened as she recognized Lady Amniset, her purple robes almost as dark as the lilies, then forced her gaze away.

The fighters spread into a semicircle as the Emperor came down to the railing. His thin features seemed strained. There was bad news from the Dorian frontier. If the Emperor sent the legions back again, it would be a victory for the priests of Toyur and the Golds.

The pairings for today's fights had been posted in the city the afternoon before, and the stands had flowered in patches of green and gold. The Emperor had reason to look tense, if the people were waiting for today's combats to decide whether the Goddess approved of his policies. Only the fighters themselves would not know how the lots had fallen until they were called into the ring.

"Slaves of Belisama!" the voices of the priests rolled across the sands. "Let the will of the Goddess be served!"

Shanna stared at the fire, and all existence narrowed to a terrible simplicity. The words that had become a part of her being roared in her ears as fifty swords flamed from their scabbards.

"I swear to fight for the Goddess, forsaking all other obligations and loyalties." As the oath rolled on, swords lowered until their points were toward the fire. "Before Belisama's holy altar, and in the presence of my Emperor, I offer my life to her as priest or sacrifice. As I do battle, so shall the soldiers of Bindir. May the will of Belisama be revealed!"

*　　*　　*

May the will of Belisama be revealed . . . As Shanna

waited, the phrase haunted her. She had survived three years in the Arena by using this time to become the weapon of the Goddess, as passionless and as pitiless as her own sword. She must not think about Culain. . . .

Think about the sword move he described, she told herself. Again and again, she worked through the sequence, trying to ignore the roar of the crowd. She saw Zennor throw himself on the body of the man he had downed and tear at his throat like a dog. Kallios killed his opponent with equal savagery. It was clear which warriors had submitted to Saibel's sorceries, if one had eyes to see.

And then the priests came to her. The sound of her own name reverberated around the Arena. Shanna strode forward, swords raised to catch the sun. They were calling her opponent's name now, its syllables shattered into meaningless bits of sound by the repetition of the crowd. Shanna turned, sight blurring as the blaze of silvered armor neared so that she would not have to see his face. And still her body went through the right motions; the salutes to the altar and to the Emperor and to the man who faced her, bright as she was dark, his every move a mirror of her own.

Her awareness was working on so many levels: the one that calculated distance and angle and motion positioning her body to meet the attack of an opponent who was bigger but just as skilled as she; the one that fluttered from one scheme to another, seeking a solution that would not leave one of them bleeding on the sand; and louder than either, the mind of the female animal that could only keen its despair.

Like an encounter long destined, they began the weapon's deadly dance. Culain's longsword cut downward and Shanna's shorter blade deflected it, but at the same time her long blade would be circling, his shortsword rising to turn it away. The weapons clashed and parted, sending one fighter or the other whirling into a new figure, arms crossing and uncoiling again. It was the harmony they had found on the practice field, but now they danced to the music of steel.

As muscles limbered and the blood sang through their veins, attacks grew bolder, defense more spirited in return. Shanna's feet scarcely seemed to touch the sand.

Somewhere in the first clash her sorrow had left her. A fight like this was the perfect marriage of coordination and skill of which a fighter dreams. She retreated a step as Culain lunged and caught his descending sword upon a cross of blazing steel; his shortsword jabbed toward her breast, but already she was whipping her own blades up and away, turning with swords extended like bright wings.

It was not the berserk rage that had brought so many fights to a grisly ending, but the true battle ecstasy. In the stands, there was silence as men strained to follow the unfolding of a fight such as they had never expected to see.

And still it continued, until at last the body began to fail. Shanna felt the breath sob in her chest, knew the moments when her footwork started to slow. But still the blades blazed through the bright air. Culain's longsword swept toward her. Turning to parry, Shanna saw him start to sink down on one knee; saw it, and understood the move he had described to her even as her own momentum carried her toward the point of his shorter blade.

She made no attempt to avoid it, accepting the appointed climax to her ecstasy. It was Culain who moved, leaving to one side so that his weapon would go past her, moving directly into the arc that her longsword was inscribing above the sand.

Shanna felt the shock jar up her arm as the keen edge bit through mesh and padding and muscle and bone. The sword had struck between the edge of his shoulder armor and the flanges of his helm. In that first moment, her only emotion was anger that the rhythm had been broken. Then the continuation of her move drew the sword from Culain's body, and she saw the bright blood follow her lifting blade.

The pattern brought her other weapon around, but Culain was already collapsing onto the sand. Her swords fell from suddenly strengthless fingers; she threw herself forward as if he had hit her, calling his name.

"Should . . . have taught you . . . how to guard!" Culain winced, coughed, and bright blood came from his lips. "Marigan!" He tried to lift his hand to her face, but it fell back again, and suddenly he smiled. "Safe now . . ." he whispered. "To tell you . . . the spell." He struggled for breath. *"Amyis Saibel!"*

With the words, his features contorted. A tremor swept through his body; he stiffened and tried once more to reach for her, fingers clawed. But the power had left him. Shanna bent closer, calling his name. But Culain's face was still constricted in rage when the understanding went out of his eyes.

Shanna ascended the stairs to the Emperor's box without seeing them. The air of the Arena boomed as the people cheered the victors, but the sound was like the noise of a battle many miles away. Culain had gone out through the Gate of Death, and with him all the color had gone from the day. The dark draperies in the Imperial box were easier to look at. Shanna drew a shuddering breath, eyes caught, despite herself, by the dark glitter of the Emperor's robes. Elisos Teyn Janufen looked older than his years; pale, with marks like old bruises beneath his eyes like a man who has not been sleeping well.

Culain will sleep well tonight . . . and I will sleep alone.

The Emperor was coming down the three steps of his dais to meet them, followed by a woman who carried a tray with wreaths of silver laurel leaves. But the woman wore purple, not black. Painfully, Shanna's mind began to function once more.

Culain is dead . . . and I killed him . . . and in a few moments Lady Amniset is going to give me my victor's crown . . .

That thought was enough to jerk her back to full awareness. The Emperor looked anxious, but Lady Amniset Aberaisi wore the smile of a well-fed beast of prey.

"Oh, my lord, what a day this has been!" said the eunuch at her side. "Such fighting! I do not know when I have seen so many die so well!"

Culain is dead . . . repeated Shanna's litany, *and he would be alive if you had not forced him to fight me*!

"And so many of them wear green," Lady Amniset replied. "Surely the gods have made plain their will. The legions will stay in Bindir!"

"I am not sure," said the Emperor fretfully. "There are complexities. I do not know what I will do!"

"My lord does not know?" An odd note in the Lady's voice set Shanna's back hair prickling. "Well, let us deal with the present, then. Here are twenty good warriors waiting for their reward . . ." She set the tray of laurel crowns on a pedestal at the Emperor's right hand.

The swordslaves spread out in a close semicircle facing him, bearing the weapons with which they had won their victories. They looked a little dazed, as if they had just emerged from some evil dream. Kolias was among them, and Zennor, whom Culain said had been given the battlespell with him. But Culain had not used it, and now he was dead, while they lived, and Shanna's evil dream went on.

She let herself be pushed toward the end of the line. The note in Lady Amniset's voice had been one of anticipation. What was she up to here?

"Servants of Belisama," said the Emperor, lifting his hands in welcome. "Bindir was well served today! Receive now the tokens of your victory—"

"And receive also a blessing," said the Aberaisi princess, her voice soft but very clear as she stepped *behind* the Emperor. "The blessing of Amyis—"

In that moment, as she had seen the inevitability of Culain's last move, Shanna understood. Before Lady Amniset had finished the phrase, the swordswoman slipped behind her.

"—Saibel!" cried the Lady. And in a single motion Shanna thrust her toward the men whose bodies were tensing, faces contorting as reason left them and they focused on the nearest foe.

"Back, my lord, for your life!" Shanna hissed at the Emperor, pushing past him. For a second he stared at her, wild eyed, then the first swords flashed from their sheaths and he scrambled backward up the stairs.

"Treason! Treason! Guards, to me!"

His cry was lost in the swordsmen's roars of fury. Like beasts they flung themselves on the thin figure in the violet robe.

The eunuch screamed shrilly, but from Lady Amniset came no sound. There was only the struggle, and the purple cloth grew red, but by that time everything was crimson, for the Valkyr guards were methodically cutting down the swordslaves, who still saw only the demon of their dreams.

"There have been confessions . . ." the Emperor said heavily. His throne room was draped in black, but Elisos himself wore a white robe. Shanna nodded. He did not need to explain how the confessions had been obtained.

"The plotters needed funds. At first the spell on the swordslaves was only a way to change the odds on the betting, but then the Aberaisi woman realized that the men she had bespelled could be used to assassinate me."

"What good would that have done her?" asked Shanna, sitting back on the cushion they had placed for her below the throne. There was always a breeze here, at the summit of the citadel. The cool air caressed her neck and she touched it, still surprised to find the neck-ring gone. The breeze brought her the music of the fountains on the terraces below. She had forgotten there could be such peace in the world.

"She had found a cousin of mine," said Elisos, "who agreed to keep the legions home and restore the cult of Saibel. A man of my own family, whom I had always treated well!"

He lives in fear as I did in the Arena, thought Shanna, *but his is worse, never knowing from what direction the danger will come*!

"How did you persuade the priests of Belisama to release me?" she asked then.

"A hundred have been executed already," the Emperor said grimly. "And there will be more. Their blood is shed on Belisama's altar, but the priests have agreed to accept them as your kills."

Shanna shivered. If he had lived, Culain's life would still have been forfeit, along with the others who had fallen under the spell. And yet it was Culain's stopthrust that had shown her how to defeat Lady Amniset in the end, using her opponent's own strength against her.

"—surely you will accept some additional reward?" Shanna realized that Elisos had been speaking for some time.

Give me my brother— she thought. But asking about him might be as dangerous as the plot she had just foiled. She needed a position in Bindir from which she could continue to follow his trail.

"A house in the City?" asked the Emperor. "I like talking to you."

Shanna stared at him. Culain's face had concealed nothing. This man's face was all contradictions, half-masked by the sculpturing of power. Culain had feared nothing, not even death. This man was afraid of everything. But Elisos Teyn Janufen was alive, and the master of Bindir.

"I am a swordswoman," said Shanna abruptly. "If you want to talk to me, give me a place in your Valkyr guard!"

The Emperor looked at her, and for a moment the fear in his face was hidden as he smiled.

ELYNNE DRAGONCHILD
by Phil Brucato

It's reached a point in these anthologies—since at first I
went as far as I could to avoid the male version of sword
and sorcery fiction, in which the women were sidekicks
or bad-conduct prizes for the heroes instead of having
adventures of their own—that male writers have taken
the role of the "token male." Or at least they are often
perceived that way.

As a matter of fact, I have bought and will continue to
buy many stories by men; for example, Bruce Arthurs,
Jessie Eaker, and Dave Smeds have appeared many
times each in these anthologies and will continue to do
so—or at least we hope they will. (All have stories in the
present volume.)

This story was good enough to overcome my known
prejudice about dragons, who have become something
of a cliché in fantasy fiction. But Phil seems to have
thought the subject through, and brings us a different
dragon story, about a maiden who became a dragon's
foster child. I'll guarantee this isn't a clone of every other
dragon story you've read this year.

The dark man in the metal dragonskin seized Elynne's arm. She cried out and pulled away. He
grabbed her again roughly and shook her, barking
words she could not understand. Another armored man

laid his hand on the first man's shoulder, speaking to him in soft tones. The first man quieted but held Elynne firmly, the leather of his gloves warm and sticky with fresh sweat and spilled blood.

Across the vaulted rock chamber, two other men gazed at three charred corpses in smoking armor. They fanned their faces to chase the smell of fiery death that choked the cavern. Elynne's own gaze blurred and swam. Spilling tears mingled with sweat as she sobbed hot fetid air. Her wails echoed within the twisting cavern complex.

The dark man rattled her again. The second man, pity in his gaze, pulled a cloak from his pack and draped it about her bare shoulders. It itched. She shrugged it off. He wrapped it about her again, murmuring soothingly. The cloak and the closeness of the two men pressed in, crushing her. A ringing rose in her ears. Not two dozen paces away, a gore-splattered man struggled to rip the heart from the massive dead beast sprawled in its last-stand corner. Elynne's stomach lurched, her legs gave way. The two men caught her as she fell into darkness.

They hadn't even let her say good-bye.

Elynne. Her christened name was one of the few things she could remember from the days before the riders came, sheathed in iron and leather. Barely six summers old, Elynne had slipped away into the forested hills while her village burned. She'd wandered for days, going ever higher in the hills her people had shunned, and had been near death when the dragon found her.

Elynne had frozen like a rabbit in the dragon's shadow, and she'd dropped to her knees in both awe and supplication as it swooped from the sky. The dragon seemed to stretch across the clouds as it landed, blotting out the sun, sending Elynne sprawling in the buffeting blast of its massive wings. Lying stunned on her back, the starving child had felt her terror give way to wonder and admiration at the majesty of the beast. Its scales shimmered in the autumn sun as the dragon's muscles shifted and slid beneath the armor. Elynne lay transfixed as the dragon's supple neck gracefully lowered a massive head to sniff her, its hot breath snorting like a blacksmith's bellows. Then it withdrew and regarded her with washtub eyes. Elynne giggled as the beast sat back on its haunches like some gargantuan puppy dog, and the creature cocked its head at the unfamiliar sound. After a moment, the dragon reached for her with a massive talon.

Screaming terror shot through Elynne, but days of starvation and exposure robbed her of the ability to do anything but howl as the dragon wrapped her in its paw and flapped its ponderous wings, rising away from the ground, the trees, the hills where she had wandered. It was like both dream and nightmare, this flight, and after a while, Elynne stopped screaming and simply watched the land spill away beneath the dragon's wings.

The girl had been near breathless when the dragon alighted at last. It set her gently on the ground before a great cave and withdrew its claw. Fear returned. Would the dragon eat her now? Elynne stood trembling, unwilling to meet the monster's gaze but unable to avoid it. The dragon stared back, waiting, then flicked its head impatiently at the cavern mouth. Elynne started forward, hesitant, waiting for the slash of teeth or a blast of fire. None came. The dragon only waited. When she'd reached the stone arch doorway, Elynne had stopped cold, unwilling to trespass. The musty air inside was sweet with the dragon's strangely pleasant scent—a smooth, leathery musk, not an animal smell. To the girl's surprise, the creature seemed to nod and grant her access to its lair. She stepped across the threshold and the dragon unfurled its great wings again and rose impossibly into the sky. She watched in wonder as it left, then entered the cave.

Inside, it was surprisingly warm, a marked contrast to the windy chill outside. A towering hallway narrowed and snaked inside and up a short distance to an anteroom where the smell of smoke and dragon hung like incense in the air. The cavern floor was worn smooth beneath her sore bare feet, and the great walls, sloping upward like the battlements of a fabled city, glowed polished in the light of a huge fire burning near the center of the room. The smoke from the firepit floated into dark chimneys far above, and smaller, twisting passageways ran off in several channels from the main room. The stonework, though obviously natural, had just as obviously been carved and smoothed by giant claws and tempered with fiery breath. To Elynne, the cavern seemed like a story-teller's dream world, a faerie kingdom or a playground for elves. But then, was this not a dragon's cavern? Suddenly all the fireside tales the older children mocked seemed real, and Elynne's hunger and fear washed away, melted into a gentle, drowsy peace. Whatever the dragon intended, she seemed safe for the first time in days. A small stream bubbled from a cleft near the floor, and thirsty Elynne drank her fill. Exhausted, the little girl lay down beside the firepit and slept.

She bolted awake to the clack and scrape of claws on rock flooring. The dragon had returned, and with it, her fear. As the monster approached the firepit, Elynne realized that it carried a limp and mangled stag in its nightmare jaws. She screamed. The dragon stopped beside the pit and cocked its head, puzzled, then dropped the stag and quickly rent it to pieces with deft passes of its claws. Being a rustic village girl, young Elynne was not so much shocked by the swift dismemberment of the animal as she was by the method. When the dragon dropped chunks of meat to sizzle on the rocks beside the fire, Elynne's stomach roared with hunger.

That night, Elynne and the dragon shared the first of many meals together.

"Tell them to look harder! After losing three good men, I don't intend to go away empty-handed!"

"Don't let your thirst for gold get the better of you, Fredrick. If nothing else, today we've saved a young girl from the jaws of Satan's hosts. And come through alive, by the grace of God. Surely that's enough to be thankful for!"

"It isn't that I'm ungrateful, Father, but gratitude won't pay the men or feed the widows. Blast it, the gold must be *somewhere!*"

Elynne heard the voices from far away. She could not understand the words, but the tone was clear enough. Hollow pain sang behind her forehead and sickness tugged at her throat and stomach. She forced her eyes to squint open to the blinding sunlight outside the cave. Wheels creaked. Bridles jingled as horses snorted. Elynne lay wrapped in soft leather on the back of a wooden wagon, nestled beside sacks that smelled of bread and oil. Groaning, she forced herself to sit up.

Outside the dragon's cave, armored men ran to and fro like ants. Another wagon sat waiting off to her left. A few paces away, the dark-haired man sat high in the saddle while a bald man, the one with the soothing voice, sought to calm the dark one's temper. Hearing Elynne moan, the two men turned to look at her. Elynne shivered. Though she'd held no shame of her body, she felt exposed before these two men's gaze, and clasped the bald man's cloak before her breasts. The standing man smiled and spoke gently to her as he moved to her side and drew a sloshing sack from the stock beside her. She stiffened as he clambered aboard the wagon and offered her the water skin. The dark man dismounted as the bald man coaxed Elynne to drink. She wanted to scream, to spit the stale water in their faces and fling herself at them with sword in hand and hack them all to pieces. But she felt dizzy and weak. Later, she consoled herself. Later, when her strength returned.

The dark-haired man's voice rang out across the clearing. The man beside her scowled while the first man strutted between the wagons. Elynne's eyes burned as she glared at him. As he built to the crescendo of his speech, the dark man leapt aboard the second wagon and whipped the leather tarp from the dark trophy underneath.

When Elynne saw the dark man's trophy, she screamed out and was sick.

She had grown up wild and strong after the dragon took her in. As she matured, Elynne had thrown off the clothing, tools, and language of mankind. She hunted, fished, and foraged with her bare hands and grew accustomed to the weather regardless of season. As there was no one who could listen, Elynne ceased to speak. She and the dragon did not need words to converse, and in time Elynne forgot what words she had known.

Near winter that first year, and for every year thereafter, the dragon and the girl would forage and build themselves a winter store within the caverns, piling extra wood to keep the fire going. Her guardian would then hibernate through the cold season, leaving Elynne to her own devices. The caverns trapped the heat of the fire and the living earth, and they remained warm all year round. During these months alone, Elynne grew bored. Sometimes she would drape herself with fur and wander barefoot in the snow, delighting in the winter's clear and cleansing bite until the cold became too bitter. Other times, she would heft a brand or two from the fire and explore the endless warrens of their home beneath the hills.

In the warmer seasons, all the world was hers to explore. She swam the lakes and streams, hiked the endless forests, and scaled the granite hills. She grew strong and self-assured, her hair a wild dark mane. Nothing was beyond her. Each year she ranged farther, dived deeper, climbed higher, and the dragon seemed to be pleased as she grew to womanhood.

The day she finally reached the summit of the highest of the hills, she stretched her bruised and aching limbs and basked in triumph, wind, and sun. For leagues in all directions lay unspoiled land, gorgeous and terrible as the dragon, or as Elynne herself. As the sun began to color the horizon, the dragon rose and soared above the hills. Laughing, Elynne called to it. The mighty beast circled the mountain she had climbed, gazing at her in concern, but Elynne had laughed and danced upon the hilltop, and the dragon understood. Fading sunlight glittered rainbows on scale and leathern wing as the dragon danced on air. Elynne motioned it home again, and, with a nod of its head, it flew off across the sunset. Alone, she drank in the sun-washed sights as nightfall came, then picked her way down the hill again in darkness.

She bolted when the wagon struck a rut. The draft horse yelped as the harness snapped it to a stop. The wagon pitched, and Elynne leapt to the ground. Men shouted behind her, and horses whinnied. She rolled to her feet on the stony turf, flung off the cloak, and ran.

If they'd hit the rut in the forest, she'd be clean away. Even many leagues from home, she knew the woodpaths well, and they'd never have caught her. But the track they'd chosen was open, bordered by trees but clear for passage. As she pounded across the naked ground she heard the thud of hooves behind her. She flung herself down and rolled as the dark man rode past, grabbing at empty air. Another man pulled up short before his horse could trample her. She scrabbled rocks from the earth and hurled them at the riders, but to no avail. They surrounded her, bore her down, and carried her, lashing and spitting, to the wagons. Against the protests of the bald man, she was bound.

As a child, Elynne and the dragon would sometimes play. She found her guardian a willing and gentle, if formidable, playmate with a keen sense of fun and an endless imagination. Yet, despite the dragon's power and gargantuan size, Elynne was never hurt beyond the usual childhood scuffs and bruises.

The girl often watched with longing as her adopted parent would fly away on some errand or another, remembering her first ride in the dragon's grip. But, until she grew older, the dragon refused to carry Elynne into the sky again.

As the years passed, Elynne realized that the dragon, though larger than a cottage, was far smaller than it had seemed. Ten summers, give or take, following her adoption, Elynne had grown enough to straddle the dragon's back. As they played one day, she grabbed one wing and slipped across her playmate's shoulders. Its tough cool scales, familiar to her touch, seemed to slide beneath her thighs. The beast rose on its haunches and raised its head to question her. Elynne's heart thundered and her bare skin tingled as she hugged the dragon tighter with arms and legs, willing it to spread its wings and hoist them both into the sky. Tendons tightened and huge veins throbbed beneath the dragon's armored hide. Her fingers clenched at scales. She met the dragon's gaze and nodded. Mighty wings, furled to the sides, lifted and spread, flapped. Feeling the speeded pulse beneath her skin, Elynne feared her hammering heart would explode as her breathing deepened, quickened. Dust and leaf clouds stirred, rose, blew away as girl and dragon lifted and the ground fell away.

Wind blasted and caressed Elynne, whipping hair and rippling skin. She felt her stomach lurch as the trees danced far below with their passing. She strained to clutch pounding wing muscles and cobbled dragonhide. Startled birds squawked and wheeled out of their way. The air grew colder. A league or so above the trees, the dragon leveled out into a glide. Elynne raised her head and shook the hair from her eyes. Her heart skipped and hitched as wide eyes gazed down upon the world spread out forever. Even the mountain was nothing like this. All below was green and brown, the sun seemed closer, the clouds wisping near enough to touch. Freedom sang within her, the freedom of gods. Vertigo and exultation whirled and warred and stole her breath. Gripping tightly with her legs, Elynne pulled back, sat up, and spread her arms in joy, boundless joy. She sucked breath from the wind that roared in her ears and bellowed her soul's song. The dragon peered over its shoulder to confirm her safety, but Elynne's eyes were closed and her mouth was wide and her throat sang wordless praises for a long, long time.

Though they rode the skies many times together, Elynne never forgot that first time she dared to ride.

The somber hall flickered firelight, and the courtly ladies tittered as Elynne's long fingers fumbled with her eating dagger. The stench of animals and unwashed bodies seared through cooked food and rich perfume. The dragon would never have tolerated such a stink. Her long gown itched, and she fought against tight corsets for each breath of foul air.

They'd brought her to a castle larger even than the dragon's cave, but instead of wild nature or solitude, the place was packed with reckless pets and ill-mannered people. They'd forced her body into tight and scratchy clothes and her feet into graceless, clumsy shoes. They tried to twist her tongue around their words and her deeds around their manners, and cuffed her when she would have none of it. The dark-haired man, called Lord, wooed her with gentle words and gifted her with finery pleasing to the eye. But of what use was finery to one who had ridden naked on a dragon's back Elynne loathed him, and found his new-found honeyed manner insulting. The others clearly thought her mad, and treated her accordingly, though with restraint. From daggered looks and appraising glances, she guessed that others found her appealing, but dressed in their clothes, weighed down by the stone castle walls, she felt ugly and alone. Only the bald one, called Father, could soothe or cheer her, and then only a little.

Now she sat at Lord's table, blushing at the chuckles of the ladies. Two hands of days and nights following their arrival at the castle, a crowd of strangers packed the banquet hall. Elynne had been wrapped in stifling gowns and led to the table. As she had entered the room, Lord had bellowed some speech or other, and the assemblage had cheered. "Smile," said Father, one of the words he had taught her. Stiffly, she obliged. Then came the food, and the fumbling, and mocking laughter. Father sought to scold the snickerers, but Elynne couldn't care less. The banquet was torture.

After much eating, drinking, and suffocating shame, Lord leapt upon the table and addressed the crowd again. Elynne couldn't catch one word out of ten, but she knew that Lord was bragging again. She sighed. Lord bragged a lot. At length, he clapped his hands and hollered. Two servants came in dragging a small cart. Elynne stopped chewing as Lord approached the shrouded cart with a jaunty step. Her throat clenched around the food and she shuddered, remembering the wagon and its trophy. He reached for the drape. She tried to tear her eyes away and could not. Lord gripped the drape and pulled. The crowd gasped. Elynne choked on her food and screamed.

The dragon's head was mounted on a huge wooden shield covered in the dragon's own skin. Elynne spat food, grabbed her eating dagger, and flung herself, shrieking, at Lord and his trophy. The table tumbled as she leapt upon it, and food flew in all directions. Guests screamed and guards scrambled. She thrashed to her feet and dashed toward Lord, holding the dagger high. Father grabbed at her and missed. Lord stumbled back in surprise and guards rose in Elynne's path. One blocked her with his halberd. The other clouted her with a heavy mailed fist. Pain flared, but Elynne had wrestled with a dragon's claw and tail and felt much harder blows. She swung the knife and felt it bite into mail. One guard cried out. The other dashed her across the wrist with the butt of his weapon, driving the knife from her grasp. Other guards grabbed at her arms and shoulders. From behind her, she heard Father crying out. Now he was before her, shaking her and pleading while the guards pinned her arms behind her. Elynne's vision reddened and swam. Strong as she was, she was helpless. Lord's voice bellowed as he pointed to the corridor, and the guards bore Elynne away while Father followed, begging at her with his soft, soothing voice.

Only once had Elynne roused the dragon's anger. Dragons, being long-lived and wise, had almost infinite patience. But a growing, willful child, she had found, could tax even a dragon's calm.

Once, she had refused to bathe. The dragon's finicky nose could not tolerate uncleanliness, and it had insisted from the start that Elynne bathe, as it did, on a regular basis. That day Elynne chose to test her limits, as children will. She threw a tantrum, yelling and kicking and refusing to budge.

The dragon was unmoved.

Elynne started to run away, howling. The dragon merely stepped in her path. She spun around, but the dragon blocked her. She stood and shouted. The dragon paid no attention. She kicked its foot, and hurt her own. She burst into tears and threw herself on the ground. The dragon waited. She rose and stalked away. It blocked her again. She stood firm. The dragon scooted its paw across the ground, gently pushing her as she stood. Snarling, the child picked up a rock and pitched it at the paw. It bounced off with no effect. She heaved a larger one. Same thing. The dragon lowered its head to glare at her. The child threw a rock at the dragon's eye. It connected.

The dragon whipped back its head in pain. The shock threw Elynne to the ground. Horrified, she watched the dragon thrash its head. Then it stopped, blinking, and turned again to her. She blanched, paralyzed with terror. The dragon growled, a sound that would have sent a whole village trembling. Fire burst from its flaring nostrils. Tears welled in its eye. Its huge jaw dropped open, baring teeth near as large as Elynne herself. Slowly, deliberately, the dragon raised its talon and lowered it over the whimpering child. Just as slowly, it tightened its grasp. To the dragon, its grip was gentle. Elynne feared it would crush her.

Child in hand, the dragon hobbled to the pool's edge and lowered claw and child into the pool. Then it shook her, dragged her out, put her back, and shook her again. Several shakes later, the dragon released the clean and chastened child on the pool's rock edge, glared at her again, and stalked off.

Elynne never again dared the dragon's anger. Strong and stubborn though she might be, the dragon was unstoppable. Or so she had thought.

The courtyard outside the tower window was quiet now. The revels had ended, and all seemed asleep but the night watch. And Elynne.

Inside the room, the finery was dashed. The guards had locked the door, and Elynne let fly her rage on every object in the room. Even Father had wisely stayed clear. She had shredded her gown and strangling underthings and hurled the clattering shoes through the window. Hours later, all was quiet.

Elynne sized up the climb from the window to the cobblestones. It was far steeper than the rocks that she had climbed at home, but better death now than continued misery. She waited until the watch passed by, then lowered herself out the window, tying a fur wrap about her waist for later use. Hugging bare flesh to cold rough stone, she hearkened back to mountain climbs by darkness as she sought toe-and-finger holds. Every floor or so, she would rest and flex in a window crevasse. She reached the courtyard without incident and crept stealthily toward the castle wall. Once, twice, she ducked the approach of passing guards, moving and freezing like a forest hunter. At length, she reached the battlements.

She padded to the top of the stairs and froze. Father stood gazing from the wall to the distant hills. He glanced over his shoulder at her, then quickly averted his eyes.

Elynne stood warily and approached the wall, poised to strike if need be. Father whispered to her, but she understood little of what he said. Then he sighed and turned to face her, deliberately ignoring her nakedness. She spread her hands and tried to explain, but could not find the words. In Father's eyes, however, she saw that she didn't need to. "Go with God," he said, and that much she understood. She nodded, gauged the distance between herself and the moat, and leapt.

During the winter months Elynne had laid claim to many passages and rooms within the cavern, many too small for the dragon to enter. She often entertained herself by drawing on the walls there with burnt wood, sharpened sticks, and homemade dyes.

The men who had killed the dragon, her protector, playmate, and friend, had left disappointed. She remembered that dragons in her childhood tales hoarded gold, jewels, and riches. Her dragon had kept none of these things. So they took its head, hide, and foster daughter as their prize.

But the dragon had left a treasure, one the men had missed. And Elynne set off for home to claim it from a painted room set deep within the hill.

She traced their path by memory skirting villages and townships as she went, living off the land. Nearly three seasons later, she returned.

A strong scent of old decay greeted Elynne's homecoming. She tossed aside her walking stick and tattered wrap and descended, trembling, into the cavern. Fading dark stains marked the way. Tears spilled, but she kept on walking.

Grief hit her as she entered the largest room, burning worse than dragon's fire. The tattered carcass lay ravaged by killers and scavengers alike. She dashed across the smooth stone floor and fell sobbing at the dragon's feet. She wept for a very long time.

Rising at last, she swept the tears away and turned her back on the remains. The firepit, too, was cold and dead. She returned to the surface and retrieved a stolen tinderbox from a makeshift pocket in the discarded wrap. Gathering deadwood, she built a small fire, lit a torch, and carried both wood and torch inside. She relit the firepit and built it up with winter-stock wood. Then, carrying a large brand, she went off in search of the painted rooms.

A handful of seasons past, the dragon had taken Elynne aside and led her to its treasure. In the silent way they had, the dragon had bade her hide the treasure. Elynne, shaken by both the honor of the request and the nature of the treasure, agreed, and buried it beneath the dirt floor of her favorite painted room.

As she reached the room, she found the floor disturbed, the treasure missing. Brittle fragments littered the floor. Was she too late? Desperately, Elynne searched the room, then followed the tracks upon the floor. She traced them through the corridors, to a refuse heap in a crevasse where she'd tossed winter food remains. She fell to her knees and dug in sharp-edged bone till she found what she had sought.

The hatchlings grumped and whined as she uncovered them from their hiding place. She figured they were hungry. Even now they were a heavy armful, but Elynne carried both back to the largest chamber and set them by the fire. It was cold outside, but as dark fell, Elynne went off to hunt.

As the dragon had done for her, so she would do for the dragon's children. And, perhaps, if she lived long enough, she might ride the winds again.

FREEING SOULS
by Lisa Deason

Lisa Deason submitted her first story to me with what I'd call a perfect "letter to the editor"—namely, almost none. She basically wrote "enclosed find my story and a postage paid envelope for its return if you can't use it."

Now some editors may like the kind of chatty letter with submissions which tells them all about the writer—including the names of all her children and cats. Personally, having made my sales when I was living in a small town in Texas, and not knowing a single person in the editorial offices, I prefer to think of your letter to the editor with your first story as your job interview, and feel the writer should let the story speak for itself. For if the opening letter is your job interview, you wouldn't—or I hope you wouldn't—walk into the boss's office and park your feet on his desk. I always recommend being brief and businesslike at first; when I buy your story and send a contract, I'll ask for your biography, and then you can be as clever as you want to in telling me all about your children and cats.

Lisa Deason, as I found out when I asked her (having bought her story, I cared), is 18 years old, and plans a career in merchandising. We hope she keeps some time out for writing. She says that "like everybody else," she is working on a novel. Good; I hope we get to read it soon.

From the look on his face, Illy guessed her partner was nearly blinded by his headache. The acolytes marched the two of them into the heart of the Shalu'val temple with the single-mindedness of the possessed.

Helena, Illy mentally spat in disdain. *She always vowed to control the Crystle one day and it seems she's done it.* She glanced over again to Kel as he passed a hand through his shoulder-length blond hair. Stepping closer, unimpeded by their acolyte guards (hell, they had let her keep her sword so they were more of an escort party than guards!), she asked softly, "How are you holding up?"

He grimaced, "Empathy's not what it's cracked up to be. Whoever Helena has in there is in absolute terror, the whole bunch of them. I haven't felt this much mass hysteria since that giant snake incident in Helder."

"Can you tell what's going on?"

The sorcerer shook his head. "No, I'm just getting disjointed feelings. In fact, *disjointed* is a good description of their tone, like souls disconnected from their bodies," he shrugged helplessly. "Sorry, *kerana mia*, I can't explain any better than that."

She laid her hand briefly on his arm before falling back a pace to ponder. Kel's headache wasn't the original reason that brought them to Greelin, but it soon took precedent over her terrible nightmares.

The demons of her sleep had been with her ever since she left five years earlier but never to the degree they were reaching now. When her torment began spilling into Kel's sleep as well, she decided enough was enough. Starting for Greelin as soon as they finished their job contracts, they were half a day away when Kel was bombarded. As they drew nearer the city, the overwhelming emotions increased quickly into pain. Illy had weighed the length of time it would take to break in the temple against the intensity of Kel's headache and decided it was better—and quicker—to let the possessed acolytes "capture" them.

Kel's rich baritone interrupted her musing. "I sense the possession wavering." Indeed, the acolytes were stumbling to a halt, their glowing green eyes momentarily reverting to normal.

"Her power must be low," Illy said, the realization heartening her. If Helena's power was fluctuating, then she couldn't be fully tapping into the Crystle, the use of which brought raw magic into Greelin through its natural magic dampener. Should Helena manage to divert the magic from its course into the city into herself instead, she would gain unlimited power.

And we'd all be dead, Illy added to herself.

Kel put a hand to his forehead and his piercingly blue eyes lost their focus. "You're right. Her power's very low but . . ." he trailed off and his breathing became laborous. "There's something . . . a—a *need*, a *search* for . . ."

It always disturbed her to see her partner in the grip of such turmoil, but she had long ago learned to quiet her own worries to keep them from interfering. "For what?" she prompted.

"For . . ." he suddenly straightened. "Oh, no you don't! I don't care how many other mages you've drained, you're not making me the next!"

The acolytes came to life again, turning on Illy while her attention was on Kel. Taken by surprise, she was pinned to the wall by a crush of bodies before she could react.

She spotted the danger and cried out a warning to shake Kel from his trance. He saw the tattered ray of green light questing down the corridor toward them and he raised his hands to send forth a reflecting spell. Only after the fact did he realize his mistake. The ray, attracted to the use of magic, homed in, snatched him clear off his feet, and whisked him away without further ado.

The acolytes released the stunned swordswoman and prodded her into motion.

"Bloody hell," she murmured. "She's after the magic after it leaves the Crystle, the leech!"

"Dear Ilhixthiara," a raspy voice said softly from the thick shadows of the Crystle's chamber. "Oh, yes, I remember you. How could I forget my training-mate, the greatest failure in the history of the Shalu'val?"

The more things change, the more they stay the same, Illy thought as she scanned the darkness for a hint of her partner or the "disjointed souls" that had given him such a migraine. *Helena's practically a step away from godhood and she's still smarting because my magic was a tad stronger than hers in training!* She felt a pang of regret. If only she still had her magic. . . !

"Nothing to say, dear? Then how about a hug for your old friend?" With that, the torches flared to reveal Helena twenty or so paces away. Noting Illy's shock, she preened, "Ah, you've noticed how good the years have been to me."

Helena, quite frankly, was a corpse. The skin stretching over the sharp bones of her skull was as yellow as rotting parchment paper and full of open, oozing sores. Her feverish eyes were sunken into her head and her lank brown hair hung in greasy strings. Some disease seemed to be eating her inside out, turning her into the very likeness of corruption and death. The sticklike arms raised and she chuckled when Illy backed away.

"Can you appreciate the face of power that you'll never have for yourself?" The ravaged lips formed a mockery of a pleasant smile. "So do you wonder what happened to your sorcerer? Let me give him to you." Her skeletal hand lazily tapped the man-sized Crystle's compartment, easing the wall open.

Body upon body poured out, many in the gold robes of the High Sisterhood and, at Helena's command, a ray extended from the misshapen lump that once was the perfect Crystle and a body was flung at Illy.

She staggered under the impact and lowered the body to the floor, knowing it to be Kel even before she looked. All coherent thought ceased and the next thing she knew, she was a breath away from Helena, sword high over her head and invisible ice locked around her, trapping her like a fly in amber.

"So vehement!" Helena leered. "If I'd known your lover inspired such passion, I would've kept him for myself! Why don't you use your magic and bring the dead to life?"

Illy managed to spit in her face.

The sorceress shrieked, wiping furiously at the moisture. The Crystle pulsated unevenly, a ray shooting forth to yank an acolyte spread-eagle onto its bumpy surface. A moment later, another body hit the floor and the Crystle swelled.

In utter desperation, Illy *reached* (how? how?) to block the sorcerous flow and in doing so, discovered the truth.

She's feeding from herself, from her own life-energy. How can she not know?

Helena doubled in agony, then stiffened, soulless eyes blazing with arcane power, and howled the phrases that began the spell of Obliteration. The temperature plunged.

"Tell me your full name!" Helena thundered and a ray whipped into the swordswoman.

The power wormed in her veins and she struggled. *Oh, sweet Mother*, she mentally begged, *help me!* Her thoughts unraveled into an entirely different plea a heartbeat later.

How dare you leave me like this, Kel? Help me, blast you!

But she had to answer, "Ilhixthiara DiCantahino el-Savven Meyr."

"I order thee to die, Ilhixthiara . . ." the hideous brow furrowed in concentration. *That cursed name!*

She could not under any circumstance be allowed to finish for then Illy wouldn't merely die, but be obliterated soul and all from any other world she might pass on to. Her soul might have chains weighing on it, but it certainly deserved better than that!

Betting that the freeze spell would loosen as more of Helena's depleting energy went into the Obliteration spell, she strained with all her might and her foot slid an inch.

Ah, what comes next? DiSavventimo? Helena was thinking when she noticed the movement. "Repeat the rest of your name!" she ordered.

The spell began to crack and her arms jerked. "DiCantahino el-Savven Meyr."

"DiCantahino . . ."

The blade started to swing.

". . . el-Savven . . ."

The spell broke and the blade split the air.

". . . M—"

Helena's ruined head was parted from her body, the final name dying with her.

Illy stood, chest heaving, the tip of her sword lowering to the ground, then she automatically bent to clean it on Helena's robe before sheathing it. Her eyes drifted to the body behind her. Kel—who called her *kerana mia*, my dearest friend, who treated her with respect as a woman and a warrior.

Kel—who was dead.

Better this, perhaps, she thought wildly, *than for him to live as a cripple as I am, a mage with no magic.*

She whirled on the Crystle. "This is all your fault," she accused, weaving on her feet like a drunkard, staggering forward to strike the uneven surface with her bare hands.

At that instant, a chorus of screams invaded her mind. She jerked away and the cacophony died. Immediately sobered, she took a moment to consider, then hesitantly touched her fingers to the Crystle again. The chorus returned, but there was also a solid beacon that kept her from withdrawing.

Kerana mia . . . kerana mia, *I hear you.* . . .

"Keleric, sweet Mother, is it you?"

Yes, along with the ones I was picking up before. Helena tried to make the Crystle do something it simply couldn't do. Magic can't be recalled once it's been bonded with a soul. Like you, Illy. Your magic's still with you, I feel it, the Crystle knows it.

You must reverse the damage that's been done before it becomes permanent.

She wanted to protest but didn't. She wanted to run but stayed. "I'll try," she said simply.

The demons of her nightmares blocked the way with a hardy shove that sent her reeling.

"So easy, she thinks!" they laughed. "She makes up her mind and poof! we're gone. No, no, Ilhixthiara. It's not that way at all."

"I'll have my magic back," she said as firmly as she could. "I need it back."

They roared gleefully at that. "You have no magic, fool. You destroyed it during your final test along with your dreams of High Sisterhood!"

"I never wanted to be a High Sister," she retorted, forgetting she intended not to argue with them. "I just wanted to learn to control my talent, to bring it to its highest potential."

"Ah yes, your *talent*," the word became an obscenity. "Your wonderful talent that everyone praised until you became cocky and believed yourself that you had such *talent*. The Crystle showed you better, eh? It burned out your magic because it wasn't nearly as strong as you thought!"

Oh, sweet Mother, it was the truth. The High Sisters had tried to convince her to postpone her final test until they were sure her system could withstand the awesome stress, but she had persuaded them to let her go on. After all, wasn't she strong? How proud her family had been, how the other acolytes had eyed her enviously as she completed her training in half the usual time. Her potential seemed unlimited, her future shining and bright, but she failed in a way that denied her the chance to try again. . . .

The demons cast chains of molten lava around her. "Your soul is ours!" they cackled. "You have no future. You're a failed sorceress and will never be anything more!"

In the midst of the hurricane of shame and guilt, she suddenly found an island of calm. Thoughts of her mercenary jobs, of the ecstatic freedom of roaming the lands and undertaking countless adventures . . . *surviving* countless adventures, buoyed her and she saw for the first time how untrue the words were. "You're wrong. I'm a free woman and mercenary. I've a new and better life with a partner I dearly love and trust. I created you when I thought I had destroyed my only shot at happiness and now I see I was wrong. I've been wrong all along. There's no place for you here. Begone."

The demons squawked and visibly paled.

"Begone," she repeated louder. "I want my soul and my magic back and I want it NOW!"

The chains around her vanished, followed a moment later by the howling demons and something tore loose inside her. Wonderingly, magic coursed through her and she directed it to correcting the Crystle, so to keep the flow going. Then it was a simple thing to restore Kel and the others to their bodies.

Kel opened his eyes and smiled knowingly at her as she whispered a tiny flame to life in her hand, just to see that she could. She snuffed it out, a grin spliting her face as wide as the world.

That night, her sleep was untroubled and she dreamt she was a hawk soaring through a vast and endless sky.

BLADEMISTRESS
by Jessie D. Eaker

Jessie Eaker, despite the female-looking spelling of his name, is male, and has appeared before this in S&S VI and VII. Like all the stories by men chosen for this anthology, his story deals as much with emotions as with barren technology. It is also a story which portrays something I'm very wary of usually: a "positive" message. All too often these "positive" stories deteriorate into sloppy (or even soggy) sentiment. But this one doesn't.

He and his wife Becki are anxiously awaiting their next child. He has children, birds, and hamsters; currently, he says, the kids have the run of the house, and the birds and hamsters are in cages—but he's thinking of reversing this. I, too, have thought wistfully that kids old enough not to be portable should be kept in cages; but I doubt if child psychologists would agree.

This story, he says, is dedicated to his mother Geraldine, who taught him to love fantasy and science fiction. That's a gift which you never outgrow.

A twig snapped.

Amara awoke instantly but feigned continued sleep. Under the cover of her blanket, she eased one of her daggers from its sheath and strained to detect the intruder's location. Behind her, she finally decided.

Just beyond the campfire's feeble flames. And the noises were getting closer.

In a blur of movement, Amara flung off her blanket and rolled to a crouch. Ignoring the pain in her side, she reared to throw her deadly weapon. . . .

At a surprised, dirty-faced girl.

Unable to stop the fluid motion, Amara altered her aim. The dagger flew past the girl's throat, narrowly missing it. The weapon impaled itself into a large oak.

The girl's eyes widened in terror. She put her hands over her mouth and stood paralyzed with fear. Her shoulders trembled.

Amara cursed and gently held her side. She could not believe that she had reopened her recent wound for a dirty-faced urchin! Amara fixed her with a withering stare and used her othersense to scan the area: they were alone.

"What do you want, *girl!*" Amara spat. "I do not take kindly to thieves. Especially those that sneak up on me while I sleep!"

The girl stood silently.

Amara strode to the oak and angrily jerked out her blade. Already, she felt fresh blood oozing through her crude binding. "Well!" Amara demanded.

The girl spoke softly. "I am not a thief."

"Then why are you sneaking up on me! I should cut your throat right here!" Amara made a slashing gesture.

"I smelled your fire." Defiance was gradually creeping into the girl's voice. "I have not eaten all day and I hoped to trade my services for some food."

Amara snorted rudely. "Sorry. I do not partake of *those* services, especially not from a child!"

Puzzlement passed over the girl's face to be quickly replaced by a deep red blush. She stammered. "All . . . all I meant was to carry and fetch."

Amara sighed. The girl could not be more than a dozen summers old. What in the name of the Goddess Mother was she doing alone in the forest? The nearest village was leagues away. Her tattered dress and patched coat—just slightly better than rags—labeled her a peasant, but her accent indicated a well-to-do family. She would be pretty if she were properly groomed. Her chest-

nut hair was matted and snarled, and Amara could smell
her unwashed body. And from the way her clothes hung
on her lean form, Amara was sure the girl had missed
more than one day's meal. She must have been in the
forest for several days at least.

And she reeked of trouble.

Amara held her side. "I do not need your help. I have
been managing by myself long years before you were
born. Now leave, before I really do cut your throat."
Amara made to throw her dagger again, but flinched at
the pain it caused.

The girl noticed. She took a step forward. "You are
wounded. Let me tend it for you. My father taught me
some of the healing arts."

Amara considered the offer. The wound was high on
her side and difficult for her to reach, let alone clean
properly. It *was* paining her, and this girl hardly posed
a threat. Amara slowly nodded. "All right, then. A meal
and a place beside my fire tonight in exchange for a little
tending. But tomorrow you are on your own. Agreed?"

The girl nodded emphatically and began gathering
some dry branches to build up the fire. Amara sat down
cross-legged next to it and began unsuccessfully to wres-
tle off her vest and blouse. The girl came to her aid and
helped her strip to the waist. Amara winced when the
girl removed the crude binding and examined the injury.

"The wound is deep and needs cleaning," the girl said.
"It is beginning to fester."

"In my sack there is an old shirt which will do for a
binding. Beside it are water and wine skins. Bring them
both: the wine for me and the water to cleanse the
wound."

The girl fetched the items and then opened one of the
skins. She smelled it and then handed the other one to
Amara. The warrior opened it and leaned her head back
for a big swallow. She quickly spit it out.

"You dolt! You gave me the water instead. . . .
OUCH!" Amara howled at the unexpected burning in
her side. Her eyes watered. She spoke through clenched
teeth and tried to rise. "What did you do? Pour fire on
it!"

The girl put a gentle restraining hand on Amara's

shoulder. "Hold still. I am using the wine to clean out the festering. I wanted to be sure I got some before you drank it all."

"You insolent brat. I should cut you into tiny . . . OUCH!"

"If you want this to get better, then let me work. Otherwise, give me my meal and I will be on my way."

Amara snarled, but remained silent for the rest of the cleaning. A bargain was a bargain. Amara imagined how she would cut the girl to pieces when she finished. The brat really was being insolent . . . but she had spirit. Not like some of the peasant girls she had seen: lifeless, eyes downcast, and afraid of their own shadows. No, this child was tough. Amara liked that. She had been the same way.

After dressing the wound, Amara gave the girl some travel bread and dried meat. The girl began to wolf them down hungrily, but she caught herself on the third bite—making herself nibble and chew slowly. Amara hid a smile. The girl had been hungry before and knew her shrunken stomach would not tolerate a quick filling. Amara felt a twinge of guilt for not feeding the girl until after the wound had been bound. Neither spoke until she was finished.

"What are you called, girl?" asked Amara. "And what brings you to this Goddess forsaken region."

"I am called Callise," she answered. "And I am looking for my mother."

Amara suppressed a groan. *Trouble. More trouble.*

Callise looked to her lap and watched her hands twist the cloth of her dress. "She left to become a guardswoman when I was a babe. My father says she could not tolerate life as a peasant. She had only married him because he was a prince. But the ruling powers shifted and they were lucky to get away alive." She sighed. "I lived with my father until a few days ago. A fever took him, leaving me all alone. My mother is the only relative I have left." The girl paused. "My father once said she had gone to Sanesse." Callise looked up expectantly. "Have you heard of a great warrior called Karasa?"

Amara shook her head. "Sorry, child. I myself hail from Sanesse and I know of no warrior by that name."

The girl was undaunted. "It has been many seasons since she left. She may have gone to another city. Someone in Sanesse may have heard where she has gone."

"Would you know your mother if you found her?"

"Oh, yes," Callise said dreamily. "Father told me. She has brown eyes and hair like I do. Although it probably has specks of silver in it like yours. . . ." The girl gave her a puzzled look. "And she is probably about your age, too."

Amara did not like that look. "Listen girl, I know what you are thinking. But I am *not* your mother. Only in childish tales do long lost parents come jumping out of the forest. I have never had a child."

The girl's hopeful gaze crumbled.

Amara chose not to notice. "I must leave at first light. You may sleep close to the fire." The girl nodded sleepily and lay down on the bare ground beside the dying flames. She curled into a ball and wrapped her arms about her chest.

Amara settled into her blanket and turned her back to the girl. But her mind would not leave her alone. It was going to get cold toward morning. Amara glanced over her shoulder at the child. There she lay, her head cradled in the crook of her arm. She looked comfortable enough. *I am not going to share my blanket. She smells bad and will toss and turn all night.* Amara lay back down, then she again looked over her shoulder at the girl. *I REFUSE to share my blanket.* With that, she stubbornly closed her eyes and tried to sleep.

When the sun was barley risen, Amara awoke. Her first impression was that she not alone under her blanket. A soft snore from behind her confirmed her suspicion: that *girl* had sneaked beneath her blanket. To her credit, Amara had not even known she was there. Well, no use crying over it now.

The older woman arose and prepared to leave. Her side felt better, but was stiff and sore. Overall, it was a small price to pay for tangling with King Larse's men. When that merchant offered her gold to retrieve his stolen jewel, he failed to mention that the thief happened to be King Larse's tax collector. Amara shook her head.

That money would have bought her a shop in Sanesse. She was getting too old to be a warrior. Her reflexes were slowing and speed was what kept her alive. It would be best to retire soon; she was not ready to die just yet.

Amara nudged the sleeping girl with her foot. "Time to wake up, sluggard. I need my blanket."

Stretching, Callise slowly sat up and rubbed her eyes. After another quick stretch, she jumped up, shook out the blanket, and folded it neatly for Amara. The older lady was impressed.

"I hope I did not bother you last night," said Callise. "It was cold last night and the fire was not helping. I crawled over beside you. I hope you did not mind too much."

Amara did not answer. She handed the girl a few pieces more of her provisions and picked up her pack. She winced at the wound's soreness. Without saying a word, she turned her back on the girl and started up the trail.

Callise called after her. "Let me accompany you to Sanesse? Please. I could carry your pack for you and look after your wound. I will be quiet and not cause any trouble."

Amara took a few more steps, but slowed. Already her side was throbbing and promised to pain her throughout the day. She should rest for a time and allow her body to heal, but it would not be wise to stop while still inside King Larse's territory. She fixed her eyes on the trail ahead. *This girl was trouble.*

The warrior slipped the strap from her shoulder and lowered her pack to the ground. She left it and walked on. Without looking back, she said, "You might as well come along. I would not feel right if a bear got indigestion from eating you."

Grinning, Callise hurried to scoop up the burden.

For the next two days they made good progress. Because of the girl's care, Amara's wound began to heal properly. It hardly hurt her at all. True, the girl slowed her down, but the more relaxed pace kept her from straining the injury. Overall, Amara was pleased with their progress. The girl's back was strong and she did not whine and complain. She was even halfway intelligent. So Amara was not surprised when the girl made a request.

They were sitting around the evening fire. Callise had finished clearing the remains of their simple meal and had raked together a bed of dry leaves for them to sleep on. Amara took the time to oil, sharpen, and clean her five daggers. The warrior looked up to find Callise kneeling in front of her.

"Amara, I have seen how you use your dagger. You handle it like it is a part of you, just another limb. And as you clean them, it is like you are worshiping them. Only a *blademistress* would do that. Only a blademistress has such skill."

Amara chose not to answer. She returned to polishing her blade.

Callise took a deep breath. "Would it be too much . . . I mean, could you . . . please . . . teach me to throw the dagger?"

Amara snorted. She did not look up from her work. "Listen, girl. Learning to throw is not easy. Very few have the combination of skill, patience, and outright *will* to learn."

"But I can do it," the girl responded. "I will make you proud of me."

Amara stopped polishing and gazed at the girl levelly. "And what do I get in return?"

Callise looked down at the ground in disappointment.

Amara frowned. Best to show her how fruitless the attempt would be. In one swift movement, the warrior rose to her feet. The girl watched her hopefully. From the nearby path, she selected a small stone and pointed to a tree ten paces away. "See that sapling with the fork in it about chest high," said Amara.

The girl nodded. Its trunk was only two fingers wide.

Careful of her side, Amara threw the stone. It struck the tree dead center, just below the fork. "When you can do that five times in row, I will teach you."

Callise came to stand beside her. The girl picked up a stone and threw it at the tree. It went wide to the right and far too short. She threw another, but it also missed completely.

"See, girl," said Amara, grinning. "It is not easy."

The girl glanced at her defiantly and picked up another stone. She managed to hit the base of the tree. Undaunted she gathered up a small pile and began to throw them. She practiced until it was too dark to see. Amara had to give the girl credit, she had strong will.

The next day, they camped early beside a small but deep river. Amara was tired of trail food and wanted something more substantial. She went off alone to hunt, leaving the girl to set up camp and with instructions to bathe.

But the game was uncooperative. Even using her othersense, she had to stalk farther than she had expected. It was nearly evening when she turned back toward camp with only a small rodent to show for her efforts.

As she approached, her othersense warned that two humans were close by. And they were very near where she had left Callise. She hurried on. She had to protect her needed provisions from any thieves.

When she drew close to camp, she heard laughter—male laughter—coming from the river. Amara dropped her prize and approached the stream bank cautiously. She peered through the bushes. Two men, burly sorts, were standing on the bank. One had an arrow notched, while the other was trying to coax the girl out of the water.

"Come on, dearie. You must be freezing your rear off in that water. Comes right off the ice, it does. So why don't you step on out here, so we can get you all warm. Me and Lile here promise to do a real good job of it." They both snickered.

The girl was covered to the neck with the cold water. She shook her head and tried to back away.

Lile, the man with the bow and arrow, said, "Now don't think'n about run'n from us, girlie. I'll shoot ya good. I will." He glanced at his partner. "Why don't ya just go in after 'er. I'm tired of wait'n."

"What! And get all wet! It tain't good fer ya. Besides it's interest'n me to see what dearest decides." He held up her clothes. "We won't even have to strip her." They both roared with laughter.

Amara cursed. The girl was nothing but trouble. She could even attract it out of an empty forest. Thank the Goddess that they were completely ignoring her sack. It would not be too difficult to retrieve it and be on her way. Best to avoid a fight wherever possible, was her belief. The girl would just have to fend for herself.

She crept through the bushes until she was right behind her sack. Reaching carefully through the bushes she groped for it, but drew up short. She shuffled forward slightly and strained to reach it.

Unfortunately, Lile chose that moment to glance her way. "Hey! We got us a visitor over there." He swung the arrow to point at her.

Amara tried to retreat into the bushes, but in her over-balanced position, her feet slipped and she fell.

He grinned at her with a mouthful of decayed teeth. "Luck's with us today. We just caught the mamma, too!" He pulled the bow taut to fire.

Just then, a thrown rock struck him in the shoulder, and he howled with unexpected pain. The arrow shot off harmlessly to one side.

Seizing the opportunity, Amara acted. She quickly rolled, pulled a dagger from her sleeve, and threw it in one smooth motion. A blade suddenly appeared in the man's arm. The bow slipped from his fingers and he dropped to his knees.

By the time Amara had rolled to her feet, another knife had already found its way into her hand. She drew back to throw and looked at the other man. "Unless you want another hole to breathe through, you will pull out that knife, lay it on the ground, and then run like the demoness herself is chasing you."

The other man obeyed and helped his partner up, then, together they marched off. Amara watched them out of sight and looked toward the girl still immersed in the river. "Well, are you just going to sit there? Get out and get some clothes on. You will be ill if you do not." The girl slowly waded out.

"Thank you for saving me," said Callise as she dressed. "I thought I was doomed. I will not forget it." Amara quickly turned away and said nothing.

*   *   *

The next day the girl resumed her practice in earnest. She woke Amara with her throwing. She threw while they traveled and even threw until dark. But the girl did not slight any of her duties. She fetched, carried, and prepared—even better than before. Amara could not help admiring the girl's determination.

One evening after supper, when they were just one day out from the city, Callise spoke, "I have something to show you." The girl held out five stones and pointed. "See that tree."

Amara looked where she indicated to find a sapling about two fingers wide. Five times the girl threw and five times she hit the tree dead center.

The warrior nodded, silently pleased. But Amara knew it was hopeless; she was not about to take an apprentice. And being a warrior was not an easy life, especially for a blademistress. You made many enemies and very few friends. And when your arm slowed, no one would have you.

But the girl had earned the privilege and Amara was not going to go back on her word. "You have done as I said. I will show you."

Lending the girl one of her daggers, the blademistress showed her how to care for it and a simple throw to master. The girl was delighted and practiced the move until it was too dark to see.

Amara decided she and the girl would have to part in the city.

Even in Sanesse, Amara did not let down her guard. With the numbers of people, her othersense was useless. It made her feel exposed.

Callise walked beside her through the streets, staring in amazement at the booths of hawking vendors, the brightly dressed people, and the smells of unknown spices.

Amara stopped before the house of Yhalla, a healer of good reputation. On her last visit, Yhalla had complained she could not find decent assistants. Amara hoped she could get the girl apprenticed there. She had decided this last night, but had not yet told Callise. She did not want an argument.

The blademistress stopped and turned to face Callise. "Girl," Amara said, searching for words. The girl's face, shining in adoration, did not help. "There comes a time in everyone's life for parting . . ." The girl nodded and glanced over Amara's shoulder. She gasped.

Amara knew that look.

Immediately, the warrior whirled and pulled a dagger from her sleeve. Time moved to a crawl; it almost seemed to stop. *Moving too slow! I will never make it!*

Close behind her stood the man at the river, good old Lile. He had an arrow notched and the bow pulled taut; people fought to get clear of his path. Amara could see the muscles in his arm straining at the effort, and his face was a mask of triumph. The man would loose his weapon before she could complete her throw . . . and he knew it.

Leap aside! Screamed one part of her mind. But if she did, Callise would take the arrow full in the chest. Either way, one of them would die.

The man's muscles tensed toward release. Amara made her decision.

The arrow leapt from the bow and buried itself within the blademistress' chest. Exquisite pain ripped through her being and she staggered back. She groped with her fingers and felt the warm stickiness flow from around the shaft. She collapsed backward and Callise caught her and lowered her to the ground.

The world began to fade. In dreamlike reality, she saw the man roar with laughter . . . she saw Callise slowly rise, a deadly expression on her face . . . she saw the girl reach to her belt and pull the dagger she had been given. Then, faster than the eye could follow, Callise threw the blade and it suddenly spouted from the man's throat.

Amara closed her eyes, ready for death to take her.

Sound came to her first—the sound of whispers, the snuffling of feet, the clanking of pots. This was followed by the rich smell of herbs, the softness of fresh linen. Finally, she opened her eyes to see the girl leaning over her wearing a concerned expression. Amara glanced around the unfamiliar room.

"You are in Yhalla's home. She has gone to get some

more herbs." The girl looked away and wiped a tear from her eye. "She did not know if you would live."

Amara could feel unconsciousness hovering just outside her vision. She licked her dry lips and tried to move reluctant lips. "Did you. . . ?"

Callise nodded grimly. "That one will not bother us again."

Amara smiled weakly. "A good throw."

Callise looked to her lap. "You could have leapt out of his way," she accused. "I have seen you move before. But you did not."

"Too old," Amara whispered. "Too slow."

"You're lying." Callise leaned forward, her long hair brushing the warrior's cheek. "You deliberately took that arrow to shield me. I do not deserve your sacrifice." A wet drop landed on her brow.

For the first time in many long years, Amara felt her own eyes grow wet. "You are a very special girl. And it is I who do not deserve your affection."

Callise sat back up and wiped at her eyes. "I still need a teacher. I would like to become a blademistress like you."

"But what about your mother? Do you not want to find her?"

Callise smiled. "I may find her one day, but for now I have all I need."

Amara grinned. "You are nothing but trouble, girl."

SORCERERS' GATE
by Patricia Duffy Novak

Patricia Duffy Novak has appeared in several of my anthologies about Darkover and in *Marion Zimmer Bradley's Fantasy Magazine*, but this is her first sale to SWORD AND SORCERESS. This story demonstrates clearly that women are capable of writing a relatively uncomplicated adventure story. This one fascinated me from the first line; I've never understood why (among literary critics) it's not quite kosher to read anything for the pure delight of finding out *what happens*.

Ms. Novak is an (associate) Professor of Agricultural Economics and is working on a degree in English just for help with writing. Because she works with a land-grant university, her work is a twelve month round-the-clock business; no long summers off to write. Grading gets done late at night, and stray hours while the baby is napping produce short stories like this. I've always said nobody ever *has* time to write; you *make* time.

Pat has a young daughter, who, like Ara in this story, is "fascinated by combs, and dogs"—of which she has three. Dogs, that is.

The chubby hand reached over the edge of the table and grasped the prize. "See?"

"Yes, sweetheart. You have the comb."

"Comb," the little girl repeated solemnly.

"Now bring it to Tavia." Octavia held out her hand, and Ara trotted toward her, tiny feet thump-thumping against the smooth wooden floor.

Octavia extracted the gleaming silver comb from the small hand and began to untangle Ara's mass of white-blonde hair. "Aren't you pretty," said Octavia encouragingly as Ara threatened to squirm away.

"Done!" said Ara hopefully, and Octavia laughed.

"Yes, I suppose you think so, but those tangles still need work." As she turned to get a better grip on Ara, a shadow flickered across the sunny room. Octavia looked up and saw a woman draped in long blue robes passing by the window.

Octavia's heart fluttered. She had not been expecting a visit from a Blue Sister. Normally, one of their order came once a month, very regularly, and the last visit was less than two weeks past.

She scooped Ara into her arms and went to open the door. The Sister stood on the swept earth path, the oval of her face a mask of cold indifference, the sapphire eyes hard as stones. Unbound hair the color of moonlight streamed down her back. All the sorcerous kin had hair that color, the same white-blonde as Ara's. The hair marked the sorceress more clearly than the costume of her order.

A few feet away from the dark-robed figure, Sorrel, the stray dog that Octavia had taken in, circled and whined. "Hush, Sorrel," Octavia pleaded, concerned that the Sister would take offense and blast the dog with a spell. The dog slunk back a few paces and quieted, although his hackles remained raised.

"Come in, your grace," Octavia said, stepping back from the doorway with a bow, a hard maneuver to accomplish with Ara riding a hip. The Sister nodded curtly and stepped into the house, where she stood for a moment looking around with an expression of distaste.

Octavia did not recognize this Sister. She had seen several of the order over the past eighteen months, but never, she was sure of it, this particular sorceress. "My poor home is unworthy of this honor," said Octavia, feeling far more anxious than honored, but there were certain polite phrases one uttered to a Blue Sister if one wished to continue living.

The Blue Sister turned her impenetrable gaze on Octavia. "I have come to see my child."

Instinctively, Octavia's hands tightened around Ara. "Your child? I did not think—" She stopped, remembering to whom she spoke, and stood rigidly, feeling the heat of the sorceress' stare.

The Blue Sister's thin lips twisted into a slight smile. "You did not think we knew our children? But of course we do. How else could we keep the bloodlines pure?" The Sister's smile faded, replaced by a stern look of command. "Bring her to me."

Octavia took a reluctant step forward. Ara, as if sensing her foster mother's fear, clung hard and whimpered.

"Here, now." The Blue Sister pulled the baby from Octavia's arms. Ara's whimpers turned to screams, but the Sister paid no heed. She turned Ara this way and that, frowning. "It's no good. I simply can't tell." She handed Ara to Octavia and stood scowling, hands on narrow hips.

"Do you think there's something wrong with the baby?" Octavia ventured, once she had comforted Ara enough to quiet her.

The Blue Sister's vivid blue eyes focused on Octavia. "She's my third. The others didn't have enough magic, but this one was sired by a Gold Adept. I thought she'd already be showing the signs, but—" The sorceress shrugged. "I do not seem to breed true."

Octavia felt a faint stir of hope. "Then she will not be a sorceress? She will not be collected?"

The Blue Sister raised a narrow brow. "Whether or not she will become a sorceress remains to be seen. But she will be collected, have no fear. We do not leave our mistakes alive to breed new magics. The Blood Demons always thirst."

Octavia's heart seemed to freeze in her breast. Oh, it could not be true! She had heard rumors of the wickedness of the Sisters, that each year they sacrificed half their children, but she had not believed it. Not when the Sisters who had placed Ara with her had seemed so kind.

Octavia remembered her first sight of the wrinkled,

red face of the tiny newborn. For a year and a half now, Octavia had been the only mother Ara knew. Now, seeing Ara's true mother, Octavia finally understood why the system of fosterage had developed. A cat had more feeling for its kits than this sorceress had for her child. Had the Blue Sister raised Ara herself, she could not possibly have been so cavalier about the child's fate. No, not even the hardest-hearted witch on the island would be able to make such a sacrifice.

The Blue Sister laughed, a dry chuckle. "Oh, do not stare at me so. Every peasant on the island is aware of our customs. I have merely spoken openly of what is whispered behind hands." She gathered her robes about her. "Take care of her until I come again. She might, after all, have the magic." She glided from the cottage, blue robes floating behind her slender form. From outside, Octavia could hear Sorrel's soft whine as the sorceress passed.

Octavia put a hand to her mouth, stifling the scream that threatened to pour from her throat. By all that was holy, by the name of Melyra, Goddess Protectress of babes and beasts, she could not let the Sisters take Ara. She had known all along that the parting, which was scheduled to take place on Ara's second birthday, would be difficult, wrenching, for she had grown to love the chid as much as she would have loved a baby of her own. But she would not let the Sisters spill Ara's blood, no matter how powerful they were. Even if Ara did have the magic, and her life was not at risk, she would not turn her over to an order that bred such women as Ara's natural mother. Octavia shuddered.

But what to do? Their city was on an island, surrounded by a rapidly moving river that no boat could traverse. The three bridges that led to the mainland were heavily guarded. She could not smuggle the child across the bridges, and she certainly could not hide her anywhere in the city. Even if she dyed Ara's silver hair, the color that marked her as part of the sorcerous breed, there was no corner of the island that could conceal them from the Sisters. Ara's very blood would call them. To be safe, they must leave. The Sisters' magic could not reach across flowing water. But to leave was impossible.

Octavia's throat constricted, and tears welled up in her eyes, but she would not let herself cry. She could not surrender to despair. There were another six months before the Sisters came to collect Ara. Octavia must think of something by then, and she could not waste her time mourning.

A scratch and a woof at the door caught her attention. "Have I forgotten your dinner, old boy?" she asked. She set Ara down and went to the kitchen where she kept a pan of scraps for the dog. She placed the food on the doorstep and then stood with Ara watching Sorrel eat. The little girl was fascinated by the animal, always eager to watch him. Sorrel in turn had developed a fierce protectiveness toward the baby.

Octavia ran her fingers through Sorrel's shaggy coat. "You'd save her if you could, wouldn't you, fella?" The dog looked at the baby and then at Octavia, a slow steady stare. Octavia gave a short, nervous laugh. "I'm starting to have fancies, thinking you can understand me. Ah, well. You're a good dog just the same."

She picked up a flat, woven basket she used for carrying her purchases home from the market and slung it over one shoulder. "Shall we go for a walk, then, to the market, the three of us?" Whatever else she needed to do in the future, right now she needed to buy some food for the three of them.

"Walk," Ara repeated, reaching her hands up, her signal that she wanted to be carried. Sorrel fell in behind them.

"Alms, my lady, alms." The blind beggar at the entrance of the market held up a cup. Almost without thinking, Octavia dropped a coin, as she did whenever she had money to spare. Although the money the Sisters gave her to care for Ara was not extravagant, it was sufficient for their needs.

"Blessings on your head," the beggar woman called, but Octavia was already moving away, toward the booths.

"Come on, Sorrel." The dog was lagging behind, circling the beggar and wagging his tail. "Come on," Octavia repeated, but Sorrel seemed oblivious to her command. He dropped his muzzle into the beggar woman's hand and yipped softly.

"I'm sorry," Octavia said, shifting Ara so that she could grab a handful of Sorrel's coat. "He doesn't usually bother people."

The beggar woman looked up, and Octavia was surprised to see that beneath the coating of grime, the woman was young and pretty. Octavia had never looked closely at the beggar woman before, but had always believed her to be old. The woman's vacant eyes were night-dark, with silver flecks that shone like stars. "He is not bothering me," the woman said. "Leave him with me, if you would, while you shop. I am fond of dogs."

Octavia looked at Sorrel, who was nestling contentedly at the beggar woman's feet, and could see no reason to object. "If he will truly be no trouble to you?" When the beggar shook her head, Octavia resettled Ara and started forward again, to make their purchases.

When she returned, basket full of bread and fruit, Sorrel rose reluctantly from his spot beside his new friend, heaving a doggy sigh. Octavia reached into the sack and picked out a plump orange. "Here," she said, dropping to her knees beside the other woman and placing the fruit on the ragged skirts. "Thank you for watching my dog."

The long, tapered fingers grasped the fruit and manipulated it. "Thank you for this." The woman smiled. "Wait, and I will tell you a secret." Octavia waited, and the woman beckoned. "No. Come closer. What I have to say is for you alone."

Octavia dropped to her knees, feeling a little foolish. Ara, clinging to her, watched the beggar with wide eyes.

"There is another way out of the city," the woman said. Octavia squeaked in surprise, but the beggar woman shushed her with a quick wave of a hand. "You have heard of the Sorcerers' Gate on the far side of the island. The Gate leads to a tunnel that passes under the water all the way to the mainland, to the Kingdom of Alworyn. You would be safe there. The Blue Sisters cannot cross the water, nor do they guard that gate."

Octavia stared at the woman, too stunned to speak. First, she had no idea how this beggar had divined her

deepest wish. Secondly, the very name of the Sorcerers'
Gate was enough to strike fear into the heart of any
rational being. The Sisters did not guard the Gate because there was no need. The Gate held its own wards;
even the Sisters themselves could not pass through it.
She had never seen the Gate, but she, like every other
soul on the island, was keenly aware of its location and
was careful to avoid passing within a quarter mile of the
ancient construction.

"Do not be afraid," said the woman. "Trust yourself,
and you will be safe."

The beggar turned her Stygian eyes on Octavia again,
and the silver flecks seemed to grow, sparkling brighter
and brighter until Octavia could no longer bear to look.
Octavia's heart filled with wonder and dread. "Melyra,"
she whispered. "Goddess Protectress, forgive me for not
knowing you." Octavia bent to touch the hem of the
other's garment. "Help us, Great One. I beg you."

"What, who's there?"

Octavia looked into the wrinkled face of an old woman
with milk-blind eyes. Whatever help the Goddess would
give had already been granted.

The months passed. Octavia had thought often of the
advice she had been given, but she had not been able to
bring herself to attempt the Sorcerers' Gate. All her life
she had heard stories of the Gate, an artifact from the
Old Ones, sorcerers with magic a hundred times more
powerful than that of the Sisters and the Adepts. Those
who had tried to pass the Gate always ran screaming
back, gibbering and crying, with no trace of reason left
in their eyes.

She had seen a thief once who had tried to escape
through that Gate. He had been led babbling through
the streets, toward the gibbet, no longer rational enough
to realize he was to be hanged for his crime. "The Gate
took his soul," she had heard an old woman whisper.

Octavia was afraid; but each day that passed brought
her closer to Ara's second birthday. She would not let
the Sisters take the baby, but could she risk the child's
sanity as well as her own?

She prayed over and over again to the Goddess, but

no answer came. Only sometimes, when the wind blew through the trees, or when a stray dog howled, Octavia thought she heard the formless noise fashion itself into words. "Trust yourself." But still she was afraid.

Finally Octavia ran out of time. In a matter of days the Sisters would come for Ara, and then there would be no more chances. It was the Gate or nothing, and Octavia would rather let herself be destroyed than let the Sisters take Ara. She packed a few items of Ara's clothing in the bottom of her market basket, along with a bit of food. She could take no more than this pittance for fear the Sisters' spies would discern her motives, but in her pockets she put all the coins she had saved during the last six months, money she had hoarded for their escape.

She took Ara's small hand in her own and let the child totter along on her own. The island was not large, but the Gate was at the far end of the city, a walk of several miles, and she would be exhausted if she had to carry Ara the entire way.

She had left as much food as she could scrape together for Sorrel. She saw no point in risking him as well as herself, but her heart was heavy as she bade him stay behind. He flattened his ears and lay down in the grass beside the path, a rumbling whine emerging from his shaggy muzzle. "Good-bye, old friend," Octavia said with a catch in her voice. "You must try to find a new mistress when I am gone." She prayed silently to the Goddess for Sorrel's sake. Then she set off down the path and did not look back.

After an hour of walking, sometimes carrying Ara, sometimes letting the child trot by her side, Octavia sat down to rest on the grassy bank of a small stream. She took an orange from the sack, peeled it, and offered a juicy segment to Ara. Then she herself began to eat. As she stared blindly at the horizon, thinking of the Gate and the babbling thief whose hanging she had witnessed, she was startled to awareness by the rustling of the grass.

She jumped instantly to alert, scooping up Ara to protect her from whatever creature, human or beast, plowed its way toward them. Then she saw the familiar red-brown, shaggy coat, and she let out her breath in a gulp of relief. "Oh, Sorrel, you should not have come. What shall I do with you now?"

The dog rubbed against Octavia's skirts, nuzzling her ankle with his cold, wet nose. Ara squealed in delight, truly happy for the first time since they had begun their journey.

Octavia touched the dog's broad head with her hand. "I suppose you'll have to come. We are over halfway to the Gate, and if I turn back now, I shall never have the courage again." And so when they set off again, the large, shaggy dog trotted at their heels.

When Octavia spied the Gate, her resolve nearly faltered. Rank weeds grew all about the stone archway, and a smell of pestilence and decay wafted from the gloom within. Standing an arm's length away with a good grip on Ara, she looked down the passageway. Although the tunnel led deep under ground, the walls glowed with an unearthly white-green light, and she could see clearly along its length. Here and there on the floor of the tunnel pits had been dug. From the ceiling hung sharp spikes. But the traps seemed pointless to Octavia; a sighted person could easily avoid them.

She began to walk forward toward the tunnel, one-handedly clutching Ara against her breast, but before she could enter, Sorrel caught her gown in his teeth and yanked. Then he ran in front of her, growling and snarling, refusing to let her pass.

Octavia's spirits sank even further. Clearly the dog, with some instinct or ability humans did not possess, was able to sense the danger in the Gate. Octavia shook her head. "I know you want to protect me, old friend, but there is no other way. We cannot let the Sisters take Ara."

Sorrel barked excitedly and then turned and raced into the tunnel. Octavia heard his nails clicking on the old stone. Before she could follow him, he bounded out, nearly knocking her off her feet. He licked her hand and whined, his tail moving in an expectant wag.

She studied him. "You're all right, aren't you? Whatever is in the tunnel doesn't bother you." She shifted

Ara to the other hip. "There is a way through, isn't there? You're trying to tell me about it."

She thought again of her few moments in Melyra's presence, of the words of the Goddess. "Trust yourself." But there was something she was not yet seeing. Then she almost laughed aloud. *Not yet seeing.* There was the answer to the puzzle. Why else had the Goddess presented herself to Octavia as a blind woman? Whatever madness lurked in the tunnel acted through the eyes. A blind woman would be immune to the magic, but would fall prey to the traps. But Sorrel, whose vision differed from the human kind, could guide them safely through the tunnel. That was what he was trying to tell her.

Octavia pulled some of Ara's clothing from the sack. "Honey," she said to the child. "We need to play a game. I will put a bandage around your eyes so that you can't see anything. You must leave it in place until I say it's okay. Do you understand? It's very important to Tavia."

Ara nodded solemnly. "Bandage. Game." And Octavia quickly wrapped the child's eyes and then her own.

"Hold on to me now," she said to Ara, grabbing a fistful of Sorrel's warm fur. Sorrel walked forward, slowly and purposefully, and soon the dank air of the tunnel filled Octavia's nose.

She knew she would never forget that long, horrible trip through the tunnel under the water. She prayed aloud the entire time, entreating the Goddess to forgive her doubts, begging mercy of the dark spirits she seemed to feel all around her. At last, when she thought she could endure no more, she felt the path begin to curve upward. Finally, there came the feel of sun on her face, the touch of warm, fresh breeze, and the sound of Sorrel's excited yips.

With tremulous fingers, she pulled the bandage from her eyes and then from Ara's. Around her lay the green hills of Alworyn, a land she had only dreamed of seeing, a land untouched by the blight of the Blue Sisters. She set Ara on the grass and danced around her, laughing and clapping her hands if she herself were a child again.

Ara laughed too at first, but then stood silently, staring

over Octavia's shoulder. Sorrel gave a squeal and bounded off. Octavia turned, her joy frozen in her breast. There on the hilltop only a few feet away was a woman on horseback. She was clad in dark leathers, and the hilt of a sword protruded above her shoulder. The horse shifted impatiently as the woman stared down at Octavia and Ara.

None of this would have frightened Octavia—she had expected the Alworians to guard their borders—but the hair that flowed in long strands down the arms of the warrior woman was the color of palest silk. Only the Blue Sisters had hair that shade. Octavia had been deceived; Alworyn was not a free land.

She flung herself to her knees and threw her arms about Ara. "Go!" she screamed, "You cannot have her. You must kill me first."

"Wait!" The woman swung down from the horse, hands raised and empty. Sorrel danced after, not growling, seeming only curious as the woman approached Octavia and Ara. "Do you think you are the only woman who has ever won free of the island?"

The woman bent down and touched Octavia gently. "My own foster mother took me through that very Gate. I felt in my heart that someone was coming. I am here to help."

Octavia let the other woman help her up. Ara blinked and then smiled tentatively at the stranger. "Come along," said the woman, holding out her hands to both Ara and Octavia. "It is time to go home."

THE BIRTHDAY GIFT
by Elisabeth Waters

One of the old fairy tales everybody knows is about the princess from whose lips pearls and rubies fell whenever she spoke. Elisabeth Waters, my cousin, and my housemate for about twelve years now, has written a number of short stories which cast a slightly different light on the old stories. It will be a long time before I forget her new twist on the Orpheus myth, "Shadowlands" in S&S VI. Just as in that story she showed that recalling the dead back from the Elysian Fields might not be altogether the act of a loving wife, so she shows that magical gifts are not always an unmixed blessing.

I guess I've been doing these anthologies for a long time; my kids, in high school when I started, are now in their middle twenties, and Lisa, substantially my junior, is now nearer forty than thirty. (Well, even Betsy Wollheim, a little kid when I first knew her, is now an editor-in-chief and has kids of her own, being, as W.S. Gilbert would say, "And a right good captain, too.") Time, as I seem to have observed before this, does pass.

Lisa makes order out of the chaos of my Berkeley office, and has won Andre Norton's Gryphon Award for her first novel, CHANGING FATE, which will be published by DAW—if my affairs ever get sufficiently untangled so that Lisa can finish rewriting it.

"**A**unt Frideswide, how could you?" Princess Rowena glared at the diminutive figure in the sorceress' robes across the amethyst, emerald, topaz, ruby, and daisy that had dropped from her lips as she spoke.

Frideswide winced. *Oh, that voice! How could such a small girl have such a loud, shrill voice?* "Rowena, dear, remember your manners! Aren't you even going to say good morning? And do, please, moderate your voice."

"I can still say 'morning,'" Rowena growled, "but I'm deleting the other word from my vocabulary. Rose thorns *hurt* when they scrape across your lips." The pile of precious stones and flowers on the table in front of her grew. "Why did you do it?"

"But, my darling child, it was always your favorite fairy tale—it seemed the perfect gift for your fourteenth birthday, and besides it will add to the value of your dowry, now that you've reached marriageable age. I know your father was worried about that." *Really,* Frideswide thought to herself, *what's the matter with the girl? It's an elegant solution to all of our problems, and she's behaving like a sulky brat.*

"Oh, I see." Rowena's dark eyes blazed. "You think this will make a prospective husband willing to overlook my dreadful voice. You'll buy me a prince—but I have to do the suffering to earn him! Well, I don't want a prince, I don't want a husband, and I'd rather take a vow of silence than go around like this! Take this spell off me! Now!!" Her voice had risen almost two octaves above her usual piercing treble during this speech, and a beaker on the top shelf shattered on the last word.

"But, Rowena, dear," Frideswide protested moving to the other side of the table to stir nervously the contents of her big cauldron, "I'm afraid I can't do that. I don't know the counterspell—indeed, I had difficulty enough getting the spell in the first place."

"No," Rowena said grimly, "not difficulty enough. I'm going to lock myself in my room, and I'm not coming out until you find a way to take this spell off me!"

A soft tap on the door was followed by a maidservant carrying Frideswide's breakfast tray. She dropped a curtsy when she saw Rowena. "Happy birthday, Your Royal Highness."

Rowena rushed past her and out of the room without replying. The maid stared after her in bewilderment, for Rowena was normally one of the friendliest people in the castle.

"She's overtired," Frideswide said hastily. *What a lame excuse; it is only breakfast time.* "All the excitement of her birthday."

"I hope she'll be recovered in time for the party this afternoon," the girl remarked. "I hear all the princes of the Five Kingdoms will be there."

"I hope so, too," Frideswide said fervently, stepping in front of the pile of the jewels on the table. "Put the tray on the end of my workbench, please, and then you may go."

When the girl had left, she sat on the stool at the end of the bench and took the cover off the tray. Immediately there was a scrabbling sound, and a dark-green newt appeared from among the clutter on the workbench to collect his share of the food. The newt had only one eye, the other having been sacrificed to a charm some time back. Frideswide also had a pet frog who was missing one toe, but that had not been one of her more successful charms, so she had not repeated it.

"Well, what do you think?"

The newt chewed several times and swallowed before answering. "*I* think she's an ungrateful brat. When I think of the trouble I took researching the spell, visiting that old dragon and bargaining—I could have been flambéed, and all she says is 'take it off'! It's a beautiful spell, one of the best you've ever cast, and it will make her rich and buy her a good husband and all she can do is yell and complain." He took another mouthful and paused to swallow it. "Why, with that spell, her husband wouldn't mind if she nagged at him day and night!"

Frideswide, however, was beginning to have second thoughts. "Maybe I *shouldn't* have done it. It was such a beautiful fairy tale—but I never thought about the practical aspects, like whether the roses would have thorns and exactly where they would come from. And what if she talks in her sleep and chokes on a ruby or something?"

The newt shrugged. "Then we wouldn't have to listen to her anymore. Her speaking voice is bad enough—but why, in the name of all the gods and goddesses, does she have to love to sing?"

"Be fair; at least she goes deep into the forest to do it."

"Which is probably exactly why King Mark wants to marry her off—he hasn't been able to get any decent hunting for ten years." He snagged another mouthful off the plate, chewed, and swallowed. "Though part of that can be blamed on our Lady Dragon."

"Speaking of our Lady Dragon," Frideswide began hopefully.

"Absolutely not!" The newt's reply was emphatic. "I went last time. If you really want to take this spell off Rowena, *you* go ask the dragon for the counterspell." He ran down the bench and disappeared through the crack in the wall that led to the ledge. He'd lie there all morning, happily sunning himself and carefully deaf to any pleas.

Frideswide gathered the spilled jewels into her belt pouch, swung her cloak around her shoulders, and set off for the dragon's lair.

The dragon looked impressed when the stones were set in front of her. "So you did manage to work the spell." She looked consideringly at Frideswide. "But obviously something went wrong, or you wouldn't be here. So what is it?"

"I'm afraid that Rowena isn't taking it at all well. She made a dreadful scene, saying that we had done this to buy her a husband, and she didn't want one anyway, and—"

The dragon chuckled. "I can fill in the rest. My daughter was like that for a time, too. Don't worry, they grow out of it in a few centuries."

"We don't *have* a few centuries!" Frideswide protested. "She's locked herself in her room, and she says she won't come out until I take the spell off, and what her father will do if she doesn't appear for her party this afternoon I don't even want to consider!" She stopped for breath, and the dragon shook her head.

"You mortals. Always frantic, always needing everything done *now*. When will you learn to relax and take the long view?"

"Doubtless when our lives are as long as yours, my Lady Dragon," Frideswide snapped. "But at present, our time moves more quickly. Do you have any *useful* suggestions?"

The dragon leaned back and blew a small gust of flame toward the roof of the cavern. "I shall ponder this matter. In the meantime, I suggest that you go home and try to reason with your wayward child. Is there anyone she might listen to—a playmate, perhaps a sweetheart? Think on that."

Frideswide got up and reached for the pile of jewels. A thin stream of flame missed her hand by half a hand's span and the heat made her jerk away.

"You can leave those." The dragon, damn her, sounded amused. Frideswide seethed all the way home.

By evening, she had gone from seething to near explosion, and so had King Mark. In his usual heavy-handed fashion, he had ordered Rowena's door broken down when she refused to come out. Rowena had fled to the balcony, from whence the dragon had neatly picked her up and carried her off. All that was left was the pearl that had dropped when Rowena screamed. Frideswide quickly pocketed it before anyone else saw it.

With a castle full of princes (there were six of them still there even after the party was canceled—five visiting from neighboring kingdoms plus King Mark's son Eric), there was, of course, an immediate proposal that someone should go kill the dragon and rescue the princess. After all, it *was* the proper princely thing to do. *But hardly*, Frideswide thought, *proper mealtime conversation*, particularly when Prince Eric described, in graphic detail, what the corpses of the last few knights to challenge the dragon had looked like after she had dealt with them. (The dragon, who valued her privacy, had a habit of depositing the body of any knight who disturbed it in the middle of the market place, in a generally successful maneuver to discourage future attempts on her life. It was obvious that Eric, at least, wasn't planning to make one.

"But don't you feel honor bound to rescue your sister?" one of the other princes asked.

"And leave me without an heir and my kingdom open to invasion or civil war?" King Mark inquired acidly. "Is that what you would like to see? We've no way of knowing that the girl is even still alive, and I forbid my son to embark upon such a dangerous and unprofitable venture. And," he added, looking around the table, "I forbid anyone else to disturb the dragon—just in case one of you feels superfluous and suicidal enough to try. The dragon gets very annoyed when some idiot tries to kill her, and it will be my land and my people that she vents her annoyance on and *I won't have it!*" He glared menacingly around the table. "Is that *quite* clear, gentlemen?" The princes all nodded, looking relieved. They had all seen— and heard—Rowena, and while rescuing her could certainly have been considered the duty of any knight or prince, in the face of a clear prohibition from the king no one could expect them to attempt it. The wine flowed, and the conversation turned to hawking and tourneys.

"But I do wonder why the dragon carried off my daughter," King Mark said to Frideswide as they left the table.

Frideswide tensed. *Did someone tell him about the spell? If anything could make him want Rowena back. . . .*

Apparently he didn't know, for he continued calmly, "You're the sorceress in the family, Frideswide. Find out what happened to my daughter—and why." He started to leave her, then turned back. "But don't upset the dragon while you're finding out!"

Doesn't want much, does he? Frideswide thought. *Oh, well, at least he isn't demanding Rowena's immediate safe return. And I am curious as to what the dragon has done with Rowena anyway.* She got her cloak, checked the sky—full moon and no clouds, plenty of light, and headed up the trail to the dragon's lair for the second time that day.

As she approached it, she could hear the most awful sounds; part rumbling, part screeching and part twanging, as if someone were plucking at random on the strings of a very badly tuned harp. She edged cautiously up to the cave entrance and peered inside.

There was a fire in the firepit, and the dragon was stretched out by it. Rowena was leaning back, propped against the dragon's side, plucking at a harp held loosely between her knees. The rest of the noise was coming from the dragon and Rowena, and presumably both of them would call it singing. Frideswide, not being tone-deaf, would not.

The dragon saw her first. "Come in, Frideswide." She sounded amused. "Have you come to check on Rowena's welfare or demand her return?"

Rowena jumped to her feet, dropping the harp with a clang that made Frideswide wince, and dashed to the dragon's far side, peering at her aunt over the dragon's shoulder. "I won't go back!" she declared hysterically. "I like it here, and I want to stay here!" Jewels fell from her lips, bounced off the dragon's shoulder blade, and slid down her scales.

"But Rowena," Frideswide began.

"I won't go back there! Nobody there likes me, nobody listens to me—at least here the dragon likes my singing."

"And what am I supposed to tell your father?"

"Tell him I'm dead," Rowena said flatly. "I'm not going back there. Never."

"Are you sure that's what you want?" Rowena nodded. "What if you change your mind later?"

The dragon said lazily, "Rowena is free to come and go as she chooses, but nobody is going to take her from here as long as she wishes to stay. Do you have a problem with that, Frideswide?"

"Not in the slightest, Lady Dragon," Frideswide said calmly. "Although if Rowena truly wishes to stay here, it might be best to say that she's dead."

"True," the dragon agreed. "Knights intent on 'rescuing a captive princess' *are* a nuisance."

"King Mark has already forbidden the lot currently at the castle to bother you."

The dragon grinned, exposing rows of long sharp teeth. "I'm sure he has."

"He did, however, ask me to find out what had become of his daughter—and why."

"He doesn't know?" the dragon said in surprise. She twisted her head to look at Rowena. "Since your aunt does not appear determined to drag you away, child, you may as well sit down and be comfortable." Rowena returned to the fire and leaned back against the dragon's flank. At a nod from the dragon, Frideswide dragged a stool near the fire and sat down, too, shedding her cloak. It was certainly warm enough here, a nice change from the castle, where even the tapestries on the stone walls didn't keep the cold out. *Perhaps Rowena would be happier here. She's right in thinking that her father and brother don't care for her, poor child. She's always been rather plain, and between that and her voice, she wouldn't have much choice in a husband unless her father was willing to give her a large dowry, which he's not . . . and then I, with the best intentions, finished the process of turning her into a freak.* It was a sobering realization.

"Are you saying," the dragon asked, "that King Mark doesn't know about the birthday present you gave his daughter?"

"I really don't think he does," Frideswide said.

"Nobody knows," Rowena said. "Nobody except the three of us."

"Are you sure?" Frideswide and the dragon asked in chorus.

"Absolutely."

"Well, that frees us from any necessity to conform to the truth," Frideswide said, turning to the dragon, "so why did you carry off and kill the king's daughter?"

The dragon thought for a moment. "Tell him it was a dietary imbalance—that every few centuries a dragon has to eat a virgin. Tell him I would have warned him and given him time for a sacrificial lottery and all that nonsense, but the need came upon me suddenly. Convey my sympathy for his grief, and," the prehensile tail reached out, snagged a golden goblet heavily encrusted with precious stones, and dropped it in Frideswide's lap, "give him that as his daughter's blood price. Will that serve, do you think?" She looked at Frideswide, but it was Rowena who answered.

"He'll love it," she assured the dragon. "That goblet's much more to his taste than I am."

Frideswide nodded. "Mark doesn't want you upset," she told the dragon, "so he'll swallow any halfway plausible story, and yours is quite plausible." She stood up to go, then remembered something Rowena had said that morning. "Rowena, are you sure no one else knows? You said 'good morning' to someone; who was it?"

Rowena looked at her blankly. "I didn't talk to anyone but you all morning, Aunt Frideswide."

"You told me you were deleting the word 'good' from your vocabulary because the rose thorns hurt your lips."

"Oh, that." Rowena giggled. "I was talking to myself in the mirror. I *told* you no one ever listens to me at the castle." She laughed, and jewels fell from her lips and piled up in her lap.

TANGLED WEBS
by Laura Underwood

On the letter of agreement we send out with each of these stories is a clear warning that if a writer doesn't send me an update of her biography I'll make something up, which the writer probably won't like as well. Since Ms. Underwood neglected to update her biography, you are free to imagine that she lives alone in Afghanistan with seven cats and fourteen crows, or that she has, like Harriet Beecher Stowe, ten children.

What we know beyond doubt is that she wrote a beautiful story, and that this story, like its title, is very artfully woven.

Terra saw the bright-colored silks of the Spider Woman weaving a path among the drab browns and grays of the peasant folk milling about the market. The Lady was tall and graceful, her thin face pale and eldritch among the ruddier folk of the village who passed Terra's stall. The Spider Woman actually had a name, Lady Lyndora of St. Creed, but Terra had called the ageless creature Spider Woman since childhood when Terra first saw the pendant hanging about the Lady's neck, a gilded spider on a miniature web. That was long ago when Terra's mother was weaver here, and in sixteen years of life, Terra had yet to see any sign of the Lady aging.

With a sigh, Terra glanced at her loom and frowned. Aaron was late, and it would be dark soon. "Just a few songs at the Black Crow," he said before leaving on an errand for their father Gordon. "I'll be back at twilight." Then Aaron kissed her cheek and whisked away, gittern strapped to his back, the instrument's strings catching glints of the afternoon sun like his shoulder length blond hair. Her brother may have been a year her elder, but he was somewhat simple and sweet. Their father was a leather crafter, and Aaron's thin fingers were useless for working the stiff material, so Aaron made the deliveries and gathered the goods that needed repair. Besides, her brother had other talents at his disposal. His nimble fingers could coax a song from the gittern, accompanied by his own voice. Bard craft was a rare gift for one of his station, and Father didn't seem to mind, but as he often pointed out, a good voice didn't put supper on the table in St. Creed.

Terra smiled at the thought of her handsome brother. One day, he would find a wife and move away to start a family of his own—perhaps—if he would just keep his feet on the ground. Father often threw up his hands in dismay and wondered what gods had blessed him with such a lackwit for a son, but the words were never spoken in anger. Still, if Aaron were much later, her father might have words for the youth that were less kind. Already, two sons of the village, lads her brother's age, had disappeared. Will, the blacksmith, lost his son last spring with nary a word or trace, and before that, just prior to the autumn feast, the Widow Savin's boy had disappeared, never to return.

"Can't blame them," her father would say. "Not much promise in these parts to keep a lad at home." Secretly, she knew her father feared Aaron would one day feel the same and leave. Life would go on, but Father was crippled and could not make the deliveries himself, and Terra had her own promising trade as a weaver since her mother's untimely death.

"How lovely," a voice crooned, and Terra was startled from her thoughts. The Spider Woman stood before Terra's stall, fingering the corner of a rug Terra had woven. "Your work is as good as your mother's was, child."

Black eyes rose to study Terra for a moment. *Not much to see in me*, the little weaver mused. Her own face was rather cherublike, but plain. The Spider Woman was beautiful, and not a wrinkle showed, not a gray hair among the sable tresses drawn back and curried under a coif of silver net.

"Thank you, my lady," Terra said. "Did you know my mother well?"

Lady Lyndora smiled, faintly, almost like a knife had left a thin, red line across her face with the corners slightly curled. "Yes, I knew the weaver." The dark eyes took on a feral gleam, and Terra found it hard not to shrink away in fear. "Her *talent* was well known to me. I have several of her tapestries in my estate. Fragile things, these weavings. One has only to pull the right thread. . . ." Terra gasped as the long white fingers gave a tug, and watched the threads seem to spill into a tangle before her eyes. "And the whole thing falls apart."

The Spider Woman rose to her full height. "But I have ruined your fine work now, child, and you must forgive me." Her hand dipped into the folds of her gown and produced a silver coin. She placed it on the pile of weavings and moved away.

What a rude thing to do! Terra watched the slender figure drift down the street, like a wisp of web caught in a gentle breeze. Around Terra, other stalls were beginning to close. She glanced across the way and saw the widowed bakerwoman shake her head. Mistress Savin made a warding sign after the Lady before gathering loaves and wrapping them. Terra collected her own wares, watching the silver coin glitter under the fading sunlight. She took up the coin, then dropped it with a squeak. A black spider scuttled out from under the silver and ran for a crack in the table. Terra's heart beat against her ribs. She could swear she saw a bright swatch of red on the creature's underbelly, like an hourglass of blood. Terra shivered, tending to her weavings, carefully shaking every piece before gathering them into her arms and fleeing for the dark interior of the shop.

The scents of oil and leather assailed her. She placed

her bundle next to her work space, cleared for her mother so long ago by her father, and hurried toward the back room to begin a meal. Father was hunched over his bench, carefully slicing a strip of leather to make a headstall for a harness.

"Father, you'll ruin your eyes!" Terra scolded and kissed his grizzled cheek. She lit a taper for him and used it to ignite the oil lanterns, filling the shop with a warm glow. Satisfied, she continued toward the kitchen

"Has Aaron returned?" Father called.

"No, Father," Terra said, brushing coppery locks out of her eyes.

What he said after, she couldn't tell. It wasn't really meant to be heard, she was sure. Terra rushed about to light the fire and heat water, throwing in dried beef and vegetables to make a stew. The loaf she had brought that morning from Mistress Savin still lay on the counter. Terra had the table set by the time Father got his crutches under him and thumped into the kitchen. She helped him into his seat at the table and cast a nervous glance toward the front of the shop. Still no sign of Aaron.

"Your brother's not back yet," Father said, shaking his head. "Lackwit, he is. Probably down at the Black Crow, warbling like a bird for the wenches."

"If it earns him a few coins, Father. . . ."

"Very little coin to be earned in our tavern, child. More likely to earn him a drink. How was your day?"

Terra smiled. "I sold two small blankets to the butcher's wife. Her little one's due any time now."

"Didn't I hear you speaking to someone else?"

Terra nodded. With the door open, she often forgot her father could hear sounds and voices from the street. Just because his legs didn't work, didn't mean his ears were crippled.

"It was the Spider Wo . . . I mean, Lady Lyndora." Terra felt her face redden and saw her father's eyes twinkle.

"Did she buy anything?" he asked.

"No, Father, though she did pay for the rug she unraveled."

"Unraveled?" Her father's ruddy face darkened with anger. "Why would she do such a thing?"

Terra shrugged. "I suppose, if you own the village, you can do as you please."

Father shook his head. "Been naught but hard times since the Lady wed our late Lord. Sad, him dying like he did, a man so young and healthy, withering like an old codger and wasting away. And all so fast. Of course, that was back before. . . ." Father paused, and Terra knew what he was thinking. *Back before the accident that killed Mother and crippled you.* Terra had been just ten when the horse went crazy and overturned the family cart, breaking Mother's neck and crushing Father's right leg. The cart was ruined and the horse had to be put down, struggling to the end. The poor beast had taken fright when a spider crawled into its ear, a large one at that. Father did what he could to raise his young ones once the pain and swelling left. The village healer often said it was a miracle he didn't lose the leg, but useless was useless all the same. His skill didn't require more than an able pair of hands, and so he continued his trade, but without a horse and cart—and Mother's gentle voice singing as she wove the intricate cloths that brought her such local fame. Aaron had learned to sing from their mother, and Terra had learned to weave.

"Father, did Mother know Lady Lyndora well?" Terra said.

"Aye," Father said, and the pain of remorse left his eyes for bitterness. "They came to St. Creed at almost the same time. One married the local Lord, and the other gave her heart to a poor leather worker." He managed a hint of a smile. Terra could still remember her mother, tall and eldritch like the Spider Woman, but with flaming hair and crisp green eyes. Except for that, one would think they were sisters. *Surely not!* Terra's mother had always possessed a mystical quality, something fey which Terra sometimes felt in her own heart. Mother seemed to know things—could do things Terra thought strange, and even now she wondered if those magical memories were more than the active imaginings of a small child. There was a night, under a full moon, when Terra had risen to the gentle sound of Mother's humming and crept into the workroom to find Mother standing at her loom, fingers spread. And the threads seemed to weave themselves into a wondrous cloth that shimmered with the light of the moon. When she found Terra, Mother had not been angry or scolding. Instead, she carried Terra back to her pallet and told her to sleep, that it was all a dream. *Was it?*

"Father," Terra said. "Where was Mother from?"

The question seemed to unsettle him. He refused to meet her gaze. "Over the mountains, not that it matters. Finish your meal and go look for Aaron. Like as not, he's charming some tavern wench with his songs."

"Father!"

He ignored her, lowering his head and devouring his food as though he wanted no more of her questions. Terra finished her own stew and shoved the bowls aside while her father thumped back into the shop to finish the harness. She snatched up a shawl of her mother's weaving, an old one with a pattern reminding Terra of a dove spreading its wings as it flew over an array of forests and valleys. She threw the shawl about her shoulders and took to the streets.

Aaron often went to the Black Crow to entertain. His voice alone had earned him enough coin to purchase the old gittern. Terra had gleaned what she could from her weaving to buy him the strings. In spite of Father's teasing words, her brother did manage to earn a coin or two for his songs.

"Father!"

He ignored her, lowering his head and devouring his food as though he wanted no more of her questions. Terra finished her own stew and shoved the bowls aside while her father thumped back into the shop to finish the harness. She snatched up a shawl of her mother's weaving, an old one with a pattern reminding Terra of a dove spreading its wings as it flew over an array of forests and valleys. She threw the shawl about her shoulders and took to the streets.

Aaron often went to the Black Crow to entertain. His voice alone had earned him enough coin to purchase the old gittern. Terra had gleaned what she could from her weaving to buy him the strings. In spite of Father's teasing words, her brother did manage to earn a coin or two for his songs.

The Black Crow was noisy inside. Terra peered through the open door at a room filled with the amber and golden glows of fire and torch. Men were gathered at the tables, laughing or just talking about the events of the day. Farmers and crafters and merchants. Not a large crowd, for St. Creed was not a large village. A single barmaid danced through the crowd to deliver food and drink. Terra sighed. Not one voice sounded like the sweet tones of her brother. She couldn't see him anywhere in the room.

"Terra?" The voice came from a table right next to the door. Will, the smith, smiled and rose from his seat to saunter over to the door. "So, old Gordon's letting his daughter haunt the tavern as well as his son, eh?"

Terra shook her head. Will reeked of sulfur and sweat, and towered like a bushy giant. "Have you seen Aaron?" she asked.

"Seen him? Why I had to wait for him to clear the tavern door just so I could get in a short span back. He was carrying old Tinker's saddle under one arm and his instrument under the other, and needed the whole door just to pass."

"Did you see where he went?"

Will shrugged. "Sorry. He did seem awfully excited about something. Wait a minute." He turned back to the room. "Hey, Brandon! You came in after me. Did you see Gordon's son in the street?"

"Aye," a man replied from across the crowd. "Near run me down, he did. Seemed in an awful hurry to catch the Lady."

"The lady?" Terra felt a chill creep over her arms. "What lady?"

"Why, the Lady of St. Creed," Brandon said. "She was waiting for him at the end of the street."

Terra thought her blood was turning to ice, making her shiver. Why should she be so afraid? "Did he say anything?"

"Not much. He was rather eager to be on his way. Seems the Lady promised him a goodly sum if he'd entertain her at supper tonight."

"Not a lady I'd care to entertain," Will said with a glare into his mug. "Heard a rumor once that she was a sorceress."

"Sorceress?" Brandon laughed.

"Aye. No one knows where she came from, but it was over the mountains, I think." Will made a warding sign over his heart.

"Why should that be so bad?" Terra said, wild thoughts filling her head. *My mother came from over the mountains!*

"Tale I heard as a lad," Will said. "I always wanted to go up there to search for ore, but my father who was smith before me forbade it. Said folk from over the mountains were not like us—lived with strange creatures and conjured magic, they did. Weren't even human, some said. I scoffed his fears until one day when I went up there and saw what I never should have seen. A lady sang to a flower in a sweet voice, and the flower turned into fruit, and she ate it."

"Sounds like a dream to me," Brandon said with a sneer.

Will shook his head. "I never saw a man cross those mountains to the valley beyond who came back again. I was lucky!"

A few men around the door murmured in agreement. Terra was shaking now. Aaron had gone to the Lady's keep. Why? For what purpose? *My mother came over the mountains.* So had Lady Lyndora—*the Spider Woman!* A spider had been under the coin. *The horse went crazy because there was a spider in its ear!* A woman who sings to a flower—*Mother sang to her loom under the moon.*

Terra turned, needing fresh air to settle her reeling head. She leaned against the outer wall, letting the cool breeze chill the sweat now soaking her face. *Aaron, you are a fool!*

The Lady promised him a goodly sum if he would entertain her at dinner tonight!

What possible harm could there be in that? Yet every time she tried to convince herself there was nothing wrong, Terra found her heart filling with the dread that something terrible might happen to her brother. Will's son last spring and Mistress Savin's son the autumn before. Had they been tempted with stories of what lay over the mountains? The turmoil of thoughts welled in Terra, and she clutched her mother's shawl as though the soft wool had the power to bring comfort and answer the nagging fear within. Terra pushed herself away from the wall, heading for the outer road and the path that would lead her to the keep of St. Creed. If anything, she could reassure herself that her brother was all right. She could pretend she wanted to see the tapestries her mother had woven for the Lady.

Better to be a fool and be sure than to wait and hope—and never know.

She would feel the fool if Aaron returned with a pocket full of silver. The nagging refused to abate, the belief that he would not return if she did not go up there and see for herself that her brother was safe and well.

Squaring her shoulders under the shawl, Terra set herself on the path to the keep. It was fair dark now. The sun had long ago fallen behind the mountains to the west. *The mountains my mother came over.* There were woods leading up to the keep, and here and there she saw the greenish glow of foxfire on rotting logs and stumps. She hugged the shawl tighter, trying to keep her thoughts from straying to the dangers a forest could hold after dark. The warm wool of the shawl about her shoulders felt like a shelter against the threat. She let her eyes drift to the soft fabric, and was startled to see a faint glow of light emanating from the threads—like moonlight. Her eyes followed the complex weave of the threads, reminding her of Mother's lessons concerning the craft. "You have a calculating eye," Mother once said. "That is important for a weaver, for you must be able to follow a thread to its source if you wish to learn the strengths and flaws of the cloth. Weaving fabric is a lot like weaving a spell. You must know how to unbind the fabric if you are to know how it is put together."

Like weaving a spell! The words of a woman who sang to her loom and made the cloth weave itself under the moon. *Sorcerous folk live over the mountains.* Terra shook the thoughts aside.

She was at the gate before she knew it. The monstrous

structure of stone rose over the road like a sentinel. Long ago, the fields close to this keep were clear, green and prosperous with grain and fat cattle. Since the Lord's death, the Lady had little use for open land and had allowed the forest to reclaim its own. Strange. Terra thought forests took many more years than her lifetime to grow so thick and dark. These woods had a strange feel to them, and as she peered about, she realized there was a weblike pattern to the collection of trees. The gate itself lay open, and the moment Terra stepped under the arch of stone, she had the impression of being watched by many eyes. There were no guards, no servants—not even livestock here. Instead, cobwebs of great size hung everywhere, dancing in the wind. Terra glimpsed spiders crawling among the webs. She shivered and pressed on, recalling too well the creature that crawled out from under the coin.

The path to the keep was clear of webs. Terra climbed steps crumbling with age. A few cobbles fell loose as she passed over them. Even the walls of the keep looked rotten, bound in a shroud of webs that seemed to be holding the stones together. She shook her head with wonder and stopped before the door.

What now? To knock seemed proper. She raised a fist and hesitated. From a distance, she thought she could hear a voice raised in song. Aaron? Her heart quickened. Quietly, she laid hold of the door and pushed. It fell open, leaving her facing a torch-lit hall lined with tapestries and canopies of web. *Spider Woman is becoming a more appropriate name for her*! Terra crept forward into the gloom, following the open paths, listening to the voice.

She came to a door that was closed. The song seemed to float out from behind it. Gently, she tested the latch and found the door would open. She pushed it in slowly, fingers numb.

The room that faced her was a huge hall. Every wall was draped with webs, and in the center, her brother sat on the floor, legs crossed, facing a dais with a table and chair. The Lady of St. Creed sat above him like a queen at her supper, yet there was no food on the table. Her dark eyes were hungrily riveted on the lad who sang in such a sweet voice.

Aaron finished his song and rose quickly, bowing to the Lady. "I really must leave now, my lady," he said. "I know Father and Terra will be fretting for the hour."

"Nonsense," Lady Lyndora said. "I spoke with your father myself. He was pleased to hear I was willing to pay handsomely for your songs before I dine."

Liar! Terra nearly screamed the word aloud. The Lady had risen from her chair and was rounding the table, descending to the floor. She towered over Aaron in a predatory manner, her dark eyes narrowing.

"And now that I have listened to your songs, my lovely, I think I shall dine."

Her eyes seemed to turn to flame, paralyzing Aaron to the spot. The lady's hand lashed out to catch his throat, thin fingers digging into his flesh. With a cry, Aaron raised a hand to drive her back, dropping his gittern. The crack of wood when it hit the floor snapped through the room like a thunder clap. Before he could even defend himself, a silky strand skittered across his arms, issuing from the Lady's fingers, weaving around him so close, he could not fight. She opened her mouth, revealing fangs.

"No!" Terra screamed and lurched into the room.

The Spider Woman turned with a hiss, angry over having her meal disturbed. Aaron fell, struggling in the grasp of the webs. The Spider Woman glared at Terra. "How dare you enter this place uninvited," the Lady screamed.

Terra continued to rush forward, not sure of what else to do. The Spider Woman raised her hand, and a web sprang at Terra like a snake. She twisted away as it touched the edges of her shawl. Before the strands could snare her as well, Terra flung the shawl away. She continued her charge, determined to reach her brother.

More web flew at her, and this time she could not avoid the scattering of silks. They caught her, winding about her like tendrils of ivy, refusing to break under her struggles. Strands like steel locked her arms to her chest and tethered her ankles so she fell, wriggling like a worm in a cocoon.

"You are most certainly Avera's daughter," the Lady

hissed. "Meddling child! You shall struggle to the last, I'll wager!"

"Why are you doing this?" Terra cried. "What are you?"

"The what does not matter, little weaver, though your mother certainly knew! She followed me to this land to stop me, and in the end, I stopped her!"

"Why?"

"Do you not know what your mother was, child? Can it be Avera never told her children she was a sorceress? Your mother was a weaver mage. She could move anything woven at will, including my webs! I came here because my hunger drove me to find a place where I could feed on such weak creatures as yourself, but your mother followed, determined to keep me from feeding. If I do not feed on the fluids of youths, I grow old and wither. So I shall feed upon your brother, little weaver, and for an extra treat, I shall feed on you as well. Those born of sorcerous flesh are sweeter than normal mortals by far."

The Spider Woman knelt beside Aaron as she spoke. Terra strained against her silken bonds—useless. The strands refused to give. She heard Aaron whimper, heard him struggle, and she twisted away, not wanting to see, concentrating instead on the webs across her body. . . .

Her eyes beheld a pattern and followed the strands to the source. *A weaver must have a calculating eye.* If she stared hard enough, she could make out individual strands—the rows—the patterns—the ends. . . . The foundation strand lay so close to her fingers. She wriggled them, sliding them between the weavings of silk until she could hook them around the end of the strand. Closing her eyes, tugged. . . .

The web unraveled as easily as her rug, falling away from her and setting her free. Terra rose to her feet, and grasping the loosened strands of web, she rushed across the room.

The Spider Woman was bent over her prey, unaware of the young woman. With a shout, Terra wrapped the strands of spider silk about the Lady's throat, jerking them taut. Lady Lyndora gasped and reached up to claw at the strands. Her hands sought the weaver, gouging

Terra's arms and hands with talonlike nails. The pain was like salt in each wound, but Terra refused to let go—refused to release the strands, and watched as the lady of St. Creed turned blue, then ceased to struggle at all. Terra let the Lady fall, watched her roll over onto her back. The gilded spider on the golden web began glowing with a life of its own, and before Terra's startled gaze, the pendant detached itself and scurried for the nearest curtain of webs.

Terra quickly knelt at Aaron's side, finding the strand that bound him in silk and tugging it to unravel the web. His breathing was shallow. She touched his cheek, startling him. His eyes flitted open, staring at her in horror before a glimmer of relief filled them. *Silly lackwit*, she thought as her own cheeks grew damp. She helped him off the floor. A new remorse came to his eyes when he saw his gittern was smashed beyond repair.

"We'd better go now," Terra said.

Aaron nodded, looking glum as he followed her to the door. She reached to widen the gap she'd made in the wooden structure by her entrance.

Gold streaked out of the webs by the door, a whir of tiny legs, and dropped on her hand. Terra screamed as the gilded spider skittered up her arm, racing toward her throat. Fear locked her limbs until she heard Aaron shout. She snapped her own hand up, smacking the creature away. It fell to the floor, bouncing twice before coming to rest on its back. And before it could escape, Aaron ground it under his heel. A woman's shriek of agony filled the air. Terra covered her ears at the horrifying sound. When she looked at Aaron, he was pale and shaken.

"Come," she said, reaching for him and tugging him toward the door.

Outside, in the dark, she felt cold without her mother's shawl, but finding it under the webs would take too long, and she wanted to leave. She stopped just long enough to stare at the pattern of the webs woven about the crumbling stone that seemed to strain against their bonds. She touched the silky surface, tracing it until her fingers found the thread she wanted. Fragile things, these weavings. One had only to pull the right thread. . . .

The web fell into a tangle at her feet. A groan of stone and wood filled the night. Aaron caught her arm and pulled her through the gates. The keep of St. Creed collapsed once its webbing fell away, tumbling in on itself as though nothing more than the silken strands had held it together for too many years.

WINTERWOOD
by Stephanie D. Shaver

Young as she is (she is fifteen), Stephanie Shaver is no stranger to these anthologies; she has now sold the requisite three stories to become an Active Member of SFWA (Science Fiction Writers of America), and she is probably their youngest full member.

She says she has three cats, since the kittens of Mama Hitler still live; and she's still not old enough to drive. She lives in San Clemente with three siblings, and hopes to go to her first science fiction convention this year. (What I wouldn't give to go to my first one again, when they were still small enough to know everybody there!)

She says that the reason I was not besieged by additional stories this year was due to the death of her grandfather, who left a strong influence on her work. She asked me to dedicate this story to "the memory of Carl Jones, Papo, whose stories will never be forgotten."

She says that she is neither married nor pregnant (well, I should hope so—the one usually implies the other, or anyhow it beats the alternative), likes "good filk"—there's no accounting for tastes, especially those of teenagers—and concludes that she's said enough, commanding me to get on to the other biographies.

"Halt!"

Astride his over-sized gray, Captain Medici rode forward through Winterwood to the front of the Legions, his face pulled down into a scowl.

"All right, what the hell's going on down here, Aritric?"

The lieutenant looked up at his commanding officer and winced. Medici's strong, muscular body looked tight even in the custom-fitted Evermist plate.

"Well, sir, there's something obstructing our path through the wood."

Medici looked at the uneasy men and then back down at the lieutenant. "Well, move it!'

"We can't, sir. She won't let us, sir."

"*She?* Are you telling me a *woman* is obstructing the path of the Red Legion?"

"Not really a *woman*," replied the voice behind him. "More like the keeper of the Wood."

Medici turned quickly enough to give an average man whiplash. A small, pale form in a green and brown gown stood to the side of the Legion, her green eyes shadowed beneath her cowl.

"I am asking nicely," she said in a simple, clear voice. "You may all either go back to the road and quit this one, or you may all die."

"And just who are *you?*" snarled Medici.

"That is of no consequence. However, if you *don't* stop chopping my flora and fauna and return to the original road, I will be forced to kill you."

"*You* kill *us?*" He laughed at the small, childlike form. "The Red Legion bows to no one but our Lord, and if a direct path through Winterwood is the only way to get to him, that path we shall take!"

A cheer went up. The woman-child sighed. "Ah, well, I warned you. You could have learned something from this." She looked the men over and shook her head. "Good night, gentlemen. Keep it in your minds that it is your last."

No smoke, no flare of light, the woman simply disappeared.

The following silence where once there had been birdsong and the gentle *shirk-shirk* of boughs was enough to make up for her lack of departing flash.

Wary, the Legion continued.

That night, they slept beneath the trees of Winterwood, and despite all his puffed-up bravery and pride, Medici set up a double watch.

As the captain sat inside his tent, puffing on a pipe, there came a gentle, "Sir?"

"Come in."

Lieutenant Aritric stepped in. Shy farmer's eyes going down, he dropped a sack at the Captain's feet. Puzzled, Medici opened it to find a score of the Four Sword badges all soldiers of the Lord wore. He looked up and noticed suddenly that Aritric wasn't wearing *his* anymore.

"I—I resign, sir."

"You *what?* Why?"

Aritric looked around uneasily. "It's Her, sir. You don't know what you're dealing with! You were cityborn, sir. There are stories, sir . . . stories we Winterwood farmers know about. Stories about *whole armies*—not just one legion—entering Winterwood and *never being seen again*. Almost . . . almost as if the forest ate them. . . ."

The Captain scowled, nibbled on his mustaches, and blew up.

"You pig-sticking whoreson! You scum-eating farmboy! Your brains fermented along with your balls out in the field years ago listening to child's tales! *Trees can't kill you, you stupid ox!* Mud-brained cow—don't you think *someone* would have seen trees munching on humans by now if it were true?! OUT! Get out, faerie-tale sissy! I'll have you and the rest of your little mommaclutching friends court martialled just as soon as we get out of here! Go back to your farms and put your skirts and bonnets back on, you little—"

Aritric departed swiftly, along with the other men, never looking back.

Medici settled back, puffing smoke out his ears and eyes as well as his nose and mouth now, steam gently lifting from his brow. After a while, he drifted to sleep, muttering about effeminate sons-of-bitches who were scared of hermit druids who knew some parlor tricks. . . .

The tree his tent was pegged to trembled once, and then, ever so gently, began to wrap strong roots around the relatively weaker body of the Captain.

Outside, guards were abruptly entangled in vines and moss and ivy, leaves filling mouths and ears, twisting around bodies.

Tangled in strong green fibers, the entire Red Legion (save twenty) were gently, sadly suffocated before they could reach so much as a dagger or a sword or a bow. . . .

Later, they would be pulled beneath the earth.

A voice came softly over the sound of forest trees holding fast to the legion. It rang out over the leaves, and the former twenty members of the legion heard it as they rode away on the original road . . . even though later all memory of the druid and her words was wiped from their minds. It reached the ears of Medici and Medici's men in their last moments, the words dying away along with their life-forces.

"Oh, trees *do* kill, Medici," she said, "but *they* do not do it for a Lord or a piece of land. *They* only do it for survival, *they* never take prisoners, and *they*, unlike men, only do it when they're sure no one's looking. . . ."

RED WINGS

by Josepha Sherman

Josepha Sherman says she is that comparative rarity, a New Yorker who was actually born there. She sent me an impressive *curriculum vitae*; she has written two fantasy novels, one of which won the Compton Crook Award, and over fifty short stories, including stories in SWORD AND SORCERESS IV, V, AND VIII. She has also written two nonfiction books and a couple of children's books. I guess that she's still rubbing it in that I carelessly referred to her as an amateur in one of these volumes; but I think I explained that—being then just out of the hospital, it's a miracle I spelled my own name right—or hers.

Anyhow, the real meaning of amateur is someone who does what they do for love. In that sense I, too, in spite of fifty-odd books in print—some of them, as I've also often said, very odd indeed—still think of myself as an amateur; I love what I do.

Ahé, to fly, to soar, to catch the wind with one's wings! To fly!

She laughed, the one who called herself Riss or Sha'arh as the fancy took her, laughed a wild, high, hawk-fierce cry. And if some human heard her, if some meek peasant saw her, bright against the sky, and made

130

the sign against evil after her—why, let him, the fool! Let him!

For Sha'arh was never human. Oh aye, her mother had been so, the poor, pale, frail thing who had died in the birthing. But he who had been father to Sha'arh— one need but look at the great red wings, strong as leather, sleek as silk, at the blazing red hair flying stiffly back, at the small, slim, supple body and fierce, hawk-proud face, to know her father for one of those the humans in their limited words called Demons of the Upper Air.

Sha'arh laughed again, beating her wings fiercely, rising until she found the strong current she sought and rode that effortlessly, soaring down the sunlit sky. The flame of her eyes quieted to red embers, and sharp white teeth—predator's teeth—glinted as she smiled, abandoning herself to the sheer sensuous pleasure of the silken winds about her, afternoon sun warm on her outspread wings. She could almost sleep like this, buoyed by the wind, at home in this her element.

But a prickle of hunger disturbed her. A winged body demanded frequent new energy, and Sha'arh sighed and looked down to the earth far below, hunting, focusing her attention on the small deer she saw standing alone. Where were its fellows? Why wasn't it seeking shelter in the forest? Was it lost to injury or age? No matter. Sha'arh twisted in the air, banking sharply and spiraling downward till she was in range. Spilling the air from her wings, she dove, striking with enough force to break her prey's neck and slay it outright.

She feasted then, feeling renewed strength flowing through her, then rose, following the sound of rushing water to a fast-moving stream. And if the forest through which it raced was gloomy, one inheritance from her father's kind had been night-keen eyes; darkness was no obstacle. She bathed cheerfully in water too shallow for one of the Water Folk to try drowning one of Air out of jealousy, then scrambled out to dry in a patch of sunlight, drowsing in the warmth.

Sha'arh awoke with a start. What . . . humans? Hunters?

Aie, yes! Hunters all about—and they were hunting *her!*

Fool that I was for having slept!

She half unfurled her wings—but these cursed trees didn't leave room for flight. And now there wasn't time to waste wondering what the hunters wanted of her. But a Sha'arh grounded wasn't a Sha'arh defenseless. She sprang at the nearest human, teeth bared, and the man fell back in alarm, breaking the circle they were forming about her. She saw her chance—

But they had a net, and even as Sha'arh tried to dodge, it settled over her. And silver wire had been woven into its meshes, the metal she could no more endure than could any of her father's race. It burned at her, weakened her till at last she collapsed, the humans all around her, pinning her to the ground. Panting, Sha'arh glared up at the one who was surely their leader: an ugly man, even for a human, painfully lean yet tall and coldly proud of bearing. His eyes were the dead eyes of one who'd dealt too long with the Dark Ones.

Just then, the furious Sha'arh couldn't have cared if he *was* a Dark One. "Why?" she snapped.

"I need you," he answered coolly. "For my Patron. I'm delighted you made my hunt so simple."

She snarled. "I shall taste your blood!"

"I think not. Bring her."

Senses confused by silver, Sha'arh's next clear awareness was of darkness . . . a cavern. The hunters had untwined the net from her, though there were enough of them to hold her light-boned body helpless. She suspected only too well that they'd removed that net only because her captor's Patron could bear silver even less than she.

They dragged the fighting Sha'arh forward. She glanced about wildly, craning her head back, seeing a gap in the cavern's roof through which the first free stars of evening could be seen. Sha'arh gave a low cry of longing and renewed her struggles, only to have one man, more daring or more reckless than the rest, get his arm around her neck and all but choke her into submission.

But what was their cursed leader doing? Tracing runes on the cavern floor with a black-hilted dagger. Aie, aie, she knew those signs!

She wasn't the only one afraid. The men were muttering among themselves, very softly, trying to convince themselves the gold they'd been paid was worth the risk, trying to reassure themselves they were in no danger thanks to the circle, murmuring, "We'll simply toss one demon to another."

What! Sha'arh struggled with renewed panic, hearing their leader beginning what could only be a summons, and was nearly choked anew by the humans. By the time she had managed to draw air into her aching lungs again, there was suddenly another Presence in the cavern. Her head shot up, and she stared wildly at That Other swirling within the protective circle, the Earth Demon of the deep and sterile blackness that is the bitterest enemy of the Air. From that swirl of darkness came a whispered, chill distortion of human sound:

"Why, what is this small, struggling thing?"

Even the cold-eyed sorcerer shivered. "An offering, Lord. One of the Sky Folk."

Sha'arh felt the Other's contempt flick over her. "Only partially," It murmured. "Some semi-human hybrid."

"Is she . . . not acceptable, Lord?" For the first time, uneasiness quivered in the sorcerer's voice.

There was a moment's silence as the Other contemplated Sha'arh. "He doesn't understand, little thing," It said in the Silent Language common to Air, Earth, Fire, and Water. "He doesn't know the hatred among the Four Kindreds. But you know."

"Yes, curse you!"

"So-o! The little thing has the Sky Folk's spirit, at any rate. And what shall I do with you? Drink the essence of your life? Cage you like a little bird and watch you flutter like a moth against the light? Yes . . . captivity is what you Sky Folk fear the most, is it not?"

"We fear nothing!"

"Brave words. But you tremble, little thing." The Other shifted back to Its chill imitation of human speech. "Yes," It said casually. "She is acceptable. Bring her."

As the humans dragged Sha'arh forward, she realized with a shock of horror they meant to cast her into the Circle. Oh, being mortal, she had, at times, thought of death, but she'd always imagined one last, clean fall from the skies to the waiting earth—not this! They were hurling her off her feet—No!

In that instant's freedom, Sha'arh flung herself straight up, wings flapping frantically, hitting humans, hitting empty air. Her body wasn't designed for this, but sheer lust for life kept her airborne, struggling up toward the gap in the cavern's roof, straining every muscle. Below her, she heard the wild confusion of the humans, and for a savage moment ached to swoop down, a hawk among pigeons, and close her teeth on their leader's throat. But the Other's anger was down there, too, and Sha'arh fought up and out into the free night.

But what was this sudden chill? Sha'arh glanced back over the curve of a wing and cried aloud in shock. The sorcerer, desperate for his Patron's favor, must have broken the Circle to free It. And though the Other was as clumsy in air as Sha'arh in water, It was far swifter than she, with her taint of human blood. It surged up after her, a darkness, coldness that drained the strength from her tiring wings. Sha'arh abandoned pride, shouting out a frantic plea to her half-kin, her father's folk. Would they hear her? Rather, would they heed her? Would they let even a half-blood of their kind die like this?

All at once she heard them, *felt* them all around her, and a wild wind roused itself. Caught, the Other was swept spinning away, helpless as a leaf in a storm.

But even as It fell back out of the world, Its dark aura brushed one red wing. Sha'arh screamed as that wing went limp and useless. As the last of the wind faded, and her indifferent kin-folk vanished with it, she plummeted down, the earth spinning dizzily below her as she twisted, turned, catching at the slightest of air currents to slow her fall, pulled off-balance again and again by her crippled wing. Beneath her, trees seemed to grow from twigs to monsters, reaching out to stab her on their branches—

But no, first there was an invisible something, someone's magical barrier, soft and heavy as the substance humans called glue, and her fall was slowing . . . slowing . . .

Without warning, she was through the barrier, and helplessly falling again. The earth rushed up to meet her. There came stunning pain, and darkness.

*   *   *

She hurt. From head to foot, she hurt, and for one irrational moment was afraid to open her eyes lest she find herself broken and dying on the forest floor.

But . . . this wasn't the ground.

Confused, Sha'arh opened her eyes and tried to rise. That was definitely a mistake. As she sank back with a hiss of pain, a voice cried out, too late:

"Don't move!"

Sha'arh turned her head sharply to the sound. That was a mistake, too, because her vision swam sickeningly.

"Gently," murmured the voice. "I mean you no harm."

Sha'arh hadn't a choice. She waited, eyes shut, with a predator's patience till her mind cleared enough to realize she was lying facedown on several soft thicknesses of blankets, her wings a warm cloak about her.

Her wings! Sha'arh stiffened as she realized the one the Other had brushed was swathed in bandages. Her suddenly urgent attempt to move it met with failure and, frightened, she tried again to rise.

"Ah no, lie still, you'll hurt yourself!"

Gentle hands were trying to hold her still, but Sha'arh had had quite enough of being helpless, and turned her head savagely, sharp teeth bared. She narrowly missed contact with a brown-sleeved arm, then overtaxed muscles gave way and she collapsed, panting. The gentle pressure of those restricting hands vanished, and Sha'arh turned her head again, warily.

A woman knelt beside her, clad in a priestess' simple brown gown. Sha'arh stared at the unexpected beauty of the clean-lined face and the mass of flowing hair softly golden in the sunlight. Not yet thinking clearly, she touched a tentative hand to that shimmering, the woman never flinching as sharp talons came near her face.

"Are you satisfied?" There was a hint of amusement in the woman's voice. "I'm quite human, really I am."

Sha'arh started, letting her hand fall, eyeing the woman with sudden new wariness. "Who are you?" Her throat ached from her human captors' rough handling, but she persisted, "Where is this place? A garden?"

"Yes. And the wall beside you belongs to my house.

I'm sorry I couldn't take you inside; there wasn't room for your wings.''

Sha'arh inhaled the scent of herbs. "You are a wise-woman? A priestess?"

"Of the Lady, yes, and a healer. My name is Amalia."

"A priestess, yet you would help me?"

"You certainly needed it!"

"You're not afraid? Other humans fear. Or hate."

"I saw your fall. You passed through my protective barrier, and nothing evil could have done that. But enough talking for you, with those ugly bruises on your throat. Just tell me this: are you in pain?"

Sha'arh was not about to admit weakness. "Not badly." But she couldn't keep the fear from her voice when she asked, "My wing. . . ?"

"Will heal." The woman frowned slightly. "But a sorry sight it was, the bone dislocated and the flesh bruised and bleeding, almost as though a great hand had closed on it." The frown deepened. "You never got that from a fall, nor the bruises on your throat, either."

"No." But Sha'arh was too weary for explanations. She sank back to the cushioning blankets, and felt a quick, tentative hand brush her sleek hair.

"Sleep," the priestess said, "and have no fears. This small land of mine is guarded well against . . . whatever pursued you."

Sunlight in her eyes woke her. It was early morning, and noisy with birdsong. Sha'arh stretched, gingerly, and sat up, gingerly, wincing. The side on which she'd fallen was spectacularly bruised. But bruises seemed to be the worst of it, and after a moment she struggled to her feet. Her injured wing ached dully, and she went in search of a pool to serve as mirror.

The priestess, Amalia, was already there, gathering water plants. Sha'arh watched for moment, enjoying the woman's grace. "Priestess."

Amalia gave a little shriek, whirling, and Sha'arh drew back in surprise, good wing half spread, because magic was flickering at the human's fingertips.

The flickering vanished. The priestess laughed, embarrassed. "I didn't hear you approach."

"Are you a sorceress?"

"No!" But the blue gaze faltered. The woman glanced down at her hands, up at Sha'arh. "I . . . can cast illusions, weak ones. And set magical barriers, as you know. How are you feeling?"

Sha'arh shrugged. "Well enough."

"Enough to answer a question? Just what attacked you?"

"An Other," Sha'arh said flatly. "One of Earth. As I am of Air, we were enemies. It sought me as prey. I escaped." She stirred uneasily, awkward afoot. "I wish to see how my wing is healing."

"Of course. Ah . . . this Other isn't likely to come a-calling?"

"No. My father's kin drove it away."

"Your— Tsk, wait, let me help you. You won't be able to reach the bandages."

Sha'arh's muscles tightened at the touch, and the woman drew back, eying sharp talons warily. "Did I hurt you?"

"No." But there was a sudden nervous wildness in her eyes.

Amalia sighed. "I had an eagle here once," she murmured, "a wild one with a broken wing—yes, I heal animals as well as humans. Now, that eagle knew me. And yet every time I tried to touch it, that lovely wild thing would threaten me. Every instinct must have been crying that a human's touch would endanger its freedom."

Sha'arh turned sharply to her. Amalia continued mildly, "Yet, when its wing was healed, the eagle was free to fly away, the unbound thing the Lady had intended it to be." She raised an eyebrow. "Clear enough?"

Sha'arh gave a fierce little laugh. "Clear enough."

"Riss?" The human had long since given up trying to pronounce that wind-sound name, "Sha'arh."

"What is it?"

"I thought you were ill, you've been so quiet. Does your wing still pain you?"

It did. But Sha'arh said shortly only, "It does well enough." She never looked up from the rock on which she was moodily perched, but she heard the priestess sigh.

"You must feel as though you'll never heal."

Sha'arh glanced angrily up at that. "I will not be pitied!"

"I'm not pitying. Only worrying."

"Don't."

"No? With you as frustrated and short-tempered as that broken-winged eagle?"

"You're in no danger from me."

"I wasn't worried about myself! Riss, you've been here for . . . what? . . . two weeks now, and eating no more than will just keep you alive."

Sha'arh stirred restlessly, unfurling and refolding her good wing. "If I don't hunger, I don't eat." She glanced up at the woman, determined to change the subject. "You are beautiful, as humans see beauty. Yet you have no man."

"What of it?"

"Most human women seem to be either wed or in service."

"I *am* in service, to the Lady." Amalia paused, uneasy under Sha'arh's steady, curious gaze. "Look you, I don't believe in false modesty. I know very well how I look. But I chose not to wed. Leave it at that."

Sha'arh shrugged, accepting; the inhuman folk rarely questioned each other. But Amalia, true-human, misunderstood. "I come," she said reluctantly, "from what's best described as highly impoverished nobility. I had no dowry. No dowry meant no high marriage. And, the Lady help us, my father wasn't about to waste his daughter on some marriage of low degree! Which was fine with me. I never did believe the . . . proper idea that a woman is property to be bought and sold."

"How can a thinking being be property?"

"Exactly. But . . . my parents died. And there I was, with no man to guard me and no rights under the law. The crown confiscated what little property there was to satisfy my father's debts, and I was left with nothing. Save this—handicap of beauty."

Sha'arh frowned, puzzled. "Handicap?"

"Oh, Riss, who would hire me? What wife wants a

fair-faced young woman in her household?" Amalia's eyes were dark with memory. "Of course there were . . . other offers . . . brothels and such. But I . . . just . . . couldn't. I tried selling my magics. But there's a law against sorcery in these lands." Amalia smiled faintly. "At last I did what my heart for years had been telling me to do. I turned to the Lady, and learned healing and a joy in my own company." She paused. "But all this must seem very, very alien to you."

"No. You must live free. *I* must live free."

"Mm." There was a flicker of humor in the blue eyes. "Are you hinting we're not so very different, you and I?" As Sha'arh blinked in confusion, uncomfortable with the thought, the priestess sighed. "But you've turned the conversation from yourself very neatly. Riss, what's wrong?"

Sha'arh glanced away. "Don't try to snare me with soft words."

"And why are you so afraid of softness?"

Sha'arh uncoiled from her rock, eyes blazing. "I am not weak!"

Amalia wasn't impressed. "Don't bate your wings at me. I've tended enough wild things to know how they fear helplessness. But—Lady's mercy, you're not some empty-minded eagle!"

"Don't lecture me!"

"I'm trying to keep you alive, dammit! Look you, you want to be free of me and my—soft words, don't you? Then stop wasting time on this—this *weak* apathy! Look!"

The priestess pointed sharply upward at a hawk circling far overhead, high above the trees, its wings flashing golden in the sunlight. Sha'arh gave a low moan of longing. Her injury, her earthbound days were forgotten as she ran forward and fiercely launched herself into the air. For one free, glorious moment she was soaring upward—

Then her injured wing gave way and she fell back to earth. Stunned, anguished, Sha'arh lay full-length and stabbed her taloned fingers savagely into the ground.

"Riss! Dear Lady, are you hurt?"

If the human touched her, she would attack, she would attack!

But Amalia must have realized the danger, because her footsteps slowed. Sha'arh stared at her, eyes glazing with despair. "Why? Why offer me empty hope?"

"I didn't mean—"

With a snarl, Sha'arh turned away, stabbing her talons into the earth once more.

There was silence for a long while. Then the priestess asked quietly, "Can you listen to me now? *Will* you listen? If I'd wished you harm, I would have left you where I found you, to die of exposure or live with a crippled wing."

Sha'arh let out her breath in a long sigh. "I . . . know you mean me well. But why show me freedom I couldn't reach?"

"To rouse you! I was afraid you were losing the will to live; I've seen that happen with earthbound birds."

"I'm not a bird. And I do not die so easily." Sha'arh sat up suddenly, good wing wrapped about her. "But you were right to rouse me." She glanced down at her taloned hands, flexing them thoughtfully. "I cannot bear your human food. But I can still hunt, on foot if I must. There should be enough small game to—Aie, what are you doing?"

"Making sure you haven't injured your wing all over again. I don't have to remind you, do I, that a hunter needs patience?"

"It will heal?"

"It will heal."

Words were easy. Patience was not so easy to keep, for all that the bewildered Sha'arh found herself enjoying Amalia's small, warm tales of her life, of the people she healed (bewildering, to *want* to heal the weak!), for all that Sha'arh found herself trying to tell the woman what her own life was like: alone yet never lonely even though there were none quite like herself. How could there be room for loneliness with wild wind and freedom filling every space?

Patience. This day found Sha'arh in her restlessness on the very edge of Amalia's magic-guarded lands, by the side of that unseen Barrier itself. It had been a long walk for a body not meant for foot travel, and she was glad to stop and rest.

Amalia thinks my wing's healed enough to hold my weight. But I—I—I don't know. If there were to be another so heartbreaking fall . . . Sha'arh hissed. *Why should the woman care what happens to me, why? Is this . . . kindness . . . what it means to be human?*

It was bewilderingly pleasant, talking with the woman, laughing with her, simply two women together despite the differences. Human women—

"I'm *not* human!" she cried aloud. "I will not *be* human!"

Still . . . she admitted she was glad there were humans like Amalia, who—

But then Sha'arh was springing to her feet, straining to hear. She snarled, very softly, and the sound of it was never human. No mistaking the *feel* of that cold, dead aura: it belonged to the sorcerer of That Other, and with him his twelve followers. Sha'arh's eyes glared crimson with hatred, her wings spread as though stooping to the kill.

But then she folded her wings again with a little shiver of worry. Why was the sorcerer here after so long? Could he still be tracking her? Surely such persistence was beyond anything human? Or . . . was the threat to Amalia? That Other would surely love to destroy a priestess symbolic of a Lady who *was* Life. Could Amalia's Barrier hold against true sorcery? Panicked, Sha'arh sprang forward to warn the woman, wings spread—

And the injured wing held her weight, and she soared upward with a cry of sheer wonder. She could fly again, she could fly!

Wild with joy, Sha'arh beat her wings fiercely, spiraling up and up where the winds played, catching the strong currents, riding them down, soaring, diving, gliding, clumsy at first then graceful, graceful as the red wings flashed in the sun and she danced with the winds about her, laughing in hawk-wild exultation. She forgot the sorcerer, forgot his followers, forgot even Amalia, drunk with the sheer glory of soaring, and she flew, she flew, she flew.

How far Sha'arh traveled that day, she never noted. When hunger overtook her at last, she found her prey in the shape of a small deer, and feasted well for what seemed the first time in an eon, fierce joy in her heart at the swift dive and the clean kill.

It was night when Sha'arh had finished, and she was weary to the last muscle. Wrapped in her wings, Sha'arh slept, and dreamed of flight.

But when she woke, it was with full memory of Amalia, and a vague, unfamiliar sense of guilt that she'd never warned the priestess. Wings spread, she launched herself once more into the air, flying this time with all her skill and speed, catching and rejecting wind after wind, racing across the sky, arguing with herself that surely Amalia would have safely fled from danger, surely would have taken sanctuary with the villagers not too far from her hut. . . .

But if she hadn't known of danger. . . ?

Aie, but the Barrier was gone from Amalia's lands! Sha'arh's soft cry of worry turned to a sharp shout of horror. She spiraled downward, spilling the air from her wings, recklessly dodging branches, not slackening speed till she had landed and was staring stunned, at the charred ruin of what had been Amalia's home.

There had been no warning, no escape. The sorcerer had broken the protective Barrier and trapped Amalia in her house.

And he had destroyed her.

Sha'arh threw back her head and gave one long scream of fury and anguish, a terrible sound and never human. She cast up her arms to the sky and called fiercely, and it never once occurred to her that she was of mixed blood, that she might not be answered. Sha'arh did not plead, she summoned, and the full power of her father's kind was within her.

The winds rose, hurling great dark clouds before them. Sharp tension built and built in the waiting air as Sha'arh continued her commanding call, until at last the storm broke and lightning flashed blindingly. Sha'arh gave a wild, high, savage laugh and threw herself up into the storm. The lightning didn't strike her, the winds didn't hurl her down, and she knew the storm was hers to control. Laughing, she set out for vengeance.

The humans had not gone far. Ahé, there they were, the murderers of Amalia, riding along the rim of a cliff—

"They will meet their fate *now!*"

The savagery of the storm swept down on the humans, and with it, the savagery of demon-eyed Sha'arh. Their horses shrilled in terror, throwing their riders, but she ignored the panicked animals. Poised on outspread wings, she called to the humans, voice clear as ice above the shrieking of the winds:

"Why? Why did you slay her?"

She saw their eyes glint as they looked up at her, and the faintest chill stole through her at what she read there; they had been callous enough before, mercenaries willing to ignore anything but coins, but they had still been human. Now . . .

"She was weak," one answered, tone lifeless, "fit only for sacrifice," and Sha'arh heard the dim echo of the Other in the words.

A second continued, voice just as hollow, "Had we the time, she would have made fine sport. For us. For the Master."

Their emptiness was beginning to shake her storm-wildness. "Could you not see her beauty? Could you sense nothing of her goodness?" Her blazing gaze flicked over them all, seeing the truth, seeing how they had, knowingly or out of simple, stupid greed for gold, let that Other leach all life, all joy from them. "You're no longer men, only slaves!" she cried in disgust. "Slaves fit only for your filthy Master—Aiee, *go to It, then!*"

Sha'arh brought both arms sweeping savagely down—and the storm winds followed her command. When they whirled away, the rim of the cliff was left empty.

"A reckoning for you, Amalia! A cleansing for you!"

But those had been only the servants. Where was the sorcerer?

She had her answer as the storm was rent about her and the rain at last poured down. The winds' force was broken, and Sha'arh landed at the cliff's edge to face the man.

They stood in silence in the rain for a tense while. Then Sha'arh snapped, "They are dead, your twelve."

The sorcerer's thin face showed no emotion. "What of it? You saw how Power had warped them; they were useless. I can always find other fools."

"You'll have no time!"

But the sorcerer raised a hand, and the force of his will held her back. "No, creature." Then, with the first hint of emotion she'd seen from him, he added, "Oh, come, do you really think I've come all this way to die at the hands of some misbegotten little hybrid?"

Sha'arh studied him a moment, really seeing him for the first time, seeing with inhuman clarity a hint in the man of the boy he must have been: deprived, abused, hungering for anything that would give him a chance to strike back, a chance for Power . . . "So you bartered yourself to Darkness," she mused aloud, then shrugged. "What is that to me?"

"Your life. My Power is a gift from my Patron. And said Patron wants you."

Sha'arh snarled, glistening with rain, sharp teeth bared, wings spread in menace. "Why did you kill her?"

"Kill— Ah, the priestess." He smiled thinly. "She sheltered you, and my Patron wouldn't permit that. And she served that simpering Lady, and that, my Patron wouldn't permit, either. She did scream most piteously . . ."

Sha'arh's thin control snapped. With a wordless cry of fury, she leapt at the man, talons outstretched—just, as she realized an instant too late, as the sorcerer had intended. His blast of will hurled her aside with stunning force.

"Enough, hybrid," he murmured. "My Patron waits."

His Patron . . . Sha'arh, struggling to marshal her senses, knew enough of the inhuman kindreds to realize the sorcerer's life was a focus for the Other, the key for It into this world. *Double reason for him to die!*

Predator-wary, she waited, trembling with tension, pretending she was still dazed. She heard the sorcerer approach warily, ready to strike . . . a moment more. . . .

Sha'arh sprang up with a shout, and her sharp teeth closed on the flesh of his arm. With a harsh cry, he wrenched himself free, throwing her aside, right off the cliff's edge, but wide red wings caught the air, brought her back to face the sorcerer, her eyes flame, a streak of scarlet staining her mouth.

"I've tasted your blood, human. I'm shielded. Now you can't work your spells on me."

She lunged at him and sent them both hurtling back over the cliff's edge into space. Yet even as he fell, the sorcerer struggled free of his encumbering robe and shape-changed. Face contorted with the pain of the shifting, still human and human-clad from the waist down, he soared up on great, leathery wings.

Sha'arh laughed in sharp delight—*Oh, fool, to fight me in my element!*—and dove to the attack. The sorcerer dodged awkwardly, unused to his new shape. He caught at Sha'arh's arm in passing, but lost his hold on slippery, rain-wet flesh. Sha'arh dove past him, then banked sharply, catching the wind, spiraling up and up, rain beating at her upturned face but nictitating membranes keeping her vision clear.

Which was fortunate, because the sorcerer was diving to meet her, dagger clenched in his fist. Sha'arh laughed again, softly, and slipped neatly aside. The man turned, too sharply, and lost the wind. His flailing wing slammed into Sha'arh, and both fliers went tumbling helplessly.

But Sha'arh, child of the sky, caught the wind again, beat at it, spiraling up once more, up and yet up. She glanced down to see that the sorcerer, now far below her, had just managed to regain his balance. And Sha'arh smiled without humor, sharp teeth glinting.

"Amalia, my vengeance is yours."

She folded her wings and dropped like a hawk to its prey. The sorcerer saw his danger, too late—

Then Sha'arh struck, and felt bones break beneath her. As she pulled sharply up, she saw the sorcerer fall.

"Ah, yes, fall! Fall, and know the terror I felt!"

He struck, and lay broken on the ground, body sliding helplessly back into its human form. Sha'arh landed warily, seeing that he still breathed. But how long could life remain in so damaged a body? What agonies might he be suffering were he conscious?

And for one long, terrible moment Sha'arh debated

something truly foreign to her. What if she let him suffer for Amalia's death? What if she forced him to endure all the torments of slow, helpless death?

Sha'arh spat in disgust. Amalia would never have condoned anything like that. And she—oh, she was a slayer, yes, but never a torturer.

The sorcerer was conscious now, and in his eyes terror and the beginning of pain. Sha'arh bent over him and said, almost gently, "For the sake of Amalia, priestess of the Lady, I grant you swift death."

Her teeth were sharp, his throat was unprotected. . . .

When it was done, Sha'arh got slowly to her feet, trembling. The rain had stopped at last, and a clean wind blew. She walked a few weary steps, then, in one wild burst of strength, leapt into the air and flew back to the top of the cliff.

And there, to her utter amazement, Sha'arh crumpled, weeping with the awkward, racking sobs of one unfamiliar with tears. After a time she caught her breath, huddling where she'd fallen, wings wrapped tightly about herself.

"Riss?"

Her head shot up. And then she was springing backward, wings outspread, crying out in sheer terror, "Amalia!"

"Riss, wait. I'm not some demon. I'm not dead!"

"But—but I saw your house— The sorcerer heard your screams!"

"My dear, I knew your wing was healed. So when you didn't come back to me yesterday, I was sure you'd flown away for good. It never occurred to me you might return, and—and mourn."

"But how did you escape?"

"I felt the Barrier fall. I'm no mighty sorceress, you know that. But people are always willing to believe what they want to believe. Particularly when they're helped along with a bit of illusion."

"Ah! You tricked the sorcerer!"

"Precisely. When he burned my house, I was safe in my root cellar. As soon as he and his men left, I scurried off to the village, and— But what of his men? They're dead, aren't they?"

"The winds swept them from the cliff. At my bidding."
Sha'arh never blinked. "They were dead, inside, long
before the winds touched them."

"Lady, yes." Amalia's fingers traced a quick sign of
benediction. "May their souls be cleansed."

Sha'arh shrugged impatiently. "The sorcerer is dead,
too."

"I . . . know. I saw the end of— He would have given
you far worse than death, and yet you gave him mercy.
Why?"

Sha'arh shivered. "I don't know. For you. For him.
For—for me—Aie, don't do this! Don't trap me into
human thoughts! Let me be free!"

"Is it so terrible a thing to be human?"

"Yes! No. Amalia . . ."

The priestess sighed. "There really is more of sky than
human in you, isn't there? You should know by now, by
seeing me, living with me, that 'humanity' doesn't mean
'chains.' "

"No." Sha'arh shivered anew. "What of you?"

"Is that what's bothering you? Worry about me? No
harm was done, not really. I'm not hurt, and my friends
from the village will help me rebuild." She hesitated,
studying Sha'arh a moment, then smiled slightly. "No.
It's not just worry. Riss, what you're feeling is called
friendship."

"It's . . . confusing."

"Sometimes."

"Amalia, I . . ."

But the priestess was drawing back, deliberately creat-
ing an open, neutral space between them. Sha'arh froze,
suddenly tense with excitement.

"I will not hold you against your nature," Amalia said
softly. "Remember that broken-winged eagle, Riss. I set
you free, my fierce young eagle-friend. You *are* free."

Sha'arh laughed in sudden fierce delight. "Ahé, yes!
Amalia, I will remember you, but I— Yes!"

Overwhelmed, she ran and leapt up into the wind,
soaring wildly out into the open sky with a wild, high cry
of freedom and the joyous flashing of red wings.

ABOVE THE GROUND
by Eric Haines

Eric Haines says that this is the third story he has sent out, and he is dutifully resisting all kinds of "third time's the charm" jokes. I admire his forbearance.

He says he wrote this story to give me a break from what I've often complained of; the general humorless, not to say grim, aspect of most sword and sorcery stories. As I think this will show, the sword and sorcery story is an admirable vehicle for a very funny story; characters in such stories are always being accused of not having their feet firmly on the ground.

Eric is 21 years old, and without any cats, dogs, or other pets. He has sold, in addition to this, only a couple of computer articles—nonfiction. Of course, computers themselves are fantasy—or at least science fiction.

Eric lives in Winthrop, Maine.

Jenda Highwood came from a long line of Highwoods, and that family had always been respectable, or nearly always. She herself was considered perhaps a bit too headstrong for her rank, but sensible enough. So it was definitely not dignified for her to be leaning against a door and puffing like she had just climbed a mountain.

The door was weather-stained and warped inward a

148

little, the wall around it was faded granite, and the tiny
castle the wall belonged to leaned decidedly to one side.
In fact, the castle was on top of a large hill, but the hill
was not particularly steep and Jenda considered herself
to be in reasonably good condition. But she panted and
sweated and when she looked down at her leather boots,
they were still, frustratingly, not touching the ground.

It was quite hard to climb even a little hill when one's
feet did not reach the ground. For one thing, it was slippery. Her boots were always at least an inch off the
earth, following the contours of rocks and pebbles but
never touching them. Climbing a sheet of ice would have
been easier, almost.

She was still panting when the door was yanked away
from her. After regaining her balance, she found herself
staring into two sad, doe-brown eyes that looked woe-
fully out of place in the aged face they gazed out from.

"Who are you?" demanded Yil, the sole inhabitant of
the castle and the sorcerer to whom she had come for
help.

"Highwood," she said, somewhat breathlessly, and
waited. The name impressed many people, but it seemed
Yil was not one of them. "Jenda Highwood," she
amended.

The old man studied her for a moment, and she knew
what he saw. A rather young woman, brown-haired,
wearing clothing that was perhaps a bit more plain than
one of her station ought to be wearing, and a short silver
blade (which she knew how to use). "Jenda Highwood—
Yes, well, come in, then," he mumbled, and turned his
back on her.

Jenda followed him into a large room that was fully as
decrepit as she imagined it would be, and more. Not only
were there shelves tumbling from the walls and upturned
tables scattered across the floor and bottles and flasks
strewn everywhere, but the shelves were half-rotted and
the tables were, too, and most of the bottles and flasks
were broken. Yil merely strode over it all, crushing more
jars into shards and pushing a table or two out of his
way. Shrugging, she followed him, and of course her feet
touched nothing.

He stopped in the middle of the room quite suddenly

and pulled a silver sphere out of the rubble. There was a rusted chain attached to the orb (which was itself actually quite shiny) and he slipped it over his neck. "Now, then," he said, and coughed, fingering the sphere possessively. "Which is it? Spells? Curses? Neither or both?"

"I'm not sure," she said. She also wondered why none of those who had visited Yil before had mentioned anything concerning the state of his abode, but she thought it best to say little about it. Instead she pointed at her boots. "But I want something done about that."

Yil looked down and blinked several times. "About that—your boots?"

"My feet. You'll notice they aren't touching the floor. I mean assuming there is a floor under all this anyway."

The old man brightened. "They aren't touching the floor . . . but that's wonderful! Have you tried walking on water? Very useful, I imagine—"

"No, I haven't tried walking on water, and in fact I would rather be walking on the ground instead of on the air. If it's not too much to ask. Say fifty in silver?"

Yil sighed and sat down on something that looked like a bench. "Fifty in silver."

"*After* you get rid of—of whatever's doing it."

"After I get rid of—anyhow, who did that? And why? Impressive bit of magic in a way," he muttered.

Jenda thought it was a good thing she had a fair amount of patience. "I haven't any idea who did it, or what did it, and if I knew why I wouldn't tell you anyway since it isn't any of your business. All I know is that I got up this morning and there I was, an inch off the floor. How about if you just get rid of it?"

He sighed again. "I'll just get rid of it." He closed his eyes and bent over his silver sphere which, disappointingly, did not glow or shimmer or do anything impressive like that. She would have shifted from foot to foot after a few minutes during which nothing happened, if she hadn't thought she would slip and fall. But then he opened his eyes again and said, "It's not an enchantment. Is it a curse or an evil spell?"

"Is there a difference?"

Yil muttered something about cross-mental influences in the ether, which she ignored, and he bent over his orb again. "It's neither a curse nor an evil spell," he pronounced, then looked something at a loss.

"Well?"

"Well. I suppose it could be an incantation."

"So?"

"So—I'm afraid there's no such thing as an incantation. That's just a myth."

Jenda came to the end of her patience before she thought she would and snarled at him.

"Now, now," he said. "Are you sure it's not your boots?"

"No," she said after taking a deep breath, "it's not. I tried bare feet, but that was almost worse. I still wasn't touching the ground and I couldn't take two steps without slipping."

"A problem," he mused.

"I would say so," she agreed. "Now what?"

The old man fingered his silver sphere again and looked at the floor. Reluctantly, he said, "We might visit Harren."

She stared at him. "Harren? The priestess? Harren? *Harren?*"

"All right!" Yil shouted hoarsely, then looked embarrassed that he had raised his voice. "But what else do you want to do?"

They set off toward Hillspring, a small village on the other side of the hill. The noon sun struck golden glints off a lake spread out to their left, and tall green pines grew in a forest in the distance. The hill itself was bare except for patches of grass and weed.

They were not yet halfway down the hill when Jenda's feet finally slid out from under her. It was then she discovered it might be nothing but air she had been walking on, but it was very solid air indeed, and even more slippery than she thought. She landed with a slap, and before she had time to think Yil disappeared behind her and rocks and weeds were sliding under her at a savage rate.

By the time she glided to a stop over a flat grassy field, the wind had chilled her, her hair was lashed about her face, and she was quite thoroughly dazed. The stones and other obtrusions had not hampered her slide, but they had certainly made themselves felt if only indirectly. She was sure she would have been very angry, or very annoyed, or perhaps both, if only she could assemble her thoughts from the many pieces they were in. So Jenda stayed where she was, lying on her back, and watched the breeze slowly shred the passing clouds above her. Then she realized her sword had gotten left behind somehow, but still she made no move.

Eventually she heard footsteps in the grass behind her. It was Yil, she knew, and when she turned her head to look at him, she saw him carrying her blade rather gingerly. There was a strange expression on his face—she could have sworn he looked as if he was trying not to laugh, and trying to remember how to laugh, both at the same time.

She groaned when she reached out and took her sword back.

"Are you injured?" the sorcerer asked, but then he covered his mouth with both hands and coughed. At least she thought it was a cough.

Jenda managed to climb to her feet, slowly and carefully and as dignified as possible, only slipping a little. "No, but I hurt all over. And I'm not climbing any more hills until someone does something about—about this." She waved a hand at the ground, or rather at the space between the ground and her feet.

"Until someone does something about this, yes, hmmm. So Hillspring is this way," he muttered as if to reassure himself, and tramped off toward the lake.

The town was quiet under the afternoon sun, or at least quieter than usual. There were few people in the streets and most of the windows in the small whitewashed houses were shut. Jenda soon discovered why; most of the villagers had gathered in the common ground.

There was a great square block of granite standing in the middle. Two long upright rods were set into the granite, one gold and the other silver, and they were crossed, symbol of the Contesting Gods. Inevitably, Harren stood before them, looking years younger than she actually was, clad in a robe half of saffron-colored cloth and half of white. Also inevitably, she was shouting.

"Ridiculous nonsense as usual," Yil mumbled. Jenda silently agreed but thought he was not one to say such things.

Not really listening, they waited for some minutes before Harren finished her speech, so either it was a shorter speech than usual or they had come in quite late. Some of the crowd dispersed then, wandering off to the work they had left, but many stayed to talk and gossip for a little while. Jenda pushed past a few small groups until she stood at the base of the slab where Harren still stood conferring with one of her acolytes.

"Greetings," Jenda said, using her most civil tone. "Perhaps you might help me with a problem I have."

The priestess said, "One moment," to her acolyte, and stared coldly down at Jenda. "Only the Contesting Gods can help you."

"Then perhaps you could persuade one of them," she said, and took the jingling bag of silver from her belt and hefted it. "With the help of this."

Harren continued to stare at her for a long moment, but she met the priestess' gaze with a slight smile and said nothing more. "We shall see," Harren said finally, and then she seemed to notice the old sorcerer for the first time. "Yil," she stated flatly, and thereafter ignored him. He was pointedly looking elsewhere.

"You see my feet aren't touching the ground," Jenda said pleasantly as if there was nothing at all amiss. "And I'd rather they did."

At least the priestess wasted no time; she looked a little suspicious but bowed her head and slowly knelt before the crossed gold and silver bars. She also did not bother with invocations, at least not out loud. Jenda was rather relieved.

Soon enough Harren lifted her head and stared piercingly out across the common ground. Yil glanced in that direction briefly and muttered and scuffed his feet in the dirt. "There is something," said the priestess of the Contesting Gods. "Something. A disturbance, a confusion, in the life flow. I know not what exactly." Her voice grew louder as she spoke and Jenda looked around hastily, embarrassed, and found several villagers now staring at them.

"If you don't know exactly, then I suppose you can't help me either," she said quietly and steadily.

Harren seemed not to take the hint, and proclaimed, "Perhaps it might be demons." Her gaze suddenly focused on Jenda. "Yes, it might indeed be the work of the hell spawn!"

"Demons?" asked someone in the now-silent crowd.

"A demon!" a child's voice shouted gleefully from the edge of the common ground, followed by her mother's loud shushing.

Now the crowd began muttering all at once, looking at Jenda covertly and sometimes openly, and she put her hand on her sword because she knew what mobs could do. Then she reflected that perhaps doing so was not the best of all possible actions. The muttering of the crowd turned angry or fearful, the word "demon" rising clear and often above the noise, and she wondered what Harren had been telling them that afternoon. Then she drew her short silver blade and cried, "Stay back! You heard wrong—I'm no demon!"

Though she swung her sword in an arc and back swiftly and competently, the crowd pressed forward, pushed no doubt from behind by those who were eager for something new and dangerous. Rather than hurt anyone, she sheathed the blade and desperately shoved herself away from the granite slab. Thus she half-ran and half-slid through the crowd, knocking people aside and leaving Yil behind.

The ground from the village to the nearby lake sloped gently downward and soon Jenda was concentrating on nothing but keeping her balance. There were still shouts from behind her, but they grew no nearer and she could spare no attention for them anyway. The blue-gold lake lake slid swiftly closer and she stared wide-eyed at it and knew there was nothing she could do to stop herself.

And then she glided out over the calm surface of the lake. She heard the frustrated clamoring of the crowd behind her and noisy splashes as a few villagers—children, no doubt—tried to follow her. Eventually, some distance from the shore, she came to a stop, and fell over.

The situation, she decided, was absolutely intolerable.

If hovering an inch above the ground was bad, then doing so above water was much worse. At least she could walk over ground. As for water—it would have been better, much better, to try crossing a sheet of the smoothest and slickest ice.

Jenda tried to stand, but fell. She tried to crawl, but her hands and knees slipped above the surface of the water and she made no progress. She drew her sword and hacked at the lake savagely, but the blade only sliced a thin line through the water and left nothing more than ripples. She tried to scream her frustration at the unfairness of it all, but nothing came out.

Looking up at last, gasping, she saw the villagers. They were still strung along the shore, but their shouts of "demon!" had changed into something else. For now they were sitting on the grassy banks and laughing.

Her cheeks flushed, she glowered, but in the end all she said was, "Gods blast it to hell and back several times over! And then some!" Which evidently carried easily over the lake, and made them laugh all the harder.

The villagers were now plainly enjoying themselves. They sat there (some had gone and brought their afternoon meal) and watched her try to escape her predicament. She did her best to ignore them, and so she wriggled and crawled, struggled and slipped, but none of her efforts brought the shore any nearer. Eventually she gave up and lay on her back, staring at the slowly fading sky, and tried not to think about anything.

There came a soft splash from near the bank. Jenda looked up and saw a girl tying one end of a rope to a pine that stood nearby; the other end was attached to a large stick floating in the water. The girl finished and turned to wave at her and went back to sit with her family. A long while later, the stick finally floated within reach, and to her relief she found she could take hold of it.

A cheer came from the shore; many of the villagers had left, finally bored, but still a good number remained. Several men began pulling the rope in and she slid swiftly back across the lake, now tinged with amber from the lowering sun.

And then she had reached the grass and the men were grinning at her. "To the tavern!" one said. "And tell us your story!" She managed to stand, and the small crowd set off toward the village alehouse.

It was a rather small, dim place, with few windows, and evidently held more people now than it usually did. They were noisy and boisterous (it seemed some had already been there for some time), and had neatly forgotten about calling Jenda a "demon." Now they called on her to provide the drinks—one thing they had not forgotten was her small bag of silver. She relented; it seemed the silver would not be of much other use that day. Against her better judgment she drank a mug or three of watery wine herself, and told her story, of how she had come to stand an inch above the ground for no reason, and how Yil and Harren had done nothing to help her. But then she told of her flight over the lake, and the villagers now laughed and shouted, especially when she described her attempts to rescue herself.

Eventually her silver ran out along with the sun, and when she finally noticed her surroundings again the tavern seemed like a badly-lit cave. Jenda said good-bye to the villagers, but they had long since been caught up in their own stories and hardly seemed to notice. She walked out into the clear evening air feeling a bit relieved. It was only as she walked across the shadowed common-ground and neared the large white granite block, staggering only a little, that she noticed.

Yil and Harren were sitting on top, next to the gold and silver rods that gleamed in the last light of the sun, and they were having an almost civil argument about something, but that was not what stopped her. It was her feet.

"They're touching the ground again," she murmured, astonished. "They really are. . . ."

"They really are?" Yil said, glancing down at her, and then he seemed to recognize her. He grinned grotesquely. "They really are. Of course, you see—I knew it. My spells only took a little while to work, that's all. Now you can pay me—"

"I think not," Harren interrupted as she stood. "It was the work of my prayers, and the will of the Contesting

Gods. I'll accept your donation now, if you would be so kind."

Yil muttered, "It was my work, I think."

"Not so, sorcerer. Your spells never work. Only the Contesting Gods—"

"But it was *my* work—"

Jenda stared up at them both, and suddenly she laughed for the first time that day. The sound of it carried in the evening dimness, but the two, the sorcerer and the priestess, seemed not to notice. "Only the Gods!" Harren exclaimed, followed by Yil's, "My work!"

She merely laughed again and left them behind, and set out over the hill again to her own town, and this time her feet quite firmly touched the ground.

If there was any good to be had out of the whole thing, it was only that Jenda Highwood rarely had to pay for wine in the Hillspring tavern again. For the villagers there still liked hearing the story, especially the last bit, as they said, and they were kind enough to pay her back for buying the rounds the first time. She never did find out what exactly had happened, or why, but after a while it did not seem to matter very much. And the last she heard, Yil and Harren were still arguing about it.

ON A NIGHT LIKE ANY OTHER
by Mark Tompkins

Mark Tompkins is twenty years old and no stranger to writing. Like everybody who comes to it early, he is not an absolute beginner; he has been writing since he "could hold a pencil." His stepfather Joe Schaumburger is an old friend from DAW. Too many of Mark's stories verge on horror for me to print many of them; since I am firmly dedicated to the proposition that horror and fantasy do not really overlap that much, but here is a story of shapechangers that very deftly overlaps categories and avoids all the old clichés about were-anythings.

Which inevitably reminds me of a classic Tony Boucher story; Tony being the (lamentably) late editor of *The Magazine of Fantasy and Science Fiction*. Tony—actually William Anthony White—had a weakness for stories which were just a setup for a one-liner joke. This one dealt with a very strange man in the moonlight; and, after going through all the old shapechanger clichés, "the stranger shuddered and changed into a weremouse." Groan. At least Mark's story is not a gross anticlimax like that.

Mark goes to Manhattanville College in Purchase, New York.

"A lone?"

Varoola, sitting at the bar, turned to see who had spoken. Beside her sat a tall, reasonably handsome young man dressed in motley, a wide sword at his hip.

"Yes," said Varoola, not bothering to conceal her disinterest. A very attractive young woman, she was tired of contending with libidinous young men who were constantly trying to pick her up—and constantly being rejected.

The man handed her a tall glass of bright yellow fluid.

"For you," he said.

At least, Varoola thought, this precludes the "may-I-buy-you-a-drink" bit.

"Thank you," Varoola said reflexively, and took a few sweet swigs.

"My name is Roderius," said the man. "You are. . . ?"

"Varoola," she said, and deliberately let out a heavy sigh.

"I assure you," said the man, "I'm not trying to pick you up or anything like that."

Varoola cracked a slight smile. "That's a good one."

"No, seriously. I'm concerned for you, that's all. You've heard about the attacks?"

"No. What attacks?"

"A little while ago, a dangerous creature, probably from the jungle on Green Hill, wandered into Cheethra. So far, it has killed and eaten twelve people in this general area."

"What kind of creature?" Varoola said.

"Nobody is sure. Everybody who has supposedly seen it describes it differently. Some say it is a two-headed panther, some say it is a gorilla with golden fur, some say it is an enormous spider, some say it is a walking snake-monster—people have given all kinds of crazy descriptions. The most popular beliefs are that it is a two-headed panther, or a gorilla with golden fur. Anyway, regardless of what it looks like, I don't think you should be outside by yourself. Are you going home when you leave here?"

"I might."

"Then I would ask that you allow me to walk you home. It would be much safer for you."

"I can take care of myself, thank you."

"Really? Against a creature that's killed and eaten twelve people? Do you have a weapon?"

"No," she had to admit.

"Well, I do," Roderius said, gesturing to the sword at his hip. "Let me come with you. It really would be foolish to do otherwise. It's not safe for anyone to be outside alone until the creature is caught."

Varoola considered. He sounded genuine, as if all he wanted was to walk her home because it was the safest thing to do. It wouldn't hurt, she figured. Besides, he seemed nice.

"All right," Varoola said. "When I leave, you can walk me home."

The two sat and drank for a bit, lightly chatting. When they were through, they left the tavern and headed out into the warm night.

"This way," Varoola said, and the two headed down the dirt road.

It was very late, and the village was quiet. As they walked and continued to chat, Varoola examined her companion's body surreptitiously.

Roderius was a big man, with a lot of meat on his bones. Probably he was very tasty. Her mouth watered with the thought of a good meal. Discreetly glancing up and down the dirt road, she saw no one and decided that now was the time.

In a sudden motion, she lashed out with her hand, drew Rodrius' sword, and hurled it a great distance down the road.

"Hey, what. . . ?" Roderius began, but he ceased to speak when she made the change come over her.

As usual, it only took a few seconds, and where a woman had stood before there was now a snarling, two-headed panther, its fangs like ivory daggers and gleaming with saliva. The panther tensed its muscles, ready to spring for the kill.

Suddenly, where a terrified man had stood, there was now an ape with golden fur, roaring fiercely to expose teeth like the panther's, and beating its chest with enormous fists. The panther froze, baffled and afraid.

For an intense moment the two creatures stared at each other. They communicated with their eyes—the panther's, green; the ape's, yellow—reading and sending messages only beasts can comprehend. Finally they reached an understanding, and gradually they relaxed. If they had had human visages, they would have smiled.

As a dark cloud drifted across one of the two full moons, the panther and the ape set out to hunt, side by side.

A WOMAN'S WEAPON
by Mercedes Lackey

Mercedes Lackey and her characters Tarma and Kethry are certainly no strangers to the readers of these anthologies; they have even attracted their own fandom, a rather dubious blessing (I know, since I was one of the first writers to attract a specialized fandom).

"Misty," however, is also known in "filk" fandom; someone wrote me about seeing a filk song about one of Tarma's spirit guides; which strikes me as about as desirable as those kooky "friends" of mine who approach me and ask in soulful tones, "How much of your work is *channeled?*" I can hardly be polite to such people; but maybe Misty's more tolerant than I am.

She has written a number of stories, several novels—how time does pass; after however many novels she can hardly be called a "young writer" any more. She has recently married and keeps a kestrel—or rather kept it—until it could be released in the wild, after its broken wing healed. She has also recently written a novel about Kethry's granddaughter. (I haven't read it yet, so my impression is only a vague one.)

Anyhow, she's come a long way from a kid filksinging at conventions.

The weather was usually more of a plague to a traveling freelance mercenary than something to be enjoyed, but today was different. Such a bright fall day, warm and sunny, should have been perfect. As Tarma and her partners rode over golden-grassed hill after undulating hill, even the warsteeds frisked a little, kicking up puffs of dust from the road with each hoofbeat, and they were at the end of the day's journey. But Tarma shena Tale'sedrin suddenly wrinkled her nose as a breeze so laden with a foul odor it could have been used as a weapon assaulted her senses.

"Feh!" she exclaimed, jerking her head back so violently that one of her braids flopped over her shoulder. "What in hell is—"

Her answer came as she and her partners, the sorceress Kethry and the great *kyree* Warrl, came over the crest of the next hill. The unsightly blotch on the grassy vale below them could only have been put there by the hand of man.

Huge, open vats, and the stack of raw hides piled like wood beside the entrance identified the source of the harsh chemical reek. The amber-haired sorceress curled her lip in a scowl at the sight of the tannery at the bottom of the hill, though her distaste might as well have been for the cluster of hovels around it.

"That's 'progress,' " the sorceress said, flatly. "Or so the owner would tell you. Justin warned me about this."

Tarma narrowed her eyes in self-defense as another puff of eye-watering potency blew across her path. "Progress?" she said incredulously, while their dappled-gray warsteeds snorted objection at being forced so close to the source of the stench. "What's progressive about this? Tanneries don't have to stink like that. And that village—"

"I don't know much," Kethry warned her partner. "Just that the owner of this place has some new way of tanning. It takes less time, supposedly."

"And definitely makes five times the stink." Tarma would have lifted her lip, but she didn't want to open her mouth anymore than she had to.

:And five times the filth,: Warrl commented acidly. *:The place is sick with it. The earth is poisoned.:*

Well, that certainly accounted for the unease the place was giving her. All Shin'a'in had a touch of earth-sense; it helped them avoid the few dangerous places left on the Plains, the places where dangerous things of magic were buried that were best left undisturbed.

"If this is change, progress, I don't like it," Tarma said. "I know you sometimes think the Shin'a'in are a little backward, because we don't like change, but this is one reason why we prefer to stay the way we are."

The sorceress shifted in her saddle and shrugged. "Well, that isn't the only thing the man's changed," Kethry continued. "And until just now, I didn't know if it was a good change, or a bad one."

Her partner's troubled tone made Tarma glance at the sorceress sharply. "What change was that?"

"There's no Tanner's Guild members down there except the owner," Kethry replied. "And I thought that might be a good thing, when I first heard of it. Sometimes I think the Guilds have too much power. You can't get into an apprenticeship if you haven't any money to buy your way into the Guild, unless you can find a Master willing to waive the fee. I thought that something like this might open the trades, give employment to people who desperately need it. But that—" she waved at the cluster of shacks around the tannery building. "—that mess—"

"That doesn't look as if he's doing much for the poor," Tarma finished for her. "But there isn't much that we can do about it. We're just a couple of free-lance mercs on the way to interview for a Company." At Kethry's continued silence, she added sharply, "We are, aren't we?"

Kethry smiled a little from behind a wisp of wind-blown, amber hair. "Need isn't complaining, if that's what you're worried about. By which, I assume, Master Karden isn't interested in providing females with employment."

"Possibly." Tarma shrugged leather-clad shoulders. "Whatever the reason, at least we aren't going to have to fight your sword and its stupid compulsion to rescue women whether or not they deserve rescue—or even want rescue."

Kethry didn't even answer; she simply touched her heels to Hellsbane's sides and gave the mare her head. The warsteed, sister to Tarma's Ironheart, threw up her head and moved readily into a canter, all too pleased to be getting out of there. Ironheart was after her a fraction of a heartbeat later.

The stench proved to be confined to the valley. Once they were on the opposite side of the next hill, the air was fresh and clean again. Tarma could not imagine what it must be like to live in that squalid little town.

:Presumably, their noses are numb.: Warrl supplied, running easily alongside the road, his lupine head even with Tarma's calf. His head and shaggy coat were the only wolflike things about him; if Tarma squinted, she would have sworn there was a giant grass-cat running at her stirrup, not a wolf. In reality, Warrl was neither; he was a *kyree,* a Pelagir Hills creature, and bonded with Tarma as Kethry's spell-sword Need was bonded to the sorceress.

Once out of the reach of the stench, the horses slowed of their own accord. Warrl looked pleased with the change of pace. He looked even happier with the village built of the yellowish stone of these hills that appeared below them, as they topped yet another rise.

This would be their last stop before Hawk's Nest, the home of the mercenary company called "Ydra's Sunhawk's." Tarma had no doubts that between the letters of introduction they carried, letters from two of Ydra's former men, and their own abilities, Ydra would sign them on despite their lack of training with a Company. After all, it wasn't every day that a Captain could acquire both a Shin'a'in Swordsworn and a Journeyman White Winds sorceress for her ranks. When you added the formidable Warrl to the bargain, Tarma reckoned that Ydra would be a fool to turn them down.

And no one had ever called Captain Ydra a fool.

But that was ahead of them. For tonight, there would be a good meal and a bit of a rest. Not a bed; that single-storied country inn down there wasn't big enough for that. But there would be space on the floor once the last of the regulars cleared out for the night, and that was enough for the three of them. It was more than they'd had many times in the past.

It was an odd place for a village, though, out here in the middle of nowhere, surrounded by grassy hills. "So, did Justin tell you why there's a town out here, back of beyond?" Tarma asked out of curiosity.

"Same thing as brought that slum here," Kethry replied. "Cattle. This is grazing country. There's a real Tanner's Guild House here, that's made leather for generations, and the locals produce smoked and dried beef for fighter-rations."

"And sometimes it's hard to tell one from the other," Tarma chuckled.

Kethry laughed, and the sound of her merriment made heads turn toward them as they rode into the village square. Her laughter called up answering smiles from the inhabitants, who surely were no strangers to passing mercenaries.

Even Warrl caused no great alarm, though much curiosity. The dozen villagers in the square seemed to take it for granted that the women had him under control. It was a refreshing change from other villages, where not only Warrl's appearance, but even Tarma and Kethry's, was cause for distress.

In fact, no sooner had they reined in their horses than one of the locals approached—with the caution a war-trained animal like the mares or Warrl warranted, but with no sign of fear. "The inn be closed, miladies," the young man said, diffidently, pulling off his soft cloth hat, and holding it to his leather-clad chest. "Beggin' yer pardon. Old man Murfee, he died 'bout two weeks agone, an' we be waitin' on the justice to figger out if the place goes to the son, or the barkeep." He grinned at Tarma's expression. "Sorry, milady, but they's been arguin' an' feudin' about it since the old man died. It ain't season yet, so 'twere easier on the rest of us t' do without our beer an' save our ears."

"Easier for you, maybe," Tarma muttered. "Well, I suppose we can press on—"

"Now, that's the other thing," he continued. "If ye be members of the Merc Guild, the Tanner's Guild Hall be open to ye. Any Guild member, really. Master left word. One Guild to another, Master Lenne says."

That brightened Tarma's mood considerably. "I take it you're 'prenticed there?" she asked, dismounting with a creak of leather and a jingle of harness.

"Aye," he replied, ducking his head. "Ye'll have to tend yer own horses. We don't see much of live 'uns at the Guild. Ye can put 'em in the shed with the donkey."

As the young man turned to lead the way across the dusty, sunlit square, Tarma glanced over at her partner. "Worth our Guild dues, I'd say. Glad now that I insisted on joining?"

Kethry nodded, slowly. "This is the way it's supposed to work," she said. "Cooperation between Guilds and Houses of the same Guild. Not starting trade-wars with each other; not cutting common folk out of trades."

"Hmm." Tarma held her peace while they stabled the warsteeds in the sturdy half-shed beside a placid donkey, and took their packs into the Guild Hall. Like the rest of the village, it was a fairly simple structure; one-storied, with a kitchen behind a large meeting hall, and living quarters on either side of the hall, in separate wings. Built, like the rest of the village, from the yellow rock that formed these hillsides, it was a warm, welcoming building.

"Ye can sleep here in the hall, by the fireplace," said the young man. "Ye can take a meal when the rest of the 'prentices and journeymen come in, if that suits ye."

"That'll be fine," Kethry replied vaguely, her eyes inwardly-focused, her thoughts elsewhere for a moment, the faint line of a headache-frown appearing between her eyebrows.

"Where's the tannery?" Tarma asked curiously. "I haven't caught a whiff of it—"

"And you won't, sword-lady," said a weary if pleasant voice from the shadows of one of the doorways. A tall, sparse-haired man whose bulky scarlet-wool robe could not conceal his weight problem moved into the room.

He's sick, Tarma thought, immediately. The careful way he moved, the look of discomfort about him, and a feeling of *wrongness* made her as uneasy as that foul tannery.

:I agree,: Warrl replied, startling her. *:He has been ill for some time, I would say.:*

"No, you will not smell our tannery, ladies," the man—who Tarma figured must be Master Lenne—repeated. "We keep the sheds well-ventilated, the vats sealed, and spills removed. I permit no poisoning of the land by our trade. I am happy to say that tallen-flowers bloom around our foundations—and if we find them withering or dying, we find out *why*."

Tarma smiled slightly at his vehemence. Master Lenne caught the smile, and correctly surmised the reason.

"You think me overly reactive?" he asked.

"I think you—feel strongly," she said diplomatically.

He raised his hands, palm-up. "Since the arrival of that fool, 'Master' Karden, and his plague-blotch, I find it all the more important to set the proper example." He tucked his hands back in the sleeves of his robe, as if they were cold. Tarma read the carefully suppressed anger in his voice, and wondered if the real reason was to hide the fact that his hands were trembling with that same anger. "I was not always a Tanner, ladies, I was once a herder. I love this land, and I will not poison it, nor will I poison the waters beneath it nor the air above. There has been enough of that already." He turned his penetrating brown eyes on Tarma. "Has there not, Swordlady Tarma? It *is* Tarma, is it not? And this is Kethry, and the valiant Warrl?"

Warrl's tail fanned the air, betraying his pleasure at being recognized, as he nodded graciously. Tarma spared him a glance of amusement. "It is," she replied. "Though I'm at a loss to know how you recognized us."

"Reputation, ladies. Songs and tales have reached even here. I know of no other partnering of Shin'a'in and sorceress." The Master chuckled at Tarma's ill-concealed wince. "Fear not, we have no women to rescue, nor monsters to slay. Only a meal by a quiet hearth, and a bed. If you would be seated, I would appreciate it, however. I'm afraid I am something less than well."

The four of them took seats by the fire; something about the Master's "illness" nagged at Tarma. What hair he had was glossy and healthy; at odds with the rest of his appearance. Short of breath, pallid and oily skin, weight that looked to have been put on since he first fell ill—his symptoms were annoyingly familiar—but of what?

It escaped her; she simply listened while Master Lenne and Kethry discussed the rivalry between the Guild and the interloper outside of the village.

"Oh, he couldn't get villagers to work there," the Master said, in answer to Kethry's question. "At least, not after the first couple of weeks. The man's methods are dangerous to his workers, as well as poisonous to the land. He doesn't do anything *new*, he simply takes short-cuts in the tanning processes that compromise quality and safety. That's all right, if all you want are cheaply tanned hides and don't care that they have bad spots or may crack in a few months—and you don't give a hang about sick workers."

"Well, he must be getting business," Kethry said cautiously.

Master Lenne sagged in his chair, and sighed. "He is," the man said unhappily. "There are more than enough people in this world who only want cheaper goods, and don't care how they're made, or what the hidden costs are. And—much as I hate to admit it, there are those in my own Guild who would agree with him and his methods. There were some who thought he should take over all the trade here. I only hold this Hall because I've been here so long and no one wants to disturb me." He smiled wanly. "I know too many secrets, you see. But if I were gone—well, the nearest Master is the same man who erected that disaster outside of town, and no doubt that those others would have their wish."

"So who *is* doing the work for him?" the sorceress persisted.

"Cityfolk, I presume," Master Lenne said, with an inflection that made the word a curse. "All men, a mixture of young ones and old men, and he works them all, from youngest to eldest. And work is all they seem to do. They never put their noses in town, and my people are stopped at the gate, so more I can't tell you."

At that moment, the young man who had brought them here poked his head into the hall. "Master, can we schedule in 'bout twenty horse-hides?"

"What, now?" Master Lenne exclaimed. "This close to the slaughtering-season? Whose?"

The young man ducked his head, uncomfortable with something about the request. "Well . . . my father's. Ye know all those handsome young horses he bought without looking at their teeth? 'Twas like you warned him, within a week, they went from fat and glossy to lank and bony. Within two, they was dead."

Master Lenne shook his head. "I told him not to trust that sharper. He obviously sold your father a lot of sick horses." He heaved himself to his feet. "I'd best get myself down to the tannery, and see what we can do. At least we can see that it isn't a total loss for him. By your leave, ladies?"

Glossy and fat . . . glossy and fat. . . . Tarma nodded absently and the Master hurried out, puffing a little. There was something about those words. . . .

Then she had it; the answer. A common horse-sharper's trick—but this time it had taken a potentially deadly turn. Horses weren't the only things dying here.

"Keth," she whispered, looking around to make sure there was no one lurking within earshot. "I think Master Lenne's being poisoned."

:Poisoned?: Warrl's ears perked up. *:Yes. That would explain what I scented on him. Something sick, but not an illness.:*

But to her surprise, Kethry looked skeptical. "He doesn't look at all well, but what makes you think that he's being poisoned?"

"Those horses reminded me—there's a common sharper's trick, to make old horses look really young, if you don't look too closely at their mouths. You feed them arsenic; not enough to kill them, just a little at a time, a little more each time you feed them. They become quiet and eat their heads off, their coats get oily, and they put on weight, makes them look really fat and glossy. When you get to the point when you're giving them enough to cover the blade of a knife, you sell them. They lose their appetites without the poison, drop weight immediately, and they die as the poison stored in their fat gets back into their blood. If you didn't know better, you'd think they simply caught something, sickened, and died of it."

Kethry shrugged. "That explains what happened to the horses, but what does that have to do—"

"Don't you see?" Tarma exclaimed. "That's exactly the same symptoms the Master has! He's put on weight, I'll bet he's hungry all the time, he obviously feels lethargic and vaguely ill—his skin and hair are oily—"

Kethry remained silent for a moment. "What are we supposed to do about it?" she asked slowly. "It's not our Guild. It's not our fight—"

Perversely, Tarma now found herself on the side of the argument Kethry—impelled by her bond with Need—usually took. Taking the part of the stranger. "How can you say it's not our fight?" she asked, trying to keep her voice down, and surprising herself with the ferocity of her reaction. "It's our world, isn't it? Do you want more people like Lenne in charge? Or more like that so-called 'Master' Karden out there?"

It was the poisoning of the land that had decided her; no Shin'a'in could see land ruined without reacting strongly. When Master Lenne died—as he would, probably within the year—this Karden fellow would be free to poison the entire area.

And if he succeeded in bringing high profits to the Guild, the practices he espoused would spread elsewhere.

It wasn't going to happen; not if Tarma could help it.

As she saw Kethry's indifference starting to waver, she continued. "You know who has to be behind it, too! All we have to do is find out *how* Lenne is being poisoned, and link it to him!"

Kethry laughed, mockingly. "All? You have a high opinion of our abilities!"

"Yes," Tarma said firmly. "I do. So you agree?"

Kethry thought for a moment, then sighed, and shook her head. "Gods help me, but yes. I do." Then she smiled. "After all, you've indulged me often enough."

Tarma returned the smile. "Thanks, *she'enedra*. It'll be worth it. You'll see."

By the time dinner was over, however, Tarma's certainty that the task would be an easy one was gone. For one thing, both questioning and close observation had shown no way in which poison could have been slipped to Master Lenne without also poisoning the rest of the Guild. They ate and drank in common, using common utensils, serving themselves from common dishes, like one big family. Tarma and Kethry ate with them, seated at the table in the middle of the hall, and they saw that the Master ate exactly what everyone else ate; his wine was poured from the same pitchers of rough red wine as the rest of them shared.

Each member took it in turn to cook for the rest, eliminating the possibility that the poisoning could be taking place in the kitchen. Not unless every Guild member here hated the Master—and there was no sign of that.

It *could* be done by magic, of course. But Kethry was adamant that there was no sign of any magic whatsoever being performed in or around the Guild House.

"In fact," she whispered, as the Guild members gathered beside the fire with their cups and the rest of the wine, to socialize before seeking their beds. "There's a spell of some kind on the Guild House that blocks magic; low-level magic, at least." The fire crackled, and the Guild members laughed at some joke, covering her words. "I've seen this before, in other Guild Houses. It's a basic precaution against stealing Guild secrets by magic. I could break it, but it would be very obvious to another mage, if that's what we're dealing with. That spell is why I've had a headache ever since we came in the door."

But Tarma hadn't been Kethry's partner all this time without learning a few things. "Maybe it blocks real magic, but what about Mind-magic? Isn't there a Mind-magic you can use to move things around?"

:There is, mind-mate,: Warrl confirmed before Kethry could answer, his tail sweeping the flagstones with approval. Kethry added her nod to Warrl's words.

"Ladies, gentlemen," Master Lenne said at just that moment, calling their attention to him. He stood up, wine-cup in hand, a lovely silver piece he had with him all through dinner. The glow of the firelight gave him a false flush of health, and he smiled as he stood, reinforcing the illusion. "I am an old man, and can't keep the late hours I used to, so I'll take my leave—and my usual nightcap."

One of the 'prentices filled his cup from the common pitcher of wine, and he moved off into the shadows, in the direction of the living quarters.

"Keep talking, and keep them from noticing we're gone," Tarma hissed to her partner, signaling Warrl to stay where he was. "I'm going to see if anything happens when he gets to his room."

Without waiting for an answer, she melted into the shadows, with Warrl taking her place right beside Kethry. There was no other light in the enormous room besides the fire in the fireplace, and Master Lenne was not paying a great deal of attention to anything that was not immediately in front of him. Still, she made herself as invisible as only a Shin'a'in could, following the Master into his quarters. *Can I assume that if someone used Mind-magic around here, you would know it?* she thought in Warrl's direction, as she slipped through the doorway on Lenne's heels.

:Possibly,: he answered. *:Possibly not. I think it will be up to your own powers of observation.:*

She waited at the end of the hallway, concealed in shadows, for the Master to take his doorway so that she could see which quarters were his. When he had, she waited a little while longer, then crept soundlessly on the flagstoned floor after him, opening the same door and slipping inside. She had thought about making some pretense at wanting to talk further with the Master, but had decided against the idea. If this poisoner was using Mind-magic to plant the poison, he might also be using it to tell whether or not the Master was alone.

Kethry knew more of Mind-magic than she did—but Tarma had a good idea what to watch. That business about a "usual nightcap"—if the poisoner knew about this habit of Master Lenne's, it made an excellent time and place to administer the daily doses.

Then, once he's got the Master up to a certain level, he stops. The Master loses his appetite, like the horses, stops eating, and drops all the weight he put on. And the poison that was in the fat he accumulated drops into his body all

*at once. He dies, but by the time he dies, there's no exter-
nal evidence of poisoning.*

And of course, everyone would have known that the
Master was ill, so this final, fatal "sickness" would come
as no surprise.

Once inside the door, she found herself in a darkened
room, with furniture making vague lumps in the thick
shadow, silhouetted against dim light coming from yet
another doorway at the other side of the room. She eased
up to the new door, feeling a little ashamed and voyeuris-
tic, and watched the Master puttering about, taking out
a dressing-gown, preparing for bed. The winecup sat on
a little table beside a single candle near the doorway,
untasted, and unwatched.

Master Lenne entered yet another room just off his
bedroom, and closed the door; sounds of water splashing
made it obvious what that room's function was.

Tarma did not take her eyes off the cup; and in a
moment, her patience was rewarded.

The surface of the wine jumped—as if something invisible had been dropped into the cup. A moment later, it
appeared as if it was being stirred by a ghostly finger.

Then Master Lenne opened the door to the bedroom,
and the spectral finger withdrew, leaving the wine out-
wardly unchanged. His eyes lighted on his winecup, but
before he could take the half-dozen steps to reach it,
Tarma interposed herself, catching it up.

Master Lenne started back, his eyes as wide as if she
had been a spirit herself. Before he could stammer anything, she smiled.

"Your pardon, Master," she said, quietly. "But I think
we need to talk."

The arsenic had not completely dissolved; there was a
gritty residue in the bottom of the cup that proved very
effective at killing a trapped mouse, eliminating Master
Lenne's doubts.

The three of them were ensconced in his parlor; he
was wrapped in a robe and dressing-gown, looking surprisingly vulnerable for such a big man. There was a fire
in his tiny fireplace, and candles on the table between
them, and the light revealed the shadows under his eyes

mercilessly. "But who could be doing this?" he asked, looking from Tarma to Kethry and back again. "And why? They say that poison is a woman's weapon, but I've angered no women that I know of—"

"Not a woman's weapon, Master," Kethry said, tapping her lips thoughtfully with a fingernail. "Poison is a *coward's* weapon. It is the weapon of choice for someone who is too craven to face an enemy openly, too craven even to come into striking-range of his enemy himself. It's the weapon of choice for someone who is unwilling to take personal risks, but is totally without scruples when it comes to risking others."

Tarma saw by the widening, then narrowing of Master Lenne's eyes that he had come to the same conclusion they had made.

"Karden," he said flatly.

Tarma nodded, compressing her lips into a thin, hard line.

Kethry sighed, and held up her hands. "That's the best bet. The problem is proving it. It's hard enough to prove an attempt at murder by real magic—but I don't think there's anyone in this entire kingdom with enough expertise at Mind-magic to prove he's been using it to try to poison you. By the way, where did you get that goblet?"

Lenne seemed confused by the change in subjects. "Every Master has one; they're given to us when we achieve Mastery."

Kethry nodded, and Tarma read satisfaction in her expression. "That at least solves the question of how he knew where the poison was going. If he has the match to that goblet, that gives him a 'target' to match with yours."

"But that also compounds the problem, Greeneyes," Tarma pointed out. "If every Master has one of these, *any* Master could be a suspect. No, we aren't going to be able to bring Karden to conventional justice, I'm afraid."

Master Lenne, sick or no, was sharper than she had expected. "Conventional justice?" he said. "I assume you have something else in mind?"

Tarma picked up the now-empty goblet, and turned it in her hands, smiling at the play of light on the curving silver surface. "Just let me borrow this for a day or so,"

she replied noncommittally. "And we'll see if the gods—
or something—can't be moved to retribution."

Kethry raised an eyebrow.

"This might not work," Kethry warned, for the hun-
dredth time.

"Your spell might not work. It might work, and Karden might notice. He might not notice, but he might not
drink the wine in his own goblet when he's through play-
ing with it." Tarma shrugged. "Then again, it might. You
tell me that Mind-magic is hard work, and I am willing
to bet that a sneaky bastard like this Karden gets positive
glee out of drinking a toast to his enemy's death and
refreshing himself at the same time when he's done every
night. If this doesn't work, I try something more direct.
But if it does—our problem eliminates itself."

They were outside the protected influence of the Guild
House, ensconced in the common room of the closed
inn. Just she and Kethry; Lenne was going through his
usual after-dinner routine, but this time, he was not using
his Master's goblet for his wine. That particular piece of
silver resided on the table in the middle of the common
room, full of wine. With a spell on the wine. . . .

Not the goblet. Kethry was taking no chances that
bespelling the goblet would change it enough that Karden's Mind-magic would no longer recognize it. The two
of them were on the far side of the room from the goblet;
far enough, Kethry hoped, that Karden would judge the
goblet safely out of sight of anyone. The inn's common
room was considerably bigger than Lenne's quarters.

That *was* assuming he could check for the presence or
absence of people. He *might* be getting his information
from a single source within the Guild House. But Kethry
was of the opinion that he wasn't; that he was waiting
for a moment when there were no signs of mental activity
within a certain range of the goblet, but that there was
wine in it. That, she thought, would have been the easiest
and simplest way for Karden to handle the problem.

All of it was guess and hope—

Kethry hissed a warning. Something was stirring the
surface of the wine in the goblet.

Something tried to drop into the wine. Tried. The wine

resisted it, forming a skin under it, so that the substance, white and granular, floated in a dimpled pocket on the surface.

"Ka'chen," Tarma said in satisfaction. "Got you, you bastard."

The pocket of white powder rotated in the wine, as the invisible finger stirred. Quickly, Kethry's hands moved in a complex pattern; sweat beaded her brow, as she muttered words under her breath. Tarma tried not to move, or otherwise distract her. This was a complicated spell, for Kethry was not only trying to do the reverse of what Karden was doing, she was trying to insinuate the poison back into *his* wine, grain by grain, so that he would not notice what she was doing.

Until, presumably, it was too late.

It was like watching a bit of snow melt; as the tiny white pile rotated, it slowly vanished, until the last speck winked out, leaving only the dark surface of the wine.

Tarma approached the cup cautiously. The spectral "finger" withdrew hastily, and she picked the goblet up.

"Well?" she said, "Can I bet my life on this?"

Kethry nodded, wearily, her heart-shaped face drawn with exhaustion. "It's as safe to drink as it was when I poured it," she replied, pulling her hair out of her eyes. "I can guarantee it went straight into the model-cup. What happened after that?" She shrugged eloquently. "We'll find out tomorrow."

Tarma lifted the cup in an ironic salute. "In that case— here's to tomorrow."

"Now don't forget what I told you," Kethry said firmly, from her superior position above the Master's head, where she perched in Hellsbane's saddle. "I may have pulled most of the poison from you with that spell, but you're still sick. You're suffering the damage it caused, and that isn't going to go away overnight."

Master Lenne nodded earnestly, shading his eyes against the morning sun, and handed Kethry a saddleroll of the finest butter-soft leather to fasten at her cantle. Leather like that—calfskin tanned to the suppleness and texture of fine velvet—was worth a small fortune. Tarma already had an identical roll behind her saddle.

"I plan to rest and keep my schedule to a minimum," Lenne said, as obedient as a child. "To tell you the truth, now that I no longer have to worry about Karden taking my trade and exerting his influence on the Guild as a whole—"

"So tragic, poisoning himself with his own processes," Tarma said dryly. "I guess that will prove to the Guild that the safe old ways are the best."

Master Lenne flushed, and looked down for a moment. When he looked back up, his eyes were troubled. "I suppose it would do no good to reveal the truth, would it?"

"No good, and a lot of harm," Kethry said firmly. "If you must, tell only those you trust. No one else." She looked off into the distance. "I don't like taking the law into my own hands—"

"When the law fails, people of conscience have to take over, Greeneyes," Tarma said firmly. "It's either that, or lie down and let yourself be walked on. Shin'a'in *weave* rugs; we don't imitate them."

"I don't like it either, ladies," Master Lenne said quietly. "Even knowing that my own life hung on this. But—"

"But there are no easy answers, Master," Tarma interrupted him. There are cowards, and the brave. Dishonest, and honest. I prefer to foster the latter, and remove the former. As my partner would tell you, Shin'a'in are great believers in expediency." She leveled a penetrating glance at her partner. "And if we're going to make Hawk's Nest before sundown, we need to leave now."

Master Lenne took the hint, and backed away from the horses. "Shin'a'in—" he said suddenly, as Tarma turned her horse's head. "I said that poison was a woman's weapon. You have shown me differently. A woman's weapon is that she thinks—and then she acts, without hesitation."

:Usually, she thinks,: Warrl said dryly. *:When I remind her to.:*

Put a gag on it, furface, Tarma thought back at him. And she saluted Master Lenne gravely, and sent her warsteed up the last road to Hawk's Rest, with Kethry and Warrl keeping pace beside her.

BEHIND THE WATERFALL
by Mary Frey

There isn't a lot to say about this story except that when I was reading it, I wanted to keep reading until I finished it. That's good enough for me. Mary Frey is a high-school teacher of French in rural Pennsylvania; and says that her pupils read my introductions to her stories—she has appeared in two S&S's and two Darkover anthologies—to find out things about her they didn't know before. When I was a kid, a teacher who sold to anthologies of paperback fiction, or of fantasy, would have been risking her job. Now kids are encouraged to read science fiction—though I meanly suspect it isn't because schools are convinced of its literary merit, but it's one of the few things they can get the kids to read at all! (As a drop-out of three teachers' colleges, I have no illusions about the education process.)

I *have come for the child.*

Mikel felt an itch between his shoulder blades and then a drop of sweat slid down his spine. The afternoon sun was warmer than he would have expected this far into the foothills. He shifted his weight in the saddle, wondered how it could be taking so long to do something as simple as locating a witchwoman, and pushed a lock of graying hair off the dampness of his brow.

It wasn't often that someone as important as the High Prince's lord chancellor and a detachment of swordsmen from the garrison came to a tiny village like Waterfall even though it lay on the main trading route to the infidel lands. The officer to whom Mikel had given his instructions was diligently questioning each of the local men from the innkeeper down to the smithie's half-witted assistant. His men, doubtless sweating as heavily in their pale dress uniform tunics as Mikel was beneath his ornate wine-red chancellor's cloak, looked thoroughly bored. Their eyes strayed more and more often to the doorway of the village's only inn.

Possibly some of them did not appreciate what a momentous event was about to occur: the lord chancellor was going to discover the whereabouts of a princess who'd been missing since she was but two days old. Once the villagers had divulged the location of the witch-woman, Mikel and his troops would ride there. The captain would have the old woman brought out of her hut, and Mikel would speak his part.

I have come for the child.

That was how he and the witchwoman had planned it.

It had been another inn, different only in the fact that it was half a realm away from Waterfall, and the lord chancellor and the witchwoman were but two of nearly a dozen travelers stranded by an unseasonably fierce storm. The hostel's wine cellars were well stocked, and as the evening wore on, the general conversation became less guarded.

Perhaps it was the caravan master who mentioned it first, once someone else had commented on the impending dispute between High Prince Donalt's nephews over who would succeed him on the throne. Mikel, traveling on a family matter rather than in his official capacity and so bearing none of the identifying regalia of his rank, had prudently contented himself with listening to what the others had to say.

"I've heard naught good of Prince Morvan, Carinthia's son," the caravan master shook his head. "But young Prince Roderic would have more to recommend his cause if he had a sister to bear his heir."

"He's got his cousin—" someone else began to say. "More than once in the past, a man with no sister to fulfill the ancient custom has turned to his nearest female cousin."

"Morvan's own sister," another pointed out. "If she's to bear the heir, why wouldn't she prefer to do it for her brother's claim rather than Roderic's? Kehlia and Morvan were raised in the same household."

Mikel nursed his wine carefully so that it would not loosen his tongue.

"It was a common story at the time Falada's son was born," commented the older woman sitting at the far end of the table. "They said that the High Princess had given birth to two babes, a boy and a girl. There were those who feared the old superstitions about twins, and so one of the infants was taken away secretly in the night and given to the Goddess' service."

Several opinions were expressed about how likely the story was to be true before Mikel set down his goblet and stood up to speak.

"This is nonsense," he declared, fixing his eye on the woman who had mentioned the old tale. She wore the telltale charms of the witchwomen woven into her hair. Mikel knew that in some places such women were considered the Goddess' servants. "If there were a daughter, if Falada had any daughter, twin or not, don't you think someone in the palace would have spoken of her openly before now? It's nothing but a rumor put about by some who think it would help Roderic's claim to the throne."

He did not add, *and since I am the leader of Faladin faction, I certainly ought to know.* But when he lay down that night in the soft featherbed which the innkeeper had, as promised, warmed for him with a curvaceous female form, he could not dismiss the idea of a girl-child who was supposed to have been Roderic's twin.

After half a night's sleepless tossing, he'd determined to question the witchwoman about what she really knew. He sat up, put match to candle, and discovered she'd anticipated him. The woman in his bed was not the buxom, auburn-haired waitress whose charms he thought he'd enjoyed in the dark.

Before daybreak, they'd conceived their plan.

* * *

As directed by the local shopkeepers, the lord chancellor and his escort followed the trail which led along the lake beyond the village. They would, the men said, find the witchwoman's hut in the shelter of the cliff, hard by the waterfall which gave the place its name.

Mikel pretended to listen gravely as the captain explained that this proximity to free-flowing water was the most natural location for anyone who claimed to work magic in the Goddess' name. He frowned, but did not comment, at the obviously low level of the lake and the mere trickle of water dropping over the top of the rocky facade ahead of them. Perhaps his erstwhile partner in this venture was not as powerful a witch as she had claimed a few weeks ago.

He'd told her to find a girl the right age whose coloring and face could be made to approximate young Roderic's. It was vital, he had said over and over, that no family members exist who could put the lie to who they were going to claim she was. The witchwoman had assured him the towns along the trading routes had orphans aplenty as a result of the infidels' raids. She had understood immediately that the lord chancellor sought a young woman clever enough to learn the role she must play, but not bright enough to think for herself.

Mikel was surprised when he saw the crude wooden building ahead of them in the shelter of the cliff. He would not have housed a donkey there, he told himself, and while he wanted a pliable "child," he did not want one who would have to be taught all the rudiments of civilized living as well.

Of course, if this one did not suit his purposes, word could be spread that the trail of clues he and the garrison had followed had proven to be false, and another missing princess could be unearthed. There was not an abundance of time for the chore, with High Prince Donalt so near death and Carinthia clamoring for her own son and daughter to be named his heirs. Mikel wanted to consolidate Roderic's position, and thereby his own, before it became necessary to instigate a messy civil war.

The captain dismounted and approached the hut. He appeared reluctant to rap on the door—it looked as if it would not withstand the assault. In a mere blink of an eye a stooped, shawl-draped figure appeared before the doorway. The officer recovered quickly enough to ask his questions.

"You're not the one who seeks me, though, are you dearie?" an aged voice cackled. She peered around the rough semicircle of horses and riders. "I think it be some-one who stands close to a crown, a dark-haired man who wears a heavy golden chain around his neck and rides a bay gelding with one white fetlock . . ." The swordsmen looked impressed by this display.

Mikel cursed under his breath. The woman was over-doing her part. Nevertheless, he said nothing when she approached him and ordered him to dismount, but al-lowed her to continue to mutter as the crone she was pretending to be would likely do. He followed her toward the hut.

The fragile door now stood ajar, although he did not remember anyone opening it. He could not see the inte-rior of the hovel for the darkness, but he did not shrink away when she fastened a hand on his elbow and pushed him forward with the words, "The way is through there, milord."

The door swung shut behind him with a thud properly belonging to a much more substantial plank of wood. From without, he heard metal hinges creak, and there was the unmistakable sound of a heavy bar being dropped. The air around him was damp, echoing his breath as if he were in a cave rather than a hut. Total darkness prevented him seeing even his own hand.

The lord chancellor cursed himself for a fool, but he refused to give his enemies the satisfaction of hearing him shout to be released from their trap.

So slowly he almost thought he imagined it, the black-ness gave way to luminescence. He began to distinguish details: the bare stone on which he stood, a moss-covered wall to his right, the black edge of a body of water two or three steps ahead, a roughly-carved stone staircase to the left side which led up into the darkness. As the light grew, he saw a shrouded figure standing a dozen or more steps up, both arms outstretched to hold a walking stick horizontally over its head. The gray-silvery light appeared to be flowing from one end of the stick.

"Who are you? What is this place? What do you want of me?" he asked.

"You must learn patience, man." The last word sounded as if she meant it as a synonym for *fool*.

"I have come for the child!" he announced as boldly as he could.

"It is a long climb," the woman said, moving her stick so that its light fell on the flight of stairs stretching up behind her into the black. "You will learn patience on the climb, man."

"Who are you? Where do these steps lead? Shall I call you priestess or witchwoman?"

She did not answer any of those questions. "Come," was all she said before she turned and started up the stairs.

Mikel had no choice but to follow. She was right; it was a very long climb.

Although he considered himself a fit man for one nearing forty, after a while he thought his legs could bear no more. A roaring noise grew steadily, drowning the methodic echoing of their footsteps on the stairs. "What is it?" he'd shouted. "You are behind the waterfall," she replied. He considered the possible meanings of her answer. The waterfall which he had seen was nothing more than a trickle and could not be the source of such fierce gushing. *You*, she had said, as if he were behind the waterfall while she was not, even though they climbed the same flight of steps.

Suddenly he recalled a story from his childhood in the desert. When the children complained of the need to shepherd the use of every drop of the precious liquid, his grandmother had told them of the Goddess' plateau where her handmaidens sent Her life-giving water over the borders of the sacred land, to tumble as waterfalls into mortal lands. If the Goddess was displeased with human conduct, the waterfalls would dry up and drought kill all living things.

There was a city, or so the story went, built in the midst of the water and overlooking the world from the lip of the plateau where the waterfall began. A city whose streets were waterways, so that everyone must travel by raft or swim to reach each others' homes. A city whose walls were covered with leafy vines which bore fruit and flowers all the year round. Strangest of all, a city whose inhabitants were all women, dedicated to the Goddess who sometimes lived among them. They valued wine more than water, his grandmother said, the latter being so common and the former so rare.

Certainly, Mikel counseled himself as his leg muscles began to quiver from the exertion of the climb, there could actually be no such place. It was nothing more than a tale for children. When he and the shrouded figure ahead of him emerged into the fresh air once more, they would be standing on one of the wooded hillsides above Waterfall.

There was such a place.

What a tale this was going to make for the balladeers! Mikel knew that he must remember the canals which passed for streets and the rose-gold hues of the marble from which the buildings were made, the scent of the flowering vines and the sweet babbling of the fountains, the view across the desert as expansive as if they rode a cloud above it and the subtle flavors of the blossoms which were called food and placed on his plate.

And he was the only man who had ever seen this. The witchwoman told him that in an effort to put him in her power, just as she attempted to confuse him by leading him through a maze of waterways and verdant courtyards to a set of elegantly furnished rooms she referred to as her home. He understood what she was doing; he would have done the same to disconcert her were he in the place of guide.

For the time being, though, the lord chancellor was content to let her play her game. He allowed her to treat him as an honored guest to be bathed and given a change of garments by her servants, to be shown the gardens, to be wined and dined, to be told the witchwoman's true name rather than the one she had told him at the inn. He lost nothing by being charming. After all, he was the only man in the city.

But when they returned to Waterfall, and then to the capital, Solange would find that *he* was the master of their scheme. Young Roderic had little inkling as yet of what was planned, but he would never accept some strange woman and a girl he'd never seen before unless Mikel told him that was what he was to do. Falada's son was only seventeen. Even if his mother's brother died tomorrow, it would be many, many years before he was prepared to rule on his own, and Mikel had made certain that the boy relied on *his* counsel in all things.

After they had dined, they lounged on a terrace enjoying their wine and a panorama of the sunset over the desert. He wanted to ask about the girl chosen to portray the missing princess, but he recalled his hostess' words about patience and held his tongue.

"Come," Solange said at last, rising gracefully from her seat. "It is time for you to make the decision." He must have looked puzzled, for she continued, "I was able to find three young women, all of whom fit the requirements you set in one way or another. Unfortunately, none meets them all. I will leave it to you to decide which of the three is most likely to succeed in fooling your opponents."

An unspoken rationale seemed to hang in the air: *And if you fail, you cannot say any other is to blame for it.* Mikel set down his wine goblet and followed the witchwoman, reminding himself that he would not have risen to his current position if he'd permitted the possibility of failure to keep him from acting.

She led him along a corridor which became a balcony, so that they had a view down into what he first took for a garden. Later, he would look up and see an arched vault so high overhead there were three rows of walkways above the one on which he and the witchwoman stood. Solange rested one hand on the railing and pointed to ground level.

A still fountain—it was the first Mikel had seen in this city which did not spew from a center ornament—was set in the middle of a grassy plot. The whole was ringed by greenery in a profuse variety of leaves, fronds, and blossoms. Pools of light came from an arc of lanterns almost identical to the sort used in the palace gardens, a touch of normality which he found oddly reassuring.

Two female figures sat side by side on the fountain's rim. A third woman knelt on the grass near them. From above, all Mikel could see was that they wore soft, multi-layered gowns much like the one Solange had appeared in for the evening meal and all had fair to light brown hair.

"What do you think?" the witchwoman asked quietly. "Do you have any initial impression which one she is?"

"What do you mean?"

She shrugged. "I merely thought. . . . Perhaps this is no more than another rumor. I had heard talk that there was a time when you and the High Princess were lovers, that you were as likely as anyone to have been the father of—"

"I did not sleep my way to the high chancellor's post!" he hissed.

"I did not mean to infer that you must have. Whether you would have been *able* to . . ." she smiled at him. "Well, we can hardly blame people for speculating about such things when you've been given full responsibilty for Roderic's education. Is it true that in her day Falada was the most beautiful woman in the capital?"

"I won't argue it. But at the time you refer to, I'm afraid I must admit to having been nothing more than one of many very young, very naive newcomers to the court. Besides, even if I could possibly be Roderic's father, what has that to do with those three?" He turned away from the garden. "Unless you mean that one of them really is. . . ?"

"Who is to say that one of them could not be Falada's daughter? You are not a foolish man, milord chancellor. If you knew there was proof that only a son had been born, you would never have started on the course we now pursue. You would not have come this far if you did not think you were going to find the weapon you need to defeat Carinthia and her children."

"An accurate assessment," he nodded.

They stepped away from the railing and started down a flight of stairs Mikel guessed would take them to the garden.

"And would it be accurate to surmise your motives for championing Roderic's cause have more to do with your own personal ambitions than with any shortcomings of Carinthia's son?" Solange asked.

"Morvan has faults enough whether I have ambitions or not," he replied quickly. "I have been chancellor long enough to appreciate the attractions *and* the disadvantages—"

"You find it difficult to contemplate giving up your control of matters of state?"

He did not answer. The remark was a bit too close to the quick.

It appeared that the witchwoman intended him to question each of the possible sisters for Roderic. One at a time they came to the corner of the garden where Solange had directed him to sit and answered the questions he asked. If what Solange had called the weapon to defeat the Morvan faction's aspirations was to be found in the garden, Mikel quickly concluded he would not find it in the first two.

Neither of them was so much wrong for the role of Roderic's twin, as neither of them was *right*. When he spoke with the first, he thought the fault might lie in her facial features. She did not remind him of anyone he had ever seen at court, much less the people she would be claiming as kin. Better, he said to himself as he bid her a courteous good evening, to find a girl whose face will lead them to conclude what we wish them to. When the second girl arrived to sit beside him on the wooden bench, he praised his wisdom in waiting, since she had a profile startlingly like Falada's. And then she opened her mouth. While it might be possible to rid her of her mountain accent and the impression she was speaking with a mouthful of porridge, Mikel doubted he had time for it.

After the second young woman left, Mikel waited quite a while for the third one to arrive. What if she was no better a choice for the task than the other two? He was reluctant to abandon the plan entirely so long as there was a reasonable chance of success. The witchwoman had been correct when she said he would never have pursued it this far if any at court could actually prove the story of a twin sister false. If Falada were still alive, for example, he would never have dared it without her consent.

A flutter of pastel clothing caught his attention from the corner of his eye. Mikel looked up and then scowled when he saw that the third girl was walking toward him somewhat unevenly with the help of a cane. Was Solange mad to think a cripple could play the part of Roderic's twin.

She stepped into a pool of light and Mikel felt his heart thump after a missed beat. The resemblance to Roderic was nothing short of remarkable. He thought of the portrait painter who'd tried to capture the young prince three years ago, only to have to abandon the finished canvas because the young man had grown up so quickly in a few weeks after posing for initial sketches. At the time, Mikel now recalled, he had even been amused at how much more like a girl than a young man the painting appeared. He was astonished to find himself looking at the girl who could have posed for it.

"Let me help you," he found himself saying as he rose from his seat and held out a hand to her.

"I do not need your help," she replied diffidently.

"Did you, uh, hurt your leg?" Mikel did not know why he felt ashamed of the question. Certainly it was his right to ask, particularly when her appearance was otherwise so perfectly suited to his plan.

"A fall from a horse a few years ago."

"Does it pain you much?" he asked, while his mind worked on the idea of how Roderic could have been similarly maimed by a black stallion the year he was twelve. Thank the Goddess the boy had not broken his leg when the beast threw him to the bare dirt.

"No." He knew she lied. A stubborn pride just like Roderic had, Mikel told himself. Odd that in this girl he found the trait admirable, while in the boy he'd raised, he'd seen it as defiance and sought to erase it.

He noticed now that she held her shoulders unevenly, as if the right one had once been injured and not healed quite properly. "Did you hurt your shoulder at the same time?"

She shook her head. "The roof was high and slippery after a rainfall. I was only six when that happened."

"Children do have a tendency to be adventurous, don't they?" Mikel remembered that Roderic had once tried to cross the palace roof. Was it when he was six or seven? That detail failed him.

"Especially when they think they've been unjustly confined to their rooms," she agreed.

Mikel caught his breath as the memory flooded back of how he had been forced to discipline Roderick once during the boy's first months in his household. As much guidance as Falada had cared to give her child, he might as well have had no parenting at all. The spoiled, petulant little boy had been locked in his room more than once, although he'd only tried to escape once. Where would the realm be today if Falada's son had been killed when he slipped and fell from the roof that time?

"Do you recall anything of your parents?" he asked the third girl, as he had asked the other two. There was some consolation in seeing proof that Roderic was not the only child who'd experienced childhood mishaps. There was relief that the boy had fared better than this girl had, since Mikel could never have supported a cripple as High Prince.

Once again she shook her head. Mikel's attention was drawn to the faint white line down the side of her face. A scar? What in the name of all holy would a *girl* be doing to have received such a thing? She was no prince who had to learn swordsmanship no matter how little natural inclination she had for it or how clumsy she was at it despite the best teachers a lord chancellor could provide.

"What sort of treatment have you had in this place?" he cut off her recollection of an orphan's upbringing. "Blessed bones, you haven't even told me your name, girl!"

"Jemma, milord. My name is Jemma. I am treated well here. I have no complaints."

"Damn it, girl, you're lying!" he exclaimed. "Look at me and tell me the truth!" He grabbed for her hand and felt the scar tissue as his fingers closed around hers. He knew where those sort of scars came from, since he still bore the same sort of marks where his grandmother had held his hand over a candleflame to make him tell the truth about some of his boyhood pranks. It was effective discipline for a stubborn boy—or had been for him. Roderic had proved impervious to such physical inducements. Mikel had been forced to find other, more clever ways to tame the unruliness of youth.

Jemma tried to pull away from him.

"I'm not going to hurt you," Mikel assured her. "Believe me, all I want to do is help you. Your scars, your injuries—are you telling me they are all from accidents in a place such as this?" He gestured with his free hand. "In a city dedicated to the Goddess, how could anyone dare to harm a girl-child?"

"Let go of her, milord," said a calm voice behind him. Mikel twisted to look back over his shoulder and saw Solange, the stick with which she had lighted the stairway behind the waterfall in her hands once more. "If you want to leave here whole, let go of the child."

"I am not hurting her," he objected. "Tell her, Jemma, I was only asking how you came by your scars and your limp. It is *you*, witchwoman, who should be held accountable for the things that were done to her."

"Do her scars and poorly healed injuries distress you, milord?" Solange asked. She stepped toward them and something in her face told him he had best let go of the girl. "How odd."

Mikel stood up and faced the witchwoman. "And just what do you mean by that? I'm not only distressed; I'm outraged. This is the Goddess' city and yet you torture children created in her very image. I cannot believe that one little girl could have been such a trouble to you to merit what you did to her." He knew then that whatever happened to the plan, he would take the child away from this place when he left.

"Children sometimes have mishaps," she replied. "Isn't that what you said to Roderic's mother when she asked questions?"

"They gave him to me to educate and train so he would be properly prepared to take his place on the High Throne one day. Yes, children do have mishaps. He did. That's the sort of child he was."

"And what sort is that, milord? The sort of child who had to have what you termed willfullness beat out of him with a horsewhip?"

"That's a preposterous—" Mikel sputtered. "Whoever told you that I whipped Roderic? I dare him or her to repeat it to my face."

Solange beckoned the girl to come to stand beside her. "If you insist, milord, I will have her bare her back so that we can all see the scars of the whippings you say never happened."

"*Her* back?" he gasped. "What has what you witch-woman or priestesses or whatever you call yourselves did to this poor child have to do with rumors my enemies have spread about what I did to discipline Roderic?"

Solange sighed and shook her head. "You still do not understand, do you, milord chancellor?" Mikel knew he must have looked confused. "Jemma *is* Roderic's twin. The story has always been the truth."

"All the more reason for me to take her away from this place before you can hurt her anymore." Mikel took a step toward the girl who shrank away as if his touch would burn her. "Jemma, you cannot want to stay here with this woman who has hurt you. I promise you that if you come with me, no one will ever hurt you again."

"No one here has hurt me, milord," the girl said. "It was you who did all of it."

"Nonsense! I never laid eyes on you before this evening."

"I told you she and Roderic are twins," Solange offered. "Think of the old superstitions about twins, the one that led those attending the birth it was necessary to take one child away and persuade Falada she had only borne only the one baby. Do not the old tales say that when one twin suffers hurt, the other will feel it; that when one twin is cut, the other will bleed? Show him, child."

Jemma turned her back to Mikel as the witchwoman's grasp fastened on the shoulder of her gown and tore at it.

"This is the most barbaric—" The chancellor stopped in mid-sentence when he saw the criss-crossed scars across the young woman's back. "This is madness. No one will ever believe you."

A vast, bottomless pit seemed to have opened in his stomach. Even as he tried to banish it, it began to consume his courage and his ability to think rationally.

"Here, my dear," Solage shrugged off one of her shawls for Jemma to wrap around herself. "They will believe me when we are in the capital. All we need to do is prick one of her fingers and see if Roderic bleeds."

"They'll call it a witches' trick," he cautioned her. After all he had done to preserve the realm while that weakling Donalt preferred to drink and gamble with his dissolute friends, it was not fair to come to this, an accusation that he had harmed a child.

"And when my brother testifies to your treatment of him?" Jemma glared at him angrily when she'd covered herself with the borrowed shawl.

"He would never do such a thing," Mikel declared. "If he were going to accuse me of mistreatment, he would have done so long ago. Who would believe him after ten years in my care without a complaint?"

"My brother is no longer a frightened child, as he was when he was first placed in your care. When Solange and I are with him—"

Mikel turned his attention to the witchwoman, unable to tolerate the reproach he saw in the girl's eyes. "You'll not get within twenty feet of him unless I am there to verify your wild tale. Mark me well, woman, I will not do it!"

"No," she agreed. "You will not."

"I do not need you. I will find some other girl to play the role of Roderic's sister," he decided suddenly. "I refuse to stay here and listen to your foul accusations any longer."

He strode out of the garden by the first doorway to catch his eye.

"How do you plan to leave the city, milord?" a voice called after him.

He did not bother to reply. It would not be impossible to find the central square and the ornately carved door which led from the stairs behind the waterfall. If he had no light, he could nevertheless manage to find his way to the base of the stairs by feel. The garrison captain and his men would be waiting on the other side of the hut's door to let him out when he shouted for them.

No one had told the chancellor that while there was but one entrance to the Goddess' city on the rim of the waterfall, there were hundreds of thousands of waterfalls all over the world.

Even today, the desert people say that when the rainy season comes, if you stand near a waterfall, you can hear the voice of a wicked man shouting to be let out from behind it. Is it true? I do not know. I know they call themselves Faladin, since their royal family can trace their ancestry from Falada's daughter.

HOARD
by *Steven Piziks*

One of my criteria for the final selection process for this volume—since every year I receive a good many more stories than I can use, and the requirements for the magazine are just different enough that I can't use the overflow in the magazine—is that when I look over the manuscripts I spontaneously remember the story. I remembered this one because it was one of the two dragon stories I selected—out of a couple of dozen—as being different enough to overcome my prejudices about stories dealing with dragons—of which I read far too many and can print far too few.

Steven Piziks says he is a substitute teacher—and the dragon in this story is based on the persona he adapts with his students. One of the many reasons I never taught in the public schools is that while I love to teach, I have neither talent nor desire to be a police officer. Steven has written nonfiction for the MOTHER EARTH NEWS—when he was fourteen!—and so, to the delight of his students, he is listed in the READERS GUIDE TO PERIODICAL LITERATURE. I don't know how they'll react to this story; modern kids are hard to impress—do they *know* just how hard it is to sell fiction these days?

Steven Piziks asked me to include a dedication "based on an idea by Laurel Schippers." But ideas don't stand alone; you can't even copyright an idea—it's the writing that really counts.

"Excuse me," said a female voice. "Where can we find the books on local history?"

The librarian didn't take her eyes from the scroll she was studying. "Third stack from the north wall, second shelf down," she answered automatically.

"Thank you." Two sets of footsteps tramped purposefully toward the north wall, allowing the librarian to get back to deciphering a recently acquired treatise written in a forgotten language.

The librarian felt rather pleased about that treatise. It was a unique item and deserved a place in her library. The library, made of comfortably solid stone, would hold it and keep it safe for eternity.

The library itself had only one large door on the first floor and still bore a close resemblance to the small keep it had once been. The one-time central hall and kitchen now housed the main stacks. The second floor living quarters had been changed into cubicles for copying text or had become locked rooms for housing the more valuable tomes.

It was the latter that made the library famous. Scholars traveled scores of leagues to consult important works found nowhere else, and a small university had sprung up nearby. The fact that the original keep had been built in the middle of nowhere did not seem to affect the library's renown. The library had no name. It didn't need one. The scholarly community referred to it simply as "the library" and there was no mistaking what they meant.

The librarian glanced up and scowled at the north wall. The couple were gathering most of the books from the second shelf of the third stack and they were handling their piles carelessly, heedless of their value. She dug long fingernails into her palms as she quickly rose from her desk and hurried toward them. Her heels clicked sinuously on the stone floor.

The couple, a young man and woman, finished looting the second shelf in short order and began hauling their booty in unwieldy piles to a nearby table. The librarian sucked in her breath and increased her stride.

They're going to drop one, she thought furiously, her steps almost a run. *They're going to damage the books.*

"What do they make these things out of?" grunted the man behind a stack of books nearly as tall as he was. "Copper plating?"

The woman frowned as she deposited her own load heavily on the table. The pile teetered precariously. The librarian opened her mouth to roar out a warning, but at the last moment, the woman reached out and casually righted the stack. The librarian's mouth snapped shut, but she didn't slow her pace one iota.

"Wouldn't surprise me," the woman said. She had completely nondescript features; brown hair and eyes, average height, and a complexion that bespoke many hours in harsh sunlight. Her movements revealed a stolid grace and she wore practical clothes which allowed easy freedom of movement.

Her companion possessed identical eyes and hair, but his skin wasn't as deeply tanned. He also dressed in practical clothes, but he moved more carefully, as if he had to remember how to make his body work. He also treated the books with more care, the librarian noted. His stack, though tall, was straight and well-balanced, and he was treating each volume like an individual treasure. The librarian decided the woman was probably a warrior and the man was probably a scholar, perhaps even a magician.

"Watch what you're doing, Kira," the man warned as he cautiously set his collection down. He selected the top volume, sat down, and delicately turned to the first page. "Books are more fragile than they look."

The librarian nodded curtly in agreement as she clicked quickly across the floor. Books were more valuable than gold, more fragile than pearls, and he obviously knew it. She decided she liked this man. A little.

"Is there anything in particular you're looking for?" she asked briskly as she reached the table. "Perhaps I could help."

Offering assistance was a risk, but if she stayed nearby, she could be sure the books wouldn't suffer any damage.

Kira looked up from the volume she was about to examine. "We're looking for information on dragons," she replied, leaning an elbow on her pile. "One dragon, anyway."

The librarian's nostrils flared. "Please don't lean on the books," she said tartly. "Your elbow could dent the cover."

Kira straightened, startled. The man looked up from his page and grinned. "Told you," he said.

"Uh, sorry," the woman apologized lamely.

The librarian nodded. "Which dragon did you want information on?" she asked, though she was already certain she knew the answer.

"The one that used to live in this keep," Kira answered.

A tight little smile creased the librarian's mouth. She had been right. She ground her teeth in frustration. "Ah," she said. "That dragon."

"My name's Kenyon, by the way," the man said from his chair. He gestured cheerfully at the woman. "This is my sister Kira."

"We're looking for the dragon hoard," Kira stated matter-of-factly. "Can you tell us anything about it? There must be a lot of stories about it in the library."

"Yes," answered the librarian, choosing to address the last remark, "yes, there are."

"Everything we've heard so far keeps pointing us to this library," Kenyon added. "That's why we're here."

"What can you tell us about it? The dragon and its hoard, I mean," Kira asked.

A half-dozen emotions boiled up inside the librarian's consciousness and at the center of them all was the reddish tinge of rage. Then she angrily shoved them aside. She wouldn't be able to think if she couldn't control herself and she had, after all, offered assistance.

She ought to be used to treasure-seekers by now; at least half a dozen wandered into the library every year. But a burning hostility was steadily growing behind her eyes.

"There isn't much to tell." The librarian forced herself to breathe easily. She would have to answer their questions and obvious reluctance or anger would only make them suspicious. "The keep was built about two centuries ago by a man named Innis Gorath. Or he had it built, anyway," she amended, falling into the rhythm of the story. "Gorath was reputed to have been a lazy man. He was also a criminal. The king banished him and his men to this area. According to the royal record, he should have been executed, but the king was merciful."

"That we knew," Kenyon put in. "We saw the records at the capital."

"After the keep was built," the librarian continued, ignoring the interruption, "Gorath began consolidating his power. He was planning eventually to launch a rebellion against the throne. That was when the dragon arrived. According to legend, the dragon simply took the entire keep by surprise. Most of the men escaped, but Gorath didn't. The dragon settled in and stayed for almost two hundred years."

The familiar litany of words dampened the librarian's anger a bit, though it still smoldered dangerously.

"Does the library have any books on dragons?" Kenyon interjected, ignoring his sister's earlier warning.

The librarian should not have been surprised—the question was inevitable—but she had still been hoping it wouldn't come up. It would make things more difficult. The anger flared again.

"Yes." The answer was almost a hiss.

"Could we see them, please?" Kenyon seemed unaffected by her tone. "I think they'd be very helpful."

The librarian almost refused, then sharply bit back the words. That, too, would look suspicious. Not as suspicious as two dead bodies, but suspicious nonetheless.

"Of course," she replied freezingly. "They're upstairs. I'll take you there."

"Excuse me," said a new voice at the librarian's elbow. She turned sharply. The voice belonged to a short, stout man in a brown scholar's robe and she recognized him as a regular visitor from the university. A respectable man. One who knew what books were about and how to treat them.

"Yes?" she said politely. "Can I help you?"

"I'm looking for Tregard Heatherton's work dealing with the effects of folk remedies on lung diseases in horses." He ran a plump hand over his near-hairless head. "Can you tell me where I might find it?"

"East wall, first stack, second shelf, fifth book from the right," the librarian replied promptly.

"Thank you." The man bowed briefly and scurried away.

The librarian turned back to the couple and found them both staring in undisguised astonishment.

"Amazing," Kenyon said, mouth hanging open in awe. "How did you know that?"

"I'm very familiar with that work," the librarian responded shortly even as she cursed herself. She should have pretended to think before she spoke.

Brother and sister exchanged glances at her tone and the librarian could read them like one of her scrolls. For someone who offered to help us, they said, she's being terribly uncivil.

"You were going to show us the books on dragons?" Kira finally prompted.

"This way." The librarian spun brusquely on one heel and clicked her way toward the staircase. She could feel Kenyon and Kira trading looks again in her wake, but she couldn't spare the energy to think about them. The rage was back, growing with every step that led them closer to the books and she was nearly shaking with the effort to contain it by the time they reached the staircase.

She led them up the stairs and down a corridor which was faced with several closed doors. The librarian continued onward, grimly refusing to glance back. Control, she told herself, control. She channeled her fury into her heels and they clicked nearly hard enough to break the stone floor.

At the corridor's end, she stopped and produced a set of keys. Without looking, she blindly inserted one of them into a disused lock and twisted savagely. Metal scraped and muttered, but the door finally swung open.

The room was small and dark. The dust raised by the librarian's entrance made Kira break into fits of sneezing and a smile of mean gladness slid briefly across the librarian's face before she turned around.

"Not many people ask to see these books," she said, pretending to apologize. "That's why all the dust." She reached into the darkness and came up with a metal lantern which she carefully lighted from one of the many candles that studded the corridor. While they were fine for the hallways, the librarian certainly couldn't allow candles among the books. The risk of fire and dripping wax was far too high.

The room was cramped and airless. A small table companioned by an equally small chair huddled in the corner. Bookcases dominated the walls and seemed to stare ominously at the intruders in the gloom. Kira and Kenyon entered timidly.

"The books you want are on that shelf there." The librarian gestured with the lantern, then set it carefully on the table. "These works are extremely rare, so I'm afraid I'll have to stay here while you look them over."

"I understand," Kenyon said, examining the indicated shelf. "Can you tell us which—"

A sudden pang went straight through the librarian's churning stomach and a red haze suffused her vision. "Excuse me," she interrupted. "I'll be right back." She turned and shouldered her way past a surprised Kira, then flew down the corridor, her heels clicking a furious staccato beat.

She reached the head of the stairs and didn't even pause. Near the door she could see a boy wearing a student's frock. He was carrying a book. She shot down the stairs and savagely caught him by the shoulder just before he would have exited. She sank her fingernails into his flesh and yanked him sharply away from the door. He yelped in surprise and not a little pain.

"I'm sorry, young man," she snarled. "Books are not allowed out of the library."

She snatched the book from his hands and shoved him roughly out of the building. She slammed the door behind him. With a grunt of satisfaction, the librarian straightened her clothes, tucked the rescued tome under her arm, and headed back upstairs.

As she drew closer to the little room, she could hear Kenyon and Kira talking. Abruptly the clicking of her heels ceased and she eased quietly closer, gently hugging the little book to her chest as if it were a small child.

" 'Dragons can speak the human tongue but cannot lie, except by omission,' " Kenyon was saying, apparently reading aloud. " 'When conversing with a dragon, listen carefully.' Who would ever want to talk to a dragon? Don't they eat first and ask questions later?"

The Berthwin text, the librarian thought sourly. They *would* find that one first. She could imagine them seated in the little room running their greasy, dirty hands over the books and she had to clamp her lips together hard to rein in a growl.

"And listen to this," the man continued. " 'A dragon is always aware of every bit of treasure in its hoard and it instantly knows if something is moved or stolen.' "

Kira snorted. "I think the hardest part is going to be separating the facts from the stories."

"Probably," Kenyon agreed. "But we've been doing a lot of that lately."

There was the heavy sound of a book closing and a moment of silence. The librarian ground her teeth and listened further, straining to hear something, anything that might give her more information, but the room remained quiet.

She was about to reenter when she heard Kenyon's voice again.

"Kira," he said abruptly. "Why don't we go home and forget about this?"

"What?" Kira asked, startled.

The librarian froze, listening hard enough to hear the lantern sputtering in the tiny room.

"I'm tired of traveling. I'm tired of hunting clues. I'm tired of the whole search, Kira," the man explained. "Why don't we just go back to Middestown and forget this?"

"Oh, just like that?" Kira replied caustically, snapping her fingers. "I suppose we can just leave our family holdings in the hands of strangers, too."

Kenyon did not reply.

"I want that hoard, little brother." Kira's voice was tinged with a tone that raised the librarian's hackles. "I want our lands back and that hoard will buy them for us."

"To what end?" Kenyon countered gently. "Mother sold them because she couldn't run them properly. She was happy to see them pass to a family that had the training and resources to do it."

"And she's buried in a public cemetery," Kira spat. "Not on the land. Our land."

"That didn't matter to her. She said so."

"And I could run the holding now."

"Could you?" Kenyon snapped. "I suppose you learned all about running a hold in the mercenaries guild." There was an awkward pause, then, "I'm sorry, Kira. I know this means a lot to you. I'm just tired, that's all."

The librarian heard a rustling of cloth and assumed that Kenyon was now resting his head in his hands. There was another long pause. Sensing that something important was about to happen, she waited quietly in the corridor.

"Tell you what, little brother," Kira said slowly after a while. "How about we keep looking for a month? If we don't find the hoard by then, we'll go back to Middestown. Porino's been after me to train recruits for ages now. I suppose I wouldn't be unhappy doing that."

"Deal!" Kenyon agreed. "One month to find the hoard."

In the hallway, the librarian glanced upward and said a quick prayer of gratitude. Now if she could just nudge them in the proper direction, she wouldn't have to explain a sudden disappearance. She smiled at the thought as she clicked unhurriedly into the room. Kenyon and Kira looked up from their positions seated amid stacks of books on the table.

"Sorry for the interruption," the librarian said. She placed the small tome she had rescued on the table. It somehow managed to look significant despite the abundance of larger volumes nearby. "People frequently try to walk away with a book or two, though sometimes it's by accident."

"Have you lost any so far?" Kenyon asked curiously.

"Not that I know of," the librarian answered grimly. "We keep strict records here."

Kenyon nodded and opened the Berthwin book again.

"So what happened to the keep after the dragon moved in?" Kira prompted.

"Well," the librarian leaned back on the table, then backed away when it wobbled uncertainly, "the stories get a little spotty at this point." Depending on who you're talking to, she added silently. "As I said, the dragon held the keep for about two hundred years and supposedly built up an amazing amount of treasure, though no one knew exactly what it was supposed to be. The stories all agree it wasn't gold or silver or magic."

"Where did it all come from?"

The librarian shrugged in carefully calculated noncommittance. "The stories don't say. They never do, of course. As time went on, tales of a great treasure drew gold-seeking warriors from all over. None actually managed to overcome the dragon, though a few came close."

"So why isn't the dragon still here?" Kira shifted impatiently in her chair.

"I was getting to that. According to the stories, a woman named Lilire rode into the keep. She was the thirteenth warrior to challenge the dragon that summer and she was in the keep for less than an hour before she rode back out. The place was empty, she said. There was no trace of the dragon, nor of the treasure."

Kira looked at the librarian dubiously. "You mean it just picked up and left? Why?"

"Well," Kenyon ventured, glancing up, "this book says dragons don't like to be disturbed, though a few like to talk." He looked intently at the librarian. "Maybe she got tired of fighting all those warriors. Maybe she just wanted to be left alone."

The librarian shot the man a penetrating look and he returned it for just a moment before dropping his eyes. Kira opened her mouth to say something, but the librarian jumped in ahead of her.

"At any rate," she continued, "Lilire claimed the keep for herself, and it was she who eventually started the library. It's been here ever since." She looked back at Kenyon. He avoided her gaze.

"But where did the treasure go?" Kira asked insistently. She had obviously forgotten her earlier thought. "It had to go somewhere. The dragon couldn't just carry it away, could it?"

"Who knows?" Kenyon said without looking up. He carefully turned a page. "Dragons are supposed to be powerful creatures. Crafty, too." He refused to meet the librarian's eyes, though she was doing her best to force him to do so.

"Is there anything you can tell us about where the dragon might have hidden its hoard?" Kira asked intently, oblivious to the silent exchange. "It's very important to us."

The librarian looked at Kenyon again, trying to see his face. But he kept his eyes stubbornly on the book.

He knows more than he's letting on, she thought shrewdly, but he doesn't seem ready to tell his sister. The last of her tension abruptly abated.

"Well," she said aloud, deftly separating a book from one of the piles, "Leland has a couple of theories in this work here, and Kythnar," she extracted another book, "has a few ideas you would find interesting. If you have time, you might also want to consult Arkinia Marthesgrave. She teaches at the university and knows a lot of local legends."

"Damn," Kenyon suddenly muttered, patting his robe and twisting round in his chair to examine the floor behind him, "I think I left my writing case downstairs and I wanted to copy these passages."

"Smart." Kira sighed. "I suppose you want me to go get it for you."

Kenyon flashed a wide grin that reminded the librarian of a puppy. She swallowed, suddenly remembering she hadn't eaten lunch yet.

"You're such a nice sister," Kenyon said with wide-eyed innocence.

Kira merely snorted as she rose from her chair and headed out the door. Kenyon watched her go, then turned to the librarian.

"I know where the treasure is," he said slyly.

The librarian settled herself into the chair Kira had vacated. "But you're not going to tell anyone," she replied coolly.

"What would that get me? It's not exactly portable. Besides, I don't want it. Kira does."

The librarian nodded. "How did you figure it out?"

"This passage." Kenyon fingered a line in the book and read aloud, "Dragons sometimes take human form . . ."

" '. . . especially those dragons that don't mind human conversation," the librarian finished quietly.

Kenyon closed the book. "Yes." He paused. "I could learn a great deal from you. A great deal."

"I'm a librarian," she answered, looking the man straight in the eye, "not a teacher."

"No, I suppose you're not." He sighed and looked away. They sat in silence, a silence Kenyon obviously wanted to break but it was equally obvious he couldn't find the nerve.

"I didn't see your case, Kenyon," Kira said, striding into the room a while later. Are you sure you left it down there?"

"No," Kenyon replied, reaching under his chair. There was a definite touch of regret in his voice. "I did have it up here after all."

Kira rolled her eyes. "And they call you a sorcerer."

The young man smiled briefly, then looked beseechingly at the librarian. She shook her head minutely, the thin smile dancing on her lips again.

"I think we should go to the university now and see that professor," he said. "I think I've learned all I'm going to."

"What about the passages you wanted to copy?" Kira objected.

"I don't think I'll need them.' He rose and stretched. "Thank you for your help," he told the librarian.

"You're welcome." She widened her smile, enjoying the absence of tension. "Good luck to your future."

"And to yours," Kira replied automatically, moving toward the door. Her brother followed, shooting the librarian one last regretful glance as he left.

The librarian thoughtfully watched them go, then, with practiced ease, she methodically put each book they had used back in its proper place. She picked up the little book that didn't belong in that room and, meticulously locking the door behind her, clicked her way to its place in the stacks. She placed it carefully on the shelf, treating it like the treasure it was.

QUEEN OF THE DEAD
by Dorothy J. Heydt

Here's another of the heroines we've known in many of
these volumes; this one is a return of Dorothy Heydt's
Cynthia, and a return to the classical setting of those
stories. I like ancient settings because—since the art of
history until recently was to inspire rather than to in-
form—once you get back about three hundred years you
have to make it all up anyhow—and thus it's all fantasy.
Hence my major historical novels are really all fantasy,
and so are Diana Paxson's and Mary Renault's, despite
much research.

Dorothy Heydt lives in Berkeley and has appeared in
many of these volumes; she has written widely in the
STAR TREK universe, but I think personally that her
work is too good and subtle for most of the commercial
markets. She has two astonishingly well-behaved children, and a house—in Berkeley—filled with such neces-
sities of life as cats, children, and computers. Her
husband, Hal Heydt, is also a computer expert—which
comes in handy.

They had been at sea some little time, and the crying
of the gulls in the Lesser Harbor had died away,
when the bindings round Cynthia's waist were loosened and she could struggle free of the cloak that had

covered her. The light was sharp in her unaccustomed eyes, and for some moments she sat blinking and breathing. (The cloak had been dusty, and rich with the sweat of the man who had worn it.)

The man sat opposite her, unmoving and silent: a small man of twenty or so, in a rough brown tunic. His black hair and beard were trimmed short around a heart-shaped face, a broad brow above clear hazel-colored eyes and a sharp narrow chin whose tuft of beard curled up at the end like a drake's tailfeathers. He sat on his heels, his body bent forward and his hands clasped on his knees, almost an attitude of homage—and the glint of a bronze earring in his ear told her he was a slave. But nothing in his patient waiting spoke of the slave whose life depends on others' goodwill, his happiness gathered piecemeal from others' inattention. He watched her as a man watches a horse he hopes to break to the saddle, or a lover his beloved, or a sailor the morning sky.

The sky overhead—and it was now an hour before noon—was golden, and the air over the sea was hazy. The water was growing choppy, and flecked everywhere with white, but the boat cut smoothly through the waves before a strong south wind. She looked over her shoulder. The southern sky was the color of brass, cloudy with dust; a sirocco was blowing up from the African deserts. The blistering wind might blow for days. This fool of a slave had better get them back to harbor—whatever harbor he could reach—while he still could.

The boat, she saw, was a fine one, carven on siderails and steering-oar, and brightly painted. A rug lay rolled up along the portside, the colors of purple and saffron visible along its edges. A bronze ring set in the deck led the eye to a trapdoor, hinting at more riches stored beneath. The little thief had princely tastes.

She turned back to him—still silent, still waiting—and her patience snapped. "Well!" she said. "You can sit there till nightfall, like a little he-sphinx, or you can tell me what this is all about."

"I need your help," he said.

"You've chosen a fine way of asking for it." She had taken a back-alley shortcut between the fish market and the herb stalls, and he had come up behind her, bundling her parcels and herself into that cursed cloak before she could turn round to look at him.

"Forgive me, lady," he said. "I didn't have much choice. I only came to Syracuse this morning, and could not stay long. Certainly not long enough to invent a meeting in the market and to talk of this and that, slowly gaining your confidence, and all in the hearing of others—"

"Stop," she said, and looked to the west. Most of Sicily had fallen out of their sight, but Aetna still thrust its pale head above the horizon. She could navigate by that, make it to Catania maybe. There would be no getting back to Syracuse, not with this wind. "Tell me in one sentence what this is about," she said, "before I knock you overboard." (If she could. She was as tall as he was, and heavier, but the arms that had grappled the cloak over her head had been uncomfortably strong.

"I need you to save my sister's child, when it's born."

"What?" She blinked. "You need a midwife?"

"A midwife—and maybe a witch," he said. "My sister is with child by the master's son, in Panormos. The master is a pious man, and fears the gods. You know what pious Carthaginians do with first-born children."

Cynthia caught her breath. "And you thought of me," she said. "You son of a drab, you knew where my Achilles heel is, didn't you? Where'd you hear of me?"

The man shrugged. "Word gets around. What now, lady? I can't compel you any further. Will you come with me, or shall I put in to Catania and let you off?"

"Oh, I'm coming, never fear. When is your sister's time due?"

"Around the next full moon."

"And the moon is waning now. Spread out your sail, man—what's your name, anyhow? We haven't much time. The first rule of midwifery says, 'Never trust a second baby to arrive on time—'"

"My name is Komi," the man said, shaking out the sail as he was bidden. "And this is her first child."

"—and the second rule of midwifery says, 'Never trust a first baby either.' I'll take the tiller."

* * *

Running before that fierce wind, they made the Straits of Messana by mid-afternoon. Till then they had had little time for speech, two people manning a ship meant for a crew of five or six. Komi had needed all his skill to bring it from Carthage to Syracuse by himself.

Now the rocky slopes to either side of the Straits blocked the wind a little, and though Komi still must sail carefully, they could hear themselves speak.

"The master is Hanno the merchant, who ships oil and wine from Tyre to Cartagena and back. Business has not been good, and the master mutters of the displeasure of the gods.

"You know what the Punic gods are like: easily offended, seldom pleased. Hanno should have—these are his words, not mine—should have given his son Myrcan to be burnt when he was born; but he withheld him. Hanno has gone in fear ever since, and such successes as he has had, he hasn't dared to enjoy. Now Myrcan has gotten my sister Enzaro with child, and Hanno sees a chance to make up his default. Maybe to give Myrcan's firstborn to the fire will make up for not giving his own. Mind you, he's not at all sure the gods will accept his belated sacrifice, but he intends to try."

"The gods have never asked us Hellenes to sacrifice children," Cynthia said. "Or, at least, very rarely;" and she told him of Iphigeneia, whom her father Agamemnon sacrificed for good winds to sail to Troy. "Unless you care to say that when we expose children we are sacrificing them to the goddess Fortune—in the hope that someone will take them up. And in Alexandria, of course, the Ptolemy's agents take them up and sell them. Maybe they would do better to let them die."

"No, they wouldn't," Komi said, so firmly that Cynthia looked up in surprise. He stood with his back braced against the gunwales, the end of the steering-oar in the crook of his arm. "By your leave, lady, I say it who know: it is better to be alive and a poor slave than dead and wrapped in silk and gold. You spoke of Fortune: well, her wheel is always turning." He leaned on the oar, and the boat slowly edged away from the Italian coast that was coming too near. "So long as we live, we may look for better luck ahead. But all the dead are dead alike."

" 'Better to be day-laborer to a poor cottager than king over all the dead who perish.' "

"Who said that?"

"Achilles."

"He was right," Komi said, and leaned on the oar again, and smiled. His tanned skin looked like dull-finished gold under the hazy sun, and the wind blew his short hair into little peaks like the small waves that ran across the sea. "This is the place where once sailors had to sail between Scylla and Charybdis. See those sharp rocks, where once they laired? But they're gone now, and all we need to fear is the Romans on one side and the Mamertines on the other." He waved a hand toward the point on their left, where the fortress of Messenë squatted like a stony toad. The Campanian mercenaries who called themselves "the sons of Mars" had seized the city and slaughtered its inhabitants in the spring of that year.

"Yes, there's been talk of nothing else in Syracuse," Cynthia said. "General Hieron wants leave to go and burn them out, and I think the Council may give him leave to do it. Are they likely to attack us?" The boat was small, but richly fitted; it had been a prince's plaything before Komi had stolen it.

"Not if our luck holds. Pirates are practical men. Who'd come out in a wind like this? Therefore, what use to come out looking for them?"

And the wind blew up a great dust behind them, and the boat skipped across the waves, past the end of the Mamertines' point, into full sight of the big warship that crouched in its lee. Its better days were behind it, but its middle age was nothing to be despised. "Our luck just changed," Komi said. "Take the tiller, if you please, lady, and let me take that sail."

For a few moments Cynthia thought the Mamertines had not seen them, or disdained to chase so small a prey. Then a rust-colored sail opened up to take in the wind, and the ship began to move. The sail was many times the size of Komi's, and would give the ship speeds they could not match. "Hard a-starboard," Komi said. He had wrapped the sheets of his sail around his forearms, and braced his feet against the deck to hold the sail at an angle. Cynthia leaned against the steering-oar. The little boat began to slip sideways, sailing northeastward across the south wind. The Mamertine ship still followed, but now her weightier hull held her back more than her larger sail pulled her on.

"How long can we keep on?" Cynthia called, bracing her forearms against the tiller.

"As long as our strength holds out."

"I mean, before we come up against the coast of Italy."

"Ah, we're not going that far. In fact—" he glanced over his shoulder at the Mamertine ship. "In fact, we're going to go the other way right now. When I say 'three,' if you please, lady, hard-a-port." He gathered in the sheets again. "One, two, *three*." The sail billowed, nearly lifting his feet from the deck, and filled out again in the wind. The waves slapped against the brow and raised a great plume of spray that drifted away on the wind, and the boat set off toward the northwest. The Mamertine ship floundered behind them, slowly coming about and attempting to follow. Komi laughed. If he did not thumb his nose at the pursuer, it was only because his hands were busy.

"Curse him, when is he going to give up?" Komi muttered an hour later. With the Mamertine ship almost below the horizon, they had paused from sailing across the wind to rest their aching arms and shoulders. But the Campanians had a full crew on board, and could trade off on tiller and sheets; they were beginning to close in again.

"He must think we've a noble passenger on board," Cynthia speculated, "who would be worth ransom money. Or treasure."

"Maybe we have," Komi said. "There's food and drink on board; I made sure of that before I stole her. Further, I did not inquire. If we ever get rid of this bastard, we'll go below and see. Lady, the talk of you that's reached Punic lands is of two sorts. One, that you're a powerful witch, who killed a Punic sorceror sent to spread plague in Syracuse, who put down a Sikel rebellion in the hinterlands by drawing down the moon, who saved General Hieron from assassination by casting a sleep on his assailant. And the other, that you're no such thing, only a woman with a clever tongue, and it's all the lies of poets."

"Mostly the lies of poets," Cynthia said. "I learned a few tricks from a friend, but she's dead now. I did use a spell to attack the sorceror, but that one won't work here." (Turn herself into a Scylla and drag the Mamertines down? Not if she could avoid it; her last shape-change had nearly been permanent.) "I do know one spell that makes little things look large. If we found a drift of seaweed, say, with little spiny fish in it, I could make it look like a great sea-monster, frighten them away. But I don't see anything—" She let the tiller slip and strained her eyes against the glare. "Is that land ahead?"

"I think so," Komi said. "One of the Aeolian Islands, Phaneraia probably. You can see the smoke of Hephaestos to our west, but we're past him already. See the plume of cloud overhead? The beaches of Phaneraia are full of the smoke and steam of the underworld, and it bubbles out in the water offshore."

"How far offshore?" Cynthia cried, and without waiting for an answer, "Make for the island as fast as you can."

Komi obeyed, letting the blistering south wind carry them forward. Cynthia ducked under the sheets he held to crouch in the bows, her eyes on the water ahead. The Mamertine continued to gain on them.

"Do you plan to run them aground?" Komi asked presently. "It could be done, we draw much less water than they do; unless they'll have the wit to hold off."

After a while she saw, or thought she saw, smoky bubbles rising out of the water. She began to mutter the words of the spell Xanthe had taught her, and crept backward to the stern still muttering, and counting on her fingers (it was that kind of spell).

Bubbles were rising out of the water in their wake, bubbles the size of melons, bubbles the size of oxen: they burst as they reached the surface and let out clouds of thick steamy smoke that spread rapidly across the water until the Mamertine ship could no longer be seen at all.

Komi had made the sheets fast and joined her in the stern. "Well done, lady," he said. "Now, if they have any sense they'll turn around and go back, and if they haven't any sense they'll follow us and they *will* go aground. How did you do it? If it's permitted to know. Is it done with that ring?"

Cynthia looked at the ring clutched in her left hand. "No, far from it. This is the ring given me by the nymph Arethousa, before she fell silent. It prevents any magic being done to the wearer—or by her. That's why I had to take it off. How far away is the—" And the boat came to a sudden stop, with a sound like the grinding of two millstones.

"Not far at all," Komi said with a rueful smile. "Where are my sandals? There they are." He put them on and hopped over the side into the shallow water. "You can't go barefoot in these waters, the steam is like hot needles in your feet. Oh, yes, the hull is still in good shape. That's good. The town's on the other side of the island and I wouldn't like to have to go cross-country here. This shore is an old holy place, chancy to walk in—as well as hard on the feet. The old folk used to sacrifice here to the gods under the earth. No one remembers their names now; they're Sikels now in the town."

"Kinsmen of yours?"

"Ah, no." He climbed aboard again, and took off his sandals to dry. "By your leave, lady, I am a Sikan. A small but important difference. The Sikels are late-comers from Italy. We are the original inhabitants of the island. The old story is that we grew out of the rocks—"

Out in the smoky mist there was a yell, and a grinding sound like the whole mill-house falling into piles of stones. They held their breath, listening. The Mamertine ship must have run aground no more than a bowshot away.

There was a splash, and a moment's pause, and a cry of pain and some very crude Latin. Some Mamertine had leapt overboard barefoot, and had his mistake demonstrated to him in the most straightforward matter.

More splashing, and orders shouted in a mixture of

bad Latin and bad Greek. The ship-master was splitting his men into groups, sending them out to explore the beach. "Go a hundred paces out, then come back. Follow your own footprints if you have to. Gaius, beat the drum for them to find their way by."

A slow drum beat began, like the stroke for a funeral barge. Under it, Cynthia whispered, "Can we get away?"

Komi shrugged, and got to his feet. He took a long-poled boathook from its mount on the port gunwale, and bracing himself in the prow he tried to push off from the sand. The boat did not move. "Maybe if I get out and put my back against it," he muttered.

"We'll both get out," Cynthia began, but Komi held up a hand. "Rhodios!" a voice was calling. "Rhodios! Why don't you answer?" They listened as the sound of feet splashing through the shallow water came nearer, and passed them, and faded away again. "The tide is out," Komi said in the barest whisper, "and I'm afraid we may be grounded till it comes back in. But I'd rather wait till they all get back on board to try to decide what they're going to do next, before we try to push off." He sat on his heels, his back against the siderail, the boathook balanced lightly across his knees. Cynthia crept across the deck to sit beside him.

Strange are the gods' gifts, she thought. *Who, except Sokrates, would have expected a Punic slave to have such wisdom in him? Who, except Zeno, would expect him to know virtue? To spare his sister the grief of a lost child, he is risking his own life, when he might have escaped and found freedom. What god was so clever, to find Virtue buried in the slaves' quarters? Was it only Fortune?*

The drumbeat had stopped. The little waves lapped against the side of the boat, and the wind whistled in the rigging, an irritating half-sound like the thin whine of a mosquito.

The man appeared all at once on the railing, like a dagger whisked out of an assassin's sleeve. Cynthia's mind quickly looked through her handful of spells, and found none that would help. The Mamertine had armored himself as best he could before leaving his ship, and his brass-studded leather cuirass was wet up to his armpits. His helmet had been patched in two places, and was slightly too large for him. The edge of his shortsword had been nicked in a series of battles, but its point was still sharp. "Now I see," he said. "You're the witch of Syracuse, aren't you? What have you done with my mates?" He was looking along the sword's edge at Cynthia's throat.

Komi was on his feet, the boathook in his hands. "Save your trouble," the Mamertine said, and drove his sword at Cynthia's heart. Komi knocked it aside. Splinters flew, but the pole was sturdy and the edge too dull to cut it.

"You crow-bitten fool," the Mamertine said. "She'll drain the soul out of you, like she did to them." He aimed his sword's point at Komi, but the boathook kept him out of range. He tried a sudden lunge, and Komi rammed the boathook into his midriff; but for the leather cuirass, his guts would have been on the deck. The Mamertine backed off to regain his breath, but Komi pursued him down the deck, pace by pace like a little image of Nemesis. When the mercenary stopped with the stern at his back, Komi stopped, too, holding the pole steady.

"Drop the sword on the deck," he said. "And you'd better drop the helm and the cuirass, too, and then you may go overboard and swim to your own boat. Or if you'd prefer to be gutted like a tuna and pickled in salt water, that's your choice."

The Mamertine spat. "Mother-jumping slave's turd," he said.

Komi smiled with half his mouth. "Hail," he said. "And I'm Komi, son of Endreigon."

The Mamertine raised his sword over his head, roaring like a bull, and Komi swung the pole sidewise and caught him on the side of the head where the helm didn't shield it. The mercenary toppled over the gunwale into the sea. Komi and Cynthia looked over the side, but could not tell if some of the bubbles in the unquiet sea came from the drowning man instead of from the fiery sands. In any event, the Mamertine never came up.

"Damn," Komi said after a moment. "I wish I could have gotten that sword. I may yet need it. A person can't go carrying a boathook indoors, but a shortsword can fit anywhere—under your tunic, up your sleeve, in a baby's basket—" His thoughtful look hardened. "Maybe one of

the others had the kindness to die on land. I'll go look."
He picked up his sandals again and began to put them
on.

"You're not going out there!" Cynthia exclaimed, forgetting to whisper, and then too late put her hands to
her mouth. But there was no answer, no sound at all but
the waves and the wind.

"Do you hear anything?" Komi said after a moment.
"For my part, I don't. They're all dead, dead or stunned
with the earthy gases. You can wander into pockets of
the stuff in any little dip in the ground. I've been here
before, don't forget. I know how to get about safely."
His hands rested lightly on her shoulders. "There are
shadows under your eyes," he said. "Poor lady, you've
been doing a sailor's work all day in this raging wind, no
wonder you're tired. Sit and rest till I get back. I shall
be perfectly safe."

Cynthia hesitated a moment too long; before she could
speak her next "No" he had leapt over the side and
vanished into the mist. She sat down on the deck, where
the sail cast a pale shadow and the air was a thought
cooler than elsewhere. She weighed the ring in her hand,
wondering whether it would help or hinder Komi's excur-
sion if she put it on and dispelled the magical mist. She
hunched her stiff shoulders and rolled her head about,
and rested her forehead on her knees to shield her eyes
from the light.

The grass was dark under the shade of the trees, and
the little flowers that dotted the ground shone faintly,
like stars through mist. The turf was cool under foot,
and she stepped between two trees and stopped short.
Beneath a scarlet-flowered tree a woman lay giving birth.
She groaned and shrieked, although the birth was the
easiest and quickest Cynthia had ever seen, and before
she could step forward to give aid the babe lay between
the woman's feet, crying lustily. The mother picked up
the child and cradled it in her arms, singing softly, and
wiped away the birthing-blood and wax with a fold of
her dark robe, and put it to the breast.

Then she opened fanged jaws impossibly wide and ate
it in two bites.

Cynthia woke with a jerk, gasping for breath, her fists

clenched so tight the ring bit into them. What ill-omened thing had she seen? The mist had thinned away, and she could see the sun was falling toward the Gates of Herakles, an hour or two maybe till sunset. The Mamertine ship lay grounded to her west, dark against the reddening sunlight. Nothing moved except the little waves of the sea, touching the shore with little plumes of white foam. The tide had begun to come in. The beach sloped gently upward, pocked with little plumes of steam, to a ridge of compacted sand perhaps fifty paces from the water's edge. Almost opposite the boat, something lay atop the ridge, some darkish thing like a dead gull or a bit of venturesome driftwood. She jammed Arethousa's ring back onto her finger and the mist vanished with an almost audible "whoosh." And the thing along the ridge was a man's booted foot, dark with seawater, lying very still.

Sandals. Kilt up her skirt into her girdle. Where was the boathook? No, he had taken it with him. Cynthia vaulted the boat railing and splashed through the shallow water to the sand.

The sight from the top of the ridge was as she'd feared—worse than she had feared; she could not have made this up. All the men from the Mamertine ship lay sprawled along the sand, not in drifts like drowned men washed up with the high tide, but each separately, as if each had decided separately to lie down in his tracks and die there. She examined each man as she wandered among them: none was breathing, none had a heartbeat; all were beginning to grow cold. She found Komi, barely breathing, draped like a cloak over the man whose shortsword he had just picked up. Its hilt lay across his fingertips, sturdily bound with bronze wire, across fingers slender as reeds and callused with ropes and hard work. Cynthia took off the ring—and held her breath waiting for something to happen, but nothing happened—and slipped it onto Komi's finger. There was no change.

He had fallen, as the mercenary he'd robbed had fallen, almost on the lip of a shallow pit floored with smooth sand. The place smelled of sulfur and of rotten things, and she remembered what Komi had said: *Earthy gases. You can wander into pockets of the stuff in any little dip in the ground.* Maybe, if she got him away quickly enough, he could revive . . . unless she had lingered here too long herself, for the air was darkening around her and as she looked into the pit it seemed no longer shallow and floored with sand. It was as deep as a grave, as deep as the throat of Aetna, and far down below there was the uneasy movement of little flames. Cynthia felt herself poured out and swallowed down that throat as smoothly as wine.

Little flames, and pale: they flickered all about her, as if about to go out. They should have been dying down into warm red coals, but the ground beneath her was cold. She moved along the floor like a pillar of smoke drifting in a slow draft. Pale flames guttered along the floor; and she also was a flame.

She tried to resist the pull, dig in what might have been her heels and move against the flow. She slowed down, but could not stop. If she could have gotten a good running start in the other direction, she might have made it out the other way—but not from a cold start. Or she could swim downstream, add her own strength to the current's and reach the bottom sooner; but that didn't seem so wise a plan, not if she had any choice.

She was a tongue of flame—but one that could not speak. Not that it mattered—there was no one on whom she could call for help. Oh, if Arethousa had not fallen asleep, and all the gods with her. But the gods were gone—or had never been, the lies of poets, the stock-in-trade of mountebanks.

The flame Cynthia flickered and sputtered, as if with green fuel or a high wind; but she went on drifting in that little breath of a wind, down to where the long throat of that ancient lava tube widened into a chamber high as a tree and round as ripples in a pond. Its floor was a shallow funnel-shape, like a theater, still preserving the form of the whirlpool of molten rock that had been swirling down some crack in the earth at the moment it froze solid. Dying flames guttered along the rock, drifting slowly toward what lay in the center.

Dim as a star that one can see only out of the corner of the eye: look directly at it, and there was nothing to see but formless blackness. But when she turned her attention elsewhere, to the flames that struggled over the floor, then what lay in the center glowed with a dull red, blood-tinged like sunlight filtered through closed eyelids or a cupped hand. Now she remembered her dream. The thing was a grave: it was a womb: and Cynthia began to be very much afraid.

O Zeus, father of gods and men, hear me. O Persephone, Queen under the earth, rescue me. O Isis who raised the dead, hear me and come to my aid. (Lies of poets. Names without realities, empty names.) Then something spoke.

But I am Isis, and I am Persephone. Did you not know? Me you served when you brought my children into the world; me you served when you slew my children and sent them back to me. All that is living I bear into the light; all that lives I devour again and swallow down into the darkness.

Here, at the earth's navel, once my children brought their lives to me, pouring them out in their fullness into my lap. So you have done for me today, pouring out these lives and your own, and you have pleased me.

(*O Hermes*, Cynthia prayed. *Gray-eyed Athene, hear me.* The pallid little flames around her were the shabby spirits of the Mamertines, drifting around the rings of the frozen whirlpool till they reached the center and were swallowed up in the womb/gullet of earth. As she was drifting, as she would be swallowed up. *O Wisdom and the Aither of Euripides. Have you all died back into the earth?*)

All, the answer came. *To me all flesh comes, and there is no escaping me. You also shall come to me.*

She had moved halfway round the first ring of the circle when a light broke upon her, like the sun bursting through a cloud or from behind the eclipsing shoulder of the moon, and gave her its name. *Virtue, sought by gods and men.* A flame like her own, but brighter, a pure brilliance reaching high overhead—but now dangerously near the center, soon to be sucked in.

Funnels; spirals; cones. The brilliance of Komi's spirit ignited her own, and a memory opened up in her mind like a flower.

A hot day in Alexandria, long ago. The smells of dust and sweat and oil. Two philosophers on the steps of the Library, comparing notes in the mysteries of geometry, drawing cones in the air with swift fingers and slicing them through with the flat of the hand. And in the dust of the street below, three little boys played a game of rolling stones.

Cynthia neither smiled—the apparatus being absent—nor took a deep breath, nor pushed off with her toes. But she made a long swoop across the rings, picking up speed as she neared the center, where Komi hovered at the edge of the pit. And as she moved she chanted at the heart of her flame, and counted along its sputtering edges, because it was that kind of spell.

All around her the flames rose high, the greasy spirits of old mercenaries blazing like fat on the fire: a dozen times, a hundred times magnified. Invisible in a whole forest of flames she skimmed like a fishing bird over the surface, seeking the one spark that tasted of Virtue, and caught it up—

It was like being made part of the sun. Nothing stood between his flame and her own; she knew him as she was known, in the flowering of a tree full of stars. So the gods must speak, or whatever divine intelligences there were: and the language of their speaking was love.

—and without stopping sped on up the tube and burst out of the earth, like Athene from the brain of Zeus, or that slave woman's baby who had appeared after one pain, not giving Cynthia time to spread out her apron. When they came back to themselves, they were running, hand in hand, along the beach as fast as they could. Their boat lay ahead, dimly to be seen in the sunset glow and through the sand raised by the howling wind. A glint of metal in Komi's other hand told Cynthia that he had brought that damned shortsword with him after all. She had to laugh, and then she had to cough.

Komi stopped her, and held her by the shoulders. "Be easy. Breathe, love, breathe. We're safe now, I think." Then he had to cough himself, and they stood together catching their breath, their heads leaning on one another's shoulders.

The sun had gone behind the moon again, the blaze of Virtue hidden in human flesh. But she knew it was still there; she felt its hidden warmth in his breath on her shoulder. Their arms had wound round each other's bodies, holding them close as flesh would permit.

"Wups," Komi said after a moment. "We're going to have to catch the boat." The tide had come in and floated off, and it lay a bowshot's length offshore. Komi picked up the shortsword again, from the sand where he had dropped it, and waded into the water. Cynthia followed.

"Komi," she said as the water rose to her waist, "there is a god within you."

He raised one eyebrow. "Then there's one in every man. I salute them all—particularly yours." Now he must swim, awkwardly and one-handed, the sword above the water, till he reached the boat. He scrambled over the side and reached down to pull Cynthia up after him. The wind had risen till it screamed in their ears like the Furies; without trying to speak further he found the ring in the deck, raised the trapdoor, and beckoned. She tucked the rolled-up rug under her arm and followed him below.

Here it was dark as pitch, except from the little light that seeped in from the trapdoor. She could see lamps, and a tinder box, hanging by the foot of the stairs. They would be handy later. She unrolled her rug and motioned to Komi to close the trap.

Velvety darkness, and relative silence, and the sound of breathing. "Well," he said.

"Well," she echoed. "What do you say? Was that really the Queen of all the Dead? I, for one, have my doubts. People die every day, every hour; but that cavern was empty but for us and the Mamertines. I have her down for a little local goddess who hasn't had a good meal in centuries and didn't care what lies she told."

"Does it matter? To her, or to something, we must all come in the end. I pray whatever gods may be for length of days between that time and now."

Cynthia abandoned the argument. The man was sitting at her elbow, not moving. Had he gone shy, or remembered the customs of the upper world? She would make him forget them. She put her arms around him and bore him down to the rug. The joining of flesh ran a poor second to the bonding of their spirits; but it was way ahead of whatever was in third place. There were soft cushions, and water, and wine and a prince's picnic basket. With any kind of luck, the wind would last for days.

THE FLOWER THAT DOES NOT WITHER
by Dave Smeds

When I was assembling data for this volume, Dave Smeds sent me an impressive list of his previous credits, ranging all the way from volumes of well-reviewed prose to comic books and pamphlets of remedial reading to magazines from *Weird Tales* to *Mayfair*, and multitudes of short fiction, including three appearances in previous S&S volumes.

I remember he was also at the third anniversary party of *Marion Zimmer Bradley's Fantasy Magazine*. But I must be getting old; I still think of him mainly as the author of the magnificent "Gullrider" which appeared in SWORD AND SORCERESS IV and would have done much to allay my prejudices against male writers, if I'd ever had any. He lives in Santa Rosa, California, and has a wife and daughter; he has earned his living as a graphics artist and typesetter and holds a black belt in the Japanese martial art Goju-ryu karate, which he has also taught.

This new story challenges many of our assumptions about beauty. I think you'll like it.

Fawn crawled into the edge of the devastation. At her back, majestic evergreens reached toward the sky. Beside her, the trees bent double to touch the ground, like beanstalks desiccated and laid down by the coming of winter. The grass under her squirming body broke off, dead and brown as in the dregs of autumn.

It was spring. Elsewhere in the province of Foxwood, hyacinth, iris, and poppies were bursting into bloom. Songbirds were courting and building nests. Lord Eaglecry's lands were demonstrating how truly fair they could be.

But for many hundred paces around the castle, an ugliness had seized hold, killing the groves and gardens, leaving blighted ground and macabre growths of fungi in its place.

Fawn knew ugliness. She had only to look in a mirror. But she had never seen the likes of this. She wormed her way through more of the stricken trees, closer and closer to the zone where nothing of the former woodland survived. Avoiding guard spells that would have changed the turf beneath her to quicksand, she reached the crest of a tiny hillock and saw the graves.

Open pits yawned. The bodies of Lord Eaglecry's men-at-arms, pillaged of weapons and armor, steamed in the mid-morning sunshine. The naked bodies of maids-in-waiting lay casually heaped at the edges of the trenches, as if they presented too much trouble for the victors to toss in, much less cover with soil.

The breeze shifted, bringing the stench toward Fawn in a fetid, viscous cloud. She choked, struggling for breath but not daring to inhale. Mercifully, the wind shifted back before she lost her breakfast.

How could their enemies revel in such trophies? The Iron Claw seemed to deliberately enjoy surrounding themselves in putrescence. Was it to intimidate the populace? Surely, Fawn thought, they must realize it only serves to anger us.

Fawn did not move any closer. Not only might she be seen by the human sentries up on the battlements, but she did not care to approach so closely that she would recognize the dead—not that some of them would ever be recognizable. Instead, she squirmed back the way she had come. She had seen as much as her master required, and as much as any fourteen-year-old girl should have to witness.

The cool, fragrant shade of the Foxwood enveloped

her, banishing the horror around the castle, reducing the need to be alert for magical traps. Here the forest was as it had been a fortnight ago, before the Flower Queen and her escort of Iron Claw mercenaries had come up from the Kingdom of the Rivers to attack Lord Eaglecry's keep. Fawn could be an ordinary sorcerer's apprentice again, not a spy for a fugitive army.

As she passed a stately oak, she mimicked a chipmunk call. Momentarily three of Lord Eaglecry's warriors drifted out of the bracken and vines ahead of her, and formed a welcome escort. Together they wended their way through two leagues of groves and thickets to the sanctuary where the marquis had taken refuge.

A dozen newly arrived survivors of the village of Bluewater milled about the camp, still numbed from the shock of seeing their homes, livelihoods, and loved ones destroyed the night before. The Iron Claw were wasting no time in their attempts to locate the marquis, and they spared few in their path, whether the victims had any knowledge of their lord's location or not. Some of the refugees noticed Fawn's arrival and grimaced in the startled way that all people did, the first time they regarded her gnarled shape. The warriors at her side fingered the nocks of their arrows, letting all know that this was no beggar child to be ridiculed. The warriors had no need to speak out loud. Any commoner in the province knew an ugly young woman treated with such respect could only be the ward and chief apprentice of Summerleaf, the grand mage—the realm's main hope of defeating the Flower Queen. Careful, neutral expressions replaced the grimaces.

Fawn noticed each and every reaction. Nature had cursed her with a gift for observation. But she ignored them, as she had long since learned to do.

Summerleaf, bent around his cane, hobbled out from under the canopy that served as Lord Eaglecry's sanctum. "There you are," he said to Fawn. "Come. The marquis is waiting."

"It is as you warned, Master," Fawn said solemnly. "The blight has spread a hundred paces farther out the past three days. Even the stones of the citadel looked strangely dull and pocked, as if the ash from Fire Mountain had rained down again."

Summerleaf grunted, frowning. "Tell it to our patron, girl. I need no help to believe it."

As they stepped into the shade of the canvas, several men and two women turned toward them: Lord Eaglecry, his wife, his head councillor, the captain of his guard, and Mage Summerleaf's two high apprentices.

Lord Eaglecry held himself stiffly and perfectly upright, despite the red rivers in his eyes from lack of sleep, despite the livid scar across his temple that even Summerleaf's incantations had not yet managed to heal. Though in his late fifties, the marquis insisted on conducting himself like the brilliant military campaigner he had been at twenty-five.

Fawn gave her report. The lord listened with brows drawn, intimidating her with his stern glare.

"The tunnel entrance has not been discovered?"

"No, but the blight will reach it by tomorrow. Once the vegetation around it dies, it will be easily found."

"We must act tonight, Lord," Summerleaf declared. "We cannot wait for your brother-in-law to reinforce you. If we don't take this chance to kill the Flower Queen, you will never dislodge the Iron Claw from your castle in time to preserve the land. If you dislodge them at all."

The captain of the guard stiffened. The grand mage had once more made clear his lack of faith in a military assault, though without the captain's brilliant defense of the castle, Lord Eaglecry would never have escaped alive.

The marquis gestured for peace. "I don't like it. Oakroot tells me this sorcery will exhaust you for a week, perhaps more. I dare not be without the skills of my chief magician at such a vital time."

Summerleaf shot a severe glance at his male apprentice. Oakroot kept his gaze on the ground, contrite in his silence. "I'm afraid I neglected to mention that to you earlier, my lord," Summerleaf continued. "Nevertheless, it is worth the risk. You have seen what the Iron Claw can do, and you say, 'These are men, they can be defeated.' That is true, given time and lives. But even death will not stop the Flower Queen or her necromancy. Defeat her, and the Iron Claw will succumb to the internecine rivalries that kept it in check in earlier times. Defeat her, and the land will not have to suffer the fate of the Kingdom of the Rivers."

"How certain can you be that you will kill her?" Eaglecry demanded.

"Not certain at all. But I do know that I, with Fawn serving as my hands, am the only one who can succeed."

Eaglecry scanned Fawn with skepticism. "She doesn't look like much of a weapon, magician. Wouldn't your older apprentices be more appropriate?"

Fawn shrank from the inspection of the marquis. The lord, lacking the tact of his vassals, did not conceal his revulsion at her appearance. She let the dismissal wash over her. Of all people, only Summerleaf had never given her that look at least once—perhaps because Summerleaf himself wore a visage that could curdle milk.

"Her and only her," insisted Summerleaf. "If she fails, it won't matter how many men-at-arms you gather, the Iron Claw will gut them like hogs. However, if she succeeds, the Flower Queen will be dead, and the Claw will lose its focus."

Even the apprentices seemed skeptical, but they did not question Summerleaf. He was a sorceror of great power. None of those present had ever heard such worry in his voice, and all were frightened.

Even the marquis. "So be it," he announced. "Tonight."

In the sorcerers' tent, as twilight fell and Summerleaf and Fawn ate a meager supper, the young apprentice finally voiced her own doubt.

"Why me?" she asked. "I am nowhere near the level of Morningdew or Oakroot."

"It is my magic you will be using tonight, and you are adept enough at channeling that."

"But . . ."

"No. You are the only one who can do it," stated Summerleaf. In the dim candlelight, Fawn thought she saw tears on his face. Surely she imagined it. Summerleaf the grand mage did not cry.

"I cannot tell you more," the wizard said in a husky,

weary voice. "Just do as we have planned. And when you reach the witch's presence, strike quickly, before her magic saps your will."

He would say no more. They finished the meal, and together began the chant. Before it ended, Summerleaf was locked in trance, his enchantment shrouding her like a cloak. Shivering, though the night was warm, Fawn left the tent.

A mere pair of men-at-arms accompanied her away from the fugitive camp, though dozens of eyes tracked her departure. She jumped at every twig that snapped, every owl that hooted. Far too soon, they reached the hidden entrance of the tunnel that led into Lord Eaglecry's former home.

One of her companions pressed back the thick shrub that blocked the opening. The other man took the crossbow that he carried, braced his foot within the stirrup, and drew the string over its catch. In the groove of the stock he placed the black, poisoned bolt intended for the heart of the Flower Queen.

Fawn carried a knife, but that would not do for the assassination. A knife would require a close approach to the witch, and Summerleaf wanted his pupil to keep her distance. A crossbow bolt would penetrate deeply and suddenly into the witch's chest, ensuring her death.

One bolt. One chance. Fawn did not even have the strength to draw the string herself. Everything depended on the first squeeze of her trigger finger.

She accepted the crossbow, nodded to the men-at-arms, and slid into the tunnel.

She twisted and squeezed through, taking care not to bump the weapon. Soon the passageway opened up, allowing her to walk, though she had to remain bent over. This was not the wide, well-maintained escape tunnel that the marquis and his comrades had used to flee when the Iron Claw overwhelmed the castle's defenses. That tunnel had been found by the enemy as soon as they searched. This one was far older and better hidden, both magically and in the physical sense, and the enemy would have had no reason to suspect its existence.

Not, that is, until she arrived. Then the secret would be out, and Eaglecry would have lost another advantage.

How it must chafe that man-of-action to have to sit and wait while a woman-child fought his battle.

Once Fawn reached the first bend, she spat the cob-webs and dust out of her mouth and lit the lamp she had brought. The musty bricks of the passageway continued as far as the light of the flame could penetrate, leading straight under the dungeons of the keep.

She knew by the odor when she crossed into the blight. Here, where the air could not circulate freely, the mephitis smothered her. She took only short, shallow breaths, trying not to smell the air as it passed in and out. The ghostly presence of Summerleaf's sorcery was needed to fend off her fear and keep her walking forward.

At last she came to a stone wall, of different brick than the tunnel. She found the latch mechanism and, blowing out the lamp, freed the lock.

The wall swung inward like a door, silent on oiled hinges. She stepped into a dim, musty corridor. Dungeon cells confronted her to the left and right. Moans and snores issued from some of the rooms, but no one raised a voice as she passed by the tiny, barred holes of their doors.

Even if the prisoners had been paying attention, they would neither have seen nor heard her.

Summerleaf's sorcery imbued her every step now, active and paternal. She gave it full acceptance, focusing on little else beyond that and her stride. Her heart skipped a beat as she turned a corner and passed within five paces of the two jailors.

The men scratched their hirsute bellies, conversed, and played a game of dice. They did not notice her slip past and climb up the stairs behind their table, though one of them glanced straight at her.

Fawn exhaled as she reached the next floor, realizing after the fact that she had held her breath. Summerleaf and she had practiced the invisibility glamour for years, at even greater distances, but no amount of familiarity could calm her completely. Even the greatest mages could only cast the glamour for brief periods, an hour at most, and even then, it was not true lack of visual and auditory presence. The sorcery bent the mind of the perceiver. A person of strong will, a magician, or anyone suspicious of her proximity would see her if they looked straight at her, and would hear the sounds she made.

Because the spell was powerful magic, it was susceptible to detection by the minor wizards that served the Flower Queen. So Summerleaf faced a difficult challenge merely to conceal the casting.

Fawn entered the familiar confines of the servants' quarters, where she, as Summerleaf's apprentice, had been housed for the last few years. Avoiding the spoiled food and excrement on the floor, she crossed the kitchen. A pair of Iron Claw warriors were carving meat on a butcher table, sampling as they argued over which of them would get what portions. Fawn wanted to gag when she saw who they were slicing, but she made it successfully into the dining hall.

Here other warriors, despite the hour, toyed with a pair of captives—one man, one woman. Fawn refused to look closely, but the image of grinning, horned faces, slung with rotting, pock-marked flesh, haunted her all the way up the stairs into the quarters of the royal family.

The men of the Iron Claw had once been human. She shuddered, fearing that she, too, if she remained here long, might sport bristles on the backs of her hands, talons instead of nails, fangs instead of smooth teeth. And the odor. Always the same charnel odor.

By rote, she found herself in front of the bedroom door she wanted. She hesitated. The door was not guarded, as that of the Flower Queen would be, but the room might be in use. She coaxed Summerleaf's river of power into her as strongly as it would flow, released the latch, and entered.

A sleeping warrior lay sprawled across the mattress, half uncovered, while one of the castle's serving maids slept by his side. The woman stirred fitfully, brushed by the current of air wafting into the room. Fawn hurriedly closed the door. The maid settled down. Her grotesque companion did not wake at all. The scent of half the wines in Lord Eaglecry's cellar rode on his breath.

At least this woman did not seem as abused as the others, noted Fawn, but she did not dwell on such morbid thoughts. She slipped into the shadows of a wardrobe closet and found the hidden catch she had been told would be there. The back of the closet opened out, spilling her into a private stairwell.

The way led straight to the lord's chamber. The stairs were his means to conduct romantic liaisons out of sight of the marquessa. He had not enjoyed admitting to their presence, though many of the household retainers, as well as the marquessa herself, already knew of them.

Fawn climbed, trembling. Perhaps the Flower Queen would not have taken the royal bedchamber as her own, though Summerleaf assured her the witch would have no choice—an odd statement, now that she considered it. If so, the plan would fail, stillborn. At that moment, Fawn could have convinced herself she would prefer that to confronting the sorceress.

The secret door, a wall panel, opened as noiselessly as the others along her route. Fawn stepped onto thick carpets, fine weavings brought all the way from the Snow Peaks along the eastern trade roads. Her tread made no echo as she crossed the room to the canopied bed.

The Flower Queen slept. Fawn did not doubt that it was her. In the midst of the vile atmosphere of the castle, her fragrance blessed the senses. Rich, thick hair surrounded her face; even in sleep it gleamed as if just combed. Her nightgown bore a fringe of the finest lace, of the type that took a skilled seamstress weeks to create.

Fawn raised the crossbow. Be quick, her master had said. She had come so far so quickly, it hardly seemed possible that her goal could be so near, so attainable.

Her finger, resting inside the trigger guard, would not squeeze. The bolt pointed straight toward the sleeping witch's heart, but remained within its groove.

Sweat beaded on Fawn's brow, and more poured from her armpits, until her tunic turned dark with the stain. So simple a thing—just a twitch of the finger. What was wrong?

Surely, it must be magic. Yet, Fawn did not sense the telltale aura of sorcery—certainly not sorcery powerful enough to control her in such a way. Her concentration faltered. Gasping, she lost the link with Summerleaf.

Fully visible and audible, she trembled, almost unable to hold the crossbow. She checked to see if something were physically blocking the trigger. Breathing faster, heart racing, she aimed the weapon once more.

But the thought of tainting that fine, pale skin with the splatter of blood repelled Fawn. She could not shoot a poison missile between the breasts of the Flower Queen; the subtle mounds beneath the coverlet only brought images of babies suckling. She could not bear to see the gentle lips of her victim's mouth contort in pain when all Fawn wanted was to hear words of greeting issue from them.

Fawn sank to her knees, lowering the crossbow. She sobbed. Her master, her patron, and all of Foxwood depended on her, and she had failed them.

The Flower Queen opened her eyes and, drawn by the sound of weeping, sat up in bed and stared at Fawn.

"Hello," the witch said. Her voice caressed the ear, like a babbling brook. "What have we here?"

Fawn kneeled, mouth open in amazement, waiting for the woman to summon her guards, but she did not.

"Stand up. Let me look at you," the Flower Queen said.

Fawn stood. She wasn't sure why. She simply couldn't deny the request, though it did not feel as if she were magically compelled.

"You are female, aren't you?" asked the queen.

Fawn winced. It was not the first time a person had asked her that upon meeting her. "Yes."

"How are you called?"

"I am Fawn."

The witch slipped from the bed with a graceful, dance-like motion. She took the crossbow from Fawn's limp grasp and laid it on the bed.

"I am Skymist," the Flower Queen said. "You came here to kill me, yes?"

Upright, no longer concealed beneath the bedding, the witch radiated her full beauty. All Fawn could do was stare at the gentle outline of the woman's hips, the long, elegant flow of her legs, the fine structure of her hands. Fawn tried to reply, but all that came was a squeak from her dry throat.

"Never mind that now," the sorceress commanded in

a kind, sympathetic tone. "Tell me about yourself, girl. Where do you come from? What is your history?"

Surely she was imagining the question, Fawn thought. Why would the ruler of the Kingdom of the Rivers care about an apprentice magician who had come to assassinate her?

"Speak. I beg you."

Once again unable to deny the impulse, Fawn spoke. "I am an orphan. I am told that I was born in the Meadows, on the far side of the Snow Peaks. All of my life that I can remember was spent here, in Foxwood, cared for by and apprenticed to Summerleaf, the grand mage who brought me from the Meadows as an infant."

Skymist reached forward and stroked her would-be assassin's cheek. Her perfect fingers rode over the bumps, warts, and wrinkles. Fawn jerked away. Only Summerleaf had ever touched her in such a caring way.

The Flower Queen bowed her head, lifting the lace of her collar to dab at her watering eyes. "I have a story of my own to tell. Will you indulge me?"

Fawn would have listened even if she had not been at the sorceress' mercy.

"Once there was a kingdom named for the many rivers that flowed through it. It was a fine, fertile land, with a mild climate that would grow many crops each year. Into that land came a surpassingly powerful magician. Not a mere grand mage, but a sorcerer supreme, seeking a court to attach himself to. He was given a commission by the king of the land, and served well.

"Eventually, as a reward, the sorcerer was given a young cousin of the king in marriage. The bride died a year later in childbirth, but the baby, a girl, survived. The child became the center of the sorcerer's affections. He denied her nothing."

As the Flower Queen rendered her story, she paced the room restlessly, as if wishing she could tell it all at once. Fawn merely listened, mesmerized by the mellifluousness of the speaker's voice.

"The child inherited her father's gift of magic. Even when very young, she could manage spells, and she hungered for everything her father could teach her. Which he did, of course, relishing every moment they spent together.

"Unfortunately, the royal family was not a handsome one, and in those traits the child took after her late mother. As she came of age, the daughter grew more and more temperamental over her appearance. At first, she contented herself with pretty clothing, cosmetics, and on important occasions, spells of illusion. Finally she came to her father and begged him to change her, to make her truly beautiful forever."

Tingles trickled down Fawn's spine. She had never heard such melancholy as that in the Flower Queen's voice.

"The sorcerer, who was called Nightlark, warned her against such a spell, but she insisted. He gave in, and searched through his lore until he found in an ancient volume a spell that would accomplish what she wished. It was a Binding of Blood, a rite that can only be performed by a supreme mage on one of his own kin, one who is also gifted in channeling magic."

Fawn gazed at the witch, eyes widening.

"Yes. I see that you understand. With my father's magic, I became so beautiful that none could resist me. Not the crown prince, who married me. Not my father. Not the warriors of neighboring kingdoms. My beauty goes so far beyond the pale of what is natural that no human being has a defense against it. We all have the impulse to revere that which is lovely. Those who view me are slave to it."

"If you could have had any servants you wanted, why did you choose the Iron Claw?" Fawn asked.

"Don't be absurd. I did not choose them. They were drawn by my beauty just as the others were. My father's spell does not force people to obey me. No. Instead, they try to possess me, like a fine jewel. Eventually, the entire kingdom fought over me. My husband was killed, and in the end the Iron Claw attacked from the hills and conquered the land. They sequestered me in my palace, and destroyed anything they thought could be a threat to me. Don't imagine that the horror they commit is at my bidding."

"Can't you stop them, if they revere you so much?"

"No. They treasure me, but they do not obey, except in trivial ways. If they truly cared for my wishes, they would help me find a way to die."

The thought of the Flower Queen lying dead sent chills racing into Fawn's empty trigger hand. What had been a goal mere minutes earlier now struck her as an affront to all that was good in the world.

"Why wish to die?" asked Fawn. "Surely you can escape? What about your father?"

Skymist sat on the bed and picked threads from the coverlet. "It is not so simple. Have you not seen the desert that has sprung up outside these walls? My entire kingdom is that way now—degenerate, foul, *ugly*. That is the price of the spell. Magic can create illusions, but not true beauty. That has to come from a source. In my case, I steal it from everything around me. My room, my companions, the land itself . . ."

"Then . . . why not cancel the spell?"

"Only my father could do that. But he was unable to do so. He is as much a victim of the sorcery as any man. He cannot bear to destroy such beauty, not even to save his own daughter. While he was within my presence, it was all he could do to avoid killing himself, simply because he knew what a threat he represented to me."

"You speak of him as if he still lives. If so, then . . ."

Fawn's words caught in her throat.

"He lives," the queen said. "I am sure of that. Before the Iron Claw seized the kingdom, Nightlark found the strength to leave. He left when he saw what his necromancy had done to his granddaughter, the babe I bore to my poor, doomed prince." Skymist hugged herself, voice growing hoarse. "She was beautiful—in the way that all newborns are. But in my presence, all that fairness was drawn away, to increase my perfection. Before she was old enough to crawl, she had become gnarled and withered. Nightlark stole her away, he took a different name for himself and her, and he hid himself far from me, outside the influence of the spell."

Fawn was shaking her head, trying to deal with the meaning of the words she was hearing.

"Why have you come here?" the girl asked softly.

"Not by choice. The only thing that gave me joy these

past thirteen years was knowing that you were safe, far from me. But the Iron Claw discovered that Summerleaf is Nightlark, and they know he is the one means of my destruction. So they came to destroy him. They brought me along, even though it increased the danger, only because they cannot bear to be away from the sight of me for long."

Fawn forced herself to her feet, but could hardly stand. Her knees swayed, as flimsy as a puppet's. "He never told me. I knew nothing of you. On one occasion the marquis joked that he and I must be blood relatives, but even then, he denied it."

"Would it have been merciful to tell you? He knew from the moment he hid you away that you would one day have to kill me."

Fawn blinked. "But . . ."

"A Binding of Blood can only be broken by the closest kin of the object of the sorcery. And only by death. Nightlark knew he could not wield the blow. He hoped that you would be able to do what he could not."

"I can't kill you," the girl said. "I tried, when you were asleep. And now that I know you're my mother . . ."

"You must. If anyone else does it, I would die, but the spell would continue. My corpse would grow ever more gorgeous, while the land would become ever more sere and brutal. Neither my father nor I knew of this consequence when the rite was invoked, but we know it now. You *must* do it."

"But how? I've already tried."

"I'm sure my father never intended for you to face this challenge at so young an age. He would not have come after me until you were fully grown, and could channel his magic completely. The Iron Claw forced him to play his hand early. I'm afraid he did not realize how powerful the spell has grown. When it was first cast, it took me a full season to drain the beauty from a hundred paces of land. But all is not lost. I think you can succeed, if I add my strength to the attempt."

Fawn swallowed hard, remembering the morbid comments earlier. "You would truly help kill yourself?"

The Flower Queen sighed. "If I had had only myself to think of, I would have done so long since. This is not life I possess. What does it matter that I am beautiful, when everything around me is made ugly by my presence? A few more years of this, and I will fling myself off a high parapet, even though that would doom the world. Kill me, Fawn. I beg you. Do it now!"

Skymist held out the crossbow. Fawn nearly dropped it. Her palms, slick with perspiration, glided over the polished wooden stock. A finger brushed the trigger guard; she shivered.

"Open your heart and mind, feel the light that binds the world."

The ritual words calmed Fawn, turning her from a frightened child into a sorcerer's apprentice—if a nervous one. She created an empty space within herself. . . .

And from the woods, Summerleaf's energies found her and gave her strength. The Flower Queen placed herself directly in front of her assassin and closed her eyes. Fawn staggered as a torrent of power joined that coming from her grandfather.

"Now," Skymist whispered.

Fawn's arms shook, but raised the weapon. Her finger somehow found the trigger. But squeeze it she could not. "I . . . I . . ."

"Don't speak. Don't look. Just *remember*," whispered her mother.

Memories came. Memories that Fawn kept in the back of her consciousness, in a cavern deep beneath a snow-capped mountain.

—At seven years of age, Stonehand, the boy she admired more than any playmate in the children's yard of the castle, declared that he would have nothing more to do with her, merely because she was ugly. A promise he kept.

—At ten, taking shelter in a stable to get out of the fury of a blizzard, the farmer within nearly killed her with a pitchfork, thinking that someone who looked as she did must be a snow demon come to steal his livestock again.

—At thirteen, a handsome sixteen-year-old took her to a secluded glade, luring her with smooth words and what seemed to her to be sincere desire. He talked her out of her clothing, and when she was naked, he stole the garments, shouted for ten of his friends to come out of hiding, and they laughed until she ran away.

What had beauty ever done for her? The tiniest tendril of willpower leaked around the waves of magic buffeting her, just enough to make her finger twitch.

The bolt slammed from the crossbow. The vibration nearly rattled the weapon from Fawn's grip. She opened her eyes.

Skymist stood, with the end of the bolt protruding from her chest, clenching her teeth in agony. She sank slowly to her knees.

Fawn burst into tears. She knelt beside the woman, reaching out as if to pull out the missile and undo what she had done.

"My lady?!" called a guard from the other side of the door. The sound of the crossbow had been sharp.

"It . . . is nothing," the Flower Queen called. "A dropped goblet." She coughed, spotting her lips with blood.

The sentry did not open the door. Skymist caught her daughter's hand, and held it away from the bolt. With her other hand, she wiped away one of the girl's tears.

"Thank you," she said. Her eyes closed. She slumped to the carpet and was still. A dark stain spread beneath her.

Fawn remained at her mother's side until no more tears would come. Finally, goaded by the tendrils of magic coming from the Foxwood, she left the crossbow on the floor and, stumbling like a drunkard, escaped the castle the same way she had come.

In the morning, Eaglecry's army assembled on either side of the road leading from the castle, with the green flag of safe passage held high by the standard bearer, where all in the castle could see it.

Within the hour, the soldiers of the Iron Claw marched out. Their grotesque armor, as evil in appearance as ever, seemed to absorb and banish any sunlight that struck it, but the bodies within the greaves, hauberks, and black leather vests no longer hunched in twisted, deformed poses. At the head of the column rode a handsome, lean man with a faint dusting of gray amid his dark, rich hair. Gone were the horns, the filed teeth, the folds of decaying flesh.

The glittering within the eyes of the mercenaries proved that the blight on their souls had yet to disappear, but they rode firmly, like sane men. Their weapons remained tied to their saddles or undrawn at their belts. They passed without incident through the gantlet of observers and turned toward the south.

Already, green sprouts and tiny flowers were appearing at the base of the castle walls, their growth accelerated by the rebound from the release of the spell upon the Flower Queen. The trees that had not been utterly killed were straightening, their leaves and needles flushed with the vivid green of life. Workers, noses covered with moistened cloths, were spading dirt into the open graves

As the enemy soldiers receded down the road, Fawn and her grandfather carried a seedling they had found in the woods out into the zone where the trees had been destroyed beyond hope of recovery.

Summerleaf wielded the spade. Fawn set the little tree in the hole, tamped down the rich, sweet loam, and sprinkled the planting with water from her goatskin bag.

Fawn looked up at the old wizard and smiled. The sun's rays played over his face, showing her, for the tenth time that morning, the gentle, soft lines in his brows, around his eyes, and down his cheeks. Summerleaf was weather-beaten and old, but his countenance pleased the eye.

He gazed back gently, not ready yet to smile, but free of the melancholy she had always associated with him. Reaching within his pocket, he pulled out a small, oak-framed mirror.

Automatically she cringed. But as she glimpsed the image in the silvered glass, her eyes widened.

"It's only just happened within the past few minutes. You were the closest to her in the early days of the spell. You are the last to be freed of it."

Fawn saw the face of a girl at the cusp of womanhood. Others might have called the chin weak, the brown hair plain and too curly, but none would have labeled her unattractive. And compared to what she had seen in mirrors and pools throughout her childhood, she would have held herself up in pride next to the most gorgeous of princesses.

"You look much like your mother did, at your age," Summerleaf said. He sighed, shoulders sagging with the relief of a lifetime, and limped into the forest, looking for another seedling to repair the scars his sorcery had left upon the world.

TO HAVE AND TO HOLD
by Linda Gordon

What's in a name? To me, "To have and to hold" will always be the title of a historical novel laid in the seventeenth century (if memory serves me) and really more of a romance than a historical. I, yes, even I, used to read romances when I was eleven years old.

But here and now, it's the title of a good and amusing fantasy by an old friend, Linda Gordon, which like all her stories, is not quite what you'd expect. She works with her husband as a team truck driver in the hopes that some day they'll have a house in which she can devote a whole room to her writing and her "dragons and unicorns and all those characters floating about." She says she's "older than she was this time last year"—well, aren't we all? After all it's the common lot; but I've determined that I'm not getting older—I'm getting *better*. Age improves wine and violins, so why not women?

S aulsanna wanted to rip the man's heart from his chest and feed it to him while it was still hot.

Instead, she eyed the tied-up child that Raven had placed on the ground near the horses.

Saulsanna's gaze shifted to the haughty looking man, and she quietly took a deep breath.

"It is simple." Raven handed her a clay-red earthen

jar decorated with magic symbols, its lid the likeness of some obscure demon. "I want the power known only to a few. I want the magic the winds can give me." He paused, smiled, and nodded toward the jar Saulsanna held. "You put the winds in there, and I will free her." He gestured toward the girl.

Saulsanna's gaze narrowed briefly, then she regained control of herself. "If Aulsa has been harmed—"

"Your windling is fine."

Saulsanna tensed at his use of the word 'windling.' Aulsa was her child, her daughter.

"She has not been touched. Do you think me daft?"

Saulsanna's brow furrowed in consideration. "Yes, you should know enough not to cause pain to my daughter."

Raven nodded matter-of-factly.

"And you did bring the proper earthen jar." After all that had thus far occurred, Saulsanna felt a smile threaten. If the man only knew that any earthern jar would do—

She quelled a sudden chuckle. And the runes and demon's head, naught save useless decoration! Where do they get such? "No doubt the tales are still about."

He nodded again. "There are still some who know how to trap the wonders and the powers of the winds."

"Yes." It was good the rumors of how to contain the winds were still about, for they kept man busy. She looked at Raven. No matter how intruding and inconvenient man was. "But the winds are their own mistresses and seek freedom at the slightest chance offered."

"Be done with it. I have waited too long to waste time speaking of such things."

Saulsanna nodded. "It is as you bid."

First she acknowledged the four corners of the world and sky, then turned to the Northern Wind.

"Oh, Mother Northern, hear me. I seek a share of your strength, a portion of your magic, for this man who . . ."

Her voice trailed off until it became a mere whisper.

After several moments, Raven started forward to listen, but the suddenly gusting wind stopped him.

Saulsanna held the open jar toward the sky.

The sky changed from blue to purple with shades of

darkness dancing throughout. The wind whipped through the trees, reeled along the ground, then died down.

The wind stirred again, whirling and snaking about, until it formed into a small dust demon.

The dust demon twirled around Saulsanna while she spoke to it under her breath. Then it finally danced above the opening of the jar she held upward.

All at once, the dust demon entered the jar, whistling as it did so.

Raven stood transfixed, amazement on his face, an excited gleam in his eyes.

Saulsanna repeated the process three times more until she had spoken to the four winds and had raised three more dust demons. Then she replaced the demon's head lid on the jar.

Her gaze shifted to the man while she lowered her arms. "My daughter."

Suddenly suspicious, Raven looked at her. His gaze darted from jar to Saulsanna back to jar. "To fail now—" He halted and looked at her. "Tell me, windwitch, how do I know the powers are in there?"

Saulsanna shook the jar. A faint sloshing sound could be heard from the sand that had accumulated within.

Raven smiled. "I had heard there would be a scratching sound as if the winds were trying to escape." He grabbed for the jar.

Saulsanna held it out of reach. "My daughter."

Raven studied her briefly then turned to the child. "Yes, yes. Very well, witch." He held up a finger. "But do not trick me."

"You know a windwitch must do as bidden when trapped."

He grunted, a faint smile at the corners of his mouth, then went and untied the child.

The little girl got to her feet and ran to her mother.

Saulsanna quickly scooped Aulsa up. "Are you well, my little wisp?"

"Yes, mother."

"Good." Saulsanna tossed the jar to Raven who gingerly caught it. "Let us take our leave of this man's presence."

She carried Aulsa to her horse and set the child astride the winged stallion.

"It is all here." Raven shook the jar. "All the magic and power I want. All the kingdoms I will rule." He shook the jar again. "Everything."

Saulsanna nodded. "It is as you bid." She swung up on the horse, landing lightly behind Aulsa.

Suddenly, a puzzled expression crossed over Raven's countenance. "How do I get the winds out, witch?"

Saulsanna gathered the reins in one hand, and wrapped a protective arm around Aulsa. "Merely open the jar, man."

Raven's expression swirled into a whirlwind of emotions, finally settling into realization. "But should I do that, the winds will vanish into the air!"

Saulsanna laughed, a tinkling sound to her voice. "You demanded I put the winds into your jar. You said naught about getting them out."

Suddenly enraged, Raven almost threw the jar, then stopped himself. He screamed. "Nooooo!"

Saulsanna urged the winged stallion to move.

Huge blue-black wings flapped, and the horse gently rose.

As always, Aulsa's stomach felt tickled at the surge of power upon flight, and she giggled.

While they glided off into the distance, Saulsanna sang to her daughter in the language of the windwitches.

Furious, Raven paid no heed to the tinkling, wind chime sound of Saulsanna's voice as it faded in the distance.

THE CATALYST
by Lee Ann Martins

This was one of the stories of which, when I was assembling manuscripts to keep for this anthology instead of those to be returned, I found myself remembering every detail. This is a first story; but Lee Ann sent me the shortest biography on record when I bought this; she says she has "a beautiful Arabian gelding which accidentally gave me a concussion the very day my story was accepted and the two events are now irrevocably fused in my memory; as if one had something to do with the other." Since this isn't very informative, you are free to imagine that she writes Westerns for a recreation from her vocation as a dental hygienist; or that she's a teacher of Arabic in a girl's boarding school, or that she writes mysteries and Westerns under eight pseudonyms—or for that matter, that she's a plumber.

Valendral presented a wrapped package to the Priest of Azlae at the High Temple. "From Jakara Amohl," she told him.

"Yes, we have been expecting this."

As he accepted the package, Valendral looked into his face, and just for a moment felt an old yearning left over from years ago, when she had truly believed that we are all one in the eyes of Azlae the Maker. She wondered what this priest would do if she were to take his hand and ask for his blessing, or comfort, or at least a mug of hot wine. But she could see that his eyes were turned inward, self-absorbed and anxious. They were pale blue, a shade which always reminded her of pebbles and ice. Those eyes hardly saw her at all. His nose, however, expressed distaste. One did not take many baths in the middle of winter with no heat, and she knew the smell of her unwashed body must be overwhelming his nostrils just as surely as his own scent of heady incense invaded her sense of smell. She knew better than to touch him.

"About the payment. . . ?" Val ventured.

"Yes, of course," the priest said, his tone suggesting impudence on her part for mentioning it. He handed her a leather purse and huffed impatiently in the cold air while she counted the money.

"But this is only half!"

"It's the amount I was instructed to give."

"It should be double this!" Then, desperately, she cried, "My brother will kill me!"

"Nonsense, I'm sure it's for the agreed amount. If your brother has any questions about the payment, he can inquire at the Temple himself. A joyous Renewal to you." He shut the door in her face.

She could have wept. She could have killed him. She would now have to go to her brother and surely catch a beating for this day's work. Two probably, one for failing to bring back enough money, and another to make up for the one her brother would catch when he reported this to Jakara. A joyous Renewal, indeed.

Val turned for home, hugging herself against the wind. It was one of those bitter, vicious winds that come on the worst evenings of winter, cutting to the bone and making the head ache. She wore several layers of clothing, but they were threadbare and felt about as useless as cobwebs against it.

The streets of the Holy City of Beru were filled with pilgrims, here for the winter solstice Festival of Renewal. Soon His Most Holy Majesty, Elward med Azlae, who was both king and the manifestation of Azlae on earth, would preside over the sacred marriage of the God and His creation, and the young women chosen for their purity and faith to be his brides would be sent to meet their Maker. In this holy union the earth would be renewed. So strong and devout were they that they were unafraid to go to their deaths. Of course, the drugs Val had just delivered to the Temple helped; not that the bride's faith was held in doubt, it was merely wise to cover every contingency.

When she ducked into the unexpectedly open doorway, her first thought was only to stand inside the entry for a while to get out of the wind. But once inside, it occurred to her that only the rich lived in this neighborhood. Perhaps she could steal enough to make up for the lost money. It would serve the fool who lived here right for not closing and locking his door.

She crept warily into the house, listening intently for signs of life. It seemed empty. "All right," she said, "get this done fast and get out. Money will most likely be on the second floor, where the bedrooms are." She quickly found a staircase and climbed up, sticking close to the wall where the stairs would be less likely to creak.

The first door she tried opened into a large bedroom, with a wardrobe on the far side so enormous it nearly spanned the entire wall. She scuttled over and opened one of its panels; it was stuffed with clothes. She began rapidly fishing through pockets—and froze. Had that been a footstep? Val waited, counting heartbeats, a wash of sweat breaking out on her body . . . nothing. She had just decided that it had been her imagination when the door handle began to turn.

In a panic she crowded herself into the wardrobe and pulled the panel behind her, leaving a crack open to see by. The newcomer was out of her line of sight, but from the rustle of fabric Val guessed that he or she was undressing. She grit her teeth. Bloody lousy time to take a bath! Then the person stepped in front of her vision—naked—and she saw that this creature possessed all the body parts of a man, and also those of a woman.

A necromancer.

Her heart surged in terror.

Born with sorcerous power and grotesque bodies cursed by the Maker, necromancers were every nightmare, every childhood monster, everything blasphemous and evil made flesh. Far worse than the priests nebulous tales of demons, for this was evil with human dimensions, evil that could touch and be touched and take you by the throat.

For the first time in years she prayed fervently, and feared she might actually be battered to death by her own laboring heart. The prayers failed her. The wardrobe door opened, she looked full in the necromancer's face for an instant, then bolted like a deer flushed from its cover.

It was over in a few seconds. The bedroom door slammed shut by itself before Val could escape. In blind panic she veered for the window, for even a broken leg was better than letting this thing have her. It was only a drop of one story; she might get away with it. She swung the windows open, breaking the latch, felt a blast of frigid air, and jumped. She glimpsed an empty alley as she fell, and then knew nothing but pain as her right leg seemed to shatter like an icicle against stone.

Finally, darkness.

She dreamed of fire, and of tremendous heat in her legs; heat so intense it should have hurt, but did not. Gentle hands were touching her, cleaning and healing her. Most of the heat was generated by the hands. She fancied that they loved her. When they went away, she tried to cry out and clutch them. But it was only a dream and she sank back into darkness.

Val returned to herself warm and clean and without pain. She could hear the rapid snapping of a fire, and smell cooking. Someone was moving about the room, instinct told her it was the necromancer. She kept her eyes closed, trying to buy time, wanting the dream back. Please, just let me rest a while. I don't want to face this thing yet, thank you very much.

"You can open your eyes now, I know you're conscious." The voice was polite, unobtrusive.

She opened her eyes cautiously and looked around. She was in a large, soft bed piled with quilts. There was a bowl of some kind of stew on a small table by the bed, apparently meant for her. She was hungry, but thought better of eating it; there was no telling what might be in it. The necromancer itself (clothed, thank Azlae!) dragged a deep leatherbound armchair beside her, and settled down. "You," it said pleasantly, "are not a very good thief."

Despite her earlier fear, Valendral was not by nature a timid girl. She stared at the creature, her eyes traveling slowly down its body and back to its face, more fascinated and less repulsed than she should have been, and surprised to see that though its eyes returned her gaze steadily, it was blushing. It had one of those curious kinds of faces that could look good on either a man or a woman, with pale skin in sharp contrast to its very dark hair and eyes. Its body, too, except for the full breasts, was androgynous. So this was the great monster. Her courage rose.

"I'm not quite what you expected, am I?"

She ignored the question for one of her own. "What do you want with me?"

"I could ask you the same thing. Why were you trying to rob me? Are you starving? You don't look it, and if you were you'd be eating." It gestured at the stew.

"I'm not hungry," she said, just as her stomach rumbled audibly.

"It's perfectly good food. I don't eat worms, you know. And why would I trouble to heal your leg if I were going to poison you an hour later?"

There was logic in that. Besides, it would not be sensible to make this creature angry. Her mind told her this, but her tongue knew nothing of sense. "You're an evil thing, can you blame me for not trusting you?"

Moving so quickly it startled her, the necromancer snatched the stew and began eating, as if to prove that there was nothing wrong with it. After gobbling several bites, it thumped the bowl back on the table, spilling some, and turned on her with eyes full of contempt. "I'm evil," it said furiously. "And who taught you that, the priests of the Maker? Do you know how they get *their* power? In human sacrifice, something not even barbarians do any more! There is great energy released in the taking of a life, you see. The priesthood uses that energy to increase their own power, all in the name of the

Maker, of course. And that jackal of a king justifies it by proclaiming it is his, and therefore Azlae's will." It shook its head. "And they call me the evil one. At least my powers are natural, at least my kind doesn't resort to mass murder!"

Even now, Val could not leave well enough alone. "So you say," she retorted.

"Let's change the subject," the necromancer said wearily, "I can't discuss it with you, you're brainwashed like everyone in this city. I still want to know why you're so desperate for my money."

She sighed, "It's a long story."

"We have plenty of time, since you can't leave until I let you." It made a rather bad attempt at an evil leer and leaned toward her. "You tell me yours and I'll tell you mine."

She leapt out of the bed, more annoyed than disgusted, and found she was not wearing her old clothes but was dressed in a new robe too long for her. She stumbled over the hem, caught herself on a bedpost, and glared at the necromancer. That thing had stripped her, seen her naked! She struggled to control her temper, reminding herself that she did, after all, had a reason to be grateful to this creature, and perhaps a reason to fear it as well, though that possibility was getting difficult to believe.

"Well, basically it's this: I owe my brother some money, and I only have about half. That's all you need to know."

"And you're obviously afraid of going back to him without the right amount," the necromancer supplied, looking at her thoughtfully.

"So what's your story?" Val asked, not wanting to talk about her brother. "How did a necromancer get past the Guardians into Beru?" The ban against magic in His Holy Majesty's lands was rigidly enforced, especially in Beru. There were priests whose sole function was to guard the city from any sign of magic not associated with the cult of Azlae.

"Simple," it said, "I never had to get past the Guardians, I was born here. My mother was not so religious that she wanted to see her child put to death. I was hidden in this house. I grew up here, played here, studied here, learned my craft here, I've never set foot outside this house.

"I have, being very careful, managed to communicate with other necromancers and sorcerers every now and then; not often enough for me, but the priesthood doesn't hold all the power there is in the world by any means."

She felt an unexpected pang of sympathy for it; a lonely life this must have been. "Where's your mother now?"

"That," it said shortly, "is all you need to know, except that my name is Petyr. You have a name?"

"Valendral."

"Valendral. That means 'Maker blessed.' See all the foolish information you acquire when you have nothing to do but learn? So, Val, how much money do you need?"

She told it.

"Wait a moment." The necromancer went to the wardrobe and rummaged around, almost hidden from view as it reached far back for something. "It sure keeps a lot of clothes for someone who doesn't get out much," Val thought. She considered bolting for the door while its back was turned, but decided against it. If it could heal a broken leg in an hour, it could certainly keep her in this room as long as it wished. She was no longer afraid of it, anyway. Whatever the reputation of necromancers, this being hardly radiated supernatural malevolence. The aloof priest had been more intimidating. Besides, if it were going to hurt her, it would have done so earlier, when she had made it angry.

Petyr returned from the wardrobe. I have here one hundred and seventy five dulmecs, enough for your brother with some left over for you. Now, wait a minute!" It snatched the purse away from her reaching hand. "It occurred to me that you are the only person in Beru who knows of my existence. You could easily have me put to death. It may not be wise for me ever to let you leave here. However, I'm prepared to make a deal with you. I will give you your freedom, plus the money, and in return you can do something for me."

A wave of fear and anger passed over her. She had

badly misjudged the necromancer and the danger it represented. She had also been a fool for beginning to like the damned creature and for thinking she could get out of this without a price.

"It depends," she said carefully. "What would I have to do?"

"Do you know what a catalyst is? No," it answered for her, "of course you don't. How could you? Well, if a necromancer is a person who can wield magic, a catalyst is a person who *is* magic. A catalyst is a source of power, a conductor for magical energy. They have no ability to cast spells for themselves, but if I, for instance, were to work in union with a catalyst, my power would increase tenfold. Such people are extremely rare. Outside the city walls there are hundreds, thousands of my kind. But catalysts are worth their weight in diamonds. And you, I discovered when I touched you, are a powerful catalyst.

She almost laughed. "Worth my weight in diamonds." Pigshit. "If that's true, how come the priesthood never came after me?"

"Because they use blood magic, not natural magic. They never heard of catalysts."

"All you want to do is cast some kind of spell with me, and I can go?"

"That's all."

"What sort of spell are you planning?"

"That's neither here nor there. Don't quibble with me, your choice is simple. Either help me and go free or refuse and never leave."

"Damned wonderful choice you give me."

"How much is your life worth to you?"

Val stiffened, trying to control her anger. "Tell me what you want."

"I have to tap into your power . . . we have to forge a bond . . . we . . . we must . . . couple," Petyr managed at last.

Now she did burst out laughing, as much at the prim word it chose as anything else. "All that talk just to get laid? You travel a long way for a screw, don't you?"

"Perhaps I would," it said with pained dignity. "That, however, is not the issue."

"There must be some other way to do this."

"If there were, do you really think I'd waste time trying to talk you into this? Come, choose. Even I couldn't be the worst you've ever had."

She ignored the implied insult, and considered her choices. She had none. The Maker knew she had done worse things to get out of bad situations. And, in truth, she did not find him ("I better think of it as a him if I'm going to play a woman to his man") repulsive. He was rather like some exotic, undiscovered creature that might be strange, even shocking to see at first, but not unbeautiful. Not the worst she'd ever had at all. This would be considered a sacrilege, but then again, she had never been very devout. She went to him, reaching up to gently touch his breast—and pulled her hand away as if it burned as a new thought came to her.

"You're doing this to me, making me want you."

"Don't blame me if you feel desire. I would never abuse my power that way, I have morals."

"Liar."

"You can always change your mind."

"And be killed for it. Some morals you have."

Petyr exploded. "Damn you, forget it, then! Leave, go, I never saw you!" The door opened by itself at his gesture, and he looked at her dubious expression. "It's no trick. I won't hurt you or try to stop you. Take the money, even. Just get out."

Valendral hesitated in the doorway, deliberating with herself. Although she cursed herself soundly for being a fool, she could not quite bring herself to leave. She turned back to him and touched his arm.

"Look, I owe you for my leg, I'll help you. But only if you can promise me that I'm not running any risk."

"Don't worry, you'll be in no danger," he smiled happily at her.

She took a deep breath. "All right, then, let's get—"

"Wait, I must prepare the spell."

Petyr turned to the fireplace. Kneeling and spreading his hands, he began to chant something too low for Val to catch. He seemed to be talking to the flames, cajoling and seducing them. A tongue of fire suddenly leapt between his hands, and he continued murmuring until the flame had become a burning globe. He then thrust his hands forward in a gesture of throwing away, the globe shot up the chimney flue. He looked at Val. "All right," he said softly, "now I need you."

But he didn't move. Looked like it would be up to her to start things. She went to him and put her arms around his neck. He felt oddly stiff, as if he were carved from wood. It took her no more than a moment to realize why. It should have been obvious, he had never done this before, he was petrified. She pulled him close to her. "Oh, my child, let me show you something."

He surprised her. Once they began, desire quickly replaced his fear. He discovered every part of her with an eagerness and something almost like reverence she could scarcely believe. He seemed to have forgotten the mercenary purpose of their lovemaking. She found her own passion matched his, and gave as good as she got, which surprised her even more. She had thought her body was long past truly feeling anything. *This can't be real, it's sorcery. He's manipulating me.* By the time he entered her, and she felt a lash of power—and, of all things, love—she was beyond caring. She had no past, and no future. There was nothing but his body, and hers, and this never ending moment.

Petyr was digging busily in his infinite wardrobe. He pulled out a traveling pack and began stuffing it with winter clothing. Val rolled over in bed to watch him. "Going somewhere?"

"There's not much time," he said for an answer without turning around.

"Excuse me, time for what?"

"Valendral, I'm sorry. I lied about the danger we'd be in."

Her stomach tightened in apprehension. "What did you do?"

"The High Temple of Azlae is burning."

She sat in stunned disbelief. "Are you crazy, why?"

"As a diversion mostly, although I wouldn't cry to see a few priests go down with it. I want to escape the city while the Guardians' attention is elsewhere, I'm tired to death of living like this, and when I found you I couldn't let the opportunity pass. But we must leave quickly, they will soon turn their minds onto what caused the blaze. Here, wear this." He threw some clothes at her along with a heavy, fur-lined cloak.

"What do you mean 'we'? I thought they didn't know about catalysts."

"Normally they don't, but that spell used a great deal of power, with you as the source. They can trace it to you as well as me. We must both leave."

"You idiot, no one crosses the Priesthood! We'd never make it out alive!"

"We can with your power and my ability to wield it."

Val was trembling with rage and fear. "You'll get nothing from me. Not after I trusted you."

Petyr drew himself up, as if bracing himself. "We are bonded. Forever. I have your power whether you give it or not."

At this last betrayal, her mind went red. She flew at him, ready to kill him with her bare hands. He tried to defend himself and calm her down, but not very successfully; he knew nothing of fighting. He finally resorted to magic to hold her off, his nose and lip bleeding and one side of his face beginning to swell.

"Listen to me," he pleaded. "Is what I offer so bad? Look at yourself! How old are you, seventeen? You look ten years older than you are and in another ten years you'd probably be dead. I offer you a chance for something better. You need to escape as much as I do."

"Don't talk to me about offering," she snarled. "You left me no choice."

"Please, can we fight about this later? They'll be looking for us."

Abruptly, Val stopped struggling against the magical barrier he had placed between them. She turned away, filled with as much loathing as she only a little while ago had been with love, and pulled on her clothes. "Get me some weapons," she demanded.

Without a word, he brought her an assortment of blades. The one sword was only an ornamental piece, which was just as well, she had never used a sword in her life. There were, however, several useful looking daggers, and she was a wicked hand with these. She belted them on under the cloak.

"Valendral—"

She jerked away from his touch. "Petyr, I'd cut your throat myself if I didn't need you to get me out of this. Remember that."

"I'll keep that in mind," he said dryly, hoisting the pack to his shoulders. "I think we should make for Farmer's Gate. The marketplace will be deserted this time of night. Does that sound good to you?"

"Good enough."

"You'll have to lead. You know the city better."

Val made a sound of disgust and headed outside. On the street she could see the flames at the Temple a half mile away. Petyr certainly had made a good job of it. She led them toward the marketplace, wading through dense crowds of people rushing for the fire, expecting Guardians to be waiting in ambush at every turn. They were lucky. She led them on a twisting path, bringing them to the marketplace in half an hour without being accosted or even noticed.

"That wasn't so bad," she said, "now all we have to do is take out the soldiers at the gate and—"

She did not see the horse that sent her flying until it was on top of her. She knew who the riders were. Only Guardians could cloak their presence so well. Dazed and shaken, she picked herself up. There were three of them, at the moment all intent on Petyr, howling curses and striking with all their blood bought power. Even from where she was, she could see the panic on his face. He was adept at striking from a distance, but when confronted with actual violence he seemed at a loss. They were overwhelming him. She launched herself at the nearest Guardian, taking him by surprise. The last thing they expected in this battle of magic was a mundane attack with an ordinary dagger. She stabbed, dragged him off the horse and buried the blade in his throat. One down.

A sudden wave of heat coursed through her body, followed quickly by a cooling sensation. She was reminded incongruously of a cool breeze on a sweltering summer day. Then heat again. It was Petyr, drawing on her

strength to attack the second rider. What looked like
lightning flew from his fingers. Quite impressive, really,
but she had no time to admire it—the third Guardian
was bearing down on her. She threw a dagger, not aiming
at the rider, who was ready for it, but at his horse. The
animal took the blade in its chest and crashed screaming
to the ground. The Guardian arose unhurt, still coming
after her, preparing to strike. Everything turned to noise
and fear in the darkness, and muscles too sluggish to get
away, and cobblestones slippery with blood. A searing
pain shot through her spine. She screamed for Petyr.
Perhaps he answered. There was a flash of white light,
then, except for the sound of Petyr's voice beside her,
blessed silence.

"Val, are you all right?" He helped her to rise, "I
thought—"

"Tell me later," she interrupted. "We're not free yet."
She straightened up and checked herself for damages.
She was badly bruised, but not broken. She could go a
distance yet. The Guardians and the downed horse were
ashes. Not bad, Petyr.

Val caught the two remaining horses before they could
bolt. "Get on," she told him, "we'll rush the gate. If you
can blow three Guardians to ashes, you can blow the
gate open."

"No."

"What?"

"I can't ride. If I should fall—"

"You idiot! Get on that horse! There'll be more coming any second. We can't outrun them on foot!" She
practically threw him into the saddle and pricked the
horse's rump with her last remaining dagger to send it
on its way, Petyr swaying precariously in the saddle. She
mounted her horse and galloped after them, her own seat
none too secure.

The Farmer's gate was at the end of the main thor-
oughfare of the marketplace, about a half mile away.
With half the distance to go, and the sounds of pursuit
behind them, Petyr began to gather his forces. Once
again, Val felt the alternating waves of heat and coolness
as he tapped into her fathomless wellspring of power.
She felt suddenly infinite. "I can encompass the world,"

she thought foolishly. She could see soldiers, already warned of their approach, waiting for them along the ramparts. They met the gate at a dead gallop; it was holding. She thought for a second that they would be trapped between the soldiers before and the Guardians behind, but she underestimated Petyr's ability, and her own power. When they were nearly on top of the gate, it not only opened, it burst into a thousand fragments, taking the soldiers with it. They never knew what hit them.

An hour later they slowed to a walk for the horses' sake. It would do them no good to run their transportation into the ground. Petyr did not venture to speak, and Val, in no mood for conversation, let him be. But the questions of pursuit and where they would go from here nagged at her. As the silence lengthened, she broke down.

"Do you think we lost them?"

Petyr looked up wearily. "I've been casting illusions and cloaking spells since we left Beru, I think we may have. I can't detect any trace. At least we have a long head start on them."

"Oh. So, any idea where we're going?"

"Let's head east, I want to get to Medilind."

"Medilind! That's almost a thousand miles away!"

"We'd be free citizens there."

"We'd be free in a lot of places, once we cross the border."

"But I always dreamed of seeing Medilind, Val! The greatest sorcerers and necromancers in the world are there!"

"Well, we don't have enough money to get there."

"Actually, we do."

"I heard they're all crazy in Medilind."

"You also heard that necromancers are the epitome of evil."

That had been true enough, she thought, but decided to let it go. She did not like having to talk to him.

"You were brave back there, Val. I'll never have half your courage."

"Don't try to flatter me," she snapped. "I haven't forgiven you."

"I've told you how sorry I am."

"So what?"

"Would you really have preferred the life you had? Do you really wish that you had never met me?"

She relented a little before the loneliness in his voice. "Look, Petyr, I'm angry enough to hate you. Maybe it won't last forever. Maybe I'll be your friend when I'm ready, but right now I can't be anything but angry."

"Fair enough," he said softly. "Val?"

She grit her teeth. "Yes?"

"A joyous Renewal to you."

He was maddening. Yet she had to make an effort to keep from smiling. "The same to you," she returned grudgingly.

"Thank you."

"You're welcome. Shut up."

And they rode eastward.

BREAKING WALLS
by Leslie Ann Miller

Leslie Ann Miller was one of the typists in my office, and one day she produced a manuscript: a perfect example of people who read something and say, in the words of a song from *Chorus Line,* "I can do that" and do it. She's another one who neglected to give us a biography. She probably thought that knowing her, I could improvise; she doesn't realize quite how absentminded I am. But you can make up something about her as well as I can; "you know my methods, Watson."

Anyhow, we know she has written another fine straightforward adventure story. I'm a sucker for these.

Rengar Castle, Winter, in the four hundred first year of our Kings.

Dear Father and Mother,

I know you are concerned about me, but I am doing well, and learning fast. We heard a speech today from one of the veterans of the Southern War. Lady Gunhild addressed the new recruits, and her speech has inspired us all. I hope that you may find it of interest, so I relate it here to the best of my memory. It is not too long a story, and the Castle is well supplied with parchment. My evenings are my own, so tonight I write. Lady Gunhild and her shield sisters joined the King's army at a training camp before the Southerners reached the Steppes, but her story is about the great Steppes battle:

"When I and my three shield sisters, Katriona, Treshen, and Elfwyn first made our way into Camp, the Captain made sure we understood one thing: if the command was given to charge, we would charge. If we were told to charge across the water, we would charge across the water. If we were told to charge a castle wall, we would charge the castle wall. If we were told to charge the enemy shield wall, we would charge the enemy shield wall. It was simple, he said, 'Put your head down behind your shield and run. And keep running. Keep going forward until you break through the other side . . . or you are killed. Simple.' "

Pray forgive me for interrupting here, dear parents, but I should mention that at this point we recruits laughed nervously. This is exactly what WE heard when we first came to the castle. Anyway, Lady Gunhild smiled at us for a moment, then continued:

"Simple," she said. "Or is it? If it were so simple, then why did the charge at the Outlands bridge fail at the beginning of the war? The command had been given, the knights had led the charge, but no one broke through. The knights had been killed, the charge had failed, and the Southerners had won the bridge. Only the winter ice had stopped them from marching all the way to the King's City. What had happened? Did the charge not have the strength to break the Southern wall? We did not know. But as I and my three sisters sat around the campfire on the eve of the great battle, it preyed heavily upon our minds.

"I, Gunhild, as you can see, am built more like a man than a woman. I am tall and strong, and in my armor it was not likely that the Southerners would recognize my gender. But my sister Kat—you may have heard the name for she is now a knight in Her Majesty's Southern Guard—was nearly a foot shorter than myself, and Elfwyn was but a handsbreadth taller than she. Treshen, though taller than either of them, was thinner than myself, and looked a good deal more fragile.

"Now, you must understand, and please do not be offended, but the simple fact is that women are, in general, smaller than men. It is a physiological truth. And being smaller is a distinct disadvantage in battle. There are ways to overcome it, of course, in single combat. There are even some advantages. Elfwyn's sword, for example, was fondly knicknamed "kneebiter"—and for good reason. But in a shield wall, being short is downright dangerous.

"In close quarters it is easier for opponents to swing over your shield to split the top of your skull. At a distance, it is easier for spears and archers to shoot over your head to hit the ranks behind you. It also enables them to see more of what is going on behind you. But more importantly, if your opponent decides to charge, they will charge directly AT you, because you represent the weak point in the wall—you have less mass to stop their charge and they have a better chance to break through.

"Conversely, which was what we were thinking about that night: if we were given the order to charge, we would be trying to break through the Southerners' shield wall, most of whom were probably twice our height and weight. Or so rumor had it. And I, at least, was not sure we could do it. We did not want to be part of a charge as disastrous as the one at the Outlands bridge, and we most certainly did not want to be the cause of its failure.

"We each had our different reasons for being there on the eve of battle, just as you have your different reasons for being here. I was there because my King needed my sword. Kat and Elfwyn were there because they had nowhere else to go. Treshen was there because the Southerners had burned her home and killed her Lord and children. She prayed that night to take a Southern life for each of her loved ones killed. But more importantly, my friends, we spent that awful night together because we needed each other.

"And when dawn broke the next morn, we'd made our peace with our Gods. We picked up our shields and buckled on our armor and reported to our Captain, and on the field our ranks began to form. We were in the second rank, with a line of shields and spears in front. At first we could not see the Southerners—the Steppes were bathed in mist—but we could hear the clank of armor in the distance, and hear their voices chanting. It was a gruesome song they sang, and it was almost enough to quench the fire in the bravest heart among us.

"Then, as the sun rose higher, the mist began to clear, and there in front of us appeared the scarlet and gold war shields of our enemy—rank upon rank for as far as the eye could see—and their black burners whipped in the new breeze sounding like the wings of vultures close above. When I saw their vast numbers, my mouth went dry. I knew then that we were going to die.

"Our Captains shouted encouraging words to us, and we began to march forward even though our feet felt like lead and our minds filled with a numbness of disbelief. Someone in the front rank began to pound the back of their shield with their sword hilt, and soon the entire army was beating away in time to our steps. It drowned the sound of our enemy's chanting, and soon the tempo began to increase as our spirits rose. The Captains did nothing to try to slow our pace, and by the time the arrows started hissing overhead, we broke into a trot. Soon we were running full tilt, screaming at the top of our lungs like madmen. The first ranks crashed into the Southerners seconds later, and even as I charged forward to help push them through, I slammed into the back of one of our spearmen as he flew backward with an arrow through his neck. When I looked up again, the rank in front of me was disintegrating under a porcupine of spears and flailing swords. Through the screams of mortal agony and the din of battle I barely heard our captain shouting the command to retreat.

"I backed up slowly, careful to keep my shield in front of me to protect from thrown spears and arrows. And I tell you now, my friends, that I thought my heart would burst with joy when I realized that Elfwyn, Katriona, and Treshen retreated there by my side.

"We regrouped a hundred paces from the Southern wall. We could hear the sounds of battle down the line and knew that in places our forces still engaged their troops. Our eyes, however, were focused on the silent red shields across from us. Why did they not charge to take advantage of our retreat? We had been engaged less than a minute and our first rank was already lying dead in the grass at their feet. Apparently they were willing to let us dash ourselves to pieces on their wall, so much confidence did they have in its strength. It was not a comforting thought—my sisters and I were now in front.

" 'We have to break their wall,' our Captain told us. 'It's our only hope. The flanks are still fighting, but we must pierce through the center. If we can break through, we have a fighting chance to rout them.'

"Kat and I exchanged glances, and Elfwyn and Treshen did the same. This was it. It was our chance to prove ourselves . . . or . . . die . . . or both.

"The Captain gave us a moment to prepare our courage, then gave the command.

"Without hesitation we surged forward, shouting the King's name. I did not look to see where I was heading. My head was well tucked behind my shield, and I held my sword crosswise above my helm to protect from swords and maces swinging over the top. Kat to my right and Elfwyn to my left, I knew, would have the same stance as our feet pumped forward, our shields side by side.

"We hit with a force that knocked the breath out of my lungs and lifted me off my feet. The spearman behind me rammed into my back, keeping me from falling backward. My sword was pounded into my helmet by an enemy's mace and something stung my exposed shins. In desperation and terror I put my shoulder into my shield and pushed with all my might, swinging my sword wildly over the shield edge in front of me. It struck something hard, and suddenly there was less resistance to my shield.

"I shoved forward, and the red and gold was beside me. I swung to the right and felt my sword bite deep. Kat's green and white shield rushed forward as the red and gold fell back. I tripped over a body and stepped on something soft and then a spear point splintered through my shield, missing my nose by inches. Another shield pounded into my shoulders from behind, and the spear wrenched back, pulling me off my feet completely. I was saved from falling headlong in the grass by a flurry of spears hitting my shield. The combined force of their thrusts against my shield kept me upright, but another pierced the wood and jabbed my ribs. My chain turned the point, thankfully, and I spun away from the shaft as it pushed through and then pulled back again.

"My feet stopped churning as I twisted. I barely saw as Kat charged past, Treshen's shield planted firmly against her right shoulder and a press of shields and spears behind.

"As I hesitated, trying to get my balance, a halberd hooked the side of my shield and pulled the corner out, leaving me exposed to the second rank of red and gold in front. I had just enough time to see Kat, Elfwyn, and Treshen crash into it before the men behind me pushed forward again and drove me onto the spike of the halberd. I fell to my knees screaming in agony, even as Elfwyn slashed the knees of its owner in front. I was knocked flat as the charge pushed through from behind. I was trampled into the grass by my own troops' boots, but all I could think of, my friends, as I drifted into the darkness, was that we'd done it. We'd broken their wall! And I did not mind dying so much that day for I had two new friends with me there in the pain and darkness: hope and satisfaction.

"The rest, as you know, is history. We broke their ranks and the charge cut their army in half. Between our flanking cavalry and our shields piercing through their middle, they were thrown into panic and chaos and were routed entirely. They were unable to reform their shield wall, and our troops cut them to pieces until they tossed down their swords and ran away in terror.

"Treshen revenged her family three times over, then joined them in Death's Dungeon at the hands of a mounted knight wielding a morning star. Elfwyn lost her sword arm protecting Kat from a thrown ax. She is now the Queen's houndmaster. You may have seen her around the grounds. Katriona fought to the very end and led the charge that split the Southerners in two. She was knighted for her valor. And I, as you see, survived my wounds, and now help to train new recruits.

"There are two lessons I hope you learn from this story: one, that when the order is given to charge, you charge, and you follow through when a hole is made. Second, and more importantly, when it comes time to break through—or to stop an enemy's charge, it is not size that matters as much as determination.

"Each and every one of you, small though you may be, can knock a horse off its feet if you set your mind to it—and BELIEVE that you can do it. We will teach you the skills you need, but nothing will save you if you become intimidated by your opponent. You must believe in yourself as a warrior, and you must believe you can break through their wall if the order is given. I, and Kat, and Elfwyn are living proof that it can be done."

So you see, dear parents, I am determined. While I may be killed in my first battle, it is not necessarily the given you seem to fear. They train us well, and it is my goal to someday serve under Lady Kat in the Southern guard. I believe in myself, and pray that someday you may believe in me as well. Belief can break down walls.

THE ENCHANTED FROG
by Cynthia L. Ward

This is another story based on the old story "everybody knows" in several versions; about the fairy tale of the enchanted frog who is really a prince. Not too long ago I bought a mug which says "You have to kiss a lot of frogs before you find the prince." And I printed a story by Jennifer Roberson which ended with a princess kissing a frog and saying—disgustedly—something like "one hundred thirty-seven."

Cynthia Ward lives in Silicon Valley with her husband—also a computer person—and her Maine coon cats. My experience of Maine Coon cats is limited to an encounter with one owned by Madeleine L'Engle, which was the largest feline I had ever seen outside a cage at the zoo; they're about the size of a large dog. I understand they're very gentle, though. You can't prove it by me; I gave it a *very* wide berth.

Therese sat on a boulder with her cotton skirt spread about her, watching the summer-blue river slide past and remembering all the times she'd come here with her cousins, before her apprenticeship. They'd gone swimming, dived from boulders, dropped from a rope-swing, picked lilies, caught fish, and ambushed frogs. A tiny patch of sand had served as their beach. The sand had not washed away with the years. It was bare save for a little rock breaking the surface of the shallows.

The rock was not a rock, Therese realized; the jutting tip had a frog's bulbous eyes and rounded snout.

Could she still catch a frog, or had her quick reflexes been destroyed by years of reading and writing and making slow, precise gestures? The seventeen-year-old slipped off the boulder to find out.

Gathering her skirt in her left hand, she crouched with her right poised to strike. A lunge and the frog was in her grasp.

The little bullfrog instantly began squirming for freedom, its disproportionately long legs kicking against the air and its inward-turned paws pushing against her thumb and forefinger. Thin and wet, it would have slipped free if Therese hadn't cupped her left hand over it. Her skirt, released, fell into the shallows and began sopping water like a sponge. She jumped back with an unladylike curse.

The sand-brown head shoved between two fingers, the broad mouth gaping with the effort.

"Let me go let me go let me go let—"

"You're *talking!*"

The frog went stick-stiff in her hands. Then the rounded jaws snapped shut and the blunt head, more wall-eyed than a horse's, angled to study her with one round cold eye that looked like it had been pressed from gold flake.

"You can HEAR me!"

The frog's jaws didn't open; the voice was a scream in Therese's head. She blinked in pain. Then she glared at the frog and said, "Not so loud!"

"Forgive me, my lady." The silent voice, a young man's baritone, was much calmer this time. "It's just that you're only the second person I've met who can hear me."

"The second?" Therese spoke aloud, to be courteous. "Who was the first who could understand a frog's thoughts?"

"The evil magician who cursed me."

"Of course! What was I thinking? Perhaps I can break your curse."

"How could a *girl* do that?" the frog exclaimed. "All wizards are evil men!"

"I'm neither," Therese said, and put the frog back down in the shallows.

As she turned away, the frog's voice filled her head as she had known it would. "O lady, I am upset by my fate, but that is no excuse for such discourtesy. Please pardon my hasty words."

"Very well," she said, turning back. "I, too, was hasty."

She crouched, offering her hand. The frog placed his forepaws on her fingers and kicked himself up into her cupped palm.

"So, frog," she said. "Will a kiss break the enchantment?"

"A *kiss?*"

Therese frowned. "That's the cure one hears prescribed for this curse. I'm not any happier about it than you."

"The wizard who enchanted me said only *he* could break the enchantment!"

"They always say that," Therese said, and before she could lose her resolve she kissed the frog.

The frog's lips, if they could be so called, were hard, cold, and wet. "Slimy" was the word that came to mind, and as she jerked back her head she struggled to keep control of her stomach. She wanted to spit but settled for rubbing her mouth against her sleeve.

"I apologize for my rudeness," she said to the frog. He was still a frog.

"I understand." She heard disappointment in his mind-voice.

"Maybe it *must* be the kiss of a *princess*, to break the spell. But there are no princesses in this land." And none were likely to appear, with the king and queen so old and the heir lost. "There should be more than one way to break the curse. I will consult my master's grimoires."

Raising her skirt in her left hand, Therese started home with her right hand held up so the frog could see where they were going. Mindful of her burden, she moved slowly down the Roman road. The stones were warm under her river-chilled feet.

"I don't want to address you as 'Frog'," she said. "And we *have* already shared a kiss. What is your name?"

"What is yours?" the frog demanded warily.

"I am Therese de Bouton."

"I am . . . Robert."

" 'Robert'?" Therese almost stopped walking. "Who enchanted you?"

A flat cold eye regarded her. "The evil magician Thibault."

"Thibault." This time she did stop walking. "I have heard of him. A most powerful wizard. A necromancer."

"Ah, you cannot help me!"

"Give me a chance, Your Highness."

"You know me!" the frog exclaimed fearfully.

"You are safe, Your Highness," Therese assured him.

She had heard the stories that Thibault of the North had put a terrible curse on the royal heir. Certainly the prince was missing. The stories told of so many different fates for Prince Robert, and the king's and Thibault's castles were hundreds of miles away, and so much time had passed, that until Therese had heard the name "Robert" it had not occurred to her that she had found the missing prince.

Therese resumed walking, and soon came to her master's house, a weathered wood cottage which stood alone in a broad hayfield, in the center of a small herb garden. As Therese drew near the cottage the door swung open. When she stepped across the threshold, the room was flooded with sourceless golden light.

Therese stepped up to a stained, scarred table laden with alembics, vials, mortars, and other tools of her trade. As she cleared a space around the ewer and basin she said, "You need to stay damp, don't you, my lord."

"Yes. If my skin becomes dry, it is painful."

Raising the ewer in her left hand, Therese poured an inch of water into the basin, then put the frog in the basin.

"I pray you stay put, my lord. Otherwise you might activate a protective spell, or jump into something deadly."

Neither was likely. But if he got off the table, she might step on him.

She went to the shelf that held her master's fortune, ten books.

Shaking with exhaustion, dusty with powders, Therese laid aside the last grimoire, pushed back her sweat-matted red hair, and looked upon the frog.

"You are right," she admitted. "Only the magician who enchanted you can break the spell."

"I feared it." The voice was quiet but so full of despair that Therese felt her heart ache. "Three years now; how many more can I survive? How many do I *want* to survive if I must live like this?"

"There is naught for it but to go to Thibault, my lord."

"But—but he will not change me back!"

"You will change back if he dies."

"Lady, I will not put you in such danger!"

"If I don't do it, you will die a frog. And I cannot in good conscience return you to the river, and I doubt you wish to spend the remainder of your days sitting in a bowl on a table."

The frog did not reply.

"I wish my master were here," she said quietly. "He has knowledge I do not; he has been a wizard for twenty-five years, while I am naught but a journeyman."

"Your master?" the frog repeated hopefully. "Where is he?"

"Far to the south, my lord; far beyond the range of my mind-voice. His mother is ill, and he has gone to nurse her back to health or be with her when she dies. He has been gone for months and may not return for many more."

The prince might die before her master returned—frogs had short life-spans. Perhaps the prince had a human life-span. But perhaps he did not. He'd been a frog three years now, and Thibault was no charitable soul.

Therese could not wait for her master's return.

"Why doesn't your master heal his mother with a spell?"

"It doesn't work that way," Therese said. "Wizards may ease illness and heal wounds—we do all we can—

but when God calls a soul no one can hold it in the flesh."

She surveyed the cluttered table and thought of the dirty dishes piled high in the kitchen. It was clear she could not instantly depart on a long journey. "My lord, let me put my master's house in order, and tomorrow we shall be on our way."

In the morning they rode out of Bouton on the ancient Roman road, the enchanted frog in a clay jug braced between Therese's body and the saddle-horn. The jug's neck was slightly narrower than the opening, so as a precaution Therese had tied one end of a string around the neck and the other around her knife-belt. She was dressed as a boy, in dark trousers, heeled riding-boots, a loose blouson more than adequate to hide her small breasts, and a broad-brimmed hat that shaded her easily-burned face and shoulder-length hair. She'd hated cutting her hair, it was her only decent feature though it was an ugly orange, but she could not pass as a boy with waist-length hair.

They stopped thrice so Robert could catch food. Therese did not watch him hunt insects. She tried to eat, knowing she needed to keep up her strength, but she had no appetite. She was also becoming increasingly saddle-sore. Her master had taught her how to ride, but since they didn't own a horse she had little opportunity to stay in riding trim.

They barely made fifteen miles that first day. The four-hundred-mile journey was going to be very long.

Their first night's lodging was a woodcutter's hut at the edge of a forest. As payment Therese helped the woodcutter split and stack logs. He did not guess she was a woman, for she was ungirlishly tall and thin, with a plain square face and a low rough voice. He may have thought she was a runaway apprentice, but he asked no questions, just served her thick stew—which she ate with sudden voracious appetite—and tossed down a second pallet far from his. When she buried herself in her bed-roll she took her crucifix out of her blouson and prayed God and the saints would help her keep her word. She was terrified.

Her silver crucifix, which had been blessed by the Pope, had been given her by her master, whose long-ago wanderyear had taken him to Rome. His faith in the Church was weak, but Therese missed the Church—the sacraments, the power of ritual, the feeling of community—and knew she always would. She'd lost the Church when she'd begun her apprenticeship. Wizards were even less tolerated than Jews, for the Old Testament said "thou shalt not suffer a witch to live." The people of Bouton, far from cities and doctors, appreciated the wizards, and the priest of Bouton did not share the hatred of most priests for wizards. But he would not allow a witch in his church.

At dawn Therese and Robert were back on the road. As the woodcutter's cote disappeared behind the trees, the prince cried, "He really thought you were a boy!"

"It's worked before when I've traveled with my master." She didn't mention that she was older now and the chance of discovery was greater. It was fortunate she had remained skinny.

"Let's stop soon," said the prince. "I'm famished!"

Therese directed their borrowed mount off the road. As she set the jug on the riverbank she gazed longingly at the water. She remembered how shocked she'd been when her master had denigrated a saint celebrated because her only bath had been her baptism. Since then Therese had grown to like hot baths so much that she shivered at the thought of stepping into the river.

She was also far more modest than she'd been as a child swimming with her cousins. She didn't want to bathe in front of Robert. He was a frog, true, but he was still a man—and the king's heir! But she couldn't swim yards away leaving him alone; wildcats, raccoons, and snakes were quick to dine on frog.

"I'm going to take a swim," Therese said without turning to face Robert. "Call if you need anything."

She stripped quickly, rushed into the river, and knelt, gasping as she immersed herself to the neck. The water was far colder than the air; she could get no colder, she was sure, if she could dive naked into a snowbank. How had she ever enjoyed long swims? She soon left the water, to dry herself with her scratchy wool cloak. Then, modestly wrapped in the cloak, she took a clay pot from a saddlebag and slathered strong-smelling ointment on her sore legs, hoping her soft skin would soon be saddle-cured. She could heal the raw spots, but that was self-defeating; they'd just be rubbed raw again. She must let the skin toughen.

She dressed herself and turned to see that Robert had finished eating. He was perched on the jug with his back to her, staring politely into the forest. She pulled a patch of moss from the riverbank and dipped the moss in the water. Robert jumped off the rim so she could replace the moss in the jug. She hadn't been able to find a water-skin with an opening big enough for the frog-body to pass through, so she'd improvised a way to keep Prince Robert's sensitive skin damp.

"My lord," she said, "why don't we catch food and dry it for you to eat on the trail?"

"No!" Robert's voice hurt her head. "I'll *not* eat dead flies! What I must eat sickens me enough as it is! And with these accurst eyes I can't even *see* a fly unless it's moving."

Quickly she said, "We will stop for all our meals."

"Why are we bothering to ride at all?"

Therese stared at him. "What do you mean?"

"I've heard the tales of wizards who walk across the sky, and fly without wings, and ride on dragons or flying horses or giant hawks. And when Thibault turned me into a frog he brought me *instantly* to a distant forest! Why are we taking the *roads?*"

"Believe me, my lord, if there were an easier way we would be taking it. But there *are* no dragons or flying horses or giant hawks. Those are, perhaps unfortunately, naught but pagan and Saracen myths. As for walking across the sky and flying, levitating, those are possible but not practical. I'd have to spell-cast constantly so we wouldn't fall to our deaths, and I would run out of strength hours before sunset; magic-making is exhausting. I would not lose my strength if I had a demon bound to me; I could hold us aloft all day, or take us instantly to Thibault's castle, or have a demon carry us through the air. But I do not deal with Satanic powers.

"And even if I did not tire, we would be extremely visible walking or levitating across the sky. If we rose too high to be seen, we would be in the aether, the realm of the angels, in air too fine for mortals to breathe; we'd swoon and fall to our deaths! But if we were lower, we'd be visible for miles around. Don't you think Thibault might learn of such a marvel? Even if he didn't see us or hear about us, he might well sense the enormous expenditure of sorcerous energies.

"Magic is not always the right tool for the task."

"I understand." Robert could not keep his disappointment out of his mind-voice.

"Robert, I wish it were not like this."

The prince got in the jug. His head popped up. "Oh, God! I can only be heard by magicians, Thibault will hear me!"

"He won't be able to hear you until we're close to his castle. If he were listening to us, we'd be dead now. He would probably sense it if you died, but isn't otherwise watching you." She tied the jug to her belt. "My lord, why did he curse you?"

The frog looked up at her with one gold eye. "My father has always refused to have dealings with the forces of evil—as he believes all magic to be—and has never had a magician at court. When I was fifteen, Thibault came into my father's lands and soon thereafter came to my father's court, to demand the abandoned office of Court Sorcerer. My father refused him, whereupon he turned me into a frog. He said I would stay cursed until my father changed his mind. Still my father refused him. Then Thibault and I were suddenly deep in a dark forest, where he mocked my helplessness, ridiculed my father's decision, and told me no one save a wizard could hear me now. Then he threw me in a pond and disappeared. I fled the forest as quickly as my new body allowed, to find that no other human could hear me and that I was hundreds of miles from my father's palace."

"My lord, I am sorry."

"Though I am my father's only child, he would never submit to Thibault's demand. He believes he would damn his own soul and those of his subjects if he consorted with a sorcerer."

"He would if he dealt with a *necromancer*," Therese said. "And it seems Thibault realized the strength of your father's resolve, else he would not have abandoned you like that. My lord, I shall do everything in my power to end Thibault's life and free you from your curse, I swear by Almighty God." She drew her dagger and cut her finger. "My word is my bond, sealed by my blood and my power."

A drop of blood fell off her finger and turned to smoke.

"Lady, how did you come to be a wizard's apprentice?"

"My lord, I was the only child in my village who showed magical talents, and they were strong. So when I was seven the wizard Michel took me as his apprentice."

"Please, lady, call me Robert. It's ridiculous, calling a frog 'my lord' and 'Your Highness.' "

"I'm not highborn, Robert. You must call me Therese."

The second day they made twenty miles before dusk. The clear weather held another three days, allowing them to cover more distance, though never more than twenty-five miles at a time; the rented saddlehorse was no swift young courser. But on the fifth day, the day the stone paving gave way to dirt, the air cooled and the sky went dark with clouds. Thunder rumbled, growing swiftly louder. Therese put on her cloak and urged the horse to its greatest speed, knowing by the dirt road that there must be a city ahead, trying to reach it before the storm broke. But within seconds the clouds opened in a torrent. In minutes the rain soaked through her cloak and turned the road to mud so deep the mare sank to the fetlock with every step.

Therese began to chant.

A spell existed that could disperse the storm, but she would fall senseless off the horse if she cast it, and the weather would be disturbed for weeks if not months after; she might dissolve the rainstorm only to face a blizzard the next day. None of that would ease her journey, and would certainly attract Thibault's attention.

The spell she was chanting was far simpler than the weather-spell, though still demanding: it was the spell to solidify air. Not that she was about to go walking across the treetops, or even higher, during a thunderstorm. She had another purpose.

The mare was trembling violently, and whinnying at every crash of thunder and flash of lightning, but so far showed no other signs of breaking. It plodded forward unable to realize that it no longer sank in mud because it was walking on a thin, clear, hard layer of ensorcelled air.

After a miserable half hour they reached the first true town of the journey. It was a sizable city, enclosed by a high wall built of stones quarried from the Roman road. The lightning was almost continuous and the rain was still falling in thick gray sheets, so Therese went against her aunt's and her own judgment to ask a gate-guard about decent lodgings.

Before she'd rented the horse from the blacksmith, Therese had gone to exchange farewells with her family, her aunt, uncle, and cousins. Her mother had died in childbirth; the wizard Michel had been summoned too late to save her, if saving had ever been possible. No one knew who Therese's father was; the years around her birthtime had been bad ones for the barony, and bandits had ravaged the village more than once before the king sent a strong new lord to restore order. Therese's mother's older sister had raised Therese as her own.

"Your master is away, yet you are dressed for travel," she had said to Therese. "Are you off on your wander-year?"

"I may be," Therese had said, eyes widening. She hadn't thought of that. If her magic could kill the powerful necromancer, she would surely be a full wizard. "I *am* going on a long journey. I do not know when I shall return."

"Where—"

"I must not speak of it."

"So. If you *must* travel, Therese, I pray you stay out of the cities. They are huge, inhospitable places, and there are men who will"—her aunt's lined face had colored—"who will *force* even a young man. You make a very pretty young man."

"I shall avoid the cities, Mother," Therese had said, agreeing to do what she'd intended all along while silently disagreeing that she, freckle-faced, pasty-skinned, carrot-haired, stick-thin, was pretty.

Now she was seeking shelter in a city.

If the innkeeper thought it strange that a lad was traveling alone, in possession of enough coin to take a private room, he was too busy to comment or interfere. He barely had time to hand over a key and direct a serving girl to show the way to the room.

The young woman said, "Ye paid for a meal also," and led Therese into the common room. It was bigger than Bouton's entire tavern, and surely held more patrons than the village had inhabitants. The crowd made Therese's mind swim.

She grabbed the serving girl's wrist. "I don't want to eat here," she shouted over the roar of conversation.

The serving girl pointed and Therese saw stairs on the other side of the common room. The serving girl started forward again and Therese, shivering from cold, exhaustion, and uneasiness, clutched her wet cloak shut and followed, praying she wouldn't attract attention. No one spoke to her, but several men addressed the serving girl, shouting requests for drinks and ruder things; the girl responded saucily to them all. This worried Therese, but despite the girl's banter and tarty looks no one followed them up the stairs.

Therese sent the serving girl to get the meal and also hot coals for the brazier. The girl returned only seconds, it seemed, after Therese had laid down her saddlebags and jug, removed her hat and cloak, and taken a lit candle from the hall.

"Supper, handsome!" The serving girl set the wood tray on the floor and dumped glowing coals from the iron pan into the brazier under the window, then dropped the pan saying, "I don't have to return downstairs right away," and threw her arms around Therese to deliver a passionate kiss.

With a shove Therese sent her stumbling back. "I am a good Christian, and betrothed by the laws of God and man." *May God forgive my lies.*

The serving girl glared at her, then shook her head

and laughed. "Ain't it always the way?" she said, and was gone.

Therese pushed the door shut and sagged against it. In her worry about a man trying to take advantage of a lad, she had forgotten she might attract a woman's attention. And she'd never received such a kiss. She had thought the only passionate kisses she would ever receive would be in her imagination; when she'd become a wizard's apprentice she'd known that between the profession and her plainness she'd likely never marry. What had just happened bore no resemblance to anything she'd ever imagined. And there had been no pleasure in getting kissed against her will by another woman.

She thanked God she was so bony the serving girl hadn't realized she had embraced another woman.

"Therese, is it safe?" the prince asked in his silent voice.

"I'll bar the door," Therese said, and did so. "Come out."

She removed her wet clothes, without hesitation; she'd grown accustomed to bathing in front of Robert by concentrating on his frog appearance. She put on her only change of clothes, also boy's clothes, glad she had something dry to wear.

It rained the next day, and many more, but the lightning did not return and the torrential downpours were brief so Therese and Robert pressed onward. They did not stay in another city, but nonetheless Therese encountered a man of the sort her aunt had warned her against.

Night caught Therese and Robert deep in forest, but a young woodsman gave Therese a night's lodging while refusing her offer to pay with labor. As she ate gamy, reheated stew and drank sour, strong ale, she felt his eyes on her; every time she looked up he was staring at her without blinking. Perhaps he was merely uncouth, but he made her uneasy. Then he grabbed her shoulders, jarring the stew-bowl from her hand, and crushed her to his chest, pressing his greasy lips to hers.

It was a man kissing her this time, but it was no more pleasant; even less, for she was imprisoned by powerful arms. She jerked her head back, breaking the kiss, but she could not otherwise move, let alone break free or draw her dagger.

"Ye've never been with a man, eh?" The woodsman spoke in a hoarse voice and stared into her eyes with a peculiar intensity. "Lad, 'tis a far greater pleasure than ye could ever hope for with a cold fish of a female."

Therese put her arms around him and began stroking his back, caressing the muscles through the threadbare cotton, then running her fingers down the spine.

The woodsman's eyes widened. "Ah, ye understand men should be together in all ways!" he said, and he relaxed his arms but put his lips on hers again.

He forced her mouth open, a new experience that nearly broke the thread of the spell she was speaking in her mind. At least he didn't realize she was sketching precise patterns on his back.

The spell ended. The man stopped moving. The spell had worked. Therese struggled out of his arms and looked down upon him. His eyes did not open. His arms did not reach for her. He did not leap up from his stool. He was motionless as a stone statue.

Therese drew her dagger, but she could not strike. If she'd been able to free her dagger while he held her she would have struck to kill. But she could not kill a man in cold blood. That went against everything she had been taught by her aunt, her Church, and her master.

She slammed her dagger back into its sheath and spat in the man's face. Then she realized the prince was staring at her.

"Therese," Robert said softly, "did he hurt you?"

"He did not," she said, and turned to the cupboard to get a clean bowl and spoon. As she filled the bowl with stew she realized her hands were shaking. She forced herself to take a bite. She was starving, and there was a bad taste in her mouth.

"You should kill him!" Robert cried.

Swallowing was difficult, her throat was tight, but after a moment she was able to speak.

"He'll be motionless as a statue for the length of a day and a night. When he can move again he will be in terrible agony for many days. After that he'll be unlikely to try such a thing again."

"I wish I could believe that, but I think you are wrong. God, a *sodomite!* I never really believed there *was* such a sin! Such evil deserves *death!*"

"Would it be better if he'd realized I'm a woman and tried to ravage me because of that?"

"What? I—" Robert fell silent. When he spoke again, moments later, his mind-voice was quiet but intense. "You are right, Therese. But I wish I could make sure he'd do nothing like that again to anyone, man or woman. You should kill him."

The prince spoke passionately, yet did not order her to kill. Therese had noticed, with appreciation, that he never gave orders, only made requests. Probably this was less out of consideration for her than out of the humbling experience of three years trapped in a small, nearly helpless, utterly alien body. But perhaps it was that he possessed the mysterious quality nobles were supposed to have, "courtliness."

"If you cannot kill this evil man," he said, "how will you be able to kill Thibault?"

"I will not do evil I can avoid. I *will* do what I *must*. I will keep my sworn oath, my lord."

Without another word the prince disappeared into the jug.

It was far too late to resume traveling, so, no matter how much they might loathe the idea, they spent the night in the woodsman's cote. Therese knew her spell would hold but still slept restlessly; she was disturbed by how close she had come to being raped. She found herself thinking of the mother she had never known, and what must have befallen the peasant girl. Therese existed only because of the ultimate physical violation. Yet she wished her mother had had a way to defend herself.

In the morning the prince remained silent, though Therese could feel him watching her. She also felt his silence. Sometimes he slept away the hours of travel, but more often they conversed. He spoke of his raising as the only child of the royal family, incidentally telling her much about the ways of the nobility; in return she told him what she could of her apprentice days, and what she judged he would find least boring about her commoner's childhood. She hoped he would not hold to this silence.

Their long journey would be longer without another friendly word in it.

After the noon meal he broke his silence. "I must say, you do not look much like your mother."

Therese stared. "So I have been told. But how do you know?"

"I glimpsed her when we were in your parents' home."

"Ah. My aunt. My mother's sister and her husband raised me, for my mother died birthing me. I've been told she much resembled her sister, so I know I do not resemble her."

"You lost both your parents young! I apologize, Therese, for reminding you of your loss."

The prince was so obviously trying to restore the earlier, easier level of their conversation that Therese felt drawn to reassure him with a confidence.

"There is no need to apologize, Robert. I do not remember my mother and do not care to know my father. He was one of the bandits who harried Bouton before your father sent a good strong lord to restore peace. For that, though he hates all wizards, your father has my gratitude."

"Therese, you need not tell me your secrets."

"It's not a secret. For a while, it's true, I was mad with desire to know who my father was, and since I was the only villager with magical talent I was sure no mere bandit had sired me. No, the wizard Michel must be my father! Had he not taken me, a nameless peasant girl, as his apprentice? Was he not kinder to me than most parents are to their children? Fortunately, he realized what I was thinking, and gently told me that though he wished it were so he was not my father. And of course I should have realized he could not be my father; he is as short and dark as my aunt. Finally I realized it doesn't matter whether or not he's my father. He's the one who made me a wizard."

"Therese, I'm sorry. I—"

"Robert, I belive you apologize more than anyone I know! There is nothing to apologize for. Come, we should go."

"I'm sorry I delayed us—O Jesu, I'm doing it again!"

She burst into laughter. After a moment, he joined in.

So they were restored to their camaraderie, and the journey, though it took two months, passed rapidly, sped by their conversations and the warmth of summer.

Then, far sooner than she expected, they entered blighted lands. The sky was leaden, the earth was bare, and the trees were naked save for a few shriveled, blackened leaves that hung from the branches like the rotting skins of small animals. Some branches bore dark fruit: dead men, women, and even children hanging on ropes. The stink was too strong for any spell to completely filter, and Therese threw up more than once. The prince, in his alien body, had no such relief.

Once they even crossed the path of a band of walking dead, a score of bloated blue-white corpses naked but for scraps of rotted cloth. Seeing horse and rider, the corpses changed direction with hideous glad cries and charged at a shuffle, with outstretched arms from which bits of flesh fell like filthy snowflakes. Therese reined in the rearing, panic-stricken horse and reached into her shirt, then raised high the crucifix that had been blessed by the Pope. It gleamed though the sun was hidden behind thick layers of cloud.

The walking dead screamed in voices rough as broken stone, raised their worm-riddled arms to cover their boiled-egg eyes, and fled as fast as their bony legs allowed. One corpse ran right off its legs and collapsed in a heap of disconnected parts. Despite the thick odor of decay, Therese dismounted and knelt beside the thing, to lay her crucifix on the chest. Though no longer connected to the torso, the skull screamed shrilly, hurting her ears. But abruptly the scream ended and the ribs collapsed, and every body part became a pile of dust writhing with barrow-worms.

Though a necromancer could raise the dead he could not call back their souls; he animated the bodies with the most minor of demons. Therese had banished an imp back to hell. Unfortunately, the crucifix would have no effect on Thibault. Mortals were free of God's compulsion.

Therese wiped the crucifix repeatedly on her pant-leg, then slipped the sacred instrument into her pocket, mounted the horse, and rode onward. The prince said nothing, as he had since they'd entered Thibault's territory; they didn't want the necromancer to hear his mind-voice. Therese prayed silently as they crossed the increasingly rugged country.

They passed through a village. It was, unsurprisingly, empty. The sagging, filthy cotes squatted with their doors and windows gaping open. They looked like skulls.

An hour later Therese saw the necromancer's castle. It was a tall stone keep, outlandishly spindly, that seemed to grow out of the high gray crag upon which it stood. It *had* grown, by magic; it had appeared, Therese had heard, overnight.

Therese prayed until she reached the foot of the crag. Then she dismounted and looked up at the keep, craning her neck to see a bit of gray wall.

"Thibault!" she called, loud, but not loud enough to hurt her throat. He would hear her. "I seek a fit master! I would learn from the greatest wizard!"

"Why should I take an apprentice?" Thibault was standing five feet away, as solid as if he'd been there all along. He was no bony graybeard in black robes, but a brawny, handsome, golden-haired man, apparently in his prime, dressed in fine silks and velvets, with a spotless white cape on his shoulder and a jaunty bottle-green cap on his head. "What could a ragged peasant brat possibly offer me?"

"My lord, I have brought you Prince Robert," Therese said, and raised the jug tied to her belt.

"The prince?" The pale eyes narrowed as if they could see through the clay. Then the blond brows rose. "You *do* have him!"

"*Traitor witch!* God *damn* you to the lowest circle of *hell!* Jesu, forgive me for trusting a wizard—"

"So, you've brought me the prince." Thibault's quiet tenor drowned out the prince's screaming mind-voice. "I could have gotten him anytime. You've proved you have the wizard-talent, but what should I care about that?"

"I have great power," Therese said, letting the jug fall to the end of the string. "And"—she tilted her head down to look up at him with a sly smile—"I have other knowledge which might please you."

"I don't care for boys."

Therese swept off her hat and ripped open her shirt. Buttons flew. "I'm not a *boy!*" she shouted indignantly.

"Well, you're a scrawny girl, that's for certain." Thibault was wearing a faint smile now. "But it's nothing that can't be changed by regular meals and a touch of demonic art. You have something far rarer than beauty. Courage. It's been over a year since even a king's knight has dared enter my land, and you come here with the brass to summon me and demand that I make you my apprentice." He advanced on her. "We may have a deal."

Thibault held out his hand, but Therese extended her arms and looked up at him with an intensity that burned her eyes. He stared at her for a long moment. Then his thin smile widened almost imperceptibly, and he took her in a gentle embrace and placed his lips lightly on hers.

She drew her dagger and thrust.

As his head jerked up, as she slipped her dagger out of his stomach, she screamed, *"Robert! Out of the jug!"*

Without pause she struck again, thrusting upward, driving the blade hilt-deep into the soft underside of the jaw. Thibault's mouth, open in shock or pain, issued not a scream but a flow of blood. Then his eyes rolled up and he fell over backward. Therese fell with him. The impact knocked the breath out of her, but she did not pause. She sawed off the wizard's head with her dagger-blade, then laid her crucifix on the breast and threw the head far from the body, so they could not rejoin.

Therese rose up, gasping for breath, blood dripping from her hands, to find herself facing a naked man she'd never seen before. She raised her dagger.

The tall young man threw his arms up and cried, "Therese!"

"Robert?" Therese put a hand to her brow, dizzied by the realization that she'd done the impossible. She'd killed the necromancer. She'd broken the prince's curse. She'd survived.

She supposed she must have turned pale, or started swaying, because Robert stepped up and closed his hands on her arms. He looked intently into her eyes and she saw he was no handsome prince, with his long bony face,

big hooked nose, muddy brown eyes, and skin so astonishingly pale it was translucent, showing a fine blue trac-
ery of veins, like the finest marble. Actually, the skin
contrasted strikingly with his shoulder-length hair, which
was black and glossy as a raven's wing, yet looked softer
than goose-down. Did it feel that soft?

Suddenly his glowingly white skin turned fiery scarlet,
and Therese remembered his nakedness, and her own
torn shirt. She stepped back, out of Robert's hands, and
turned away holding her shirt closed.

"Not all Thibault's fine clothing is ruined," she said.
Her face felt warm. "And you are near his height."

She walked away, leaving the crucifix on the body, and
busied herself talking to the horse, scrubbing her bloody
hands on her torn shirt, and putting on her other, intact
blouson.

After a time Therese heard the prince come up behind
her, his new boots crunching on the dry, stony soil. She
flushed again, thinking of her glimpse of his naked body,
thinking of how often he had seen her naked, but she
turned to face him. Surely facing him was no worse than
facing the necromancer!

Prince Robert was dressed in all the dead man's finery
save the foppish cap and the bloodied shirt and cape. His
bare chest was lean, hairless, and alabaster pale. She
focused on his face, which was pale again, and smiling.

"Beautifully done, Therese. I thought you had betrayed me, but you were tricking Thibault!"

"I am sorry, my lord," Therese said softly, bowing her
head. "I only lately thought of trying to take Thibault
without magic, and I did not wish to discuss my plans
while in his territory. I did not think I'd be able to convince him, and if I'd put a glamour of trustworthiness or
beauty on myself he would have sensed it. I hoped your
innocent reaction would convince him."

"It did." Prince Robert went down on one knee so he
could look into her eyes. His expression was intent.
"Lady, you have saved my life, and therefore my family
and the kingdom. Any reward you desire is yours. Even
if you wish to be Court Sorcerer I will bend all my efforts
to make that so. If I must wait till I am King, I will make
you Court Sorcerer. Indeed, I do beg you to take this

office. The kingdom clearly needs the service and protection of a wizard, and no one deserves it more than you!"

"My lord, I do not deserve the office! I'm no more than a journeyman. I killed Thibault through mundane treachery!"

Curiously, Robert smiled. "Did you not tell me that magic is not always the best tool for a task?"

Startled by the reminder, Therese found herself laughing.

Prince Robert reached out and took her hand. "I hope that on the day you assume the office you will become my bride."

Therese drew in a sharp breath, astonished. Warring emotions—desire, terror, longing for power of place—filled her heart. She ignored them. "I am a nameless commoner and a witch, and you are the heir to the kingdom, and the betrothed of the Count of Savoy's daughter. We cannot marry."

Robert's face darkened. "I shall marry as I choose. I shall certainly give you titles and estates. You deserve them. I shall grant you the land you have saved—"

"I do not crave titles and estates," Therese realized. "And if you married me, you would destroy years of diplomatic effort. Your Highness, you have your duty and I have mine. My only wish is to become the best wizard I may be."

Robert bowed his head.

"Come, my lord." Therese drew him to his feet. "You've been away a long time. Your parents are waiting for you. And your father must send priests here, to banish whatever evil spirits have been released by Thibault's death. There is much work ahead. We must go."

Robert kept his hands on hers. "You would make the sort of advisor a king needs, one who demands the hard choices. Say that when you are a master wizard you shall be my Court Sorcerer."

Therese looked at him. "I would like that, my lord, but my village needs a wizard, and my master Michel is not young. If I can find another to take my place in Bouton—"

"Though Rome itself protests, I shall do all I can to help you in this search."

"Thank you, my lord."

The prince smiled, and though his eyes were dark they seemed alight as he intertwined his fingers with hers. "I am Robert, Therese."

"Robert, I shall join your court."

Leading the horse, they started walking south. They were still holding hands, an unspoken promise more powerful than the laws of men and requirements of diplomacy.

THE PRICE OF THE GODS
by Roxana Pierson

This story I had a few doubts about; on my handy rejection slip form I have a category saying "just too gruesome." I almost returned it the day I got it, since I seldom use much horror, but I found it quite unforgettable and couldn't resist the temptation to share it with you.

Roxana Pierson forgot or neglected to send me a biography; I remember when I printed her first story, "Swarm Song," in FOUR MOONS OF DARKOVER, she was at that point—maybe three years ago—one of the youngest writers ever to sell to me. Since that time she has been supplanted as youngest by Micole Sudberg, then fourteen when she first sold, now in college, and by a couple of other very young writers. Like all of Roxana's stories, this one has a twister in the tail.

Zharad bowed low and said, "The soceress, Sharala, is willing to talk with you now."

Arusha, Queen of Endor, regarded her Chief Torturer with disdain. A squat, hirsute man with no neck and long, apelike arms, he stank of blood, unwashed orifices, and hot iron.

Grimacing, the queen dabbed her nostrils with a perfumed kerchief. "Will she tell me the Secret, then?" she asked sharply.

"So she says."

"I take it she's finally broken?"

"That is difficult to say—witches are not as other women," Zharad replied. Ill at ease away from his dungeon, he twisted the thongs of his whip nervously. "Shall I take you to the dungeon?"

"No, that won't be necessary." Arusha paled visibly, picturing the stench of the dungeon with its gruesome instruments of torture. No, one visit to observe Zharad's work had been quite sufficient. She motioned to a servant for wine, and sipped the rich red liquid thoughtfully. So, the witch was ready to talk! Was it true, or just another attempt to escape? It would be interesting to see how the sorceress had fared under Zharad's tutelage. "Can she walk?" Arusha inquired.

"With assistance."

"Then bring her to me, and be quick about it—I've waited long enough already."

"As you wish, your majesty." Zharad bowed his way out and the queen resisted the impulse to hurry him with a well-planted kick. The oaf, after all, knew his job; his prisoners seldom died before their time. Just the same, it was revolting that she must employ such a creature!

Sharala arrived in the grip of two burly guards. The soceress' eyes were blackened and her lips puffed, but there was no disguising the finely-drawn features—or the long black eyes that glittered with unquenchable malice. Rage pricked at Arusha as she saw that even torture had not been able to entirely destroy Sharala's youthful beauty. With displeasure she noticed that the sorceress' tattered gown was clean and her head freshly shaven; her intricately tattooed scalp shone. That meant she still had enough power left in her voice to persuade others even against their will. A bad sign.

The guards shoved the sorceress to her knees at Arusha's feet and forced her head to the floor. The moment they unhanded her, however, Sharala dragged herself to her feet. She swayed slightly, then drew herself up to stand straight and proud. The two women glared at each other.

"So," Arusha said slowly. "Have you had enough?"

"Have you?" Sharala shot back. Her swollen tongue

stumbled over the searing stumps of freshly-broken teeth, but her words were clear enough to send a chill down Arusha's spine. "It is I who choose my hour of death, not you."

Arusha's fist tightened on her wine goblet until her nails dug into the palm of her hand. "I'll have you tortured until the end of time, if that's what it takes. So far, I have spared you, but I have only to give the order. When Zharad is done, even the dogs won't have you. Or perhaps you don't believe me?"

"I believe you. Perhaps you do not believe me?"

"Give me the Secret of Long Life, and you are free to go."

"The Secret belongs to my Order," Sharala said slowly. "To give it to one who has not had the proper training is dangerous—for both of us—as I told you before."

"I will never release you until you give it to me. As I have told *you* before. If you are not ready to tell me, I will give you back to Zharad. Is that what you want?"

"You win, my queen," Sharala said, sighing heavily. "The secret is yours, but I warn you—you may live to regret this day. The gifts of the gods are not without a price." Her shoulders slumped wearily, and Arusha had the impression that only sheer force of will kept the woman upright.

"Tell me, then!" Arusha cried, leaning forward eagerly. "What is the Secret? I must have it!"

"You must drink my blood."

"Your blood!"

"It is the only way—the Life Force is in the blood. That is how it was given to me, and that is how I must give it to you. Now, call your leech, and let us be done with this charade."

"Never mind the leech! You—" Arusha pointed her little finger at the guard on Sharala's left. "You have a knife—use it."

Startled, the man retreated a pace, protesting, "My . . . my lady, I know nothing of leechcraft."

"Bloodletting is a soldier's craft, isn't it?"

"That is not the same."

"If it must be done, I will do it," Sharala said quietly. "Give me your dagger, soldier."

Silently, the guard handed over a long, slim blade and watched with open astonishment as the sorceress gouged the razor-sharp steel across her left wrist as calmly as if she were slicing fruit.

Arusha hurriedly dashed the wine from her goblet and caught the rich, red blood as it spilled out. When the glass was filled, Sharala said, "That is enough, for what you want." She bent her arm, holding her wrist tightly.

"This had better not be one of your tricks," Arusha threatened. She wrinkled her nose in distaste, took a deep breath and drained the goblet in three long swallows. Clasping a hand to her mouth she burped and swallowed heavily several times, then extended the goblet, saying, "If a little is good, more is better! Fill it again."

Sharala gazed at her tormentor with utter contempt. "I have done what you asked. Let me go."

"No," Arusha hissed. "One more. When I have evidence it is working, then you may go, and not before."

"As you wish, then." Sharala once again let her blood drain into the goblet. Long before it was filled, however, she collapsed and would have fallen had the guards not caught her. Arusha quickly snatched the goblet away before its contents could spill. She regarded Sharala's still figure with disdain—the once-proud sorceress looked like a discarded rag.

"Take her away, and send someone to scrub the floor," the queen ordered. Grimacing, she forced herself to swallow the remaining blood and sat back against the cushions, waiting to see if she felt different. Except for nausea, she felt nothing.

Arusha stared at the canopy of her bed; the heavily embroidered cloth glowed richly in the candlelight. The queen yawned mightily, turned onto her right side and then her left; neither position seemed comfortable. Far away, the town crier announced, " 'Tis the fourth bell, and all's well."

The queen squeezed her aching eyes shut. Four in the morning, and still wide awake! Her eyes felt as though they had springs in them; they simply would not stay shut. She heard every little noise from the clop of cart horses to the patter of mice in the ceiling. Every nerve in her body felt raw.

For weeks, now, sleep had eluded her; instead, she descended into a twilight zone of horror punctuated by dreams of burning and death. Indeed, she had come to think of her bed as a torture device to be avoided. And when exhaustion forced her to rest, the visions would begin—nightmares so vivid that she wasn't always sure if an event had actually occurred or if she had only dreamed it—as though the veil between waking and sleeping was dissolving.

Nothing seemed to help, not the physician's potions, the royal masseuse or the royal consort. She was beginning to wonder if she would ever sleep again. Without the break between her days that sleep had provided, her life seemed like one long chain of unrelated events; she could make no sense of things. If only she could sleep! She knew from experience, however, that if she hadn't slept by now, she wouldn't. Wearily, she rose and called to the nearest maid—her women had learned not to bother her when she woke—with each sleepless night, her temper grew more sullen.

"Girl!"

"Your majesty?" Rubbing her eyes, the young woman staggered to her feet and bowed before the queen. She was a wan, colorless little thing, Arusha thought, but then, who cared what servants looked like so long as they obeyed?

"Bring my cloak and slippers and then come watch the sun rise with me."

The girl obeyed quickly and quietly, following like a shadow as the queen marched through the darkened halls and up the winding, tower steps to the windswept battlements. Streaks of pink and purple were just beginning to color the sky, and a rosy glow illuminated the mountains as though a furnace burned behind them. At the first sign of the sun, the birds broke into a raucus frenzy of singing and roosters strained their necks trying to outcrow each other.

The queen paced restlessly. Even though she was so tired she feared stumbling, she was unable to remain still.

It was as though some unholy fire burned in her veins—Sharala's blood. She snorted derisively at her fears. It was a bad bout of insomnia—nothing more—unless the sorceress had managed to cast some kind of spell on her. Yes, that must be it; what other answer could there be?

Just thinking of Sharala enraged Arusha. The sorceress had tricked her, and everyone knew it; the whole palace was laughing behind her back. All that nasty blood she had been forced to drink, and for what? If there was a Secret to Long Life, Sharala still kept it. The queen felt no different than ever—if anything, she felt worse. Yes, it was time to let Zharad finish the sorceress off, but first she would gloat over her one last time.

To Arusha's shock, Sharala looked near death. The sorceress had aged overnight—her hair was white and her skin wrinkled; she looked a hundred years old. With a thrill of alarm, Arusha realized that if the witch died, she would never find out the Secret. "I ordered the physician to attend you," the queen said sharply. "Has he not come?"

"He has come," Sharala said weakly. Her voice quavered and her hands trembled.

"Then why are you ill?"

The sorceress looked vaguely amused. "Ill? I am not ill, merely old."

"I do not understand."

Sharala smiled creakily. She said, "I gave you my blood and my youth. What more do you want?"

"Long life!"

"Have you felt no different, then?"

"Nothing. My hair has not grown blacker nor my skin softer. You tricked me."

"Did I? Are you sure nothing has changed?"

"I have difficulty sleeping, if you must know," Arusha replied crossly.

"Is that so?"

"Yes, that's so! If it's a spell of yours, you'd better remove it or I'll have Zharad remove you!"

"I do not fear Zharad. There is nothing more he, or anyone, can do to me now. And as for spells, I have no more; you have already taken everything I have to give."

"What do you mean?"

"Why, the Secret of Long Life, of course!" Sharala laughed, a wild, eerie cackle of mockery. For a moment, her eyes glowed with their old intensity. "Neither I nor any mortal can add to the span of your years—the time had to come from somewhere. Think, my queen. Do you not have a longer life now that you do not waste time sleeping?"

"That is not the same!" Arusha leapt from her throne and struck Sharala across the face. "Witch! What have you done to me?"

"Only what you wanted. Personally, I always found the night useful for contemplation. Of course, these days, I sleep too soundly for that."

Arusha grasped the sorceress by the neck and shook her. "Take your spell back. Undo it."

Sharala sobered. "I wish I could."

"What if I was bled?"

"It's too late. You cannot pass the Secret on unless you are already close to death—only the fire in your veins sustains you, now. You neither need to eat or sleep."

"But how long will I have to live like this?"

"That, only the gods know. It is as I said: they do not give their gifts freely. Even as I paid a price, so will you. Now, I go to seek *my* sleep."

So saying, Sharala turned away, and Arusha let her go. The sorceress hobbled slowly down the echoing hall, a tiny, bent crone of a woman dressed in a too-large gown.

TIGER'S EYE
by Syne Mitchell

This is one of the shortest stories I've ever printed, at least in part because it's more than a setup for a one-liner.

Syne Mitchell is 21 years old and lives in Tallahassee, Florida. Any more information and the bio would be longer than the story. However, she is female and her name is pronounced sine, with a long i.

Marla of the plains was a very ordinary woman, with brown hair, brown eyes, and brown skin. Her clothes were plain and unornamented. Her body was lean and strong, tempered by her life on the plains. It was to her great surprise one day, that while chasing a horse that had fallen behind the herd, the air before her opened up and she fell into a darkly lit room.

When her eyes adjusted to the red torch light, she saw a squat toad of a man on a golden ornamented throne. He wore only a silken loincloth and a beaten circlet of gold around his neck. The stones set into the necklace gleamed even when the shadows fell upon them. In his right hand he held a black stick topped by an empty grasping hand.

"I suppose," he sneered, "my little treasure, that you

are curious as to why I have summoned you. I am a collector, you see, a collector of women. Unlike my fellows, I enjoy the essence of my collection without the unpleasantries of feeding or housing." He gestured to the band around his neck. "Each of these gems is a woman bound by the power of my staff into a priceless, ageless jewel."

Marla's wide-set eyes scanned the room. The only way out was through a beaded curtain.

"This," the sorcerer continued, gesturing to a diamond that glittered fiercely, "is the essence of the sorceress Darsheel. Quite a prize. You, my little tiger's eye, will be my next adornment." At this last, he began to lower the staff. Marla leapt left and rolled to her feet. A bright flash of light exploded where she had stood.

"Here now," the mage complained, "this is most unladylike behavior."

Marla ran through the beads. She richocheted off an invisible wall that blocked the door. "You'll not leave that way," the man chuckled, again bringing the staff to bear.

Marla spun away from the door, tearing down strands of beads. Before the sorcerer could speak she fell upon him and had him trussed in a matter of moments. His flesh rolled over the tight binds and from behind the beads in his mouth, he wailed.

As Marla contemplated what to do next, her gaze fell upon the staff. She looked at the mage's necklace. Then again at the staff. She removed the circlet and with her hunting dagger prized a milky opal from the soft gold. She placed the stone in the claw. A white light blinded her. When she could see again, a soft-spoken woman with red-gold hair stood before her. Moments later, twenty-two women stood in the room.

The plainswoman addressed the crowd. "I leave his punishment to you." The mage beneath her feet squirmed against his bonds.

Darsheel stepped forward with a wicked grin upon her face and an unholy light in her eyes. "It is fitting that your courage should have some reward."

*   *   *

Marla of the plains was a very ordinary woman, with brown hair, brown eyes, and brown skin. Her clothes were plain and unornamented, except for a bit of onyx that swung fitfully from a leather thong.

MARION ZIMMER BRADLEY

THE DARKOVER NOVELS

The Founding
☐ DARKOVER LANDFALL   UE2234—$3.95

The Ages of Chaos
☐ HAWKMISTRESS!   UE2239—$3.95
☐ STORMQUEEN!   UE2310—$4.50

The Hundred Kingdoms
☐ TWO TO CONQUER   UE2174—$4.99
☐ THE HEIRS OF HAMMERFELL   UE2451—$4.95
☐ THE HEIRS OF HAMMERFELL (hardcover)   UE2395—$18.95

The Renunciates (Free Amazons)
☐ THE SHATTERED CHAIN   UE2308—$3.95
☐ THENDARA HOUSE   UE2240—$3.95
☐ CITY OF SORCERY   UE2332—$4.50

Against the Terrans: The First Age
☐ THE SPELL SWORD   UE2237—$3.95
☐ THE FORBIDDEN TOWER   UE2373—$4.95

Against the Terrans: The Second Age
☐ THE HERITAGE OF HASTUR   UE2413—$4.50
☐ SHARRA'S EXILE   UE2309—$4.99

THE DARKOVER ANTHOLOGIES with The Friends of Darkover

☐ DOMAINS OF DARKOVER   UE2407—$3.95
☐ FOUR MOONS OF DARKOVER   UE2305—$3.95
☐ FREE AMAZONS OF DARKOVER   UE2430—$3.95
☐ THE KEEPER'S PRICE   UE2236—$3.95
☐ LERONI OF DARKOVER   UE2494—$4.99
☐ THE OTHER SIDE OF THE MIRROR   UE2185—$3.50
☐ RED SUN OF DARKOVER   UE2230—$3.95
☐ RENUNCIATES OF DARKOVER   UE2469—$4.50
☐ SWORD OF CHAOS   UE2172—$3.50

DAW

MARION ZIMMER BRADLEY
NON-DARKOVER NOVELS

A note concerning:

THE FRIENDS OF DARKOVER

So popular have been the novels of the planet Darkover that an organization of readers and fans has come into being, virtually spontaneously. Several meetings have been held at major science fiction conventions, and more recently specially organized around the various "councils" of the Friends of Darkover, as the organization is now known.

The Friends of Darkover is purely an amateur and voluntary group. It has no paid officers and has not established any formal membership dues. Although the members of the Thendara Council of the Friends no longer publish a newsletter or any other publications themselves, they serve as a central point for information on Darkover-oriented newsletters, fanzines, and councils and maintain a chronological list of Marion Zimmer Bradley's books.

Contact may be made by writing to the Friends of Darkover, Thendara Council, Box 72, Berkeley, CA 94701, and enclosing a SASE (Self-Addressed Stamped Envelope) for information.

MARION ZIMMER BRADLEY'S FANTASY MAGAZINE

Fans of Marion Zimmer Bradley will be pleased to hear that she is now publishing her own fantasy magazine. If you're interested in subscribing and/or would like to submit material to it, write her at:

P.O. Box 249
Berkeley, CA 94701

(If you're interested in writing for the magazine, please enclose a SASE for her free Writer's Guidelines.)

(These notices are inserted gratis as a service to readers. DAW Books is in no way connected with these organizations professionally or commercially.)

DAW

FANTASY ANTHOLOGIES

DAW

Attention:

DAW COLLECTORS

Many readers of DAW Books have written requesting information on early titles and book numbers to assist in the collection of DAW editions since the first of our titles appeared in April 1972.

We have prepared a several-pages-long list of all DAW titles, giving their sequence numbers, original and current order numbers, and ISBN numbers. And of course the authors and book titles, as well as reissues.

If you think that this list will be of help, you may have a copy by writing to the address below and enclosing one dollar in stamps or currency to cover the handling and postage costs.

DAW Books, Inc.
Dept. C
375 Hudson Street
New York, NY 10014-3658